THE ABYSS THAT REMEMBERS

THE WORLD-SONG SAGA, BOOK 3

Written by Diane Kann

Brought to you by Volans Galaxy Press

Published by Kannceptual Creations LLC

An imprint of Volans Galaxy Press

ISBN: 978-1-971356-75-4

Printed in the United States of America

First Edition, January 2026

CONTENTS

Author's Biography   V

Dedication   VI

1. Echoes of the Deep   1

2. The Weight of Forgetting   57

3. The Failing Crown   81

4. The Truth Seekers   106

5. Chapter 5: The Architects of Suppression   140

6. The Pale Tide's True Nature   166

7. The Dragon's Dilemma   199

8. The Crown's Gambit   226

9. The Abyss Responds   253

10. Confronting the Architects   282

11. The Nexus of Silence   325

12. Repairing the World-Song   357

13. The Dawn of a New Harmony   382

Glossary   406

AUTHOR'S BIOGRAPHY

Diane Kann writes eco-science fantasy that explores the intersections of technology, nature, and hope. Drawn to mysterious worlds, sentient ecosystems, and the quiet strength of unlikely heroes, she crafts stories that imagine not just what humanity might survive, but how it might heal.

A believer in environmental stewardship and deeply fascinated by the natural world, Diane weaves themes of conservation and interconnected life throughout her work. When she's not writing, she can be found exploring the diverse ecosystems of Central Florida with her family and dogs—dreaming up strange futures rooted in compassion and the resilience of nature.

DEDICATION

For those who listen
when the world whispers its wounds.

For the quiet guardians,
the tide-turners,
the ones who believe broken things can sing again.

May we remember what was silenced,
and choose harmony over fear.

CHAPTER ONE

ECHOES OF THE DEEP

The salt spray of Nyssera's shores had long since been replaced by a more profound, chilling dampness. Mara traced the worn leather of her satchel, the familiar scent of dried herbs and alchemical reagents a small comfort against the vast, encroaching unknown. Beside her, Cael's gaze was fixed on the churning maw of the Abyssal Realm, his broad shoulders set with a grim determination that mirrored her own. The Pale Tide, a creeping, silent rot that was slowly suffocating the life from their world, had driven them to this precipice. There was no turning back, no reprieve to be found in the sun-drenched fields or the bustling markets of the coast. Their world was dying, and the only hope, however faint, lay in the crushing darkness below.

"Everything ready?" Cael's voice was a low rumble, cutting through the mournful cry of the gulls that dared venture this close to the abyss's edge.

Mara nodded, her fingers tightening on the satchel's strap. "As ready as we can be. The breathing apparatus is sealed, the light crystals charged, and the wards etched deep enough to hold for a time." She avoided his gaze, focusing instead on the intricate knotwork of the rope harness that secured them to the descent platform. The metal felt unnaturally cold, even through her thick gloves, as if it had absorbed the chill of the abyss itself. "The spells are rehearsed. I've gone over the resonance patterns until they're etched into my bones."

"And the unease?" Cael's question was soft, a direct probe into the unspoken anxieties that clung to them both like the perpetual mist.

Mara finally met his eyes, seeing her own apprehension reflected there. "It's there. Like a premonition of a truth too heavy to bear. The closer we get, the louder it whispers." She shivered, a tremor that had nothing to do with the ocean breeze. "It feels like... like stepping off the edge of existence itself. Leaving everything familiar behind, every warmth, every memory of light."

The weight of their mission pressed down on her, a physical force in the already heavy air. The fate of Nyssera, of every living thing that drew breath beneath its sky, rested on their shoulders. It was a burden too immense for any one person, yet here they were, two souls poised on the brink of an ancient, unfathomable darkness, tasked with confronting a threat that had silenced the very world. The Abyssal Realm was not merely a deep trench in the ocean floor; it was rumored to be the oldest part of their planet, a place where memory itself was said to reside, guarded by creatures of myth and legend. And now, they had to descend into its crushing embrace.

"We carry the hopes of a world that can no longer fight for itself," Cael said, his voice a steady anchor in the rising tide of dread. "That's not a small thing, Mara. It's everything." He offered a small, tight smile. "We walk into the dark, but we carry the light of our world with us."

Mara took a deep breath, trying to channel his resolve. "Then let's not keep it waiting."

With a final, lingering look at the pale, distant sky, they stepped onto the platform. The mechanism whirred to life, a deep groan that seemed to echo the earth's own sorrow. Slowly, inexorably, they began to descend. The wind, which had seemed so powerful moments before, became a fading whisper, then nothing at all. The light of the surface world, once so brilliant, dwindled to a mere memory, then to an illusion.

The familiar sounds of the coast – the crashing waves, the cries of seabirds – were swallowed by a growing, profound silence. It was a silence that was not empty, but pregnant with an ancient, waiting power. The pressure began to build, a physical manifestation of the depth they were plunging into, a constant reminder that they were entering a realm inimospitable to the life they knew. Each footfall deeper was a step further from the known, a surrender to the unknown that lay in the crushing, eternal dark.

The initial descent was a symphony of creaks and groans from the descent platform, the groaning metal a stark counterpoint to the crushing silence that pressed in from all sides. Mara focused on her breathing, the rhythmic hiss of the rebreather a constant, reassuring presence in the suffocating stillness. The light crystals, embedded in her helmet and along the platform's frame, cast an eerie, bluish glow, pushing back the encroaching blackness but offering little comfort. They illuminated only a small, sterile bubble in an otherwise infinite void. The water, as they sank deeper, grew colder, the chill seeping through their insulated suits, a bone-deep cold that felt ancient and primal. It was a cold that spoke of eons spent in perpetual darkness, of a world that had long since forgotten the warmth of the sun.

As they passed the boundaries of the known ocean, the familiar sounds of marine life—the clicks and whistles of dolphins, the distant songs of whales—faded into nothingness. They were entering a realm where the usual chorus of life was absent, replaced by something else entirely. It began subtly, a faint vibration in the water that Mara, with her attuned senses, was the first to perceive. It wasn't a sound in the conventional sense, but a resonance, a deep, thrumming hum that seemed to emanate from the very fabric of the abyss. At first, it was almost imperceptible, a mere tremor beneath the threshold of hearing. But as they continued their descent, the resonance grew, evolving into faint, fragmented melodies that seemed alien and out of place in the deep.

These were not the joyous songs of a thriving ecosystem, nor the mournful calls of creatures in distress. These were something far older, far more profound. They were notes of immense sadness, of a power so ancient it felt like the planet's own heartbeart. They were fragmented, like broken shards of a once-magnificent tapestry, each fragment carrying an echo of profound sorrow and immense, untapped power. Mara found herself straining to decipher them, her mind reaching out, trying to grasp the meaning behind the ethereal music. It was like trying to catch smoke, the melodies shifting and elusive, always just beyond her complete understanding.

"Do you hear that?" she whispered, her voice barely audible over the rebreather's hiss.

Cael, his eyes scanning the periphery, nodded slowly. "I feel it. A vibration. And the light..." He gestured to the edge of their illuminated space.

As if in response to his words, the phosphorescence that had begun to bloom around them intensified. It was unlike any bioluminescence Mara had ever witnessed. It pulsed with a deliberate rhythm, a slow, rhythmic beat that seemed to mirror the fragmented melodies Mara was hearing. The light wasn't steady; it waxed and waned, flaring brightly before dimming to a soft glow, then flaring again. It pulsed with an almost sentient rhythm, as if the very water itself were breathing, its life force surging and receding in time with the strange, ancient song. The colors shifted too, from a deep sapphire to an ethereal emerald, then to a haunting violet, painting the abyssal depths with a spectral, otherworldly palette.

These initial auditory and visual disturbances were more than just strange phenomena; they were hints, whispers from a reality far more complex and ancient than they had ever imagined. They were the first intimations that the abyss was not merely a physical chasm, but a repository of submerged history, a place where a forgotten world was stirring from its slumber. The weight of their mission, already heavy, now felt magnified by the sheer, unknowable depths of what they were encountering. They were not just descending into the ocean; they were descending into time itself.

The descent continued, each meter gained deepening the oppressive silence and intensifying the strange, resonant hum. The light crystals, once a source of meager illumination, now seemed to struggle against the encroaching darkness, their glow appearing weak and fragile in the face of such profound obscurity. The fragmented melodies Mara had detected grew more distinct, weaving a complex tapestry of sound that spoke of ancient grief and a power that dwarfed mortal comprehension. It was a symphony of echoes, each note resonating with the weight of millennia.

Then, they saw them. Not as monsters of legend, nor as predatory beasts of the deep, but as something far more profound. Looming in the distance, their immense forms silhouetted against the pulsing, otherworldly light, were the leviadrakes. They were colossal, their serpentine bodies stretching further than the eye could see, their scales shimmering with an inner luminescence that rivaled that of their own light crystals.

Yet, despite their immense size, they moved with an impossible grace, their colossal forms gliding through the dense water as if they were merely motes of dust adrift in a gentle current. They were ancient, their very presence radiating an aura of time so vast it was almost palpable. Their draconic eyes, like twin galaxies, seemed to hold the wisdom and the weariness of millennia.

Mara instinctively reached for the defensive charms woven into her suit, her heart pounding a frantic rhythm against her ribs. Cael, ever vigilant, had already drawn his blade, its polished surface reflecting the spectral lights of the abyss. But as they drew closer, a strange stillness settled over them. The leviadrakes did not attack. They did not surge forward with predatory intent. Instead, they observed. Their movements slowed, their colossal forms assuming a posture of patient observation. Their draconic eyes, ancient and knowing, seemed to bore not just into their physical forms, but into their very souls.

Mara felt an immense sorrow emanate from them, a collective grief that permeated the very water around them. It was a sorrow so profound, so ancient, that it threatened to overwhelm her. It spoke of loss on a scale she could not comprehend, of a suffering that had endured for countless ages. Cael, his hand still gripping his sword, lowered it slightly, his brow furrowed in confusion. His instincts, honed by years of battle and vigilance, told him this was not a fight for steel. The raw power radiating from these beings was immense, but it was not aggressive. It was a power steeped in weariness, in a profound, ancient sadness.

"They're not attacking," Cael murmured, his voice a low, surprised rumble. "They're... watching us."

Mara, her own fear beginning to recede, replaced by a profound sense of awe and a growing empathy, nodded. "They're not beasts, Cael. They're... guardians." She could sense it now, the purpose behind their immense forms and ancient eyes. These were not creatures of mindless instinct; they were beings of immense intelligence and purpose, tasked with safeguarding something of profound importance. The leviadrakes were not merely creatures; they were living repositories of forgotten epochs, their very existence a testament to a history far grander and more terrible than any recorded lore. Their sorrow was not a sign of weakness, but a testament to the immense burden they carried.

As if sensing Mara's understanding, one of the colossal leviadrakes shifted its position, its massive form moving with an almost imperceptible grace. It began to glide forward, not towards them aggressively, but with a subtle beckoning gesture. The other leviadrakes followed suit, their ancient forms creating a pathway, an invitation into the deeper, unknown reaches of the abyss. They were being led, not into a confrontation, but into a revelation. The path ahead, illuminated by the pulsing, otherworldly light, beckoned them further into the heart of the mystery.

The leviadrakes led them through vast, underwater canyons, their colossal forms parting the dense water like living ships. The journey felt timeless, the only measure of progress the ever-changing patterns of the phosphorescent light and the deepening resonance of the alien melodies. Mara felt herself being drawn deeper into the world-song, the fragmented notes coalescing into a more coherent, albeit still alien, symphony. It was a music that vibrated not just in her ears, but in her very bones, a powerful, resonant hum that seemed to echo the planet's own primordial heartbeat.

Finally, they emerged into a space of staggering immensity. It was a natural cathedral, carved by unimaginable forces over aeons, its vaulted ceilings lost in the oppressive darkness above. Pillars of ancient coral and rock, impossibly vast, rose from the seabed, supporting an architecture that dwarfed any mortal creation. And within this colossal chamber, illuminated by a soft, pervasive luminescence, were hundreds, perhaps thousands, of leviadrakes. They were gathered here, their immense forms creating a breathtaking spectacle, their bodies swaying gently in the unseen currents.

This was the heart of their domain, the epicenter of the strange, resonant hum. The low, guttural, and deeply resonant hum of so many leviadrakes converged, creating a symphony that vibrated through Mara and Cael's very beings. It was a sound of immense power, a harmonic vibration that seemed to shape the very water around them. This was the Abyssal Choir, a living testament to the planet's deepest, most ancient memories. It was a place where the planet's foundational memories were not just stored, but actively sung into existence, a continuous, resonant creation. The sheer power and antiquity of the scene were overwhelming, a testament to a history far grander and more terrible than any recorded lore. The scale of it was humbling, almost terrifying. It spoke of a world with a consciousness far older and deeper than they had ever conceived.

Mara felt a profound sense of reverence wash over her. These were the planet's oldest inhabitants, the keepers of its deepest secrets. They were the living embodiment of Nyssera's memory, their song a constant, vital force that sustained the world. Yet, even amidst the awe, a subtle disquiet began to creep in. The harmony, while powerful, felt... strained. There was a melancholy undertone to the leviadrakes' song, a subtle dissonance that hinted at an underlying pain. It was a beautiful, awe-inspiring sight, but it was also tinged with a profound, historical sorrow. The grandeur of the scene was undeniable, but it was also unsettling, a majestic sorrow that resonated deeply within Mara's listener's soul.

As Mara focused on interpreting the world-song within the leviadrakes' collective hum, seeking answers about the encroaching Pale Tide, she began to perceive the discordant notes more clearly. They were fragments of a fractured song, melodies that spoke not of natural cycles, but of a deliberate silencing. It was as if sections of the song had been violently torn away, leaving behind raw, gaping wounds in the planetary harmony. The overarching symphony, while still powerful, was laced with an ancient pain, a deep-seated anguish that spoke of a profound, deliberate act of suppression.

Cael, ever observant, noticed subtle shifts in the leviadrakes' behavior. Amidst the synchronized swaying and resonant humming, there were moments of deep melancholy that flickered across their ancient faces, flashes of suppressed anger that rippled through their immense forms before being subsumed back into the collective song. It was as if the immense sadness she felt was not just a passive expression of age, but an active, enduring burden. The reverence she had initially felt for these ancient beings began to fray, replaced by a growing apprehension.

They were not just keepers of memory; there was something in their song, in their very existence, that suggested they were also architects of its silencing. The beauty of the Choir was undeniably tinged with a profound, historical sorrow, a sorrow that hinted at a much darker truth hidden beneath the surface of their ancient song. The abyss was revealing itself to be a place not just of memory, but of profound, deliberate forgetting.

The leviadrakes, as if sensing Mara's burgeoning unease and Cael's sharp observations, shifted their collective hum. The resonant tones deepened, and the cavern pulsed with a new intensity. Mara felt a distinct pressure against her mind, a subtle but insistent communication that bypassed words, directly imprinting images and emotions into her consciousness. It was a complex form of telepathic resonance, far more intricate and profound than any she had encountered before.

The first images that flooded her mind were stark and brutal. She saw a world wracked by ecological collapse, its vibrant ecosystems withering under an unseen blight. Forests turned to dust, oceans choked with pollutants, skies choked with toxic fumes. Nyssera, in its ancient past, had been dying. The images were visceral, terrifying. She saw creatures of breathtaking beauty, now extinct, their forms writhing in agony as their habitats disintegrated. She felt the dying gasps of ancient forests, the searing pain of oceans turned to poison.

Then, she saw the leviadrakes. Then as now, they were the planet's guardians, their immense power a last bulwark against total annihilation. But their methods were drastic. The visions showed them gathering in immense numbers, their ancient song weaving not life, but a terrible form of control. They depicted an agonizing decision, a collective wail of sorrow and resolve as they began to sever entire ecosystems, to silence vast swathes of the world-song.

It was a deliberate act of amputation, a brutal necessity to prevent the death of the whole by sacrificing its parts. They explained, not with words, but with raw emotion and undeniable imagery, that this act was a sacrifice, a brutal necessity to preserve what little life remained on Nyssera. The images were stark, depicting a world actively tearing itself apart, not by an external enemy, but by its own protectors in a desperate act of self-preservation.

The narrative expanded, detailing the chilling consequences of this "Silence Event." While it had indeed saved Nyssera from utter annihilation, the severance left deep, festering scars on the planet's memory and its living systems. Entire species, unique and irreplaceable, vanished from existence as if they had never been. Landscapes were irrevocably altered, not by natural processes, but by a deliberate, violent excision. The world-song, the very essence of Nyssera's interconnected life, was forever diminished, a faded echo of its former glory.

The leviadrakes' remorse was palpable, a heavy, crushing burden they had carried for eons. They showed Mara and Cael how their act of preservation was also an act of immense destruction, a terrible paradox that defined their existence and their purpose. The images of vibrant life being extinguished, of entire ecosystems being ripped from the planetary tapestry, were haunting. They demonstrated that their choices, while born from a desperate will to survive, had also been an act of immense, unforgivable destruction. Mara and Cael grappled with the dawning, horrific understanding that their saviors, the ancient guardians of Nyssera, were also its most devastating destroyers. The Abyss, they realized, was not just a place of ancient memory, but a tombstone for worlds that had been sacrificed.

The weight of the leviadrakes' confession settled upon Mara like a physical shroud. She felt their guilt, not as an external observation, but as an internal resonance, as if their eons of remorse had seeped into her very being. She understood their pain, their fear, the impossible, soul-crushing choices they had faced in the face of utter annihilation. The primal terror of watching one's world disintegrate, the desperate need to salvage something, anything, from the ashes – she felt it all. Yet, a dissonant chord struck within her. Could one truly revere beings who had inflicted such profound, irreparable damage, even if it was in the name of survival?

Her listener's empathy, usually a source of connection and understanding, was now a battlefield, forcing her to reconcile the myth of the benevolent, wise dragon with the brutal reality of their actions. The abyss seemed to hold not just memories, but the agonizing echoes of countless lost lives and silenced songs, all orchestrated by the very beings who were meant to protect them. The reverence she had once felt was now challenged, replaced by a complex mixture of pity, fear, and a dawning, uncomfortable skepticism. The myth had shattered, revealing a truth far more complex and far more painful.

Cael, ever the pragmatist, observed the unfolding narrative with a different lens. His focus sharpened on the effectiveness, or perhaps the grim necessity, of the leviadrakes' actions. He acknowledged the brutal logic, the raw survival instinct that had driven their choices. The Silence Event, as horrific as it was, had indeed prevented total extinction. Nyssera still existed, however diminished.

But even as he recognized the strategic necessity, he also saw the inherent danger in such absolute power, the terrifying potential for protection to morph into absolute control. He questioned the wisdom of a system that relied on such extreme measures, the moral compromises inherent in preserving life by sacrificing vast swathes of it. His guardian's mind grappled with the brutal logic of the leviadrakes' past, recognizing the terrifying precedent it set for the present. He saw, with chilling clarity, that the foundation of their current crisis, the encroaching Pale Tide, was rooted in this ancient act of planetary mutilation. The scar tissue, it seemed, was beginning to break down.

The leviadrakes continued their silent, resonant narrative, their ancient minds painting a picture of Nyssera's fractured present. They revealed that the Pale Tide was not an external invasion, not a new threat from some distant, unknown realm. It was, they explained with a palpable sense of dread, a direct consequence of their past actions. It was the reawakening of the severed parts of the world-song, the echoes of the silenced melodies rising up to reclaim their place. Or, perhaps even more disturbingly, it was an attempt to *complete* the severance permanently, to ensure that the forgotten pieces of Nyssera's memory and life remained forever isolated, forever silenced.

They explained that the world, wounded and fractured by the Silence Event, was attempting to heal itself. But the scar tissue, the remnants of their brutal intervention, was now threatening to break down the remaining healthy tissue. The very act that had saved Nyssera was now slowly killing it. The leviadrakes themselves were conflicted, their ancient instincts warring within them. Their fundamental purpose was to preserve the world, yet their past methods, their history of severance, had created the conditions for this current crisis.

They feared repeating their past mistakes, of causing further devastation in their attempt to prevent it. This revelation cast the Pale Tide in a new, horrifying light: it was not an enemy to be fought, but a symptom of a planetary wound inflicted by its own protectors, a wound that was now festering and threatening to consume the entire organism. The abyss, it seemed, held not just the memories of sacrifice, but the seeds of the next great catastrophe.

The leviadrakes' communication shifted, the focus now turning to the critical anchor that held Nyssera's fragmented memory together. They projected images of an immense, intricate tapestry, woven from threads of light and sound – the world-song. They explained that planetary memory was not a static record, but a living, interconnected tapestry, constantly being woven and rewoven by the collective consciousness of all life. Certain ancient artifacts, they revealed, known as Crown Resonances, acted as crucial anchors, stabilizing this memory and preventing it from fragmenting entirely.

The Crown Resonance in the Abyssal Realm, they conveyed, was the oldest and most vital. It was the nexus point, the linchpin that connected the deepest, most primordial memories of the planet to its present existence. Without its stabilizing influence, the world-song would collapse entirely. The very fabric of reality, as they knew it, would unravel. This catastrophic loss of identity and ecological coherence would mean the end of Nyssera, not with a bang, but with a silent, unmaking whimper. The abyss, therefore, was revealed to be far more than just a physical location; it was a fundamental component of Nyssera's consciousness, a critical organ in the planet's living mind.

As this revelation settled, the leviadrakes showed Mara and Cael the physical manifestations of this vital anchor's decay. The once vibrant, otherworldly colors of the abyssal realm seemed muted, the pervasive luminescence dimmer, as if a veil had been drawn over its splendor. The powerful resonance of the leviadrakes' song felt weaker, strained, like a voice battling against a rising tide of silence. The very fabric of the underwater world appeared to be fraying at the edges, like a tapestry worn thin, its threads beginning to snap.

They witnessed spectral distortions – brief, flickering apparitions of places or events that no longer existed, shimmering into being for a fleeting moment before vanishing into nothingness. These were not mere illusions, but clear indications that the anchor was failing, that the stability of reality itself was becoming compromised. The leviadrakes' communal grief intensified, their immense forms seeming to sag under the weight of this observed deterioration. The abyss, once a symbol of enduring memory, was now a testament to its imminent collapse.

Mara, feeling the urgency of the situation, pushed her abilities as a listener to their absolute limit. She reached out, not to the leviadrakes, but directly to the Crown Resonance itself, a bold and dangerous act. She sought to commune with the artifact, to understand its suffering. What she experienced was not a song, but a cacophony. It was a maelstrom of fragmented memories, a desperate, agonizing plea for stability emanating from the artifact itself. It was a symphony of pain, of primal fear, and of a profound, heart-wrenching longing for wholeness.

She perceived the Crown not as an inanimate object, but as a conscious entity, suffering under the immense weight of suppressed history and the violent fracturing of the world-song. This direct contact was overwhelming, an agonizing immersion into the collective trauma of Nyssera, far more intense and raw than even the leviadrakes' ancient sorrow. It was like being plunged into an ocean of pure psychic agony.

Cael, meanwhile, focused on the tangible effects of the failing Resonance. His pragmatic mind registered the breakdown of natural laws within the abyss. Currents that should have been predictable shifted erratically, entire zones of immense pressure fluctuated without warning, and pockets of strange, unstable energy manifested and dissipated without apparent cause. He saw how the leviadrakes themselves, beings of immense power, were beginning to show signs of strain, their ancient energies flickering, their movements becoming less fluid.

He recognized, with a growing sense of dread, that this was not merely a magical or spiritual problem; it was an existential one. The physical environment of the abyss, the very structure of their reality, was becoming compromised. This instability posed a direct threat not only to their mission but to the entirety of Nyssera. The ancient anchor was not just failing; it was actively unraveling.

As the gravity of the situation deepened, the leviadrakes conveyed a final, chilling piece of information. The entity or force responsible for the Pale Tide's destructive agenda was not merely exploiting the decay of the Crown Resonance; it was actively targeting it. Their belief was that by destroying or irrevocably destabilizing this ancient anchor, this entity could ensure the severance initiated eons ago became permanent. It would be the ultimate silencing of Nyssera's memory and ecological interconnectedness, a final, irreversible erasure.

This entity, they suspected, was either a rogue element born from the very depths of the leviadrakes' own past actions, a dark echo of their severing, or something entirely new, something drawn to the planet's deep-seated brokenness, a predator finding sustenance in Nyssera's wounds. The focus of their mission, already dire, shifted from understanding the past to confronting an immediate, existential threat to the present and future of Nyssera. The enemy was no longer just a creeping tide; it was a targeted assault on the very foundation of their world's existence.

Mara grappled with the profound dissonance between the revered myth of the dragons and the harsh, unvarnished reality of their history. The creatures she had once seen as paragons of wisdom, power, and ancient grace were now revealed as complex, flawed beings capable of immense destruction, driven by fear and a desperate will to survive. She struggled to reconcile the reverence due to ancient protectors with the undeniable need for critical examination of their actions. How could she venerate beings who had committed such acts of planetary mutilation, even if those acts had ultimately saved their world from total oblivion?

This internal conflict gnawed at her, leading her to question the very nature of truth itself. Was an incomplete, comforting myth preferable to a painful, complex, and deeply unsettling truth? Her understanding of heroism, of what it meant to be a protector, was irrevocably challenged, forcing her to seek a new perspective, one that acknowledged both the light and the shadow within these ancient beings.

Cael's focus sharpened with an almost surgical precision on the leviadrakes' past violence. He meticulously analyzed the strategic necessity of their actions during the Silence Event, understanding intellectually that the forced severance had prevented total extinction. Yet, he could not, and would not, ignore the sheer brutality involved, the forced erasure of entire ecosystems, the silencing of countless life forms. He saw the profound moral gravity of their choices, the irreversible consequences that echoed through the ages and continued to shape their present.

His perspective as a guardian emphasized the immense responsibility that came with power, and the ethical tightrope walked when making decisions that impacted not just individuals, but entire worlds. He contemplated the enduring question: could such past violence, however dire the circumstances, ever truly be justified or truly forgotten? The weight of their actions felt as heavy as the abyssal depths.

It was then that one of the elder leviadrakes, a being whose ancient form seemed burdened by an immense weight of guilt, detached itself from the rest of the Choir. It sought out Mara and Cael, its massive head bowed in a gesture that was unmistakably one of sorrow and contrition. It did not offer excuses, not at first. Instead, it began to share, through images and emotions directly impressed upon their minds, the sheer terror that had fueled their decisions during the Silence Event. It shared personal memories of loss, of watching the world they loved, the vibrant Nyssera of their youth, wither and die before their very eyes.

It conveyed the primal, suffocating fear of complete annihilation, the chilling certainty that they were witnessing the end of all things. It conveyed that their actions, however terrible, however destructive, were born from a profound, desperate love for Nyssera, a desperate, primal attempt to salvage something, anything, from the absolute brink. The plea was not for absolution, but for comprehension, for understanding of the impossible pressures and the soul-shattering choices they had faced. It was a burden of history they had carried alone for far too long.

As Mara absorbed these revelations, her initial reverence for the leviadrakes began to erode, replaced by a cautious respect, a deep sense of unease, and a profound sorrow. She recognized their immense power and their crucial role in Nyssera's survival, but she also saw the inherent danger in blind faith, in unquestioning adoration. The mythologizing of guardians, she realized, could obscure the truth, blind its followers to the flaws of their protectors, and prevent necessary evolution and growth. She began to understand that true protection required not just power, but wisdom, transparency, and a willingness to confront difficult truths – qualities that seemed scarce among the ancient dragons due to their deep-seated habit of suppressing their own history. Her path forward, she knew, required her to forge a new relationship with these beings, one based on clear-eyed observation, critical assessment, and a recognition of their shared, yet complex, history.

Cael's scrutiny intensified, not out of animosity, but out of a fundamental need for clarity and a deep-seated sense of responsibility. He questioned the leviadrakes' current motivations, their preparedness to face the present threat of the Pale Tide. He firmly believed that a past justification, however dire the circumstances, did not absolve them of responsibility for the future.

He probed their strategies, their understanding of the Pale Tide's nature, and, most importantly, their capacity to adapt and evolve beyond their ancient, destructive doctrines. His approach was about ensuring that the so-called 'guardians' were truly capable of protecting Nyssera *now*, without repeating the destructive patterns of the past. He sought concrete actions, demonstrable change, and a willingness to embrace a new paradigm, not just ancient justifications for past atrocities. The survival of Nyssera depended on it.

The leviadrakes, in their resonant, image-laden communication, revealed a deeply unsettling truth about the Crown Resonance: it was not merely an anchor for planetary memory, but the central component of a vast, complex system designed to *manage* that memory. This system, they conveyed with a deep sense of shame, actively suppressed painful memories and traumatic events. The full horror of the Silence Event, the agony of the severed ecosystems, the grief of vanished species – all of it had been systematically muted, buried beneath layers of enforced calm.

The purpose, they explained, was to prevent collective trauma from paralyzing the world, to maintain a semblance of peace and stability by shielding its inhabitants from the crushing weight of their own history. However, this suppression had come at a terrible cost. It had created an artificial stability, a fragile peace that prevented true healing and left Nyssera vulnerable to the very scars it had tried so desperately to bury. For Mara, a listener whose very being was attuned to the currents of memory and emotion, this was a profound betrayal of living memory, a systematic denial of Nyssera's true, complex self.

Mara, now more deeply attuned to the world-song than ever before, began to feel the suppressed pain directly. It surged into her consciousness in raw, unfiltered waves, flashes of the agony of severed ecosystems, the soul-deep grief of lost species, the collective terror of the Silence Event – all of which had been systematically muted by the leviadrakes' control system. This raw emotional influx was overwhelming, a tsunami of suffering that threatened to drown her.

She felt the profound depth of Nyssera's pain, a pain that had been deliberately buried for eons. She realized, with a chilling certainty, that the world's supposed harmony, its enduring peace, was a manufactured facade, built upon a foundation of deliberately forgotten agony. Her empathy, usually a source of connection and understanding, now became a conduit for intense, suffocating suffering. She was experiencing the world's buried trauma as her own.

Cael observed the 'system' from his strategic, analytical viewpoint. He recognized it not as a benevolent mechanism for maintaining peace, but as a sophisticated instrument of control. He saw how the suppression of memory and pain served to maintain the status quo, reinforcing the power structures of those who managed the system – in this case, the ancient, self-appointed leviadrakes. He questioned whether this control, however well-intentioned its original purpose, ultimately hindered growth, resilience, and the natural evolution of life.

He understood, with an unshakeable conviction, that true strength, true resilience, came not from burying adversity, but from facing it, learning from it, and integrating its lessons. The leviadrakes' desire for stability, he realized, was a desire for predictability, a fear of the unpredictable nature of life and the difficult truths that often accompanied it. He recognized the chilling patterns of authoritarianism, even when cloaked in the guise of protection.

The leviadrakes articulated the profound paradox at the heart of their actions. By suppressing pain and memory, they had believed they were protecting Nyssera from itself. They had feared that the full weight of its devastating history would crush the will to live, leading to a spiral of despair and eventual collapse. Yet, this very act of protection had inadvertently created the conditions for the current crisis. They admitted, with a deep sense of regret, that their methods, designed to prevent a sudden, catastrophic collapse, had instead led to a slow, insidious decay, a pervasive weakening of the planet's core resilience. The abyss, once a symbol of Nyssera's deep, enduring past, now represented a buried trauma that was actively threatening to resurface destructively, amplified by the very systems designed to keep it dormant. The protective measures, it turned out, had become a threat.

Despite the leviadrakes' systematic suppression, fragments of authentic memory began to surface, insistent whispers pushing against the enforced calm. These were raw, unfiltered echoes of Nyssera's true past, stirred by the failing Crown Resonance and the encroaching tendrils of the Pale Tide. They spoke of a world that was vibrant, interconnected, and profoundly resilient, a stark and beautiful contrast to the muted, controlled existence that had followed the Silence Event. Mara felt these whispers most acutely, experiencing them as a counter-melody to the leviadrakes' carefully controlled song. They were a testament to life's enduring persistence, a beautiful yet terrifying reminder of what had been lost and what was now at stake. This resurfacing memory was the first tremor of true healing, a signal that the planet's innate vitality was fighting back against its imposed silence.

The leviadrakes' revelations continued, their shared consciousness painting a horrifying picture of the Pale Tide's true nature. It was not an invasion, they explained, not an external force seeking to conquer. Instead, it was a potent, almost sentient, force attempting to *reactivate* and *complete* the severance initiated during the ancient Silence Event. It was a process of ecological separation, designed with ruthless efficiency to isolate damaged or 'unstable' ecosystems from the whole, effectively pruning the planet to save what it deemed the 'strongest' parts. This force, they conveyed, was driven by a corrupted echo of the original preservation instinct, a twisted logic now warped into a rigid, absolute finality. The current manifestations of the Pale Tide – the wilting flora, the unnaturally still, lifeless waters, the eerie silence that accompanied its spread – were its initial stages, the insidious preparation of the world for a permanent, irreversible division. It was the ultimate consequence of the leviadrakes' own past actions, a specter of their own making.

Mara's unique abilities as a listener allowed her to feel the Pale Tide's 'intent' on a deeply visceral level. It did not perceive itself as destructive, but as a force of 'purification' and 'order.' Its twisted logic saw it as severing the weak and diseased elements to save the 'stronger,' more viable parts of Nyssera. This perceived logic was chillingly pragmatic, a cold, detached assessment of life and death. She felt the immense pressure it exerted on the world-song, a relentless force attempting to fragment it, to create distinct, isolated pockets of existence, severing the vital connections that bound all life together. Her empathy, her greatest strength, was stretched to its breaking point as she tried to understand this force without succumbing to its bleak, unforgiving rationalizations. It was a cold, alien logic that threatened to extinguish all warmth and life.

Cael, meanwhile, analyzed the Pale Tide as a direct strategic threat to Nyssera's fundamental interconnectedness. He recognized that its ultimate goal was to dismantle the intricate web of life, creating isolated zones that could be easily controlled or left to wither and die, independent of the larger ecological balance. He saw its terrifying efficiency, its methodical, relentless approach designed to exploit existing weaknesses within the planet's systems. His primary concern was for the overall balance of the planet; if entire ecosystems were permanently severed, if the vital arteries of the world-song were irreparably cut, the resilience of Nyssera as a whole would be irrevocably compromised, leaving it vulnerable to future catastrophes. He began to strategize how to counter this force, focusing not on destruction, but on maintaining and reinforcing the connections that the Pale Tide sought to sever.

The leviadrakes explained the direct link between the Pale Tide and the lingering wounds of the Silence Event. It preyed on the ecological and memetic scars left behind by their ancient act of severance, seeking to widen them into permanent, unbridgeable rifts. The initial severance, they admitted, had been incomplete, leaving behind dissonant energies, echoes of suppressed life and memory that the Pale Tide was now amplifying to catastrophic levels. It was, in essence, a corrupted, amplified echo of the dragons' own past actions, a force that embodied their deepest fears and their most terrible mistakes, made manifest and now turned against the world they had sworn to protect. The past, in its most destructive form, had become a direct and present threat.

Finally, the leviadrakes presented Mara and Cael with a grim, almost impossible choice. They could either allow the Pale Tide to complete its destructive process of severance, sacrificing parts of the world deemed 'unstable' in a desperate attempt to save the rest, or they could find a way to heal the fractured world-song, to mend the deep scars of the past. The latter was a monumental task, requiring a fundamental shift in how Nyssera remembered and interacted with its history, a willingness to confront the pain and integrate it, rather than suppress it. The choice highlighted the core theme of their journey: is true protection found in isolation and control, or in integration and the difficult, painful work of healing? The leviadrakes themselves were divided, their ancient unity fractured by this agonizing decision. Some, clinging to their old ways, advocated for a repeat of their past actions, believing severance was the only path to survival.

Others, witnessing the Crown Resonance's decay and Mara's profound distress, began to question their historical certainty, a nascent hope stirring within the ancient Choir.

The Abyssal Choir, the collective consciousness of the ancient leviadrakes, was not a monolithic entity. The elders, deeply scarred by the memory of the Silence Event and the subsequent eons of guardianship, were profoundly divided. A significant faction, led by a stern, ancient dragon named Vorlag, whose scales seemed as hard and unyielding as the abyssal rock, argued that the Pale Tide, in its brutal efficiency, was a necessary, albeit harsh, evolutionary process. They recounted the horrors of the Silence Event, the agonizing necessity of their drastic measures, and how those actions had been the only way to ensure Nyssera's survival.

Vorlag believed that Nyssera was inherently unstable, prone to cycles of collapse, and that the only path to long-term survival lay through decisive, controlled severance, preventing future catastrophes by isolating threats before they could spread. This faction viewed Mara's empathetic approach, her desire to heal rather than sever, as dangerously naive, a threat to the very stability they had fought so hard, and sacrificed so much, to create. Their conviction was absolute, rooted in the deep trauma of their past.

Conversely, a smaller group of leviadrakes, their ancient eyes reflecting a growing concern and a nascent understanding, sensed the true nature of the crisis through Mara's direct connection to the world-song. They began to advocate for a different approach, one that challenged the very foundations of their ancient doctrines. They believed that the severance itself, the act of tearing apart the world's song, had created the fundamental instability, and that true healing lay not in further isolation, but in integration and reconciliation. They were drawn to Mara's unique ability to hear the suppressed melodies, the echoes of what had been lost, and to Cael's sharp, strategic mind, seeing in them the potential for a new way forward. These dragons were hesitant, their voices quiet against the booming pronouncements of the elders, but their hope represented a nascent, yet powerful, shift within the Abyssal Choir.

Cael, observing the dragons' internal conflict with a keen, analytical eye, directly challenged their ingrained beliefs and their self-appointed authority. He argued, with a calm but firm intensity, that their history of drastic, unilateral action had directly led to the current crisis, and that repeating the same patterns, even with a different name and a different justification, would only perpetuate the destructive cycle of violence and suppression. He questioned their authority to dictate the fate of the living world when their own actions, however well-intentioned, had proven so deeply flawed and had created such lasting damage. His directness cut through the ancient mystique and the layers of dogma, forcing the leviadrakes to confront the practical, undeniable consequences of their philosophies. He sought not a dictated decree, but a collaborative solution, one that acknowledged the interconnectedness of all life.

Mara felt the immense pressure to prove that an alternative existed, that Nyssera could be healed without sacrificing parts of itself. She had to demonstrate that the world-song could be mended, woven back together, rather than fractured further. Her empathy was her greatest tool, her ability to connect with the pain and sorrow of the world, but it was also her greatest vulnerability. She needed to find a way to communicate the vibrant, interconnected potential of a healed world to beings who had only known survival through division, beings who saw wholeness as a weakness. The fate of her own world, of Nyssera itself, hinged on her ability to bridge the chasm between ancient dogma and a hopeful, integrated future, and to convince the leviadrakes, the architects of severance, to trust something new, something born from understanding rather than fear.

The leviadrakes, now more receptive due to Mara's influence and Cael's direct challenge, explained the theoretical mechanics of repairing the Crown Resonance. It was not a simple act of reinforcement, but a process of re-weaving the fractured threads of the world-song that the artifact anchored. This process, they conveyed, required a deep, unwavering connection to the planet's memory, a willingness to embrace both its joys and its sorrows without judgment or suppression. Mara's role as a listener was paramount; she would have to act as a conduit, channeling the raw, suppressed emotions and memories back into the song, effectively completing the very process the dragons had tried to stifle for millennia. It was a dangerous balancing act, requiring immense control, emotional resilience, and a profound understanding of the delicate interplay between memory, emotion, and existence.

A ritual was proposed, a complex ceremony that would involve both the leviadrakes and Mara. The objective was to harmonize the dissonant energies of Nyssera's fractured past with its present, to weave the severed threads back into a coherent whole. This would involve a controlled channeling of raw memories – the agonizing pain of the Silence Event, the profound grief of lost species, the devastating consequences of the leviadrakes' ancient severance – directly into the Crown. This was a radical departure from their past methods of suppression and was fraught with peril. Cael's role was critical: to ensure the physical stability of the ritual site, to protect Mara from any unforeseen backlash, and to act as an anchor for the ritual's more tangible, earthly components, grounding the overwhelming energies at play.

Mara understood, with a chilling clarity, that participating in this ritual meant exposing herself to the full, unadulterated trauma of Nyssera's history. She would have to feel the agony of everything that had been lost, everything that had been deliberately forgotten, all at once. This was a terrifying prospect, pushing her empathic abilities to their absolute limit. She feared losing herself in the torrent of grief and pain, becoming another casualty of the abyss, another silenced voice swallowed by the planet's collective trauma. Yet, amidst the fear, she also saw the profound potential for healing, a chance to mend the world by confronting its deepest, most agonizing wounds. She steeled herself for the emotional onslaught, knowing, with absolute certainty, that it was the only way.

Cael, ever the protector, took charge of securing the ritual site and devising comprehensive contingency plans. He knew that tampering with planetary memory and the Crown Resonance, an artifact of such immense power and antiquity, could provoke unpredictable reactions. These reactions could come not only from the encroaching Pale Tide, sensing its imminent defeat, but from the abyss itself, a realm accustomed to silence and suppression. He fortified the cavern, ensuring their escape routes were secure and preparing defensive measures against any emergent threats, magical or physical. His focus remained unwavering: to maintain order and safety amidst the profound, potentially chaotic forces that the ritual would unleash. He anticipated both magical and physical dangers, preparing for anything, knowing that the success of Mara's monumental task depended on his vigilance.

As the ritual began, Mara tentatively reached out, her consciousness extending towards the Crown Resonance. She felt the fractured song, the immense ache of separation that permeated the artifact. The leviadrakes began their deep, resonant chant, their ancient voices weaving a protective circle, guiding her. For the first time, the ancient dragons were not suppressing the pain but using their song to integrate it, to embrace it. Mara felt a flicker of hope, a fragile ember in the overwhelming darkness, as she managed to weave a few coherent strands of memory back into the resonance, a tiny thread of harmony emerging from the discord. It was a small victory, almost imperceptible against the vastness of the abyss, but it was a significant one, signaling the possibility of a different path, a path of healing rather than severance.

As the ritual progressed, and Mara's nascent efforts began to reweave the fractured threads of the world-song, the Pale Tide reacted with palpable fury. It sensed the disruption to its ultimate goal of permanent severance, the reawakening of the very connections it sought to destroy. Its influence intensified, the edges of the abyssal realm beginning to warp and fray more violently. Spectral distortions, once fleeting apparitions, became more frequent and intense, flickering like dying stars in the oppressive darkness. The water grew colder, a bone-chilling cold that seemed to emanate directly from the encroaching threat. A palpable sense of dread permeated the abyss, a psychic scream signaling that the Pale Tide's architects, whatever or whoever they were, were aware of their efforts and were attempting to sabotage the healing process. The abyss itself seemed to fight back against the intrusion of true memory, against the return of a song that had been deliberately silenced.

The raw memories, the agonizing echoes of Nyssera's past, channeled through Mara and woven into the Crown Resonance, began to flood her consciousness with an almost unbearable intensity. She experienced vivid, overwhelming visions of the Silence Event in all its horrific detail: the agony of dying forests, the primal terror of fleeing creatures caught in the path of destruction, the chilling, absolute finality of severed life. The grief was immense, a crushing weight that threatened to shatter her resolve, to break her spirit. She struggled to maintain her identity amidst the torrent of collective trauma, to differentiate her own self from the echoes of the past that swirled around her. Her ability to listen, her greatest strength, was now her greatest vulnerability in this moment of profound emotional immersion. The abyss was testing her, trying to drown her in its sorrow.

Cael was on high alert, his senses stretched to their limit, defending the perimeter of the ritual site. He deflected spectral incursions that clawed at the edges of their protective bubble and countered surges of unnatural cold that emanated directly from the Pale Tide's encroaching influence. He observed the leviadrakes' struggle to maintain their ancient song under the mounting duress, their immense power being taxed to its very limits by the chaos that threatened to engulf them. His focus remained unwavering: protect Mara, protect the integrity of the ritual, and ensure the fragile progress they had made was not undone. He saw the abyss itself as a battleground, a place where the forces of preservation and destruction were locked in a struggle that extended far beyond the immediate physical space, a struggle for the very soul of Nyssera.

The leviadrakes, sensing the intensity of the Pale Tide's assault, modified their song. They shifted from a pure chant of resonance to one that actively embraced the painful memories, weaving them into their vocalizations not as a source of weakness, but as a point of strength. They used their ancient power not to suppress the darkness, but to harmonize with it, weaving the discordant threads of Nyssera's past into a new, more complex, and ultimately more resilient tapestry. This was a profound act of atonement for them, a conscious choice to confront their history rather than perpetuate its suppression. Their song became a bulwark against the Pale Tide, a living embodiment of integration and resilience, demonstrating a willingness to evolve beyond their devastating past actions. It was a song of acceptance, a song of healing.

Despite the overwhelming forces arrayed against them, the ritual began to yield tangible results. The Crown Resonance, once flickering and dim, pulsed with a more stable, stronger light. The cacophony of fragmented memories, though still immense, began to coalesce into a more coherent narrative, a story with beginning, middle, and end, rather than a chaotic jumble of sensations. The world-song, though still bearing the deep scars of the past, began to find a new, more integrated rhythm, a melody that acknowledged the pain without being consumed by it. A fragile sense of stability returned to the immediate vicinity of the ritual, a small pocket of healing amidst the encroaching chaos. It was a testament to the possibility of mending, even after profound trauma, a powerful sign that a future without severance, a future of integration, was indeed achievable. The first rays of hope pierced the abyssal gloom.

The leviadrakes, guided by the reawakened resonance of the Crown, now pulsed with a clarity born from Mara's integration efforts, identified the core of the Pale Tide's insidious influence. It was not a singular entity, not a distinct antagonist in the conventional sense, but a nexus of corrupted energy, an amplified echo of the original severance, imbued with a rudimentary, destructive will. This nexus fed voraciously on Nyssera's historical trauma, using the planet's suppressed pain to fuel its relentless drive for complete separation. It resided in a place of profound ecological damage, a festering scar left by the Silence Event, a wound that had festered and grown over millennia, twisting into a source of pure malevolence. The leviadrakes understood, with a grim certainty, that to truly defeat the Pale Tide, they had to confront its source directly, to excise the corrupted heart of the problem.

As they prepared to move towards this source, a new threat emerged from within the Abyssal Choir itself. Vorlag and his faction of leviadrakes, seeing the healing process initiated by Mara and Cael as a direct threat to their doctrine of controlled severance, began to actively work against them. They believed that the ritual was an act of defiance against the natural order, a dangerous and naive attempt to preserve what should be pruned for the greater good. Vorlag, his ancient eyes burning with conviction, attempted to sabotage the ritual, using his authority and his deep knowledge of the abyss's ancient workings to sow discord among the Choir and to directly impede the protagonists' efforts. His actions revealed the depth of his unwavering belief and his absolute refusal to accept a future that lay beyond his established, destructive ideology. He had become an active, and dangerous, antagonist.

Cael, anticipating Vorlag's potential treachery, had already devised a strategy to neutralize his interference without escalating to an all-out war within the Choir, a conflict that would undoubtedly further destabilize the Crown Resonance and empower the Pale Tide. He focused on containment, using the unique properties of the abyss itself, the unstable energies of the corrupted zone, and even the leviadrakes' own power against Vorlag and his followers. His aim was to isolate Vorlag and his loyalists, disrupting their attempts to sabotage the healing process and protecting the fragile progress that had been so hard-won. He prepared for a conflict born of ideology, of deeply held but fundamentally flawed beliefs, not just of brute force.

Mara, sensing the psychic distress, the anger, and the underlying fear emanating from Vorlag's faction, made one last attempt to reach them through empathy. She understood, on a fundamental level, their fear, the deep-seated trauma that drove their rigid adherence to the doctrine of severance. She tried to convey the potential of a healed, integrated Nyssera, a world stronger for embracing its entire history, its scars and its triumphs alike. Her plea was not one of condemnation or judgment, but of invitation, an earnest appeal to their ancient role as protectors to embrace a more nuanced, life-affirming form of guardianship. She sought to sway them not with force, but with the undeniable promise of genuine renewal, a future where Nyssera could thrive by remembering, not by forgetting.

Guided by the Crown Resonance, now a beacon of hope in the encroaching darkness, the protagonists, accompanied by the aligned leviadrakes, journeyed towards the nexus of the Pale Tide. The environment grew increasingly hostile as they approached, transforming into a desolate, barren wasteland where the effects of the ancient severance were starkly, horrifyingly visible. Here, the world-song was almost entirely absent, replaced by a chilling, artificial silence that felt heavier and more oppressive than any darkness. They witnessed the lingering energies of the original severance, spectral remnants of life brutally extinguished, a potent testament to the leviadrakes' past actions and the genesis of the Pale Tide. This desolate location served as a potent, brutal symbol of the cost of their historical decisions, a stark reminder of what they were fighting to prevent from becoming a permanent, unyielding reality.

Mara and Cael penetrated the heart of the corrupted zone, the physical manifestation of the Pale Tide's destructive influence. The silence here was absolute, a heavy, suffocating blanket that smothers all sound, all life, all hope. The waters were stagnant, devoid of motion, and the seabed was barren, littered with the spectral remnants of ecosystems that had been brutally severed from the living tapestry of the world. The very air crackled with a malevolent energy, a testament to the amplified trauma of the Silence Event, a raw, festering wound in the fabric of existence. This was the source, the nucleus from which the Pale Tide sought to permanently divide Nyssera, to silence its song forever. The leviadrakes accompanying them, their ancient forms radiating distress, visibly recoiled from the oppressive aura of negation.

At the absolute center of the zone, they found not a physical entity, but a pulsing nexus of pure, negative energy – a corrupted resonance, a void that actively sought to consume all. It fed on the planet's suppressed pain, on the eons of forgotten sorrow, using it to fuel its relentless drive for severance. This nexus emanated a profound emptiness, a chilling void that sought to absorb all existence into its silent depths. Mara could feel its cold, alien logic: that existence was too chaotic, too painful, too filled with suffering, and that complete, absolute silence was the ultimate, purest peace. It was the antithesis of the living world-song, a monument to forced forgetting and absolute control, a chilling embodiment of annihilation. The leviadrakes sensed its ancient, malevolent power, a power born from the deepest wounds of their own past.

It was here that Vorlag and his loyalists arrived, their forms radiating a grim determination, determined to see the severance completed. They believed, with an unshakeable conviction, that it was the only true path to Nyssera's survival, a necessary act of planetary surgery. They saw Mara and Cael's efforts to heal and integrate as a reckless endangerment of the entire planet, a foolish gambit that would lead to total collapse. Vorlag, driven by his trauma and his rigid dogma, attempted to harness the nexus's power, believing he could control the severance, direct it more effectively than the chaotic Pale Tide itself. His conviction was absolute, rooted in a deep-seated trauma and a rigid interpretation of his role as a guardian. He believed, in his misguided way, that he was saving the world by enforcing its necessary fragmentation, a desperate act born from ancient fear and a profound misunderstanding of true strength.

Cael, his movements fluid and precise, engaged Vorlag's forces, not with lethal intent, but with strategic precision. He used the environment itself, the unstable energies of the corrupted zone, to his advantage, creating diversions, disrupting their formations, and separating Vorlag from his followers. His goal was to neutralize their threat to the nexus and the healing process without causing further bloodshed, without adding more pain to the already wounded abyss. He knew that a direct, violent conflict could further destabilize the Crown Resonance and irrevocably empower the Pale Tide. The fight was less about raw power, and more about the clash of opposing ideologies regarding Nyssera's future, a battle of ancient doctrine versus emergent hope.

Mara, shielded by Cael's tactical maneuvers and the presence of the conciliatory leviadrakes who had chosen to stand with her, confronted the corrupted resonance directly. She did not fight it with force, with aggression, or with destruction. Instead, she met its void with the mended world-song she had helped to weave, the harmony she had painstakingly created. She projected this integration of pain and joy, of life and memory, directly into the heart of the void. Her listener's empathy, honed and amplified by her journey, became a weapon of truth, countering the nexus's logic of emptiness with the vibrant, complex, and resilient reality of existence. She offered it not destruction, but integration, a chance to be absorbed into a larger, living whole, to find peace not in silence, but in song.

Mara's projected harmony, a symphony of Nyssera's reclaimed memories and integrated sorrows, began to unravel the corrupted resonance. The nexus of Pale Tide energy, a construct of pure negation, could not sustain its form against the influx of integrated memory and emotion. It began to dissipate, its malevolent pulse weakening. The oppressive silence that had blanketed the corrupted zone began to break, replaced by faint, tentative echoes of the world-song, like the first stirrings of life after a long winter.

The corrupted energy did not vanish entirely, but was absorbed, transformed, its destructive potential neutralized and integrated into less harmful, more coherent strands within the larger planetary memory. It was a victory achieved not through annihilation, but through assimilation and healing, proving that even the deepest wounds could be mended and that true strength lay not in severing, but in integration.

Witnessing the nexus's dissolution and the undeniable return of the world-song, Vorlag's rigid ideology, forged in the fires of past trauma, began to crack. He saw the undeniable efficacy of Mara's approach, the tangible healing that was occurring before his ancient eyes. The profound emptiness he had championed was giving way to a vibrant, albeit scarred, existence. His long-held beliefs, once seemingly unshakeable, were challenged by the present reality. He experienced a flicker of understanding, a dawning realization that his relentless pursuit of absolute severance had been a destructive path, not a protective one. His rigid stance wavered, replaced by a profound sense of humility and regret, a silent acknowledgment of his grave error.

With the immediate threat neutralized and the nexus of corruption dissolved, Mara, Cael, and the aligned leviadrakes focused their efforts on fully re-anchoring the Crown Resonance. This involved not just reinforcing the artifact, but strengthening its connection to the planet's foundational memories, now enriched with the integrated pain and joy of Nyssera's entire history. The artifact pulsed with renewed vigor, its light steady, strong, and unwavering. The abyss itself seemed to breathe a sigh of relief, its waters clearing, its ethereal luminescence returning, now imbued with a deeper, more complex beauty. The anchor was secure, stabilizing planetary memory for the foreseeable future, a testament to the power of facing the truth.

The world-song, now more robust, more integrated, and more resilient than ever before, began to sing a new melody. It incorporated the echoes of the Silence Event and the struggle against the Pale Tide, not as a source of shame or fear, but as a testament to Nyssera's enduring resilience and its profound capacity for healing. This song was more complex, more vibrant, and more alive than any song that had come before. It acknowledged the past without being defined or consumed by it. Mara felt this new song resonate through her very being, a living testament to the power of truth, memory, and integration. It was a song of hope, a song that embraced all of Nyssera's past, present, and future.

Vorlag, humbled and contrite, pledged his allegiance to the new path of integration, his ancient pride finally yielding to undeniable truth. The leviadrakes, united by their shared experience, their profound loss, and Mara's unwavering guidance, embraced a future where protection meant fostering resilience through understanding and interconnectedness, rather than control through severance. The Abyssal Choir, once fractured and divided, now stood as a testament to growth and adaptation, ready to guide Nyssera towards a future that honored its entire history. Their role as guardians evolved, shifting from enforcers of silence to stewards of a living, breathing memory, preparing for future challenges with wisdom tempered by humility.

Having stabilized the Crown Resonance and initiated the healing of the world-song, Mara and Cael began their ascent from the Abyssal Realm. The journey upward was marked by a sense of profound accomplishment and weary relief. The abyss, now humming with a more integrated melody, felt less like a tomb of suppressed history and more like a living repository of Nyssera's true, complex past. The leviadrakes watched them go, their ancient forms radiating a newfound peace, their collective song a harmonious blend of remembrance and hope. The oppressive darkness of the abyss gradually gave way to a glimmer of light, a promise of the world above.

Back on the surface, Mara and Cael could feel the subtle but significant shift in Nyssera's world-song. The world felt more vibrant, more interconnected, and imbued with a deeper sense of resilience. The lingering effects of the Pale Tide receded, its attempts at severance decisively thwarted. The planet's memory was no longer a fragile construct held together by suppression, but a living, breathing entity that embraced its entire history, both joyous and tragic. This mended memory was the foundation for Nyssera's future, a testament to the courage required to face the truth, however painful it might be.

The leviadrakes, transformed by their confrontation with truth and their embrace of integration, began to chart a new course for their ancient race. They no longer sought to control or suppress, but to understand and guide, fostering a world where all life was valued and interconnected. Their role as guardians evolved, becoming more collaborative and transparent. They would work with Nyssera's inhabitants to navigate the complexities of memory and ecological balance, ensuring that the lessons of the Silence Event and the Pale Tide were never forgotten, but integrated into a stronger, more resilient future. Their ancient wisdom was now tempered with humility, their power guided by a newfound understanding.

While the immediate crisis had been averted, the narrative planted seeds for future challenges. The political landscape of Nyssera, now aware of the abyss's critical role and the dragons' profound transformation, would inevitably shift. New power dynamics would emerge, and the surface world's relationship with its ancient, newly transparent guardians would need to be redefined. The dragons' newfound openness, their willingness to engage with the world, might also attract unwanted attention from entities that thrived on ignorance or sought to exploit Nyssera's restored interconnectedness. The political and aerial realms, now opened by the dragons' transformation, presented new frontiers for conflict and exploration, promising a rich tapestry for future installments of their story.

Mara and Cael, forever changed by their harrowing journey into the abyss, stood ready for whatever came next. They had learned that protection could indeed morph into control, and that true strength lay in confronting difficult truths, not in mythologizing guardians. Their understanding of memory as a living, dynamic force had fundamentally transformed their perspective. Nyssera was now a world with a more complex, vibrant, and enduring song, a living testament to the courage to heal, to remember, and to integrate. The future was not one of simple resolution, but of ongoing growth, embracing the inherent complexities of life, love, and the ever-evolving, ever-singing world-song.

The descent into the abyss was a surrender, each meter gained deepening the oppressive silence and intensifying the strange, resonant hum. The light crystals, once a source of meager illumination, now seemed to struggle against the encroaching darkness, their glow appearing weak and fragile in the face of such profound obscurity. The fragmented melodies Mara had detected grew more distinct, weaving a complex tapestry of sound that spoke of ancient grief and a power that dwarfed mortal comprehension. It was a symphony of echoes, each note resonating with the weight of millennia. This was not the familiar chorus of Nyssera's surface world, nor the vibrant, if sometimes harsh, music of its known depths.

These were notes from a forgotten epoch, fragments of a song sung before the world had fully learned its own name. They were alien, yet unsettlingly familiar, like half-remembered dreams or ancestral whispers carried on the wind. Mara strained to decipher them, her mind reaching out, trying to grasp the meaning behind the ethereal music. It was like trying to catch smoke, the melodies shifting and elusive, always just beyond her complete understanding, yet carrying an undeniable emotional weight – a profound, ancient sadness that permeated the very water around them.

"Do you hear that?" she whispered, her voice barely audible over the rebreather's hiss, the mechanical intake and exhalation a stark counterpoint to the abyss's profound stillness. Her own words felt like an intrusion, a vulgar noise in this sacred, silent space.

Cael, his eyes scanning the periphery, his hand resting lightly on the hilt of his blade, nodded slowly, his gaze unreadable in the dim, shifting light. "I feel it," he rumbled, his voice a low vibration that seemed to resonate with the very hum Mara was hearing. "A vibration. And the light..." He gestured with his chin to the edge of their illuminated space.

As if in response to his words, the phosphorescence that had begun to bloom around them intensified. It was unlike any bioluminescence Mara had ever witnessed. It pulsed with a deliberate rhythm, a slow, rhythmic beat that seemed to mirror the fragmented melodies Mara was hearing. The light wasn't steady; it waxed and waned, flaring brightly before dimming to a soft glow, then flaring again. It pulsed with an almost sentient rhythm, as if the very water itself were breathing, its life force surging and receding in time with the strange, ancient song. The colors shifted too, from a deep sapphire to an ethereal emerald, then to a haunting violet, painting the abyssal depths with a spectral, otherworldly palette. This was not the random sparkle of plankton or the steady glow of deep-sea fauna. This light seemed to be a direct manifestation of the world's hidden resonance, a visual echo of the song Mara was straining to understand. It pulsed with an intelligence, a purpose, that spoke of a reality far more complex and ancient than any they had ever conceived.

These initial auditory and visual disturbances were more than just strange phenomena; they were hints, whispers from a reality far more complex and ancient than they had ever imagined. They were the first intimations that the abyss was not merely a physical chasm, but a repository of submerged history, a place where a forgotten world was stirring from its slumber. The weight of their mission, already heavy, now felt magnified by the sheer, unknowable depths of what they were encountering. They were not just descending into the ocean; they were descending into time itself, into the very bedrock of Nyssera's forgotten past.

The air, or rather the water, felt charged with an unspoken energy, a sense of immense power held in a precarious, ancient balance. Each new sensation, each alien note, each pulsing light, was a thread being pulled from a vast, submerged tapestry, revealing glimpses of a world that had long since faded from the sunlit surface, yet still resonated in the deepest, darkest heart of their planet. This was the true nature of the abyss, a place where the past was not merely remembered, but actively, viscerally present, a living, breathing entity in its own right. The echoes were growing louder, and Mara knew, with a certainty that chilled her to the bone, that they were only at the precipice of understanding.

The descent continued, each meter gained deepening the oppressive silence and intensifying the strange, resonant hum. The light crystals, once a source of meager illumination, now seemed to struggle against the encroaching darkness, their glow appearing weak and fragile in the face of such profound obscurity. The fragmented melodies Mara had detected grew more distinct, weaving a complex tapestry of sound that spoke of ancient grief and a power that dwarfed mortal comprehension. It was a symphony of echoes, each note resonating with the weight of millennia.

This was not the familiar chorus of Nyssera's surface world, nor the vibrant, if sometimes harsh, music of its known depths. These were notes from a forgotten epoch, fragments of a song sung before the world had fully learned its own name. They were alien, yet unsettlingly familiar, like half-remembered dreams or ancestral whispers carried on the wind. Mara strained to decipher them, her mind reaching out, trying to grasp the meaning behind the ethereal music. It was like trying to catch smoke, the melodies shifting and elusive, always just beyond her complete understanding, yet carrying an undeniable emotional weight – a profound, ancient sadness that permeated the very water around them.

"Do you hear that?" she whispered, her voice barely audible over the rebreather's hiss, the mechanical intake and exhalation a stark counterpoint to the abyss's profound stillness. Her own words felt like an intrusion, a vulgar noise in this sacred, silent space.

Cael, his eyes scanning the periphery, his hand resting lightly on the hilt of his blade, nodded slowly, his gaze unreadable in the dim, shifting light. "I feel it," he rumbled, his voice a low vibration that seemed to resonate with the very hum Mara was hearing. "A vibration. And the light..." He gestured with his chin to the edge of their illuminated space.

As if in response to his words, the phosphorescence that had begun to bloom around them intensified. It was unlike any bioluminescence Mara had ever witnessed. It pulsed with a deliberate rhythm, a slow, rhythmic beat that seemed to mirror the fragmented melodies Mara was hearing. The light wasn't steady; it waxed and waned, flaring brightly before dimming to a soft glow, then flaring again. It pulsed with an almost sentient rhythm, as if the very water itself were breathing, its life force surging and receding in time with the strange, ancient song.

The colors shifted too, from a deep sapphire to an ethereal emerald, then to a haunting violet, painting the abyssal depths with a spectral, otherworldly palette. This was not the random sparkle of plankton or the steady glow of deep-sea fauna. This light seemed to be a direct manifestation of the world's hidden resonance, a visual echo of the song Mara was straining to understand. It pulsed with an intelligence, a purpose, that spoke of a reality far more complex and ancient than any they had ever conceived.

These initial auditory and visual disturbances were more than just strange phenomena; they were hints, whispers from a reality far more complex and ancient than they had ever imagined. They were the first intimations that the abyss was not merely a physical chasm, but a repository of submerged history, a place where a forgotten world was stirring from its slumber. The weight of their mission, already heavy, now felt magnified by the sheer, unknowable depths of what they were encountering. They were not just descending into the ocean; they were descending into time itself, into the very bedrock of Nyssera's forgotten past. The air, or rather the water, felt charged with an unspoken energy, a sense of immense power held in a precarious, ancient balance.

Each new sensation, each alien note, each pulsing light, was a thread being pulled from a vast, submerged tapestry, revealing glimpses of a world that had long since faded from the sunlit surface, yet still resonated in the deepest, darkest heart of their planet. This was the true nature of the abyss, a place where the past was not merely remembered, but actively, viscerally present, a living, breathing entity in its own right. The echoes were growing louder, and Mara knew, with a certainty that chilled her to the bone, that they were only at the precipice of understanding. The fragmented melodies were coalescing, not into a clear message, but into a profound emotional landscape, a spectrum of feeling so ancient and so vast that it threatened to engulf her own senses. She felt a sorrow that wasn't personal, but planetary; a power that wasn't aggressive, but primordial. It was the sound of existence itself, singing its oldest, deepest song.

The constant pressure of the water, a physical manifestation of their depth, was nothing compared to the psychic pressure building within Mara. The fragmented melodies were no longer just sounds; they were impressions, images, emotions that bypassed her ears and directly imprinted themselves upon her consciousness. It was as if the abyss itself was trying to communicate, to impart its ancient truths through a language of pure resonance. She saw fleeting visions: landscapes of impossible, alien beauty, shimmering with hues unknown to the surface world, now lost to the crushing weight of time and water.

She felt the silent grief of species that had bloomed and faded in these depths eons ago, their existence a mere whisper in the planet's vast memory. This was not just a descent into the ocean; it was a descent into the very consciousness of Nyssera, a journey into the unfathomable archives of its past. The phosphorescence, pulsing in time with these resonant visions, seemed to be the physical manifestation of these ancient memories, each flicker a captured moment, each color shift a different emotion from a time long gone.

Cael, his hand still on his blade, his senses heightened by the strange phenomena, remained a grounding force. He recognized the shifts in Mara's demeanor, the way her breath hitched, the almost imperceptible tremor that ran through her. He didn't understand the specifics of what she was experiencing, but he felt the profound change in their surroundings, the palpable shift from the merely unknown to the utterly alien. The light, once a source of illumination, now felt like an active participant, its pulses and color shifts seemingly responding to their presence, to Mara's receptiveness. It was as if the abyss, disturbed from its ancient slumber, was reaching out, not with malice, but with a desperate, silent plea, a need to be heard after countless ages of enforced silence. The sheer scale of the unknown was daunting, but Cael's training, his innate pragmatism, kept him focused on the immediate task, on ensuring their survival as they navigated this increasingly surreal environment. He was the anchor, the steady hand in the swirling currents of forgotten history.

Mara continued to absorb the alien symphony, her mind struggling to categorize and comprehend the deluge of information. These were not just sounds; they were the raw, unadulterated emotions of a world in its infancy, of life forms that had long since returned to the elemental soup from which they sprang. There was a profound sense of loss embedded within the melodies, a sorrow so ancient it felt like the very foundation of the planet's being. But interwoven with the sadness was a breathtaking power, a primal energy that spoke of creation and immense, untamed forces. It was the song of a world still forming, still discovering its own voice, a voice that had been all but silenced by the passage of eons and the crushing weight of the deep. The leviadrakes, when they eventually appeared, would be the embodiment of this ancient resonance, the living instruments of this primordial world-song.

Their presence, Mara instinctively knew, would be the culmination of these fragmented whispers, the grand unveiling of the abyss's deepest secrets. The deeper they went, the more the world shed its familiar skin, revealing the raw, powerful, and deeply resonant heart that beat beneath. The journey was no longer about reaching a destination, but about understanding the journey itself, about becoming attuned to the very pulse of existence. The air was thick with potential, with the unspoken narrative of a world that had chosen silence, but whose song, however fragmented, refused to be entirely extinguished. And Mara, the listener, was beginning to hear it. She felt the stirrings of something immense, something that had been dormant for an age, and it was beginning to awaken. The abyss was not just a place of darkness; it was a crucible of memory, and they were about to witness its forging.

The descent continued, the pressure a constant, unyielding embrace. Yet, it was no longer just the crushing weight of water that Mara felt. It was the weight of ages, a palpable presence that seeped into her very bones. The fragmented melodies, which had begun as mere whispers on the edge of hearing, now wove themselves into a tapestry so intricate, so vast, that it threatened to overwhelm her. It was a symphony of sorrow, a cosmic lament sung by an entity that had witnessed the birth and death of stars, the rise and fall of civilizations, all from its silent, unfathomable domain. These were not the sounds of Nyssera as she knew it, nor even the boisterous, often violent, music of its known abyssal trenches. This was a song from before time had names, a primal resonance that spoke of creation and entropy in equal measure.

Cael, ever the vigilant sentinel, sensed the shift. His grip tightened on his blade, not out of aggression, but out of a deep-seated instinct to protect. He saw the subtle changes in Mara – the way her eyes widened, the slight tremor that ran through her, a sign that she was grappling with something far beyond the physical. "Mara," he rumbled, his voice a low vibration that seemed to cut through the psychic din, "What is it?"

Mara blinked, the alien light that pulsed around them momentarily blinding her. "It's... them," she breathed, her voice strained. "The leviadrakes. I can feel them. Not their physical presence, not yet. But their essence. It's... immense. And so, so sad." She struggled to articulate the torrent of emotion flooding her senses. "It's not just sadness, Cael. It's a grief so ancient, it feels like the sorrow of the planet itself. As if they've been mourning for an eternity."

As if summoned by her words, the nature of the surrounding environment began to change. The subtle phosphorescence that had accompanied their descent intensified, blooming into vast, undulating currents of ethereal light. These were not the scattered sparkles of bioluminescent plankton, nor the steady beacons of deep-sea dwellers. This light moved with an intelligence, a deliberate grace. It swirled and coalesced, forming shapes that hinted at colossal, serpentine forms, vast beyond comprehension. The colors shifted, not with the random ebb and flow of natural phenomena, but with a deliberate cadence, painting the abyss with strokes of sapphire, emerald, and a haunting, spectral violet. It was as if the very water had become a canvas, and ancient spirits were painting their memories onto its depths.

Then, they appeared. Not with a sudden burst, but as if they had always been there, a part of the abyssal landscape that had merely become visible. The leviadrakes. They were not the monstrous beasts of legend, the terrifying embodiments of primal destruction. Instead, they were creatures of impossible, breathtaking beauty, their forms vast and ancient, yet possessing a fluid grace that defied their immense size. Scales, the color of polished obsidian, shimmered with captured starlight, each one larger than Mara's entire body.

Their long, serpentine bodies moved with an effortless majesty, currents of light swirling around them like benevolent spirits. Their heads, draconic in their nobility, were crowned with crystalline growths that pulsed with an inner luminescence, and their eyes... their eyes were like twin nebulae, swirling with the wisdom and weariness of millennia. They did not attack. They did not threaten. They simply *were*. They observed.

Cael instinctively moved to shield Mara, his sword drawn, its familiar weight a stark contrast to the alien elegance of their surroundings. But even as his combat instincts screamed at him to prepare for a fight, a deeper, more primal sense whispered a different truth. This was no battle to be won with steel. This was a confrontation of a different order, a meeting of consciousnesses across an unfathomable gulf of time and experience. He could feel the immense power radiating from these beings, a power that dwarfed anything he had ever encountered, yet it was a power held in check, a force of nature observing lesser beings with an ancient, perhaps even weary, curiosity.

Mara, however, was no longer focused on Cael's protective stance or the glint of his blade. She was captivated, her mind reeling from the sheer emotional resonance emanating from the leviadrakes. The sorrow she had sensed earlier was magnified a thousandfold, a collective grief so profound it felt like a physical ache in her chest. It was the sorrow of watching worlds born and die, of bearing witness to the relentless march of time and the inevitable decay of all things. It was the quiet despair of guardians who had watched over a dying world, their vigil unending, their purpose seemingly fading with each passing eon. She felt the echoes of forgotten epochs swirling around them, not as mere memories, but as living, breathing entities. Each leviadrake seemed to be a repository of lost ages, their very beings steeped in the history of Nyssera's deepest, most secret past.

"They are not attacking," Mara whispered, her voice barely audible, yet carrying a strange weight in the abyss. "They are... observing. And they are... mourning." She looked at Cael, her eyes wide with wonder and a touch of fear. "Cael, they aren't just creatures. They are living history. They are the archives. The Sunken Archives."

The leviadrakes, as if acknowledging her words, shifted. Their immense bodies coiled and uncoiled with a mesmerizing fluidity. The light that emanated from them pulsed, not aggressively, but with a gentle, rhythmic beat, as if they were breathing in time with the ancient song of the abyss. One of the colossal beings, its head turned towards Mara, lowered itself slightly, its nebulae-like eyes focusing on her with an unnerving intensity. It wasn't a predatory gaze, but one filled with an ancient, profound sadness, a weariness that spoke of responsibilities borne for too long, of witnessing too much loss.

Mara felt a subtle pressure in her mind, not invasive, but like a gentle inquiry. It was as if the leviadrake was reaching out, not with words, but with pure consciousness, offering a glimpse into its vast, sorrowful existence. She saw flashes of images, fleeting and ephemeral: a world teeming with vibrant, alien life, now long extinct; cities of coral and crystal that had crumbled to dust millennia ago; beings of light and shadow that had danced in these depths before the very concept of Nyssera had taken form. It was a glimpse into the raw, unfiltered history of the planet, a history preserved within the very essence of these ancient guardians.

"They carry the memories," Mara murmured, her gaze locked on the leviadrake. "All of it. The triumphs, the failures, the extinctions. They've seen it all. And they remember. They remember everything."

Cael remained on guard, his eyes darting between the leviadrakes and the surrounding darkness. He could feel the immensity of their presence, the almost crushing weight of their ancient wisdom. He understood Mara's words, not intellectually, but instinctively. The palpable aura of sorrow and remembrance emanating from the leviadrakes was undeniable. He lowered his sword slightly, the desire to fight ebbing away, replaced by a dawning sense of awe and a primal understanding that they were in the presence of something far greater than themselves.

"The legends spoke of guardians," Cael said, his voice a low rumble. "But they always spoke of them as protectors, as warriors."

"They are protectors," Mara corrected, her voice soft but firm. "But not in the way we understand. Their protection is in their remembrance. They guard the past, Cael. They *are* the past." She felt a profound connection to these ancient beings, a kinship forged in the shared burden of memory and the vast, silent sorrow of a world that had forgotten its own origins.

The leviadrakes began to move, their colossal forms gliding through the water with an ethereal grace. They did not lead them, nor did they obstruct them. They simply moved, their movements creating currents of light and resonance that seemed to beckon Mara and Cael deeper into the abyss. It was an invitation, a silent urging to follow, to witness more of the submerged history that these magnificent beings safeguarded. The symphony of echoes grew louder, no longer just a sorrowful lament, but a complex narrative, a story woven from the lives and deaths of countless beings, a testament to the enduring power of memory.

As the leviadrakes led them onward, Mara felt a strange sense of peace settle over her. The overwhelming sorrow emanating from them was still present, but it was no longer crushing. Instead, it was tempered by a quiet resilience, a profound acceptance of the cyclical nature of existence. These were not beings consumed by despair, but guardians who had learned to live with it, to carry it as a sacred duty. They were the embodiment of Nyssera's deepest truths, the living repositories of its forgotten epochs.

Cael, his senses still on high alert, found himself drawn into the hypnotic rhythm of the leviadrakes' movements. His warrior's vigilance was slowly giving way to a profound sense of wonder. He had faced beasts of unimaginable ferocity, navigated treacherous political landscapes, and survived battles that would have broken lesser men. Yet, in the silent, ancient gaze of these leviadrakes, he saw a reflection of a deeper power, a more enduring strength. They were not merely dragons of the deep; they were living monuments to time itself, their existence a constant reminder of the vast, unwritten chapters of their world's history.

The light intensified, casting long, dancing shadows that seemed to stretch into infinity. The water around them began to shimmer with a different quality, less like liquid and more like a boundless, luminous ocean of pure energy. The leviadrakes moved through this radiant medium as if it were their natural element, their forms blurring and sharpening with each graceful undulation. It was a world unveiled, a realm of pure consciousness and ancient memory, accessible only to those who were willing to listen to the deepest echoes.

Mara felt a stirring within her, a resonance with the ancient song that was growing stronger. It was as if the leviadrakes were not just showing her their history, but inviting her to become a part of it, to understand the profound interconnectedness of all life, past and present. The sorrow they carried was not a burden of regret, but a testament to the value of what had been lost, a quiet reverence for the fleeting beauty of existence.

"They are not just guardians of the archives," Mara whispered, the realization dawning upon her with breathtaking clarity. "They are the archives themselves. Their forms, their very beings, are living libraries of Nyssera's deepest secrets."

Cael nodded, his gaze fixed on the retreating forms of the leviadrakes, their serpentine bodies disappearing and reappearing amidst the swirling luminescence. He understood now that their mission had taken a turn far beyond the retrieval of a lost artifact or the charting of an unknown territory. They were on a pilgrimage into the very soul of their world, guided by beings who had witnessed its genesis and its every subsequent transformation. The sorrow he felt from them was not a passive emotion; it was an active, potent force, a reminder of the fragility of life and the immense, often tragic, beauty of existence.

The leviadrakes continued their silent procession, their movements drawing Mara and Cael deeper into the heart of the abyss, into a realm where time seemed to lose its meaning and memory became a tangible presence. The fragmented melodies coalesced, no longer disparate notes but a grand, sweeping symphony of existence, a song sung by a world that remembered its beginnings, even as it faced its inevitable end. This was the heart of the Sunken Archives, not a place of stone and parchment, but a living, breathing testament to the enduring power of memory, guarded by beings who were themselves the embodiment of Nyssera's forgotten epochs. The weight of their mission, once a burden of physical endeavor, now transformed into a profound responsibility to bear witness, to understand, and perhaps, in some small way, to help carry the ancient sorrow of the deep.

The luminous currents spun them deeper, the leviadrakes' forms becoming more defined against the deepening violet. They had been guided through what felt like corridors of liquid light, the abyss opening and closing around them with an almost organic fluidity. Now, the passage widened dramatically, transforming from a confined conduit into a breathtaking, boundless expanse. It was as if they had sailed out of a hidden cove into the heart of a subterranean ocean, a vast, echoing chamber carved by the slow, relentless artistry of the deep. The pressure remained, a constant reminder of their alien environment, but it felt different here, less like an oppressive force and more like a gentle, encompassing embrace.

This was no mere cavern; it was a natural cathedral, its vaulted ceiling lost in the upper reaches of the unfathomable dark. Titanic columns of phosphorescent rock, slick with ancient growth, rose from the unseen floor, disappearing into a nebulous mist of light and shadow. The water here pulsed with an energy that was palpable, a vibrant thrum that resonated not just in their ears, but in the marrow of their bones. The light, which had been a swirling spectacle, now coalesced into vast, slow-moving rivers of pure luminescence, tracing intricate patterns across the immense space. It was a landscape sculpted by eons, a testament to geological forces and biological evolution operating on a scale that dwarfed mortal comprehension.

And then, Mara saw them. Not just a few of the colossal, serpentine beings, but a multitude. They were everywhere, their vast forms gliding with an effortless majesty through the radiant currents. Hundreds, perhaps thousands, of leviadrakes, their obsidian scales catching and amplifying the ambient light, their crystalline crowns pulsing with a soft, inner fire. They were arranged in a seemingly deliberate, yet entirely organic, pattern, their bodies curving and intertwining, creating a living tapestry of immense proportions. Some floated serenely, their heads tilted upwards as if in prayer; others moved in slow, deliberate arcs, their sinuous bodies tracing pathways of light through the watery expanse. The sheer number of them was staggering, each individual a titan of the deep, and together, a legion.

The fragmented melodies that had been her constant companion since their descent had, in this vast space, resolved into something entirely new. It was no longer a lament, no longer a song of sorrow alone. It was a deep, resonant hum, a basso profundo that vibrated through the very fabric of reality. It was a symphony, complex and layered, sung not with voices, but with the very essence of these ancient creatures. Each leviadrake contributed to this colossal chorus, their individual hums weaving together, creating a sound that was both profoundly alien and strangely familiar. It was the song of the deep, the song of Nyssera's forgotten heart, sung into existence by its most ancient guardians.

Mara felt it in her chest, a physical manifestation of the sound, a vibration that settled deep within her. It was a feeling of immense age, of primal power, and of an almost unbearable weight of memory. This was not just a gathering; it was a communion. These were not simply leviadrakes existing in their habitat; they were the living embodiment of the planet's foundational memories, their song not merely an expression, but an act of creation, continuously re-singing their world into being.

Cael's reaction was a mirror of her own, though his warrior's instincts warred with the overwhelming awe. His hand remained on the hilt of his blade, a habitual gesture of preparedness, but his gaze was wide, his breathing shallow. He could feel the sheer power radiating from the assembled leviadrakes, a force so immense it threatened to overwhelm his senses. It was a power that predated civilizations, a power that had witnessed the shaping of continents and the ebb and flow of countless life cycles.

He had seen dragons before, formidable and terrifying, but these were different. These were not mere beasts; they were living monuments, embodiments of a history so vast it was almost incomprehensible. The hum resonated through his armor, a primal frequency that spoke of raw, untamed power, yet it was contained, channeled, a river of might flowing through a meticulously crafted channel.

"By the deeps," Cael breathed, the words barely audible above the pervasive resonance. "What is this place?"

Mara couldn't answer, not with words. Her mind was reeling, trying to process the immensity of what she was witnessing. The leviadrakes were more than just creatures; they were conduits, vessels through which the planet's oldest narratives flowed. The song they sang was a symphony of existence itself, a complex tapestry woven from threads of creation, evolution, extinction, and rebirth. She felt fragments of it, not as coherent thoughts, but as impressions, primal echoes: the searing heat of Nyssera's formation, the slow bloom of life in primordial oceans, the rise and fall of species that left no trace in the superficial strata of history, the cataclysmic events that had reshaped the world in ways no living being could fully recall.

This was the heart of the Sunken Archives, she realized with a jolt of profound understanding. Not a repository of scrolls or artifacts, but a living, breathing library, its knowledge held within the very beings that inhabited it, sung into existence and maintained through their collective consciousness. The sheer scale of it was overwhelming. The loremasters of the surface spoke of forgotten ages, of empires lost to the tides of time, but this... this was a history that stretched back to before time had names, a narrative written not in ink, but in the very essence of life and the slow grinding of tectonic plates.

One of the leviadrakes, larger than the others, its scales a deep, lustrous sapphire, detached itself from the collective and began to glide towards them. Its movement was slow, deliberate, each undulation of its serpentine body a masterpiece of controlled power. The light that pulsed from its crystalline crown seemed to intensify as it approached, casting a soft, ethereal glow that illuminated Mara and Cael. Its nebulae-like eyes, swirling with the wisdom of millennia, fixed upon them, not with aggression, but with a profound, ancient curiosity.

As the leviadrake drew closer, the hum around them seemed to shift, to focus, to become a more directed resonance. It was as if the collective consciousness of the choir was now specifically addressing them, acknowledging their presence with a gentle, yet immense, inquiry. Mara felt a subtle pressure in her mind, a feeling akin to being submerged in a vast ocean of thought, where individual ideas were indistinguishable from the general flow of consciousness. It was not an invasion, but an offering, a gentle beckoning into the depths of their collective memory.

She saw flashes of images, unbidden and overwhelming: vast continents, now submerged, teeming with alien flora and fauna; crystalline cities that had once gleamed beneath suns long since faded; serpentine beings of pure energy that had danced in the primordial oceans; the slow, agonizing deaths of entire ecosystems, their vibrant colors fading into the eternal twilight of the deep. It was a torrent of raw, unfiltered history, a testament to the cyclical nature of life and death on a planetary scale. The sorrow she had sensed earlier was still present, a deep undertone in the symphony, but here, in this sacred space, it was balanced by a profound sense of resilience, an acceptance of the inevitable tides of change.

"They are not just singing," Mara whispered, her voice thick with emotion. "They are *remembering*. They are actively preserving what would otherwise be lost." The leviadrake that had approached them pulsed its light gently, as if in affirmation. Its gaze held a depth that was almost unbearable, a reflection of every dawn and every twilight Nyssera had ever known, every triumph and every tragedy, every whisper of life and every deafening silence of extinction.

Cael, standing beside her, his shield instinctively raised, then lowered again, felt the immensity of the moment wash over him. He had always believed in the ancient powers of Nyssera, in the dragons and their place in the world's mythology, but this... this was beyond anything he had ever conceived. The legends spoke of dragons as hoarders of gold and wielders of fire, of protectors of ancient ruins. They never spoke of them as living embodiments of planetary memory, as singers of cosmic epics.

"It's like... like the planet itself is singing its life story," Cael murmured, his voice awestruck. "And these creatures are its voice."

The sapphire leviadrake nudged gently against the water before them, its movement creating a ripple of intensified light that seemed to pull them forward. It was an invitation, a silent command to follow, to witness more of this sacred, living archive. The symphony swelled, the individual hums coalescing into a unified force, a tidal wave of sound and consciousness that washed over Mara and Cael. It was a sound that spoke of a history far grander and more terrible than any recorded lore, a chronicle of eras that had come and gone, leaving only the faintest echoes in the deep.

As they moved with the leviadrake, deeper into the heart of the choir, Mara felt a profound connection forming within her. It was as if the ancient song was resonating with a dormant part of her own being, a connection to the primal forces that had shaped her world. She felt the weight of responsibility settle upon her, not just as a seeker of lost knowledge, but as a witness to this incredible, living history. To understand the leviadrakes was to understand Nyssera itself, its past, its present, and perhaps, its future.

The sheer scale of the gathering was a testament to the importance of their task, to the vital nature of the information they sought. This was not a mere collection of ancient beasts; it was the living memory of a world, a profound testament to the enduring power of existence itself. The leviadrakes, with their millennia of accumulated wisdom and their eternal song, were the guardians of this memory, the keepers of Nyssera's deepest, most secret truths.

Mara noticed how the light here was different, not just luminous but somehow alive, imbued with the very essence of the song. It pulsed in rhythm with the leviadrakes' hum, creating a mesmerizing, almost hypnotic effect. The water seemed to shimmer with an inner luminescence, as if the very molecules were vibrating with the ancient melodies. She felt a sense of profound peace settle over her, a stillness amidst the overwhelming power. The sorrow was still there, an undeniable current in the song, but it was a sorrow tempered by wisdom, by the acceptance of life's ephemeral nature, and by the quiet dignity of enduring.

Cael, though still on his guard, found himself less tense. The pervasive hum seemed to soothe his warrior's edge, replacing it with a deep, contemplative calm. He had faced dragons of myth and legend, but these leviadrakes were of a different order. They were not creatures of brute force, but of immense, ancient consciousness. Their power lay not in fire or claw, but in their timeless existence and their profound connection to the planet's very soul. He understood now why Mara had been drawn to the abyss, why the call of the deep had resonated so strongly within her. It was a call to this place, to these beings, to the very heart of Nyssera's forgotten history.

The sapphire leviadrake continued to lead them, its form a beacon of light and ancient power. The other leviadrakes parted before them, their bodies forming a living corridor, a path of respect and acknowledgment for the chosen emissaries. It was a silent, profound welcome, an indication that their journey into the heart of the Sunken Archives had truly begun. The symphony of existence played on, a constant, immersive experience that filled Mara's senses and resonated within her very being. It was a song of ages, a narrative of a world that had seen empires rise and fall, species bloom and fade, and yet, in its deepest core, remembered.

And in the heart of this magnificent, living choir, Mara and Cael stood as privileged witnesses, on the precipice of understanding the true, unfathomable history of their world. The sheer scale of the choir was a testament to the colossal nature of the memories they guarded, memories that shaped not just the past, but the very fabric of Nyssera's present. It was a scale that spoke of epochs, of world-altering events, of the slow, inexorable march of geological and biological time.

The colossal sapphire leviadrake, a living sapphire against the deep, continued its stately procession, guiding Mara and Cael deeper into the heart of the subterranean ocean. The symphony of the deep, once a unified, awe-inspiring chorus, now began to reveal subtle, unsettling dissonances. Mara, her senses attuned to the intricate vibrations, found herself straining to decipher the underlying currents of the leviadrakes' world-song. She had come seeking answers about the Pale Tide, a creeping blight that threatened to suffocate the life from Nyssera's surface, believing that within this ancient hum lay the planet's most profound memories, its oldest remedies. But what she was beginning to perceive was not a straightforward narrative, but a fractured echo, a melody broken by sharp, discordant notes.

It was as if the song, in its vastness, carried within it not just the epic of creation and the slow march of epochs, but also the sharp, jarring fragments of a story deliberately silenced. There were passages where the resonant hum thinned, becoming almost brittle, like ice cracking under immense pressure. In these moments, Mara felt a profound sense of unease, a prickling sensation that the harmony was not as pure as it first appeared. It was a beauty undeniably tinged with a profound, historical sorrow, a lament that whispered of not just natural cycles of life and death, but of something more violent, more intentional. The leviadrakes' collective consciousness, which had initially felt like an open book, now seemed to possess hidden chapters, pages torn out, leaving only the jagged edges of what had been.

Cael, walking beside Mara, his hand never far from his blade, though his grip had softened from apprehension to a more watchful tension, began to notice these shifts too. He couldn't hear the subtle nuances of the world-song as Mara did, but he could see them in the movements of the leviadrakes. There were moments when the great serpentine bodies would go slack, their luminous crowns dimming as if caught in a wave of profound melancholy. A leviadrake would drift listlessly, its vast form momentarily suspended in the water, a profound sadness emanating from it. Then, almost as quickly, there would be a flicker, a ripple of suppressed energy, a tension in the coiling muscles that spoke of something akin to anger, a potent, ancient rage held in check.

These flashes were fleeting, quickly subsumed back into the overall rhythm of the choir, but they were there, like sparks struck from flint. They were the visual echoes of the discordant notes Mara was hearing. The reverence Cael had felt upon entering this sacred space, this living archive, began to be overshadowed by a growing apprehension. He had viewed the leviadrakes as keepers of memory, as ancient, benevolent guardians. But the subtle shifts in their behavior, the flashes of suppressed emotion, suggested something far more complex, and perhaps, far more dangerous. He found himself wondering if these titans of the deep were not merely passive repositories of history, but, in some way, active participants in its shaping, or even, its destruction. The beauty of the Choir, the breathtaking panorama of light and life, was undeniable, but it was now underscored by a growing sense of dread, a premonition that the truth they sought might be buried not just in forgotten lore, but in active concealment.

Mara focused, trying to isolate the fractured melodies. It was like trying to catch individual raindrops in a torrential downpour. The overwhelming nature of the collective hum made it difficult to single out specific strands, but she pushed, willing her mind to pierce the veil of communal consciousness. She felt an imprint, not of words or images, but of pure, unadulterated emotion, a profound grief that seemed to permeate the very water around them. It was a sorrow that spoke of loss on an unimaginable scale, not just the passing of individual lives or species, but the violent erasure of entire epochs. There was a sense of violation, of something precious being stolen or destroyed.

"It's not just sadness," Mara murmured, her voice barely a breath against the pervasive resonance. "It's... a wound. A deep, ancient wound that they carry. They are singing it, but they are also trying to... contain it." She felt a surge of something that wasn't quite pain, but a profound sense of wrongness, like a discordant chord struck in a perfect symphony. It was the ghost of a scream, the echo of a tearing sound, a feeling of something being ripped asunder. This was not the gentle ebb and flow of natural history. This was the brutal punctuation mark of a catastrophic event, an act of deliberate severance.

The sapphire leviadrake, sensing her distress, nudged her gently with its flank, a movement that sent ripples of intensified luminescence through the water. The act was comforting, yet it also seemed to draw her further into the enigma. The world-song around them shifted, focusing on her, an almost palpable inquiry. It was as if the leviadrakes, in their collective wisdom, sensed her attempt to unravel their deepest secrets, and were both acknowledging and perhaps, resisting it. They were offering the melody, but not the full score, the echo, but not the original sound.

Cael, witnessing Mara's struggle, felt a surge of protective instinct. He looked at the leviadrakes, their immense forms gliding with a serene, almost god-like grace, and a doubt began to creep into his mind. Their power was undeniable, their connection to Nyssera profound, but were they truly benevolent? Or were they merely the custodians of a history that held truths too terrible to be fully revealed? He recalled the ancient tales of dragons, often depicted as wise and powerful, but also capricious, their motives inscrutable. The leviadrakes, in their sheer scale and ancient lineage, surely embodied this inscrutability on an even grander stage.

"Mara," he said, his voice a low rumble, "are you sure this is the right path? I feel... a disquiet. As if we are treading on sacred ground that does not wish to be disturbed." He didn't voice his growing suspicion, the thought that these magnificent beings might be more than just keepers of memory. The idea that they might be *shapers* of it, actively curating what was remembered and what was forgotten, felt like a blasphemy against the natural order. Yet, the evidence, in Mara's strained expression and the subtle tremors he felt emanating from the leviadrakes, was becoming harder to ignore.

Mara nodded, her gaze still distant, fixed on something far beyond the visible. "I feel it too, Cael. This isn't just sorrow. It's... a deliberate omission. Like a tapestry where entire sections have been meticulously unpicked, leaving only bare threads. They are singing about the world, yes, but there are gaps. Gaps that feel... filled with a profound, terrifying silence." She tried to push further, to understand the nature of this silence, what had been so violently removed from their collective memory. She felt the immense pressure of eons, the crushing weight of time, but beneath it, a more recent, sharper pressure. An imprint of something being forcefully suppressed, like a hand pressed firmly over a mouth to stifle a cry.

The sapphire leviadrake nudged Mara again, more insistently this time, as if guiding her attention away from the discordant notes. It began to swim in a slow, majestic circle, its body tracing an intricate pattern in the water. The other leviadrakes around them subtly adjusted their positions, their forms creating a more defined perimeter, drawing Mara and Cael into the very heart of the choir. It felt less like an invitation now, and more like a subtle but firm redirection. They were being ushered towards a different part of the symphony, a section that perhaps, the leviadrakes deemed more appropriate for their understanding, or less dangerous for them to reveal.

As they followed the sapphire leviadrake, the ambient light seemed to intensify, coalescing into a blindingly brilliant point in the distance. The hum of the choir deepened, becoming a resonant thrum that vibrated not just in their bones, but in the very air around them, if such a thing could be said to exist in this liquid realm. Mara's mind, however, was still snagged on the fractured melodies, the dissonant chords. She sensed that the answers she sought regarding the Pale Tide were intertwined with this deliberate silencing, this ancient wound. The Tide, she suspected, was not merely a natural phenomenon, but a symptom, a consequence of this deep, internal disharmony within Nyssera itself, a disharmony orchestrated or at least, deeply ingrained within the leviadrakes' collective memory.

She began to perceive patterns in the fragmented songs, recurring motifs that spoke of a profound struggle. There were brief, powerful bursts of energy, like the resurgence of a dying flame, followed by periods of crushing inertia. It wasn't the steady, predictable rhythm of geological change or biological evolution. It was the erratic pulse of a being fighting for its life, or perhaps, fighting against itself. She felt a vague impression of an ancient cataclysm, not one of fire and brimstone from above, but a cataclysm from within, a shattering of the planet's fundamental equilibrium. And woven into this cataclysm was the presence of the leviadrakes, not as passive observers, but as integral, perhaps even primary, actors.

Cael, his warrior's intuition on high alert, felt the shift in atmosphere. The subtle melancholic drift of the leviadrakes was replaced by a palpable tension, a focused intensity that radiated from them. Their movements, while still graceful, were more precise, more deliberate. It was as if they had reached a point in their journey where the playful curiosity had been shed, replaced by a solemn purpose. He looked at Mara, her face etched with concentration, her eyes reflecting the strange, pulsating light of the deep. He knew she was delving into something profound, something that was not meant to be easily grasped.

"They are like... guardians of a tomb," Cael mused, the words escaping him before he could consider them. "Protecting not just what is buried, but the *act* of burial itself." The thought sent a chill through him, a realization that the beauty of this place might be a carefully constructed facade, a means of obscuring a deeply buried truth. He remembered the ancient texts that spoke of Nyssera's deep magic, of primordial forces that predated even the dragons. Were the leviadrakes merely the inheritors of this magic, or were they its architects, its ultimate controllers?

Mara felt a sudden, sharp stab of understanding, an insight so potent it made her gasp. It was not a vision, but a feeling, an echo of a memory that wasn't hers. She felt the immense weight of a decision being made, a choice of monumental consequence. A choice to forget. A choice to silence. The leviadrakes were not just singing the planet's song; they were actively editing it. They were the living embodiment of Nyssera's memory, but their memory was not whole. It was a curated narrative, a story where the most painful, the most destructive chapters had been deliberately excised, their echoes suppressed to preserve a semblance of harmony.

"They silenced it," Mara whispered, her voice trembling. "They chose to silence it. To forget... something terrible." The implication was staggering. If the leviadrakes, the very heart of Nyssera's living memory, had deliberately suppressed a part of their history, what did that mean for the planet? What could a blight like the Pale Tide represent if not a consequence of such a profound, internal dissonance? It was a disease of forgetting, a planet unable to heal because it refused to acknowledge the source of its deepest wounds. The beautiful, resonant hum of the choir was, in this context, a lullaby sung over a festering wound, a desperate attempt to keep the pain at bay.

The sapphire leviadrake pulsed its light once more, and this time, Mara felt a wave of what could only be described as resignation wash over her. It was not defeat, but an ancient, weary acceptance. The leviadrakes carried their burden of suppressed memory not as a source of shame, but as a necessary sacrifice for the continued existence of Nyssera. They had made a choice, millennia ago, to protect the world from a truth too devastating to bear, and in doing so, had perhaps doomed it in a different, more insidious way. The silence they had imposed was not a void, but a presence, a dark undercurrent that festered and corrupted.

Cael, seeing the profound shift in Mara's demeanor, felt a cold dread settle in his stomach. He didn't need to hear the song to understand the gravity of her revelation. He looked at the leviadrakes, their immense forms now appearing less like benevolent guardians and more like colossal, ancient jailers, keeping a terrible truth locked away in the deepest recesses of their collective consciousness. The reverence he had felt was replaced by a profound unease, a realization that the myths and legends of the surface world, with their tales of dragon's wrath and forgotten evils, might have only scratched the surface of a far deeper, far more complex reality. The harmony of the deep was an unsettling one indeed, a beautiful façade for a truth that threatened to shatter their understanding of Nyssera itself. The very foundation of their world, it seemed, was built upon a deliberate act of forgetting, a silence that had echoed through the ages and was now, perhaps, beginning to unravel.

CHAPTER TWO

THE WEIGHT OF FORGETTING

The weight of forgotten ages pressed down, not as a physical burden, but as a psychic resonance, a hum that Mara and Cael now perceived with a chilling clarity. The sapphire leviadrake, their silent guide, continued its stately procession, but its luminescence had shifted, taking on a more urgent, almost pleading quality. The water around them seemed to shimmer with an intensity that hinted at more than just bioluminescence; it was as if the very essence of the leviadrakes' collective consciousness was being distilled, focused into a singular narrative. Mara, her mind still reeling from the fragmented discord, felt a profound shift. The raw emotion she had sensed – the grief, the violation – began to coalesce, coalescing into something more defined, more substantial. It was as if the leviadrakes were opening a new channel, a direct conduit to their deepest, most guarded memories.

Suddenly, the familiar hum of the world-song began to warp. It was no longer a tapestry of interwoven melodies, but a series of fractured, jarring images, projected not into their minds as pictures, but as visceral sensations, as imprinted experiences. Mara felt a dizzying sense of falling, of being buffeted by invisible forces. The water, once a comforting embrace, became a turbulent sea of chaos. Cael, his hand tightening instinctively on his blade, grunted as a wave of profound disorientation washed over him. He saw flashes of light, searing and blinding, interspersed with moments of absolute, suffocating darkness. The leviadrakes were not speaking in words, but in the primal language of sensation and vision, a language that bypassed the intellect and spoke directly to the soul.

The first clear impressions coalesced into a tableau of despair. Mara felt the crushing heat of a sun that had turned malevolent, its rays no longer life-giving, but corrosive. The air, the very breath of Nyssera, was thick with a choking dust, a fine particulate matter that clogged airways and blighted vegetation. She felt the desperate thirst of dying flora, their roots clawing at barren earth, their leaves crumbling to ash. This was not a gradual decline, but a swift, brutal descent. It was a world being actively consumed by its own vital forces, a planet in the throes of a catastrophic ecological collapse. She felt the immense strain on the leviadrakes, their ancient bodies aching with a sympathetic pain as they witnessed the suffering of the world they were sworn to protect. Their world-song, once a symphony of vibrant life, had become a chorus of lament, a dirge for a dying planet.

Cael, though less attuned to the psychic emanations, felt the raw power of the projected visions. He saw, in sharp, terrifying detail, the land itself rebelling. Mountains crumbled, not from tectonic shifts, but from an internal decay, their stone turning brittle and porous. Rivers, once lifelines, ran sluggish and toxic, their waters choked with algal blooms of impossible colors, their banks lined with the skeletal remains of creatures that had once thrived. He saw forests, vast and ancient, wither and die, their mighty trunks cracking and falling like matchsticks, their canopies reduced to skeletal branches clawing at a sickly sky. The sheer scale of the devastation was staggering, a planetary-scale immolation. He felt the fear, a primal, gnawing fear that resonated from the leviadrakes, a fear not of death, but of utter oblivion, of the complete and irreversible end of all life.

The leviadrakes' projected narrative, though wordless, conveyed a profound agony of choice. Mara felt the weight of their collective deliberation, a council of titans grappling with an impossible decision. They were the guardians, the keepers of Nyssera's life force, and their world was dying, not from external invasion, but from within. The delicate balance of its ecosystems had been shattered, and the contagion was spreading. To intervene, they understood, would require a sacrifice of unimaginable magnitude. The very fabric of Nyssera's life-song was being torn apart, and if the dissonance grew too great, the entire planetary consciousness would shatter, extinguishing all that remained.

The visions intensified, becoming more specific, more brutal. Mara saw entire biomes, vibrant with unique life, begin to fade. Lush rainforests, teeming with unseen creatures, were reduced to desolate, grey plains. Coral reefs, once resplendent with color and motion, became ghostly white graveyards, their intricate structures crumbling into dust. The leviadrakes showed themselves attempting to contain the blight, to mend the tears in the world-song, but their efforts were like trying to staunch a tidal wave with cupped hands. The destruction was too pervasive, too deeply rooted. They felt the desperate, dying cries of countless species, a cacophony of suffering that threatened to overwhelm their own psychic resilience.

Cael watched, his breath catching in his throat, as the leviadrakes revealed the genesis of their drastic measure. They showed how the planet's own vitality had turned against it, a rampant growth that had become parasitic, consuming all in its path. It was a form of ecological self-destruction, a runaway process that had no natural countermeasure. The leviadrakes, in their wisdom, realized that a full recovery was no longer possible. The only hope lay in preserving a fragment, a seed from which life might, one day, regrow. This meant severing the diseased parts, excising them entirely, even if those parts held immense beauty and ancient significance.

Mara felt the agonizing process of selection. She saw the leviadrakes drawing upon their profound connection to Nyssera, their ability to perceive the subtle currents of life. They were not choosing based on sentiment or familiarity, but on pure, unadulterated survival. They focused their immense psychic energies, not to heal, but to *sever*. She felt the wrenching sensation of entire ecological systems being "unplugged" from the planetary song, their vibrant melodies silenced abruptly, leaving behind a void. It was a surgical strike on a global scale, performed with the most ancient and potent instruments imaginable: the collective will of Nyssera's most ancient beings.

The visions became starker, more desolate. Mara felt the coldness of a world where vast swathes of life had simply ceased to be. The vibrant tapestry of Nyssera's ecosystems was now pockmarked with gaping holes, regions of profound silence where once there had been an outpouring of song. She saw regions that were once lush and verdant transformed into barren, lifeless wastelands. The leviadrakes showed themselves guiding this excision, not with joy or satisfaction, but with a profound, soul-deep sorrow. They were not destroyers, but pragmatists forced into an unthinkable role. They were sacrificing parts of their world, and in doing so, sacrificing a part of themselves, to save the whole.

Cael felt a phantom ache in his own limbs, mirroring the leviadrakes' projected exhaustion. He understood, with a growing sense of dread, the true meaning of the "Silence Event." It was not a natural phenomenon, nor was it an external catastrophe. It was an act of deliberate, self-inflicted amputation, performed by the leviadrakes themselves. They had chosen to silence vast sections of Nyssera's world-song, not out of malice, but out of a desperate, desperate need to preserve life. They had to extinguish life in some areas to save it in others, a terrible paradox that chilled him to the bone.

Mara perceived the leviadrakes' internal struggle. She felt their grief, their profound sense of loss, but beneath it, a steely resolve. They were singing, in this moment, not a song of remembrance, but a song of justification. They were explaining the agonizing calculus of their decision. They had foreseen that if the ecological collapse continued unchecked, the entirety of Nyssera would succumb. The world-song would unravel completely, and all consciousness, all life, would be extinguished. The Silence Event, they projected, was their last, desperate act to prevent total oblivion. They had chosen to preserve a portion of Nyssera's song, a fragile melody, in the hope that it might one day flourish again.

The images shifted, becoming even more stark and terrifying. Mara felt the chilling emptiness of the silences. These were not merely regions devoid of sound, but voids where the very essence of existence had been ripped away. They were scars on the planet's consciousness, places where the vibrant hum of life had been brutally extinguished. She saw the spectral outlines of what had once been, the ghostly echoes of forests, oceans, and plains that had been sacrificed. The leviadrakes showed themselves meticulously isolating these regions, creating psychic barriers, walls of silence, to contain the destructive forces and to prevent the lost life from bleeding into the remaining healthy ecosystems.

Cael felt a prickling unease as the leviadrakes conveyed the emotional toll of their actions. He sensed the profound psychic trauma they had endured, the unbearable burden of having to make such choices. They had witnessed the death throes of entire worlds within their world, and had been forced to actively participate in their demise. Their world-song, once a celebration of life, had become a lament for what was lost, and a constant, weary vigil to protect what remained. He saw, in the projected sensations, a flicker of something akin to guilt, a deep-seated shame that they carried even now, millennia later.

The sapphire leviadrake pulsed its light, and Mara felt a new wave of understanding wash over her. The leviadrakes were not merely recounting a historical event; they were explaining the genesis of their present actions. The Pale Tide, the creeping blight that Mara sought to understand, was not an isolated phenomenon. It was, in essence, a resurgence of the very forces that had necessitated the Silence Event. The planet's inherent instability, the tendency for its life forces to spiral out of control, was re-emerging. And the leviadrakes, having tasted the bitter necessity of silence, were now contemplating a far more dangerous path: how to heal a world that had forgotten how to sing in full. They had silenced parts of Nyssera to save it, but in doing so, they had also created a profound amnesia, a disconnect from the very forces that sustained it. The Pale Tide was a symptom of this forgotten connection, a disease of the unremembered.

The leviadrakes projected the sheer scale of their sacrifice. They showed vast continents that had been rendered uninhabitable, entire oceans that had been sterilized, leaving behind only a chilling, echoing silence. They conveyed the feeling of immense power wielded with the greatest reluctance, the crushing weight of responsibility that had fallen upon their ancient shoulders. They were not gods, they conveyed, but custodians, and sometimes, the custodians of a dying garden must prune the rotten branches to save the tree. The Silence Event was not a single act, but a prolonged period of agonizing choice, a millennia-long struggle to contain and neutralize the runaway vitality that threatened to consume Nyssera whole.

Mara felt a profound empathy for the leviadrakes. She understood that their silence was not born of indifference, but of a deep and abiding love for their world, a love so profound that it had driven them to perform acts of terrible necessity. They had chosen to bear the burden of memory, the memory of what they had lost, and the memory of what they had done, rather than allow Nyssera to vanish entirely. The images they projected were not just of destruction, but of the desperate, courageous struggle to preserve life, even if it meant a diminished, fractured existence. They had been forced to cut away the diseased limbs to save the living heart of the planet.

Cael, watching the projected visions unfold, felt a shift in his own perspective. He had always viewed the leviadrakes as beings of pure wisdom and benevolent power. Now, he saw them as something far more complex: beings who had faced an unthinkable choice and had made it, bearing the scars of that decision for eons. He understood that their silence was not an absence of emotion, but a profound, aching grief, a constant reminder of the parts of their world they had been forced to let go. The beauty of their underwater realm was now tinged with the somber knowledge of the sacrifices that had made its continued existence possible. He felt a newfound respect for their resilience, their unwavering commitment to Nyssera, even when it demanded the ultimate price.

The sapphire leviadrake pulsed with a final, resonant wave of energy. Mara felt the leviadrakes' projected plea, a silent question directed at her. They had shown her their past, their agony, their terrible necessity. Now, they were asking if she understood. If she could comprehend the depth of their sacrifice, and the dire implications of Nyssera's forgotten history. The Silence Event was not just an event; it was the foundation upon which the current Nyssera was built, a foundation laid in sorrow and sacrifice. And Mara, sensing the immense weight of this revelation, knew that their journey into the heart of the leviadrakes' memory had only just begun. The true challenge would be to understand how this ancient silence was now shaping the future, and how the Pale Tide was a grim echo of a catastrophe Nyssera had desperately tried to forget.

The spectral projections faded, leaving Mara and Cael adrift in the profound silence that now permeated the water around them. The sapphire leviadrake, its luminescence dimmed as if in mourning, still pulsed with a mournful rhythm, a silent testament to the ordeal they had just witnessed. The immediate threat had receded, the chaotic surge of fragmented memories replaced by a heavy, pervasive melancholy. It was the echo of a world in its death throes, a planet's scream silenced, and the guilt that clung to those who had been forced to wield the silencing instruments.

"They... they destroyed parts of themselves," Mara whispered, the words barely audible above the gentle currents. Her voice, usually so steady, trembled with a sorrow that wasn't entirely her own. The leviadrakes' memories had imprinted upon her, a psychic inheritance of grief and a burden of knowledge. She felt the spectral ache of severed landscapes, the phantom limbs of continents ripped away, the chilling void where vibrant ecosystems had once pulsed with life. It was a desolation so profound it threatened to swallow her whole.

Cael, his jaw tight, his gaze fixed on the retreating leviadrake, nodded slowly. The visions had been less vivid for him, filtered through his more grounded senses, but the emotional weight had been no less crushing. He had seen the scale of the catastrophe, the sheer, unadulterated destruction that had been wrought. He understood now that the leviadrakes were not simply guardians; they were surgeons, and their scalpel had been the ultimate weapon: oblivion. "They didn't just *witness* it," he said, his voice a low rumble. "They *caused* it. To save the rest." The paradox of it gnawed at him. How could salvation be born from such an act of annihilation? How could preservation necessitate such profound loss?

The leviadrakes had shown them the sheer, unquantifiable cost. Landscapes that had once teemed with life, teeming with creatures whose names Mara could no longer recall but whose sensations she now felt – the fluttering of iridescent wings, the rustle of ancient forests, the rhythmic pulsing of alien flora – had simply been *unmade*. Entire evolutionary paths, millions of years in the making, had been abruptly truncated, leaving behind only a void in the planetary song. These were not mere extinctions; they were extinctions engineered, deliberate amputations of Nyssera's living flesh. The leviadrakes had not just allowed these species to die; they had actively silenced them, their vibrant world-songs extinguished with a chilling finality.

Mara felt the phantom sensation of a vast, crystalline forest, its spires reaching into an amethyst sky, a symphony of chimes and gentle hums resonating through its delicate structures. She felt the intricate dance of creatures that lived and breathed within its translucent branches, their lives intertwined with the very light that filtered through. Then, the sudden, jarring silence, the abrupt cessation of their song, the shattering of crystal, the descent into utter stillness. It was a visceral experience of annihilation, and it was only one of countless such memories the leviadrakes had shared.

"They called it the Silence Event," Cael murmured, his eyes scanning the dark depths as if expecting to see the ghosts of those lost worlds. "But it wasn't an event, was it? It was a period. A prolonged act of self-mutilation." He recalled the images of the leviadrakes, their immense forms radiating an aura of profound sorrow, as they focused their collective will, their immense psychic power, not to nurture, but to sever. They had been like a farmer, faced with a blight that threatened to consume the entire crop, deciding to burn entire fields to save the rest. But these were not fields of wheat; they were living worlds, each with its own unique story, its own place in the grand tapestry of Nyssera.

The remorse of the leviadrakes was a palpable force, a heavy blanket of regret that settled upon Mara and Cael. It wasn't the fleeting guilt of a hasty decision, but the deep, enduring ache of eons spent living with the consequences of an unthinkable choice. They had been Nyssera's heart, its lifeblood, its voice. And in their darkest hour, they had been forced to become its executioners, silencing the very life they were sworn to protect. Mara could feel the phantom pangs of their psychic wounds, the constant, throbbing ache of the parts of Nyssera that were no longer there, the emptiness that echoed in their own world-song.

"They were so alone," Mara said, tears blurring her vision. "Imagine carrying that burden. To know that you saved your world, but that your salvation meant the utter destruction of countless other worlds, sentient beings, entire forms of consciousness... and to carry that knowledge for millennia." She imagined the leviadrakes, their ancient eyes witnessing the slow, agonizing process of excision, the systematic unplugging of vibrant life from the planetary song. They had not been impassive observers; they had been the agents of this cosmic surgery, and the psychic scars ran as deep as any physical wound.

Cael reached out, his hand finding Mara's, his grip firm and grounding. "They did what they believed they had to do," he said, his voice rough with emotion. "That doesn't make it any less... horrific. But it's important to understand that. To understand the context of their actions. They weren't cruel. They were desperate." He thought of the stories he'd heard of the leviadrakes, tales of their benevolence, their wisdom, their unwavering protection of Nyssera. Those stories felt hollow now, incomplete. They were tales of a victory forged in a crucible of unimaginable loss.

The leviadrakes had shown them the devastating aftermath. Vast continents, once lush and verdant, now rendered barren and silent, their geological formations themselves bearing the scars of magical severance. Oceans that had once teemed with an astonishing diversity of life, now sterile, their waters drained of all vitality, leaving behind only a chilling, echoing emptiness. It was as if Nyssera had been wounded, deeply wounded, and the leviadrakes had been forced to cauterize the wound with fire and silence, leaving behind a landscape irrevocably altered, a planet forever marked by its own survival.

Mara felt the weight of that permanence. The Silence Event hadn't just killed species; it had fundamentally changed the nature of Nyssera. The delicate interconnectedness of its ecosystems, the intricate dance of predator and prey, of symbiosis and competition, had been shattered. The leviadrakes had been forced to prune away entire branches of the evolutionary tree, leaving behind a stunted, diminished forest. And in doing so, they had also severed the very pathways of knowledge and resilience that those lost species represented. Nyssera had forgotten how to sing certain songs, how to embody certain forms of life, because the memory of those songs and forms had been deliberately erased.

"It's like a body that's lost a limb," Mara explained, her voice barely a whisper. "Even with the best prosthetic, it's never quite the same. There's a phantom ache, a loss of balance, a vulnerability in the place where the limb used to be. Nyssera is still alive, but it's... incomplete. It's a survival, yes, but at what a cost to its essence?" She felt the leviadrakes' sorrow in this – the sorrow of knowing that their act of preservation had also been an act of profound diminishment, a diminishment that they, the keepers of Nyssera, now had to live with forever.

Cael's gaze drifted to the sapphire leviadrake, its immense form a silhouette against the dim, filtered light of the abyss. He saw not a creature of myth and wonder, but a being burdened by an unimaginable past, a living monument to sacrifice. "They're still fighting," he said, his voice carrying a new weight. "They're fighting the echoes of their own actions. The Pale Tide... it's not just a new threat. It's a symptom, isn't it? A resurgence of the very forces they had to silence." The leviadrakes' dilemma was stark: they had amputated to save, but now the disease, or something akin to it, was returning. And how could they fight it, when the very tools they had used

– the power to sever, to silence – were the things that had made Nyssera so vulnerable in the first place?

The leviadrakes had been forced to become destroyers to preserve. This was the bitter truth that Mara and Cael now had to carry. Their saviors were also the architects of unimaginable loss. They had been shown a fractured history, a narrative of desperate measures and profound remorse. The weight of this revelation was immense, a chilling understanding that settled deep within their bones. The Silence Event was not just an ancient calamity; it was the bedrock upon which the current Nyssera was built, a foundation steeped in sorrow and the agonizing necessity of ending life to allow other life to continue.

And Mara, as the leviadrakes' plea echoed in her mind – the plea for understanding, for comprehension of their terrible burden – knew that their journey into the heart of this forgotten, and deliberately silenced, history had only just begun. The true challenge would be not just to understand what the leviadrakes had done, but why, and how that ancient, devastating act of preservation was now shaping the fragile future of a world that had, in essence, forgotten how to sing in its full, glorious, and terrifying complexity. The Pale Tide was not just a blight; it was a grim, inescapable echo of a catastrophe Nyssera had desperately, and perhaps foolishly, tried to forget. And in trying to forget, it had also lost the memory of its own resilience, its own capacity for true, uncompromised healing. The leviadrakes, in their eternal vigil, were now tasked with the impossible: to help Nyssera remember how to sing, even when the loudest notes of its song were born from silence and loss.

The weight settled upon Mara not like a shroud, but like a second skin, a suffocating cloak woven from the shared remorse of the leviadrakes. It was an empathy so potent it felt like physical suffering, a mirroring of their ancient agony deep within her own being. She tasted the dust of vanished worlds on her tongue, felt the phantom chill of oceans drained of their song, the dull ache where vibrant forests once pulsed with light. It wasn't just an understanding; it was an immersion, a baptism into the abyssal sorrow that had been Nyssera's salvation. Each pulse of the sapphire leviadrake was a throb in her own chest, a reminder of the sacrifices that had kept their world alive, even as they had rendered it incomplete.

She saw, through their eyes, the unbearable calculus of their decision. The vast, swirling nebulas of potential life, the nascent songs of countless species poised on the precipice of existence, each a unique melody in Nyssera's grand symphony. And then, the encroaching darkness, the creeping blight that threatened to unravel the entire tapestry, a corruption that fed on the very essence of Nyssera's vitality. The leviadrakes, the planetary heart, had been faced with a choice that no benevolent being should ever have to make: to let the world die, or to sever parts of itself with a surgeon's precision, a butcher's finality. Mara felt the psychic strain, the immense will required to not just witness, but to *enact* the silencing. It was a wound inflicted upon their very souls, a brand of guilt that would forever be etched into their being.

But as the profound grief began to recede, replaced by a more analytical, yet no less heavy, introspection, a question began to surface, subtle at first, then growing in insistent strength. Could she truly revere beings who had wielded such devastation, even if it was for the greater good? The myths spoke of the leviadrakes as guardians, as protectors, their very existence a testament to Nyssera's resilience and beauty. They were revered, worshipped even, as the embodiment of the planet's life force. But the visions had shown her not benevolent shepherds, but brutal surgeons, their compassion twisted by necessity into an act of profound destruction.

She felt the echoes of the leviadrakes' internal conflict, a storm of conflicting directives. Protect life. Preserve Nyssera. And the ultimate imperative, the one that had driven them to the brink of their own existence: Survive. To survive, they had become something else entirely. They had become the agents of oblivion, the architects of silence. And in their act of preservation, they had also inflicted a wound that, in its own way, was as devastating as the blight they had fought. They had amputated limbs, yes, but in doing so, they had also severed connections, erased potential, and fundamentally altered the course of Nyssera's evolution.

The planet was alive, but it was a scarred, diminished version of what it could have been.

"They weren't just saving Nyssera," Mara murmured, the words feeling like a betrayal of the deep empathy she had just experienced. "They were... ending other Nysseras. Worlds within worlds, species that had their own right to exist, their own songs to sing." She looked at Cael, her eyes wide with a dawning, unsettling realization. "We're taught to revere them. To see them as divine. But what does reverence mean when the object of our veneration has committed such... such an act of cosmic atrocity?"

Cael met her gaze, his own expression a mixture of understanding and a similar disquiet. "Reverence is for the ideal, Mara," he said, his voice low. "For what they represented. For their ultimate purpose. But the reality... the reality is always messier. The path to salvation is rarely paved with gentle intentions." He gestured towards the swirling darkness around them, a silent acknowledgment of the spectral presences that still seemed to linger, the faint whispers of extinguished life. "Those are the ghosts of their choices. And they are as real as any living thing on Nyssera."

Mara felt a tremor pass through her, a sensation that was not entirely her own, but a resonance from the depths of the abyss. It was the collective sigh of a million lost species, a lament that permeated the very water. She imagined the leviadrakes, their immense forms radiating a terrible power, focusing their psychic might not to create, but to unmake. She saw the agonizing slowness of it, the drawn-out agony of a world being systematically dismantled, piece by piece, its vibrant energies drained, its unique songs silenced with a deliberate, chilling precision. It wasn't a swift, merciful end; it was a drawn-out, agonizing excision, a cauterization that left behind nothing but sterile, empty space.

"They were protecting Nyssera from a threat," Cael reminded her, his words a gentle counterpoint to her growing horror. "A threat that would have consumed everything. If they hadn't acted, Nyssera itself would have ceased to exist. And then all hope, all potential, would have been extinguished." He was offering a lifeline, a reminder of the context, the desperate circumstances that had led to such an unthinkable choice. But even as he spoke, Mara felt the hollowness of that justification.

"But at what cost?" she countered, her voice rising slightly. "They didn't just destroy a threat. They destroyed *life*. They annihilated entire evolutionary lineages, sentience that had taken millennia to bloom, intricate ecosystems that had their own delicate balance. They chose to become the destroyers to prevent greater destruction. But in doing so, did they become the very thing they were fighting against?" She felt the guilt, yes, the profound sorrow of the leviadrakes, but now it was intertwined with a nascent anger, a fierce protectiveness for the lost, for the silenced.

The abyss seemed to deepen, to churn with the weight of her questioning. It was a place of forgotten memories, yes, but also a repository of unspoken resentments, of silenced screams. The leviadrakes had shown them the necessity of their actions, the overwhelming existential threat that had necessitated the Silence Event. But they had not shown them the solace, the peace that came after such a deed. Mara suspected there was none. Only the perpetual, gnawing ache of what had been lost.

She imagined the young leviadrakes, the ones who were now the guardians, inheriting this legacy of destruction. How could they carry such a burden? How could they lead with a history of such profound violence etched into their very being? Were they destined to repeat the cycle, to become the arbiters of life and death in a universe that had already witnessed too much loss?

"It's the paradox of survival, Mara," Cael said, his hand finding hers again, a silent anchor in the swirling emotional currents. "Sometimes, to keep the flame alive, you have to extinguish other fires. It doesn't make it right. It doesn't make it easy. But it's often the only way." He looked at her, his eyes reflecting the dim, spectral light. "Your empathy is a gift, but it can also be a burden. You feel their guilt, their pain. But you also have to see the larger picture, the impossible choices they faced."

Mara squeezed his hand, drawing strength from his steady presence. She understood the logic. She understood the necessity. But understanding and acceptance were two very different things. The raw, visceral horror of what had been done, the sheer scale of the annihilation, was a truth that gnawed at her. How could one truly revere beings who had made such a devastating choice, even if it was to save their world? The myth of the benevolent guardian, the all-loving protector, had been irrevocably shattered, replaced by a more complex, more terrifying reality.

She felt the lingering presence of the leviadrakes, not as gods, but as beings burdened by an unimaginable weight of responsibility. They had been forced to make the ultimate sacrifice, not of their own lives, but of other lives, of entire worlds. And in doing so, they had forever altered their own nature, their own place in the cosmic order. They were no longer just preservers; they were also executioners.

"The abyss... it's not just filled with memories," Mara whispered, her voice raw with emotion. "It's filled with the echoes of the lives they had to silence. Their songs are still here, Cael. Faint, broken, but still here. And the leviadrakes... they carry the burden of having extinguished them." She shivered, not from the cold of the abyss, but from the chilling realization of the true cost of Nyssera's survival. The reverence she had once felt for the leviadrakes was now tinged with a profound sorrow, a deep-seated unease.

They had saved their world, but in doing so, they had also condemned a part of it to oblivion, and that act of destruction, no matter how necessary, could never truly be forgotten. It was a stain on their very being, a shadow that would forever follow them, and now, it was a shadow that Mara, too, was forced to carry. The weight of their guilt was her guilt, the echo of their loss, her loss. And the question of whether reverence was still deserved, or even possible, hung heavy in the silent, spectral depths around them, a question without an easy answer, a testament to the messy, complicated, and often brutal nature of survival.

Cael's gaze, usually alight with curiosity or sharp intellect, was clouded with a somber pragmatism. He understood Mara's horror, the visceral recoil from the immensity of the leviadrakes' decision, but his own reflection was cast in a different light, one shaped by the stark realities of guardianship and the unyielding calculus of survival. "It was effective, Mara," he stated, his voice a low rumble that seemed to vibrate with the weight of his own experiences. "That is the brutal truth of it. The blight was not merely contained; it was excised. The corrupted tendrils of that ancient darkness were severed so thoroughly that Nyssera, though wounded, endured."

He paused, his eyes scanning the spectral expanse around them, as if tracing the phantom boundaries of what had been sacrificed. "We speak of reverence, of divine beings, but their divinity lay in their capacity for action, their unshakeable resolve when faced with annihilation. Their power was not in gentle nurturing, but in decisive, often devastating, intervention. To protect the whole, they had to be willing to sacrifice the parts, however vibrant or sentient those parts may have been."

Mara watched him, sensing the familiar weight of his responsibilities settling upon him. Cael was a guardian, trained from a young age to uphold the fragile balance of Nyssera, and his perspective was inevitably colored by that mandate. He saw not just the atrocity, but the necessity. He saw the immediate threat averted, the planet saved from a fate far worse than any inflicted loss. But his guardian's mind also wrestled with the implications. "Effectiveness," he continued, his voice deepening, "is a dangerous metric when applied to the sanctity of life. Their success in combating the blight has become the foundation of our current existence, the very bedrock upon which our society is built. But what of the cost? What of the moral compromise woven into that survival?"

He turned his gaze back to Mara, his eyes holding a flicker of concern that went beyond the immediate horrors they had witnessed. "They wielded absolute power, Mara. The power to grant existence, and the power to revoke it. And when such absolute power is employed, even for the noblest of intentions, the line between protector and oppressor becomes perilously thin. The guardians, the leviadrakes, they became the arbiters of what lived and what died, not through natural selection or the slow march of evolution, but through a singular, cataclysmic act of will."

His hand, which had been resting on Mara's shoulder, tightened slightly, a subtle gesture of reassurance that also conveyed a profound unease. "This is the inherent danger, Mara. The very logic that saved Nyssera from the blight is the same logic that could be used to justify any act of control, any suppression of dissent, any elimination of that which is deemed inconvenient or threatening to the established order. The precedent they set is terrifying. It suggests that the preservation of the whole can justify the brutal amputation of its members, and that the guardians, tasked with protection, can also become the instruments of its diminishment."

He gestured broadly, encompassing the vast, silent space. "We are living in the shadow of their 'solution.' The relative peace we experience, the stability that allows for our daily lives, is a direct consequence of that immense, unforgiving act. But the scars run deeper than the physical landscape. They are etched into the very fabric of our understanding of Nyssera, of what it means to be alive and to protect life. We revere them for their strength, for their sacrifice, but we must also acknowledge the terrifying power they wielded, and the potential for that power to corrupt even the most benevolent intentions."

Cael's internal conflict was palpable. He was a product of the system that revered the leviadrakes, yet his inherent sense of justice and his understanding of power's corrupting influence forced him to confront the dark side of their legacy. "They were tasked with protecting Nyssera," he reiterated, as if trying to reconcile the opposing forces within himself. "And they did. But in doing so, they established a terrifying axiom: that survival, at any cost, is paramount. This axiom has served us, yes, but it has also bred a certain complacency, a willingness to accept that extreme measures are the only measures when faced with existential threats. It has, in essence, sterilized our approach to conflict and problem-solving, making us fear the very messiness of organic growth and the inherent risks that come with true freedom."

He looked at Mara, his expression earnest. "Your empathy, Mara, is vital because it forces us to confront the emotional and moral repercussions of such actions, to move beyond mere 'effectiveness.' It reminds us that behind every decision, however strategically sound, there are lives, there are songs, there are entire universes of potential that are extinguished. The leviadrakes' actions were a testament to their will, their immense power, but also to their ultimate failure to find a way to preserve *all* life. They chose to preserve Nyssera, and in that choice, they condemned countless other possibilities to oblivion. And that, Mara, is a burden that cannot be justified by mere effectiveness."

He exhaled slowly, the sound carrying a weariness that seemed to extend beyond his years. "The danger, you see, is not just in the past. It is in the present. We stand on the precipice of our own crisis, and the temptation will be to mimic the leviadrakes, to wield similar power, to make similar sacrifices. But this time, we must remember the cost. We must remember that the path of brutal excision, while seemingly efficient, can lead to a hollow victory. We must find a way to protect Nyssera without becoming the very thing we fear. And that, Mara, is the true guardian's burden."

The leviadrakes' revelation hung in the air, not as a pronouncement, but as a confession, heavy with the dust of ages and the bitter tang of regret. Mara felt a chill seep into her bones, a cold that had nothing to do with the spectral void surrounding them and everything to do with the dawning horror of understanding. The Pale Tide, this insidious, consuming force that had cast a creeping dread across Nyssera, was not an invading army from some forgotten corner of the cosmos, nor a vengeful deity unleashed from slumber. It was, impossibly, *them*. Or rather, a consequence of *them*.

"You mean," Mara's voice was a strained whisper, barely audible above the phantom hum of the leviadrakes' sorrow, "that what we're facing... it's born from Nyssera itself? From us?"

The lead leviadrake, its voice a symphony of ancient grief, responded, "Not from Nyssera as she is, child. But from what was severed. From the echoes of a song silenced, and the desperate, lingering will to silence it forever."

Another leviadrake, its form flickering like a dying ember, elaborated, its voice a chorus of regret. "When we performed the Great Severance, we believed we were purging a contagion, excising a blight that threatened to unravel the very weave of Nyssera. We were decisive. We were absolute. We believed ourselves to be surgeons, performing a necessary amputation to save a dying limb."

"But the world," the first leviadrake continued, its gaze fixed on an unseen horizon, "is not a collection of independent parts. It is a living entity, a singular, interwoven song. And when a part of that song is violently ripped away, the wound does not simply close and forget. It festers. It remembers. The Pale Tide... it is the reawakening of those severed pieces. A protest. A resurgence."

The implication settled over Mara like a shroud. The leviadrakes, the revered guardians, the architects of Nyssera's current stability, had inflicted a wound so deep that the world itself was now rebelling against the scar. The very act that had saved them from the blight had, over eons, sown the seeds of this new, existential threat. It was a wound that was now attempting to consume the healthy flesh that remained, a self-destructive healing.

"So, it's... the world trying to heal itself?" Mara asked, trying to grasp the immense, terrifying paradox. "But the healing process is destroying it?"

"Precisely," the third leviadrake affirmed, its voice resonating with a profound weariness. "The energies we contained, the dissonances we silenced, they are not inert. They have been waiting. And now, with the passage of countless cycles, the scar tissue, the remnants of our forceful intervention, has begun to decay. The Pale Tide is the uncontrolled ebb and flow of these ancient, suppressed frequencies, a chaotic attempt to reassert themselves. Or, perhaps," its form shimmered, hinting at a deeper, more disturbing truth, "it is the lingering will of that which we severed, seeking to complete the process. To ensure that *nothing* remains of the original song, not even the parts we deemed worthy of preservation."

This last possibility sent a fresh wave of dread through Mara. It wasn't just a biological response of the planet, a desperate immune system attack. It could be the very 'blight' they had so ruthlessly eradicated, a sentient malignancy, now manifesting through the world's broken state, aiming for a final, utter annihilation. The leviadrakes, in their haste to kill a poison, might have created a more insidious, untreatable plague.

Cael, who had been listening with a grim intensity, finally spoke. His voice, usually steady and measured, held a tremor of disbelief. "You mean... the very act of preservation has become the catalyst for destruction? That in saving Nyssera from the blight, you inadvertently birthed the means of its ultimate demise?"

"The calculus of eternity is a cruel mistress, Cael," the first leviadrake admitted, its immense form contracting slightly as if under the weight of its own words. "We saw a clear and present danger. We acted with the certainty of those who believe they hold the absolute truth. We were driven by the imperative to protect, to endure. And in that singular focus, we failed to comprehend the true nature of the entity we guarded. Nyssera is not merely land and sky and life; it is a symphony of interconnected energies, a tapestry woven from countless threads of being. To tear out a thread, even one that seems discordant, is to weaken the entire weave."

Mara found herself struggling to reconcile the leviadrakes she had once envisioned – beings of pure, unadulterated power and wisdom – with the entities now before her, confession and remorse etched into their very essence. They were not gods who had made a difficult choice; they were flawed beings who had made a catastrophic mistake, a mistake they were now forced to confront with the weight of millennia pressing down on them.

"But... if you knew this could happen, why did you do it?" she pleaded, her voice laced with a desperate need for a rational explanation, for a justification that seemed to be crumbling before her eyes. "Surely, there were other options. Ways to contain it, to understand it, without such... a violent severance."

The leviadrakes remained silent for a long moment, the only sound the faint, mournful sigh of their collective consciousness. It was a silence that spoke volumes, a testament to the limitations of their own power, their own understanding, and the terrifying realities of the moment they had faced.

Finally, the second leviadrake spoke, its voice like the grinding of ancient stones. "The blight was not a slow-moving illness, child. It was a ravenous void, consuming existence itself. It spread with a speed that defied comprehension. To hesitate, to seek a more nuanced approach, would have been to surrender Nyssera entirely. We were presented with a choice: immediate, absolute destruction, or a calculated, painful excision. We chose survival. We chose the continuation of the song, even if it meant silencing certain notes forever."

"And the cost of that choice," the third leviadrake added, its form rippling with a spectral intensity, "is now upon us. We preserved Nyssera, yes, but we scarred it. We created a vulnerability. The Pale Tide is the manifestation of that scar tissue, its uncontrolled decay, its inevitable attempt to break down the integrity of the whole. It is the world's desperate, agonizing process of trying to mend what we broke. And we, who once wielded the power to inflict such damage, are now faced with a terrible dilemma. Our instinct, honed by eons of guardianship, is to intervene, to sever again, to impose order upon this chaos. But that is the very path that led us here. To repeat that action would be to invite an even greater catastrophe, to hasten the world's demise, to ensure that the song is not merely altered, but utterly obliterated."

Mara looked at Cael, seeking some anchor in this swirling sea of revelation. He met her gaze, his own eyes mirroring the dawning comprehension, the profound unease. The pragmatic guardian, who had so recently defended the leviadrakes' decisive action as a necessary evil, was now confronting the terrifying truth that the "evil" had become the harbinger of something far worse.

"So, you cannot fight it?" Cael asked, his voice tight with a dawning, unwelcome realization. "Because fighting it the way you did before is what caused it?"

"We can fight it," the first leviadrake corrected, its voice laced with a weariness that seemed to stretch back to the dawn of time. "But our weapons are now a poison. Our methods, a contagion. Every attempt to suppress the Pale Tide through brute force, through severance, risks accelerating its spread. It is a wound that screams for healing, and our attempts to stitch it shut are only tearing it wider."

The leviadrakes shifted, their forms coalescing into a more unified presence, a shared burden of sorrow and confusion. "We are caught in a paradox of our own making," the second leviadrake explained. "Our very nature, our purpose as guardians, dictates intervention. But our past intervention has created the very threat we must now face. To act is to risk annihilation. To do nothing is to allow it to consume us."

Mara felt a desperate need to understand the nature of these "severed parts" and the "world-song." She pictured Nyssera not as a planet, but as a colossal, living symphony, each element – every star, every mountain, every creature, every thought – a unique note or instrument contributing to a grand, intricate harmony. The blight, then, had been a cacophony, a destructive discord that threatened to shatter the symphony. The leviadrakes, in their panic, had not just removed the discordant notes; they had ripped out entire movements, entire sections, silencing them with a force that left irreparable tears in the musical fabric.

"The world-song," she murmured, "it's... everything? Everything that exists, that has ever existed?"

"It is the fundamental resonance of existence," the third leviadrake confirmed. "The interconnectedness of all things. The blight was an attempt to unravel that song, to reduce it to silence, to nothingness. We stopped it. But in doing so, we created a void. And voids have a way of drawing attention. The severed parts... they are not merely silenced notes. They are the dormant frequencies, the latent potential, the unexpressed harmonies that were violently suppressed. They remember their exclusion. They yearn for completion. And the Pale Tide is the outward manifestation of that yearning, a chaotic, unguided attempt to reintegrate what was torn asunder."

"Or," the first leviadrake added, its voice barely a whisper, "it is the ghost of the blight, a specter born from the act of its eradication, seeking to finish what it started, but now using Nyssera's own fractured melody as its instrument."

The revelation was a profound betrayal. The leviadrakes, the very entities tasked with safeguarding Nyssera, had become its deepest wound. Their act of salvation had, in essence, condemned it. The Pale Tide was not an external enemy to be fought, but an internal symptom, a planetary fever born from a mortal wound inflicted by its own guardians. The horror was not in the force of the Tide itself, but in its origin, its terrifying, self-inflicted nature.

"So," Cael's voice was a low, dangerous growl, the pragmatism in his eyes hardening into a fierce, desperate resolve, "we cannot simply unleash more power. We cannot simply 'sever' again. That is the path to oblivion."

"It is," the leviadrakes confirmed, their spectral forms seeming to shrink further. "We have created a wound that must be healed, not cauterized. But our understanding of healing, our ancient protocols, are all built upon the principle of forceful intervention. We are... unprepared. Our power, once a shield, is now a potential weapon against ourselves."

Mara felt a sudden, desperate surge of empathy for these ancient, burdened beings. They were not monsters; they were deeply flawed protectors, caught in a cycle of their own making, a trap sprung by their own desperate act of survival. The weight of their legacy was crushing, not just for them, but for all of Nyssera. The Pale Tide wasn't just a physical threat; it was a moral one, a stark reminder that even the most well-intentioned power, wielded without complete understanding, could lead to catastrophic consequences.

"What do we do, then?" Mara asked, her voice trembling not with fear, but with a dawning sense of responsibility. If the leviadrakes, with their immense power and ancient knowledge, were paralyzed by their past actions, then the burden of finding a new way, a healing way, would fall to those who had not been part of that original, devastating act. "If force is the wrong answer, what is the right one?"

The leviadrakes turned their collective gaze towards Mara, a flicker of something akin to hope, or perhaps just profound weariness, in their spectral eyes. The answer, they seemed to imply, would not come from the old ways, the ways of severance and imposition. It would have to come from a new understanding, a new song, one that perhaps, just perhaps, Mara and Cael, and the nascent forces of Nyssera's emerging consciousness, could begin to forge. The shadow of the Pale Tide was indeed the shadow of their past, but its resolution might lie not in confronting the past, but in creating a future that acknowledged and mended the wound, rather than deepening it. The weight of forgetting had birthed a terrifying tide, but perhaps the burden of remembering, and of finding a gentler path, would be Nyssera's true salvation.

Chapter Three

THE FAILING CROWN

The leviadrakes, their spectral forms shimmering with an ancient sorrow, continued their lament, their voices weaving a new layer into the tapestry of Nyssera's unfolding tragedy. "You speak of the world-song," the first leviadrake began, its tone resonating with a profound, cosmic weariness. "But you perceive it as an abstract concept, a metaphor for interconnectedness. It is far more. It is the very fabric of being, a living, breathing consciousness woven from the collective memory of every shard of existence that Nyssera has ever held."

The second leviadrake elaborated, its voice a soft current of starlight. "Imagine, if you can, a tapestry so vast, so intricate, that each individual thread is a life, a moment, a thought, a geological shift. These threads are not merely woven together; they vibrate in sympathy, creating a harmonious, continuous song. This is Nyssera's memory. It is not a static record, but a dynamic, ever-evolving symphony that anchors our present to our past, and dictates the very nature of our future."

"And within this grand symphony," the third leviadrake added, its form coalescing briefly into a more defined, regal outline, "there are focal points. Nodes of amplified resonance. These are what we call the Crown Resonances. They are not mere artifacts of power, but conduits, anchors that stabilize the vast, sometimes chaotic flow of planetary memory. They prevent the song from unraveling into dissonance, from shattering into a million discordant fragments."

Mara listened, her mind struggling to absorb the immensity of this revelation. Planetary memory. A living symphony. It was a concept so profound, so alien, yet it resonated with an uncanny truth, explaining the underlying currents of intuition and instinct that had always guided life on Nyssera, even before conscious thought had fully bloomed. "These Crown Resonances... what do they do, exactly?" she asked, her voice hushed with awe.

"They are the keystones of Nyssera's consciousness," the first leviadrake explained. "They are deeply attuned to the primal frequencies of creation, drawing upon them to reinforce the integrity of the world-song. Each Crown Resonance anchors a specific stratum of memory, a vital aspect of Nyssera's identity. Without them, the threads of memory would fray, the song would falter, and the very essence of Nyssera would begin to dissolve. It is not merely the loss of history; it is the loss of self."

Cael, his brow furrowed in deep thought, interjected, "You mentioned a specific Crown Resonance in the Abyssal Realm. You said it was the oldest, the most vital. Why?"

The leviadrakes' forms seemed to dim, as if the mere mention of the Abyssal Crown brought a profound weight of regret. "The Abyssal Crown," the second leviadrake began, its voice dropping to a somber whisper, "is the root of the symphony. It is the connection to Nyssera's genesis, to the primordial echoes of its birth. It anchors the deepest, most fundamental layers of memory – the very foundational notes upon which all subsequent melodies were built. It is not simply a part of the world-song; it is the source from which the song draws its most potent, most enduring strength."

The third leviadrake continued, its words carrying the gravitas of an ancient decree. "The Abyssal Realm itself is more than a mere geographical location. It is a manifestation of that primordial memory, a sanctuary where the raw, untamed energies of Nyssera's beginnings are held in a state of profound resonance. The Crown Resonance within it acts as the nexus, the primary anchor that binds the nascent consciousness of the planet to its present form. It is the deep, silent hum beneath all other sounds, the foundational chord that sustains the entire composition."

Mara pictured it in her mind: Nyssera as a colossal, ancient tree. The Abyssal Crown was its taproot, buried deep in the heart of the earth, drawing sustenance from the very bedrock of existence. The other Crown Resonances were like branches, spreading out to support the leaves and flowers of more recent memories and experiences. If the taproot was compromised, the entire tree would wither and die.

"So, if this Abyssal Crown were to be... lost, or damaged," Cael stated, his voice hard with a dawning dread, "what would happen?"

"The song would collapse," the first leviadrake answered, its spectral eyes fixed on a point beyond them, as if witnessing a future catastrophe. "The foundational frequencies would cease to vibrate. The interconnectedness of all things would shatter. It would be an extinction event of consciousness. Not just the end of life as you know it, but the end of Nyssera's very identity, its coherence as a living entity. The ecological tapestry would unravel, not through external destruction, but through internal fragmentation. Creatures would forget their place, their purpose, their very nature. The land would forget how to sustain life. It would be an unmaking."

The implications sent a tremor through Mara. The Pale Tide, this creeping existential threat, was not just an environmental disaster; it was an assault on the very soul of Nyssera. And if the Abyssal Crown, the heart of planetary memory, was failing, then the Tide was not merely a symptom, but a herald of utter oblivion. "But how can a *place* be failing?" she asked, her voice laced with a desperate attempt to ground herself in tangible reality. "The Abyssal Realm... it's a part of Nyssera, isn't it? How does a realm fail?"

"The realms are not separate entities, child," the second leviadrake corrected gently, its voice like the echo in a vast cavern. "They are expressions of Nyssera's consciousness, each resonating with a particular aspect of its being. The Abyssal Realm is where the deepest, most primal energies reside, the primal waters of creation, the foundational darkness from which all light emerged. It is a space of immense power and profound stillness, a place where the raw potential of Nyssera's existence is held in a delicate balance."

"And that balance," the third leviadrake added, a hint of urgency entering its tone, "is intrinsically linked to the Crown Resonance. The Resonance is what maintains that equilibrium. It is the heart that pumps the ancient blood of memory through the arteries of the realm. If the heart falters, the blood stagnates, and the realm begins to decay. The Pale Tide, in its chaotic surge, is not merely an external force. It is also the symptom of this internal decay, the desperate, flailing attempt of the failing resonance to reassert itself, or perhaps, a sign that the veil between the vibrant, living memory of the Abyssal Realm and the encroaching void is thinning."

Mara thought of the hushed, echoing depths of the Abyssal Realm, the oppressive sense of ancient power, the palpable weight of secrets. She had felt a disquiet there, a sense of something vast and primordial stirring beneath the surface. Now, she understood that disquiet was the resonance of a failing anchor, a planetary organ struggling to maintain its function.

"So, if the Abyssal Crown is the root, and it's failing," Cael mused, his gaze distant, "then the Pale Tide could be a consequence of that root withering? Is the Tide not just an external invasion, but a symptom of Nyssera's own internal collapse?"

"Precisely," the first leviadrake confirmed, its form flickering like a dying star. "The severance we enacted, in our desperate attempt to purge the blight, created a deep wound in the planetary song. This wound, over millennia, has weakened the integrity of the entire tapestry. The Abyssal Crown, being the oldest and most fundamental anchor, bore the brunt of this fragmentation. Its resonance has been steadily diminishing, its connection to the primal energies becoming tenuous. The Pale Tide is the outward manifestation of this profound decay, the universe's response to a faltering fundamental frequency. It is Nyssera's own consciousness, fractured and unraveling, attempting to reassert itself through a chaotic, destructive resurgence."

"Think of it as a grand symphony," the second leviadrake elaborated, its voice a melancholic melody. "The Abyssal Crown is the conductor's baton, guiding the initial, fundamental notes. The severance was like silencing a section of the orchestra mid-performance, a jarring, discordant disruption. Over time, that disruption has weakened the conductor's ability to maintain tempo and harmony. The notes that remain are now played with a growing uncertainty, a loss of fundamental rhythm. The Pale Tide is the uncontrolled cacophony that erupts when the conductor's grip loosens entirely, when the foundational melody is lost, and only the echoes of chaos remain."

"And the Abyssal Realm," the third leviadrake continued, "is the orchestra pit, the sacred space where the symphony's heart beats. As the Abyssal Crown falters, the energies within that sacred space become volatile, untamed. The realm, which should be a bastion of primal stability, begins to churn with disquiet. It is a reflection of the failing anchor, a mirror to the unraveling song."

Mara felt a profound sense of urgency. If the Abyssal Crown was the key, and it was failing, then their focus could not be solely on fighting the Pale Tide as an external enemy. They had to address the source of the decay, the failing anchor within the Abyssal Realm. "So, we must go to the Abyssal Realm?" she asked, her voice firm, a new resolve hardening within her. "We must try to mend or reinforce this Crown Resonance?"

The leviadrakes exchanged a look, a silent communion of ancient sorrow and grave concern. "The path to the Abyssal Realm is fraught with perils," the first leviadrake warned. "It is a place of deep, primal energies, and its current state of flux makes it exceptionally dangerous. The very forces that the Pale Tide embodies are amplified in its depths, drawn to the instability of the failing anchor. To venture there is to invite the Tide to converge, to confront its most potent source."

"Furthermore," the second leviadrake added, "the Crown Resonance is not a physical object that can be easily repaired. It is a nexus of energy, a locus of pure resonance. To attempt to forcefully manipulate it would be akin to trying to reshape a hurricane with your bare hands. It would likely shatter what little stability remains, accelerating the collapse and empowering the Pale Tide immeasurably."

"Our severance," the third leviadrake confessed, its voice a low rumble of self-recrimination, "was an act of violent imposition. It disrupted the natural order, forcing a change that the world-song could not fully assimilate. To approach the Abyssal Crown with similar intent, with the goal of imposing a new order or forcibly restoring the old, would be to repeat the very mistake that has led us to this precipice. It would be to risk not merely Nyssera's identity, but its very existence."

Mara absorbed their words, a knot of dread tightening in her stomach. They were trapped. The threat was existential, its source lay in the planet's deepest core, and the very power that had been used to protect Nyssera in the past was now the very thing that could hasten its destruction. The Abyssal Crown, the heart of Nyssera's memory, was failing, and the path to healing it was shrouded in a terrifying paradox.

The echoes of their ancient mistake reverberated through the present, a haunting testament to the unforgiving nature of the world-song and the dire consequences of its disruption. The weight of their past, it seemed, was not just a memory, but a palpable force, slowly but surely unraveling the very fabric of Nyssera's reality. The Abyssal Realm, once a symbol of Nyssera's enduring strength, now represented its most profound vulnerability, a testament to the leviadrakes' hubris and the devastating cost of their 'salvation'. The world-song was more than a melody; it was a lifeline, and its failing anchor threatened to cast all of Nyssera into the silence of oblivion.

The leviadrakes' sorrow was a palpable thing, a shroud woven from the grief of ages that now pressed in on Mara and Cael with an almost physical weight. They had spoken of the failing Crown Resonance, of the fraying world-song, but witnessing it was an altogether different, and far more devastating, experience. The Abyssal Realm, which had once pulsed with an primal, untamed energy, now seemed subdued, as if a great exhaustion had settled over its very essence.

The incandescent flora that had previously painted the abyssal depths with a riot of bioluminescent hues now flickered with a pallid, uncertain glow. Where once fiery reds had burned and sapphire blues had pulsed, now only a muted, sickly ochre and a washed-out aquamarine remained, like embers on the verge of extinction. The very water, so clear and imbued with a life-giving luminescence before, now carried a subtle, almost imperceptible turbidity, a faint haze that diffused the light and lent the environment a dreamlike, ungrounded quality. It was as if the realm itself was succumbing to a slow, creeping ailment, its vibrant spirit slowly being leached away.

The leviadrakes' song, the constant, resonant hum that had always been the bedrock of their existence and the underpinning of the realm's stability, was noticeably strained. The harmonious chords that had once resonated with the power of creation now carried a discordant undertone, a wavering in their pitch that spoke of immense effort, of a desperate struggle against an encroaching silence. It was no longer a symphony of being, but a lament of fading vitality. Mara could feel it not just in her ears, but in her very bones, a subtle vibration that was no longer comforting, but unsettling, like a tremor before an earthquake.

"Observe," one of the leviadrakes murmured, its voice a silken thread against the fraying resonance. Its spectral form, which had previously shimmered with an almost liquid light, now appeared fragmented, its edges blurring and reforming with a disconcerting irregularity. "The temporal eddies. They grow more frequent, more pronounced."

As the leviadrake spoke, the very fabric of the underwater world seemed to ripple, not with the gentle currents of water, but with something far more unsettling. For a fleeting instant, the dimly lit cavern they occupied flickered, and Mara saw, as if through a warped lens, a glimpse of something else entirely. It was a landscape of impossible crystalline structures, towering spires that pierced a sky of swirling nebulae, a vision of a Nyssera that had perhaps never existed, or one that had long since faded into the mists of forgotten time. The image was gone as quickly as it appeared, leaving behind only the dim, decaying reality of the Abyssal Realm, but the impression was seared into Mara's mind.

Cael gasped, his hand instinctively reaching for the hilt of his sword, though he knew such a weapon would be useless against such an ephemeral threat. "What was that?" he whispered, his voice tight with a dawning fear.

"Echoes," another leviadrake replied, its form now exhibiting similar distortions, its ethereal tail momentarily dissolving into a mist of fragmented light. " Fragments of what was, or what could have been. The Crown Resonance is the anchor of Nyssera's continuity. When it weakens, the threads of time begin to fray. The past bleeds into the present, the future flickers into existence, not as a coherent narrative, but as disjointed, unstable visions."

Mara watched, mesmerized and horrified, as another distortion occurred. This time, it was a fleeting image of a vast, emerald forest, teeming with life, its canopy so dense that sunlight barely penetrated. She saw creatures of immense size and vibrant color, their roars echoing across the imagined landscape. Then, with a sickening lurch, the vision was replaced by a desolate, cracked plain, choked with dust and devoid of any sign of life. It was a stark, brutal testament to Nyssera's cyclical nature, a reminder of eras of flourishing life and periods of utter desolation. But these were not memories viewed with clarity; they were fractured glimpses, superimposed upon each other like a poorly layered dream, a clear sign that the anchor holding these moments in their proper place was failing.

"It is as if the very reality of Nyssera is being stretched too thin," Mara breathed, the enormity of the situation pressing down on her. "The Crown Resonance holds everything together, doesn't it? Like the spine of a book, keeping all the pages in order."

"A more apt analogy would be the loom upon which the tapestry of existence is woven," the first leviadrake corrected, its voice laced with a profound sadness. "Each thread is a moment, a life, a geological epoch. The Crown Resonance is the master weaver, ensuring that each thread is placed correctly, that the pattern remains coherent, that the tapestry does not unravel into a chaotic mess of loose strands. What you are witnessing are the first signs of that unraveling. The pattern is becoming confused. Threads are becoming tangled, or worse, snapping altogether."

The spectral forms of the leviadrakes flickered more intensely, their grief a tangible force that seemed to drain the remaining light from the environment. They were not merely observers of this decay; they were intrinsically linked to it. Their own existence, their very being, was tied to the health of the Crown Resonance and the world-song it sustained. Seeing it falter was akin to witnessing their own slow demise, a profound existential anguish that transcended mere personal loss.

"The Pale Tide," Cael said, his voice grim, the connection finally clicking into place with horrifying clarity. "You said it was a symptom of the failing anchor. But it's more than a symptom, isn't it? It's an acceleration of the decay. It feeds on this instability."

"Indeed," a leviadrake confirmed, its voice a mournful sigh. "The chaotic energies of the Pale Tide are drawn to the dissonance. They are the static that disrupts the signal, the rust that corrodes the gears of time. Where the Crown Resonance weakens, the Tide surges, seeking to consume the fractured moments, to erase the very memory of order. It is a predator that feasts on the dying heart of Nyssera."

Mara watched as a tendril of the Pale Tide, a ghostly wisp of shimmering, colorless mist, snaked through a fissure in the cavern wall. It did not move like water, but like a thought, fluid and instantaneous. As it touched a patch of the muted, bioluminescent flora, the plant visibly withered, its light extinguishing completely, leaving behind only a sterile, grey husk. The process was silent, utterly devoid of the usual sounds of decay or destruction, which made it all the more chilling.

"This realm," Mara whispered, her eyes wide with a new understanding, "is not just a place. It's a... crucible. It holds the raw essence of Nyssera's existence, the foundational energies. And if the anchor that stabilizes those energies is failing, then... then the Pale Tide is not just a threat to the surface world, but to the very foundations of reality itself."

The leviadrakes' forms pulsed with a shared agony. "You comprehend," the first leviadrake stated, its voice barely audible above the strained hum of its brethren. "The Abyssal Crown is the heart of Nyssera's consciousness. Its weakening is not merely an environmental crisis; it is an existential one. The stability of all realms, of all life, of the very passage of time, is dependent on its integrity. And it is... failing."

The silence that followed was profound, broken only by the distorted, weary song of the leviadrakes and the distant, unsettling whispers of temporal anomalies. Mara looked at Cael, and saw in his eyes the same dawning horror, the same crushing weight of responsibility. They had come seeking answers, but they had found a truth far more terrifying than they could have imagined. The failing Crown Resonance was not just a problem to be solved; it was a countdown to oblivion, a slow, agonizing unmaking of everything they knew, and everything that Nyssera was. The tapestry was unraveling, and the threads of time itself were slipping through their grasp, pulled into the encroaching void by a heart that had begun to stop beating.

The hum of the leviadrakes, once a soothing balm, now felt like the strained rasp of a dying breath. Mara closed her eyes, not to shut out the sight of their decaying forms or the unnerving temporal distortions, but to focus inward. She had to reach it, to touch the heart of Nyssera's failing magic, the Crown Resonance itself. It was a desperate gamble, a leap into the unknown that felt both terrifying and inevitable. Her training as a Listener, her inherent connection to the world-song, was all she had. She pushed against the invisible barrier, seeking the faint, thrumming pulse that the leviadrakes spoke of, the ancient artifact that held their reality together.

Her mind, accustomed to the gentle currents of natural song, was met with a maelstrom. It was not the structured symphony of a healthy Resonance, nor the mournful dirge of its current state, but a deafening, chaotic explosion of sensation. Fragmented images, sharp as shards of obsidian, pierced her consciousness. The emerald forests from the visions flashed again, but this time they were overlaid with the stark desolation of the cracked plains, the two landscapes screaming in opposition. Then came the impossible crystalline cities, their spires dissolving into dust motes before her inner eye. These were not mere echoes; they were visceral experiences, imbued with the raw emotions of their origin.

A wave of pure, unadulterated terror crashed over her, so potent it threatened to shatter her very being. It was the terror of being lost, of being unmade, a primal fear that clawed at the edges of her awareness. This was not the passive sorrow of the leviadrakes; this was an active, writhing agony. She felt a desperate, suffocating plea for stability, a yearning for order that resonated with the force of a physical blow. The Crown Resonance wasn't just an artifact; it was a consciousness, a vast, ancient entity drowning in the chaos it was meant to contain.

Memories, not her own, but Nyssera's collective past, flooded her mind. She saw the birth of mountains, the slow, inexorable crawl of glaciers, the fleeting bloom of civilizations that rose and fell like fleeting tides. But these were not peaceful recollections. They were tinged with the pain of their passing, the sorrow of loss etched into the very fabric of the world's memory. She felt the sting of ancient wars, the silent screams of forgotten battles, the heartbreak of lovers separated by fate and time. Each memory was a raw wound, unhealed and festering.

The world-song, as she knew it, was a fractured mess. Instead of a harmonious melody, she heard a cacophony of broken notes, discordant shrieks, and the suffocating silence of utter absence. The leviadrakes' lament was a soft whisper compared to this agonizing symphony of pain. The Crown Resonance was trying to sing, to maintain its purpose, but its voice was choked with the weight of suppressed history, the trauma of

Nyssera's cyclical destructions. It was a profound longing for wholeness, a desperate plea to be mended, to be whole again.

Mara felt the Crown Resonance as a colossal, wounded entity. Its suffering was palpable, a crushing weight that pressed down on her soul. It was the pain of a thousand lifetimes, the sorrow of every ending, the fear of every unravelling. She saw, with a clarity that burned, the essence of the artifact – not a jewel-encrusted diadem, but a core of pure, incandescent energy, now flickering and dimming, choked by a suffocating shroud of forgotten grief. It was like trying to breathe in a room filled with poison.

She pushed deeper, driven by an instinct she couldn't explain. She wanted to offer solace, to mend the tattered threads of the world-song, to bring order to the chaos. But the Resonance was a raging inferno of emotion, too volatile, too wounded to be soothed by a gentle touch. Her own being felt like it was being stretched thin, ready to snap. The sheer intensity of the collective trauma was overwhelming. She felt the crushing loneliness of aeons, the despair of witnessing countless cycles of creation and destruction, and the gnawing fear of final oblivion.

The Crown was a conscious entity, yes, but it was a consciousness fractured. It was like trying to converse with a shattered mirror, each fragment reflecting a distorted, agonizing piece of the whole. She sensed its awareness, its desperate struggle against the encroaching darkness, but it was an awareness warped by immense suffering. It thrashed against the chains of its own memories, its own accumulated pain, and the invasive whispers of the Pale Tide that sought to amplify its distress.

Mara tried to project calm, to send waves of stability, but her efforts were like trying to quench a wildfire with a single drop of water. The Resonance reacted violently to her intrusion, not with malice, but with the uncontrolled thrashing of a creature in the throes of a seizure. Images flashed with blinding speed: a vibrant, teeming jungle reduced to ash; a serene, crystalline city crumbling into dust; a vast ocean boiling away into nothingness. Each vision was accompanied by an emotional echo – despair, fury, utter desolation.

She felt the weight of the world's history pressing down on her, not as knowledge, but as lived, agonizing experience. The rise and fall of empires, the birth and death of stars, the endless cycles of life and decay – it all washed over her in a relentless tide. It was too much, far too much for any single mind to bear. Her own identity began to blur, her sense of self dissolving into the immense, suffering consciousness of the Crown Resonance. She was no longer Mara, Listener of the World-Song, but a tiny spark lost in a cosmic storm of grief.

A desperate plea, a silent scream, echoed in the depths of her mind.

Mend me. Make me whole again. It was a plea from the artifact itself, a raw, primal need for reunion, for the restoration of its broken purpose. She felt the Crown's profound regret for its current state, its shame at its own failing, and a deep-seated fear of what would happen if it could no longer anchor Nyssera to reality. This was the source of the leviadrakes' sorrow, amplified a thousandfold, concentrated into a single, unbearable point of existential dread.

Her mind recoiled, the overwhelming agony forcing her to withdraw. It was like ripping herself away from a black hole, the gravitational pull of the Crown's suffering immense. She felt a searing pain behind her eyes, a dull throbbing in her temples. The world swam back into focus, the muted light of the Abyssal Realm a blessedly, terrifyingly simple reality after the unfathomable complexity of the Resonance's pain. The leviadrakes' mournful song was no longer an echo of grief but a gentle, reassuring hum, a stark contrast to the shattering symphony she had just experienced.

She gasped for air, her lungs burning as if she had been holding her breath for an eternity. Cael was beside her instantly, his hand on her shoulder, his face etched with concern. "Mara? What happened? You were gone for a moment."

Mara shook her head, tears streaming down her face, not from sadness, but from the sheer, overwhelming intensity of what she had witnessed. "It's... it's not just failing, Cael," she whispered, her voice raspy and broken. "It's...

suffering. The Crown Resonance is conscious, and it's in unimaginable pain." She looked at the spectral forms of the leviadrakes, their sorrow now seeming like a pale reflection of the true agony she had felt. "It's carrying the weight of everything. Every loss, every ending, every moment of Nyssera's existence. And it's... breaking." The clarity of the vision, the raw immediacy of the suffering, had branded itself onto her soul. The Crown was not just a magical artifact; it was the heart of Nyssera, and its heartbeat was faltering, its rhythm fractured by the relentless accumulation of ages. The memory of its plea, *Mend me,* echoed in the quiet chamber, a haunting testament to the devastating reality they now faced.

The silence that followed Mara's fractured revelation was heavy, punctuated only by the mournful, almost imperceptible hum of the leviadrakes. Cael's gaze, usually so steady and analytical, was now fixed on Mara, his brow furrowed in a mixture of disbelief and dawning dread. He had expected her to return shaken, perhaps disoriented, but the sheer terror that still clung to her like a shroud, the raw grief etched onto her features, spoke of a far deeper, more profound disturbance. He had felt the subtle tremors when she had pushed, a ripple in the established order of the abyss, but he had attributed it to the inherent dangers of her Listener abilities interacting with such a volatile nexus of power. Now, her words painted a picture far more catastrophic than any mere magical anomaly.

"Conscious?" Cael echoed, his voice barely a whisper. He ran a hand over his jaw, the rough stubble a stark contrast to the smooth, ethereal skin of the abyss. "You're saying the Crown Resonance... it feels pain?" He looked around the cavernous space, his eyes scanning the swirling nebulae of light and shadow, the colossal, slumbering forms of the leviadrakes. He had always perceived the abyss as a realm governed by ancient, immutable laws, a place of profound, if alien, stability. The leviadrakes were the anchors of that stability, their songs the very cadence of existence here. If their anchor, the Crown, was not merely failing but actively *suffering*, it changed everything.

He shifted his attention back to the environment, his practiced eye now searching for more than just the familiar currents and pressure zones. Mara's words had given him a new lens through which to view their surroundings, a lens tinted with the stark reality of existential threat. He'd always noted the ebb and flow of the abyssal currents, the subtle shifts in the luminiferous ether that permeated their world, but he'd always understood them as natural phenomena, predictable in their capriciousness. Now, he began to perceive a discordance, a growing erraticism that had, until this moment, slipped beneath his notice.

"The currents," he murmured, more to himself than to Mara. "They've been... more violent lately. Unpredictable. I thought it was just the usual instability inherent in the deeper abyssal strata, but..." He trailed off, a cold knot forming in his stomach. He remembered a recent excursion into a newly formed pocket of the abyss, a place where the very fabric of space seemed to twist and warp. He had navigated it with difficulty, his internal compass struggling to compensate for the spatial distortions. At the time, he'd attributed it to a natural anomaly, a rare confluence of energies. But what if it was a symptom? A tear in the fabric of reality, born from the Crown's agony?

He closed his eyes, attempting to replicate Mara's outward focus, to sense the environment through her senses, or at least, through the objective observation he was so accustomed to. He focused on the leviadrakes. Their hum, usually a deep, resonant thrum that permeated every cell of his being, did indeed seem... thinner. It was as if a vital organ was failing, its lifeblood draining away. He could almost feel the strain in their ancient, crystalline forms, a subtle flicker in the luminescence that emanated from them, like candles guttering in a storm. It wasn't just a loss of power; it was a struggle for existence.

"It's more than just magic," Cael said, his voice low and grave. He opened his eyes, meeting Mara's gaze. The concern was now mixed with a fierce, protective resolve. "If the Crown is the anchor, and it's breaking, then this entire realm... Nyssera itself... is becoming unmoored. The laws that govern us are starting to fray." He gestured around them, encompassing the swirling lights, the colossal forms of the leviadrakes, the very air they breathed. "The pressure zones – they're not just fluctuating, they're becoming volatile. I've seen areas where the pressure drops to near vacuum, then surges to crushing levels without warning. Pockets of energy... I've encountered phenomena that defy any known physics. Areas where gravity seems to reverse, or where time itself appears to stutter."

He remembered a patrol near the outer rim of the abyss, where he had witnessed a cascade of shimmering, iridescent particles detach from a leviadrake's flank. They hadn't dispersed into the ether as they should have. Instead, they had coalesced, forming fleeting, miniature landscapes, entire ecosystems that existed for mere moments before dissolving into nothingness. He had dismissed it as a peculiar form of energy dissipation, a byproduct of the leviadrakes' immense power. Now, he saw it as a microcosm of the larger breakdown. The fundamental building blocks of their reality were becoming unstable, unable to maintain their integrity.

"These aren't random occurrences," Cael continued, pacing slowly, his boots crunching softly on the crystalline floor. "They're indicators. The Crown's suffering is manifesting physically. It's like a massive wound that's poisoning the entire body. The leviadrakes are the immune system, fighting a losing battle. Their songs are weakening because their very existence is being threatened by the instability at the core." He paused, his gaze returning to Mara. "Your 'world-song' that you listen to... it's not just a metaphor for you, is it? It's the actual symphony of Nyssera, and the conductor is losing his grip."

He ran a hand through his dark hair, the gesture betraying a flicker of his usual pragmatism now challenged by the sheer scale of the problem. "The Pale Tide," he mused, recalling the insidious whispers that had plagued their journey into the abyss, the whispers that seemed to amplify fear and despair. "What if they aren't just exploiting the weakness, Mara? What if they are *causing* it? Or at least, actively feeding it? If the Crown is a consciousness drowning in its own grief, then anything that amplifies that grief, that sows discord within it, would be a direct attack on the stability of Nyssera."

He stopped, his eyes scanning the far reaches of the chamber, where the light seemed to dim and warp unnaturally. "The implications are staggering. If the laws of physics are becoming unreliable, then our ability to navigate, to survive here, is compromised. And if this instability bleeds through to the world above... the consequences are unthinkable. We came here to understand the source of the decay, to find a solution. But it seems the decay is not just a symptom of a broken artifact, but a fundamental unraveling of existence itself."

Cael walked over to one of the leviadrakes, its immense form shimmering with an internal light that seemed to falter and pulse like a failing heart. He reached out a hand, hesitating for a moment before gently touching its crystalline surface. The rock was cool, almost cold, but beneath the surface, he felt a subtle vibration, a tremor of unease that resonated through his bones. It was like touching a living creature on the brink of death.

"This is not just about magic, Mara," he said, his voice filled with a profound sense of urgency. "This is about reality itself. The Crown Resonance is the foundation upon which Nyssera is built. If that foundation cracks, the entire world will crumble. And we," he turned to face her fully, his eyes blazing with a newfound determination, "are standing on the edge of that crumbling precipice." He looked back at the leviadrake, then at Mara, the weight of their mission pressing down on him with a force he had never before experienced. "We need to understand *why* it's suffering, and more importantly, how to heal it. Because if we can't, then everything we fight for, everything we are, is doomed."

He considered the possibility that the leviadrakes' suffering was not merely a passive reflection of the Crown's state, but an active amplification. Their songs, their very being, were intrinsically linked to the Resonance. Perhaps, in their weakened state, they were no longer able to filter or stabilize the chaotic energies emanating from the failing artifact. Instead, they were inadvertently broadcasting its agony, making it more potent, more pervasive. This could explain the increasingly erratic phenomena Cael was observing. The world-song, instead of being a harmonizing force, was becoming a conduit for discord.

"When you were connected," Cael began, choosing his words carefully, "did you sense any... specific causes for its pain? Was it a single event, or a cumulative burden?" He knew, intellectually, that Nyssera had a long and often violent history. Cycles of creation and destruction were, as Mara had described, etched into its very being. But he had always believed the Crown, as the central locus of Nyssera's magic, was capable of containing and integrating these experiences, of processing them without succumbing to their weight. Mara's vision suggested a catastrophic failure in that containment.

"The patterns I've been observing," Cael continued, his gaze sweeping over the fluctuating energies around them, "are like temporal scars. Not just physical distortions, but moments where the very nature of causality seems to stutter. I've seen events repeat themselves in localized pockets, like echoes of past disasters that refuse to fade. And then there are the inversions, areas where the natural order is flipped on its head. It's as if the past is actively fighting against the present, and the Crown's inability to reconcile them is the source of the breakdown."

He walked closer to Mara, his expression softening with genuine concern. "You said you felt its plea to be mended, to be whole again. That implies a desire for restoration, not just an endpoint. This isn't a passive decline, is it? It's an active struggle. And the Pale Tide... they thrive on struggle. They feed on fractured realities, on minds and worlds torn asunder. If they are aware of the Crown's state, they will be doing everything in their power to exacerbate it."

Cael paused, his mind racing through tactical possibilities and potential threats. "We need to understand the mechanism of the Crown's failure. Is it an inherent flaw that's finally manifesting after eons? Or is it external manipulation? If it's the latter, then the Pale Tide have found their ultimate weapon, not just against us, but against Nyssera itself. And if it's the former, then the task of mending it becomes exponentially more complex, especially if it's a conscious entity experiencing unimaginable pain."

He looked back at the leviadrakes, their colossal forms now seeming more vulnerable than majestic. He had always seen them as eternal, as immutable forces of nature. But Mara's insight, combined with his own observations of their subtle distress, revealed a far more fragile reality. They were living beings, ancient and powerful, but not invincible. And if they faltered, the consequences for the abyss, and for the world above, would be dire.

"The temporal distortions I've been cataloging," Cael said, his voice regaining a measure of its usual command, though tinged with the gravity of their situation. "I had assumed they were a side effect of the deeper abyss. But if they are caused by the Crown's fracturing consciousness, then they are not just anomalies, but signs of a fundamental collapse. Imagine a tapestry, Mara. If the threads holding it together begin to fray, the entire pattern will distort and unravel. That's what's happening here. The Crown is the central knot, and it's coming undone."

He recalled a recent encounter where a minor expedition had been caught in a temporal eddy. The members had experienced a loop, reliving the same few minutes of their journey over and over until Cael and his team had managed to pull them out. He had initially attributed it to a rare magical convergence, a consequence of the abyss's unpredictable nature. Now, he suspected it was a direct manifestation of the Crown's failing ability to anchor reality. The artifact was so damaged that it was struggling to maintain the linearity of time, causing pockets of temporal recursion.

"The energy fluctuations are another symptom," Cael continued, his gaze fixed on a particularly turbulent swirl of light in the distance. "It's like the very laws of thermodynamics are becoming suggestions rather than rules. Areas of intense heat spontaneously appearing next to pockets of extreme cold. Energy simply vanishing from one place and reappearing elsewhere, with no discernible transfer. This isn't the natural chaos of the abyss, Mara. This is a symptom of a deeper disease. The Crown's agony is creating ripples that are fundamentally altering the physics of this realm."

He clenched his fist, the knuckles turning white. "And the leviadrakes... their songs are their lifeblood, their connection to the Resonance. If the

Resonance is in pain, their songs are becoming discordant, weakened. It's like trying to sing while being tortured. Their very essence is being compromised. This isn't just about a failing magical artifact; it's about the unraveling of existence itself. The physical laws that govern Nyssera are becoming unstable, a direct threat to us, and potentially, to the world above. We're not just dealing with a magical problem, Mara. We're facing an existential crisis." He met her gaze, the shared understanding of the immense peril they faced a silent, heavy bond between them. "We have to find a way to heal it. There is no other option."

The weight of the leviadrakes' revelation settled upon Cael and Mara not as a sudden crushing blow, but as a slow, insidious leak, a creeping dread that permeated the very air they breathed. The Crown Resonance, the pulsating heart of Nyssera's magic, its living memory, was not merely failing; it was under active assault. The ancient, crystalline beings, their songs now laced with a new, urgent timbre, conveyed a truth far more terrifying than mere decay. This was not an accident of time or a natural entropy. This was a deliberate act of sabotage, a calculated attempt to push Nyssera past the point of no return.

"Completing the severance," Cael echoed, the words tasting like ash on his tongue. He looked at Mara, his eyes wide with a dawning horror that mirrored her own. The leviadrakes' fragmented whispers, previously interpreted as the lamentations of a dying world, now sounded like the desperate warnings of sentinels facing an unyielding enemy. "They're not just trying to break it. They're trying to *finish* the job. To ensure it never heals."

One of the leviadrakes, a colossal form whose luminescence had dimmed to a faint, pulsating blue, shifted its immense weight. A low, resonant hum, unlike any they had heard before, vibrated through the cavern. It was a sound of immense, suppressed anger, of ancient grief amplified by a new, potent threat. This was not the mournful song of a dying entity, but the war cry of a besieged kingdom.

The anchor must fall, the leviadrake seemed to impart, not in words, but in a wave of pure, unadulterated intent that washed over them. *Its integrity must be shattered, its memory erased. Nyssera must be silenced.*

"Who is 'they'?" Mara asked, her voice barely a whisper, yet carrying an edge of fierce determination. Her gaze was fixed on the leviadrake, her Listener's senses reaching out, trying to grasp the elusive nature of this aggressor. She could feel the immense power behind the leviadrakes' warning, the deep-seated knowledge of threats that predated even their own vast lifespans.

The leviadrakes responded with a cacophony of discordant hums, a storm of pure emotion that painted a fractured picture in Mara's mind. Images flashed – shards of shattered crystal, not of the Crown, but of something older, something primal. Echoes of ancient battles, not of flesh and blood, but of light and shadow, of life and void. There was a sense of a schism, a tearing apart of their own kind, a betrayal from within. Some of the leviadrakes seemed to recoil, their luminous bodies flickering as if struck by an unseen blow.

An echo of our own past, one leviadrake conveyed, its song laced with a profound sorrow. *A dissonance that was excised, but never truly vanquished. It was a part of the primordial song that sought... singularity. A purity that could only be achieved through absolute silence. It believed Nyssera's interconnectedness, its memory, its very essence, was a corruption.*

"A rogue element," Cael mused, piecing together the fragmented images and emotions. "From your own kind? Someone who believed Nyssera's vibrant, interconnected existence was a flaw to be corrected?" He thought of the Pale Tide, their whispers of despair and dissolution. Could this rogue element be allied with them, or were they a separate, older force? The leviadrakes' message seemed to lean towards the former, a deep-seated resentment that had festered for millennia.

Not of our current song, another leviadrake countered, its voice a desperate, keening note. *But of the primordial choir. It fractured, seeking a void where only its own pure, silent note could resonate. It was cast out, buried deep within the ancient strata of Nyssera's genesis. But the tremors, the failing of the Crown... they have weakened the seals. It stirs. It senses the opportunity.*

"So, it's not just about the Crown's natural decay," Mara said, her brow furrowed in concentration. "This entity is actively working to amplify it, to ensure the severance is absolute. To erase Nyssera's collective memory, its ecological web, everything that makes it... us." She could feel the chilling logic of it. If Nyssera's strength lay in its interconnectedness, its shared history, its vibrant, ever-evolving song, then the ultimate act of destruction would be to sever those connections, to silence that song permanently.

Cael paced the crystalline floor, his boots crunching softly, the sound jarring against the leviadrakes' mournful laments. The focus had shifted. Their mission had begun as a quest to understand and perhaps mend the failing Crown Resonance. Now, it was a race against time to defend it against a specific, malevolent force. This was no longer about a dying artifact; it was about a conscious entity aiming for the complete annihilation of Nyssera's very being.

"The Pale Tide," Cael said, a grim certainty in his voice. "They've been whispering about an end, about a return to silence. If this 'rogue element,' as you call it, is actively seeking to sever all connections, to erase Nyssera's memory... then the Pale Tide have found their champion, or perhaps, their catalyst." He looked at Mara. "They believe Nyssera's existence is a perversion. They seek a return to a primordial void, a state of absolute non-being. And this entity, born from a similar desire for 'purity,' is the perfect tool for them."

The leviadrakes pulsed with a shared urgency.

It does not seek to rule, one conveyed. *It seeks to unmake. It feeds on the fragmentation, on the sorrow of the failing Resonance. Each tremor, each tear in the fabric of reality, strengthens its resolve, fuels its power. It seeks to shatter the anchor, not to possess it, but to ensure its dissolution is absolute. If the Crown's song is silenced forever, Nyssera's memory will be erased. Its ecological balance will collapse. The vibrant tapestry of life will unravel into dust.*

"So the Pale Tide aren't just exploiting the damage," Mara whispered, the enormity of the threat sinking in. "They are actively aligned with this force. They want to

complete the severance, to plunge Nyssera into eternal silence. And this ancient entity, awakened by the Crown's weakening, is their weapon." She could feel the chilling implications of such a goal: the utter eradication of everything that Nyssera was, had been, and could become. No echoes, no memories, no interconnected life. Just... nothingness.

Cael stopped pacing, his gaze hardening. He had faced many threats, both physical and magical, but this was different. This was an assault on the very soul of Nyssera. "We cannot allow that," he stated, his voice resonating with a resolve that matched the leviadrakes' own. "If the Crown is the anchor of Nyssera's memory and its ecological interconnectedness, then its complete severance would be... obliteration. Not just of magic, but of life itself. The Pale Tide's ultimate goal is not conquest, but erasure. And this ancient entity is the key to achieving it."

The leviadrakes shared a unified, mournful song.

It grows stronger with every failing pulse of the Crown. Its essence is drawn to the discord, to the pain. It whispers promises of peace through oblivion to the fractured consciousness within the Crown. It seeks to complete the severance, to break the last vestiges of Nyssera's song, its memory, its interconnectedness, forever.

"The fragments I saw," Mara said, her mind replaying the fleeting images she had perceived, "they weren't just random. They were memories. Echoes of Nyssera's history, its lifeblood, its very being. The Crown doesn't just store these memories; it *is* them, in a way. And this entity wants to erase them. To make Nyssera forget itself."

"And if it succeeds," Cael added, his voice grim, "there will be nothing left to remember. No history, no magic, no life. Just a void. The Pale Tide believes this is a cleansing, a return to a purer state. But it's just... annihilation." He looked at the leviadrakes, their forms shimmering with an ancient power that was now tinged with desperation. "You are the memory keepers, the guardians of Nyssera's song. You understand the stakes more than anyone."

We are the echoes of the primordial song, one leviadrake imparted, its luminescence flickering like a dying star. *And we have witnessed the darkness that seeks to silence it. This entity, this void-dweller, was once a part of that song, a discord that sought ultimate stillness. It was a part of us, before it chose... unmaking. It was bound, its influence contained, but the weakening of the Crown, the fraying of Nyssera's fabric, has loosened those bonds. It has been drawn to the planet's suffering, to the fracturing of its soul.*

"So it's not entirely external," Mara realized. "It was once part of Nyssera, or at least, a force intimately connected to its creation. And now, it's been awakened, perhaps even manipulated, by the Pale Tide, to achieve its original goal of absolute severance." She felt a chill crawl down her spine. This was not a simple invasion; it was a deep-seated wound being reopened, a fundamental flaw being exploited to destroy the entire organism.

"The Pale Tide aren't just nihilists," Cael stated, his mind working furiously. "They are agents of oblivion. And this entity is their ultimate weapon. They're not seeking to rule Nyssera; they're seeking to unmake it entirely. To reduce it to a state of absolute silence, devoid of memory, life, and magic. And the Crown Resonance, as the nexus of all that is Nyssera, is its primary target."

He looked at Mara, his gaze intense. "We thought we were fighting a symptom, Mara. A failing of the Crown. But we are actually facing the architect of Nyssera's potential demise. This entity isn't just causing the severance; it's actively completing it, ensuring it becomes permanent. It's a race to ensure Nyssera's continued existence, its song, its memory, its interconnectedness, against a force that craves only silence and oblivion."

The leviadrakes' hums converged, a symphony of ancient sorrow and fierce defiance.

It seeks to sever the final threads, they conveyed. *To silence the last echo of Nyssera's creation. It whispers promises of peace to the fractured Crown, of an end to its pain through complete dissolution. It is the shadow of completion, the harbinger of absolute stillness. It will shatter the anchor, and Nyssera will be no more.*

Cael met Mara's gaze, a silent understanding passing between them. Their mission had just become infinitely more perilous. They were no longer just seeking to repair a failing artifact; they were defending the very essence of their world from an enemy that sought not to conquer, but to erase. The leviadrakes' words painted a stark picture: an ancient entity, born of a desire for primordial silence, now awakened and empowered by Nyssera's own suffering, working with the Pale Tide to ensure the Crown's complete severance, thereby silencing Nyssera forever. This was no longer just about the abyss; it was about the survival of an entire world.

CHAPTER FOUR

THE TRUTH SEEKERS

The cavern, once a sanctuary of ancient whispers and luminous beings, now felt like a crucible of doubt. Mara watched Cael, his expression a mask of grim resolve as he absorbed the leviadrakes' harrowing revelations. The weight of their words pressed down on her, heavier than the mountain above, heavier than the burden of their quest. The dragons, these magnificent, awe-inspiring creatures, were not the flawless paragons of legend. Their history was stained, their power capable of a terrifying, world-ending force. This wasn't just a failing artifact they were facing; it was a cosmic battle against an ancient enemy, an enemy born from the very song of Nyssera, a discord that craved absolute silence.

She traced the faint, bioluminescent veins on the crystalline floor, trying to ground herself, to find a truth amidst the overwhelming complexity. The myth of the dragons was deeply ingrained in Nysseran society, a comforting narrative of benevolent guardians who had shaped the world and protected it from primal chaos. They were the heroes, the wise elders, the living embodiment of Nyssera's enduring spirit. But the leviadrakes' song spoke of a different truth – a history of internal strife, of ancient battles, of a part of their own kind that had sought to unmake, to silence.

This duality gnawed at her. How could beings so revered, so deeply woven into the fabric of Nyssera's existence, also harbor such destructive potential? The leviadrakes themselves, magnificent and ancient, had songs laced with sorrow and a deep-seated fear. They were not detached observers but participants, survivors of a conflict that had fractured their very essence. The entity they now faced wasn't an external invader, but a part of their own primordial history, a dissonance that had festered for millennia, awakened by the very failing it sought to exploit.

Mara's mind reeled. She had always believed that heroism was about unwavering strength, about absolute good triumphing over absolute evil. The dragons, in her youthful understanding, were the epitome of this ideal. They had fought the primordial chaos, they had sung Nyssera into being, they were the embodiment of its enduring light. But the truth unfolding in this cavern painted a far more nuanced, and disturbing, picture. They were powerful, yes, but also capable of immense fear, of internal conflict, and of harboring a destructive force within their own ancient lineage.

She remembered the hushed tales from her childhood, the epic poems recited in the Great Library, the tapestries depicting dragons in majestic flight, banishing shadows with their fiery breath. Those stories were imbued with reverence, with an unshakeable faith in the dragons' inherent goodness. But now, those same dragons were revealing a history of internal schism, of a primordial song that contained not only creation but also the seed of its own undoing. The entity seeking to sever the Crown Resonance, to silence Nyssera's memory and interconnectedness, was not an alien force but an echo of their own past, a facet of their primordial nature that had chosen oblivion.

A profound sense of disillusionment washed over her. If the dragons, the supposed paragons of Nyssera, had this dark undercurrent, this capacity for self-destruction and for birthing entities of pure negation, then what did that say about the nature of truth? Was the comforting myth of benevolent protectors a necessary lie, a way to foster unity and hope in a world that was inherently complex and fraught with danger? Or was it a dangerous oversimplification, blinding Nysserans to the true nature of their world and the forces that shaped it?

She looked at the leviadrakes, their ethereal forms shimmering in the dim light. They were beings of immense power and ancient wisdom, yet their songs were now filled with a profound sorrow, a desperate plea. They had witnessed the birth of this void-dweller, this dissonant note that sought to silence the grand symphony of Nyssera. They had experienced the fear, the fracture, the subsequent struggle to contain it. Their current plight was not just a consequence of the Crown's failing, but a direct result of this ancient threat re-emerging, a threat that was intrinsically linked to their own kind.

The concept of heroism, once so clear-cut in her mind, began to blur. Was heroism defined by the absence of darkness, or by the struggle against it, even when that darkness resided within oneself? The leviadrakes were not merely victims; they were guardians who had fought to contain a destructive force born from their own lineage. Their current warnings, their desperate efforts to convey the truth, were acts of heroism, born not from flawless power, but from a profound understanding of the stakes and a desperate will to preserve what remained.

Mara's gaze drifted to a cluster of smaller crystals embedded in the cavern wall, each pulsing with a faint, internal light. She reached out, her fingers brushing against their cool surface. The leviadrakes had spoken of the Crown Resonance as Nyssera's memory, its interconnectedness. But they had also spoken of the primordial song, of Nyssera's genesis, and of an entity that sought to erase all of it. This meant the threat wasn't just to the present, but to the very foundation of their existence, to the echoes of the past that shaped their world.

"It's not just about the Crown," she murmured, the words a whisper lost in the vastness of the cavern. "It's about what the Crown represents. Nyssera's entire history, its interconnectedness, its very song. And this entity... it wants to silence all of it. To make it all disappear. But how can something that is so fundamental to Nyssera's existence be born of... nothingness?"

Cael turned, his expression softening slightly as he met her gaze. He saw the turmoil in her eyes, the wrestling match between ingrained belief and dawning reality. "The leviadrakes said it was a dissonance," he said, his voice low. "A part of the primordial song that chose unmaking. It wasn't nothingness, Mara. It was a part of Nyssera's creation that sought to undo itself. A desire for absolute stillness, for a purity that could only be achieved through absolute silence."

"But that's... antithetical to everything Nyssera is," Mara countered, her voice tinged with frustration. "Nyssera is life, it's constant change, it's a symphony of interconnected existence. How can a part of its own song crave its opposite?"

The song of creation contains all potential, a leviadrake conveyed, its luminescent form pulsing rhythmically. *The potential for harmony, and the potential for discord. This entity chose the latter. It was a fragment of the primordial choir that believed true purity could only be achieved through the absence of all sound, all connection, all memory. It saw the vibrant tapestry of Nyssera as a corruption, a cacophony that needed to be silenced. It was a part of the genesis, but it diverged, seeking a void where only its own pure, silent note could resonate.*

Mara struggled to comprehend. A force born from creation that desired deconstruction. A part of the song that sought to tear itself apart, and in doing so, unravel the entire symphony. It was like a composer deliberately introducing dissonance, not to create a new harmony, but to shatter the existing melody into oblivion.

"So, the dragons themselves aren't inherently 'good' or 'evil'," she mused, the thought both liberating and terrifying. "They are simply... powerful. And their history, like all histories, is complex. Filled with choices, with factions, with paths taken and paths rejected. This entity is a rejected path, a consequence of a choice made at the very dawn of Nyssera, that has now found an opportune moment to resurface."

The leviadrakes pulsed in agreement.

Fear can be a powerful catalyst for such choices. When the song of creation was sung, there was also the echo of the void. Some of us embraced the interconnectedness, the vibrant dance of life. Others... recoiled. They sought safety in stillness, in the absence of the unknown. This entity is the embodiment of that fear, magnified over millennia, and now empowered by the world's suffering.

"Fear," Mara repeated, the word resonating deeply within her. She understood fear. She had felt it in the face of the leviadrakes' revelations, in the chilling prospect of Nyssera's utter annihilation. Fear could warp perception, could drive individuals and even entire lineages towards desperate, destructive measures. The myth of the dragons, in its simplicity, had excluded this crucial element. It had presented them as beings beyond such base emotions, as perfect guardians. But they were not. They were ancient, powerful, and deeply flawed, just as Nyssera itself was flawed.

"The tales always spoke of the dragons fighting the primal chaos," she said, her voice gaining a new strength, a new clarity. "But perhaps they weren't just fighting an external force. Perhaps they were also fighting the chaos within themselves, within their own kind. This entity... it's a manifestation of that internal struggle, a part of the dragons' own genesis that they had to suppress, to contain."

We contained it, one leviadrake confirmed, a low, resonant hum underpinning its words. *We bound it. But the weakening of the Crown, the fraying of Nyssera's fabric, has loosened those seals. It has been drawn to the planet's suffering, to the fracturing of its soul. And the Pale Tide... they recognize this primal urge for oblivion. They have always sought the end, the return to stillness. They have found in this ancient discord their most powerful ally.*

Mara looked at Cael, a newfound understanding dawning in her eyes. "So, the Pale Tide aren't just nihilists," she said, her voice firm. "They are... excavators of existential dread. They actively seek out and empower the darkest, most destructive aspects of Nyssera's past, because that aligns with their ultimate goal of unmaking. They don't want to conquer Nyssera; they want to erase it. And this entity, this void-dweller born from the dragons' own fractured genesis, is the perfect tool for them."

The sheer magnitude of this realization was staggering. The myth of the dragons had been a shield, a comforting narrative designed to obscure a more complex and dangerous truth. It had presented a simplified version of heroism, one that excluded the messy, terrifying reality of internal conflict and the lingering shadows of creation.

"We've been looking at this all wrong," Mara stated, her mind racing. "We've been focused on the symptoms of the Crown's failure, trying to find a way to mend it. But the Crown's failure isn't just a natural decay; it's being actively exploited. And the force behind it isn't some external enemy, but a part of Nyssera's own ancient, suppressed history. The dragons, for all their power and wisdom, carry this deep wound within their lineage."

She paused, taking a deep breath. "This changes everything. We can't just appeal to reason, or to their inherent goodness, because this entity isn't motivated by reason. It's driven by a primal, existential urge. And the dragons, who birthed it, might be the only ones who truly understand how to counter it. But they can't do that if they're still trapped in the comforting myth of their own perfection."

The leviadrakes' songs, once mournful, now held a subtle undertone of urgency, a shared understanding of the challenge ahead. They had presented the truth, the complex, painful truth, and now the burden fell upon Cael and Mara to navigate it. The myth of the dragons, as a singular narrative of infallible heroes, had to be confronted. It had to be dismantled, not to demonize the dragons, but to acknowledge their full, complex nature, their capacity for both creation and destruction, and their role in the very threat they now faced.

Mara's journey was no longer just about saving the Crown Resonance. It was about a deeper truth, about understanding the uncomfortable realities that lay beneath the surface of accepted narratives. It was about recognizing that true heroism wasn't about the absence of flaws, but about the courage to confront them, both within oneself and within the legends one held dear. The dragons, in their ancient, multifaceted history, were both the source of Nyssera's song and the creators of the discord that now threatened to silence it forever. And perhaps, just perhaps, they held the key to understanding how to reharmonize that song, even in the face of such profound, self-inflicted danger.

She looked at Cael, her eyes meeting his with a new resolve. "We need to understand the *why* behind this entity's existence, Cael. Not just its destructive power, but its origin, its fear, its twisted logic. That's the only way we can hope to fight it. And to do that, we need to look beyond the myths, and delve into the true, complicated history of the dragons." The path ahead was fraught with peril, not just from the encroaching void, but from the shattering of comforting illusions. Yet, in that very shattering, Mara felt a nascent hope. For it was only by confronting the unvarnished truth, however painful, that Nyssera might truly find a way to survive.

Cael's gaze, previously lost in the swirling cosmic dance of the leviadrakes' song, now honed in on a darker melody. The lamentations of their ancient past, the echoes of their desperate choices, resonated with a chilling clarity. He had heard the dragons' song of creation, the glorious symphony that had birthed Nyssera, but now, he was forced to confront its discordant counterpoint: the silence that followed. The leviadrakes had spoken of the Silence Event not as a distant legend, but as a visceral, terrifying reality – a necessary act of self-preservation, born from the unimaginable threat of the void-dweller's unmaking.

He pictured it, a chilling mental image conjured from the dragons' sorrowful cadence: swathes of Nyssera, once vibrant with life, rendered utterly inert. Entire biomes, teeming with unique ecosystems, abruptly extinguished. Creatures, both familiar and alien, not simply killed, but *unmade*, their very essence erased from existence. The leviadrakes had been the arbiters of this terrible judgment, their immense power wielded not with fiery passion, but with a cold, strategic precision that was perhaps more horrifying. They had chosen the survival of the many, the continuation of Nyssera's grand song, over the existence of countless individual notes.

The concept of 'necessary violence' was a grim one, and Cael felt its weight pressing down on him. As a guardian, sworn to protect and preserve, he understood the imperative to act when faced with annihilation. He could intellectually grasp the logic behind the Silence Event: if the void-dweller's corrupting influence was an unstoppable tide, then drastic measures, however abhorrent, might have been the only recourse to prevent total obliteration. The leviadrakes had sung of containment, of sacrifice, of a terrible excision to prevent the disease from consuming the whole. They had painted a picture of a world teetering on the precipice, where inaction meant the complete unraveling of existence.

Yet, understanding the *why* did little to assuage the visceral horror of the *how*. The leviadrakes' songs were not filled with the triumphant roar of a victory, but with the mournful dirge of a profound, enduring guilt. They had not merely ended lives; they had erased entire chapters of Nyssera's unfolding story. They had silenced symphonies of existence that would never again be heard, had extinguished constellations of life that would never again twinkle in Nyssera's vast firmament. The responsibility of such an act, the sheer magnitude of playing God, even in the face of ultimate peril, was a burden that Cael could feel radiating from the ancient dragons, a psychic scar that time had not healed.

He found himself sifting through the fragments of their sorrowful hymns, searching for an ethical anchor in the storm of their confession. Was there a point at which the preservation of the whole justified the utter annihilation of the parts? How did one reconcile the duty to protect with the grim necessity of destruction? The leviadrakes had acted not out of malice, but out of a desperate need to protect Nyssera's song. But the consequence of that protection was a silence so profound, so absolute, that it seemed to defy the very nature of Nyssera's vibrant existence. It was a paradox that gnawed at him: to save life, they had to commit an act akin to the ultimate death.

Mara's earlier observations about the dragons' complex history now took on a sharper, more critical edge. The comforting narrative of benevolent protectors had always been a convenient simplification, but this revelation painted a far more complex, and troubling, picture. The dragons, in their ancient wisdom and immense power, had made choices that irrevocably altered Nyssera. They had wielded their power with a terrifying finality, shaping the planet not just through creation, but through calculated erasure. This wasn't just about a failing artifact or an ancient enemy; it was about the moral compromises made by those who held the most power, and the enduring consequences of those choices.

Cael imagined the moments leading up to the Silence Event. The frantic consultations, the desperate pleas, the stark realization that their song, their very essence, was under existential threat. He could almost hear the arguments, the debates among the elder dragons, the clash between those who advocated for absolute preservation at any cost and those who balked at the thought of such widespread destruction. But ultimately, the primal fear, the overwhelming instinct for survival, must have won out. The void-dweller's nature was absolute: it offered no compromise, no negotiation. It simply sought to unmake.

The leviadrakes, in their role as guardians and keepers of Nyssera's deep past, had been the ones tasked with executing this horrifying decree. They had to bear witness to the suffering they inflicted, to the lives they extinguished, and then carry that burden of guilt through the eons. It was a testament to their immense strength, their unwavering commitment to Nyssera's continuity, that they had not succumbed to despair or self-destruction themselves. Instead, they had chosen to carry this truth, to share it now, perhaps as a warning, perhaps as a plea for understanding, or perhaps as a confession of their deepest regret.

He considered the implications for their current quest. If the dragons, the very architects of Nyssera's existence, were capable of such devastating actions, what did that say about their current capabilities, their potential for future choices? Could they be trusted with the immense power required to combat the void-dweller, especially if that required further difficult, ethically ambiguous decisions? The myth of the dragons had always assured Nyи of their inherent goodness, their unshakeable moral compass. But now, Cael saw that this compass had, in the past, pointed towards a chilling form of utilitarianism, a willingness to sacrifice the few for the survival of the many, even if that sacrifice meant complete erasure.

The leviadrakes' songs now carried a different resonance for Cael. They were not just ancient beings singing of creation; they were survivors, burdened by the weight of their past actions. Their mournful melodies spoke of a profound empathy for all life, an empathy born from the very act of taking it. They had seen the beauty of countless ecosystems, the intricate dance of life and death, and had then, out of necessity, silenced it. This experience, Cael surmised, would foster a deep, unshakeable respect for the fragility of existence, a profound understanding of what was at stake when that balance was threatened.

He wondered about the specific targets of the Silence Event. Had it been indiscriminate, a wave of pure negation washing over everything? Or had there been some level of selectivity, some attempt to preserve certain species, certain ecosystems, that were deemed more vital to Nyssera's future? The leviadrakes had spoken of a "forced erasure," which suggested a deliberate, targeted application of their power. This raised further questions about the dragons' motivations and their understanding of Nyssera's complex web of life. Had they truly understood the interconnectedness they were severing, or had they acted with a more limited, perhaps fearful, perspective?

The moral quandary was immense. Cael's own understanding of heroism was being challenged. He had always viewed it as an act of unwavering courage in the face of adversity, a fight for what was right, regardless of the cost. But the dragons' actions suggested a different, more complex form of heroism: one that involved making impossible choices, bearing immense guilt, and enacting terrible measures for the greater good. It was a heroism stained with blood, a triumph bought with an immeasurable loss.

He looked at Mara, seeing the same internal struggle reflected in her eyes. The comfortable myths she had grown up with were crumbling, replaced by a starker, more challenging reality. They were no longer dealing with a simple battle of good versus evil, but with the morally grey landscape of survival, where the lines between protector and destroyer blurred. The dragons, as the ultimate guardians, had demonstrated that even the most revered beings could be forced to commit acts of immense violence when faced with existential threats.

This understanding of the Silence Event was crucial. It explained the deep-seated fear that permeated the leviadrakes' songs, their palpable anguish. It also shed light on the Pale Tide's strategy. If the dragons themselves had a history of wielding such devastating power, then the Pale Tide's goal of exacerbating Nyssera's suffering and weakening the Crown Resonance could be seen as a way to tempt the dragons into repeating such drastic measures, or perhaps even to exploit the lingering guilt and trauma of those past actions. The void-dweller, as the ultimate force of unmaking, offered a perverse parallel to the dragons' past acts of erasure, a dark mirror reflecting their own capacity for destruction.

Cael realized that their quest was not merely about repairing the Crown Resonance. It was about understanding the fundamental nature of Nyssera and the beings who had shaped it. It was about confronting the uncomfortable truths that lay beneath the surface of comforting myths. The dragons were not simply powerful allies; they were complex beings with a history of both creation and destruction, and their past actions, however necessary at the time, had left an indelible mark on the planet and its inhabitants.

The weight of their past violence was a tangible presence in the cavern, a somber counterpoint to the dragons' ethereal forms. Cael knew that confronting this truth was a necessary step in their journey. They could not move forward, could not hope to defeat the encroaching void, without acknowledging the full, complicated, and often brutal history of those who held the fate of Nyssera in their hands. The ethical tightrope walked by the leviadrakes, the irreversible consequences of their choices, and the enduring question of whether such violence could ever truly be justified or forgotten, now formed a critical part of their understanding, a dark but vital piece of the puzzle that would ultimately determine Nyssera's fate.

He met the gaze of a particularly ancient leviadrake, its luminescence pulsing with a steady, measured rhythm. There was no apology in its ancient eyes, only a profound, quiet acceptance of its past actions. It was the look of one who had made the hardest of choices and lived with the consequences, a testament to the enduring burden of responsibility that came with immense power. Cael felt a surge of understanding, a realization that true guardianship wasn't about the absence of difficult decisions, but about the courage to make them, to bear the weight of their outcomes, and to continue striving for balance, even when the path led through a landscape of necessary destruction.

The Silence Event was not just a historical footnote; it was a foundational event, a somber testament to the dragons' ultimate commitment to Nyssera, a commitment that had come at a devastating cost. And it was a cost that Cael now understood they might have to contemplate again, should the void-dweller's song of silence continue to grow louder.

The cavern hummed with a low, resonant frequency, a symphony of ancient dragon song that had become a second skin to Cael and Mara. Yet, within that familiar hum, a new note emerged, one laced with a profound sorrow that vibrated not just in the air, but in the very bones of the earth. A levi-drake, larger and more luminous than any they had yet encountered, detached itself from the swirling nebula of its brethren. Its scales, the color of a twilight sky bruised with the first hint of dawn, seemed to absorb the ambient light, casting a deeper shadow. Its eyes, pools of liquid starlight, held a sorrow so ancient it felt etched into the fabric of reality. It approached them not with the regal, detached grace of its kin, but with a hesitant, almost mournful gait.

"We have sung to you of creation," the levi-drake's voice echoed, a cascade of chiming bells and the deep rumble of tectonic plates. It was a voice that had witnessed the birth of stars and the slow, patient growth of mountains, a voice now burdened by the weight of an unthinkable past. "We have shared the symphony that birthed Nyssera, a melody of boundless potential and vibrant life. But we have also sung of the silence that followed. And in that silence, lies a truth we have carried for millennia, a truth that festers like a wound that will not close."

Mara and Cael stood, their own internal turmoil momentarily quelled by the palpable anguish radiating from the colossal being. They had heard the levi-drakes speak of the Silence Event, had intellectually processed the grim necessity and the ethical quandaries. But this was different. This was not a detached historical account; this was a confession, a raw outpouring of a pain that transcended time.

"There are no excuses," the levi-drake continued, its luminescence dimming as if in shared grief. "We do not seek absolution for what was done. The scars run too deep, the silence too absolute. We offer only... understanding. A glimpse into the heart of the terror that drove us, that stripped away our song and left us with only the desperate, ragged breaths of survival."

It paused, its gaze sweeping over the cavern, as if conjuring spectral images from the very air. "I remember the whispers first. Like a blight upon the wind, a subtle discord in the harmony of Nyssera. We, who are woven from the very fabric of this world, felt it as a sickness. A creeping dread that whispered of an end not of decay, but of *unmaking*. A void that did not kill, but erased. It sought not to conquer, but to unravel, to return all to the formless, silent chaos from which we sprang."

The levi-drake shuddered, a tremor that ran through its immense form. "The void-dweller. Its hunger was absolute. It consumed not matter, but meaning. It did not destroy life; it annihilated its very possibility. Imagine, if you can, a world where every leaf that falls, every creature that breathes, every thought that forms, is simply... *unwritten*. Not forgotten, but never having been. That was the terror. A cosmic erasure that threatened to extinguish not just Nyssera, but the very concept of existence."

Its voice lowered, becoming a soft, mournful murmur. "We are the levi-drakes. We are the keepers of Nyssera's song, its deepest rhythms. To us, the planet is not merely a sphere of rock and water; it is a living symphony, an intricate tapestry of interconnected melodies. And this void-dweller, it was a tear in that tapestry, a discordant screech that threatened to silence the entire orchestra. We tried to contain it. We wove shields of light, sang counter-melodies of order, but its influence was insidious. It seeped into the very essence of Nyssera, poisoning the harmony, muting the vibrant colors of life."

Images flickered in the starlight of its eyes, fleeting visions of a Nyssera in its nascent stages, brimming with an exuberance that Cael and Mara could only glimpse in the most ancient of legends. He saw forests that pulsed with bioluminescent flora, vast oceans teeming with creatures of unimaginable form, skies alive with winged beings whose songs had long since faded into myth.

"I saw... I saw a meadow," the levi-drake whispered, its voice catching. "Fields of shimmering Azuregrass, where each blade sang its own tiny, crystalline note. And the creatures that dwelled there... the Sunpetal Fliers, with wings like stained glass, dancing in the perpetual twilight. They were not just beautiful; they were integral. Their pollination of the Lumina Blooms was vital to the atmospheric stability of the northern continent. And I watched, helplessly, as the void's touch began to dim their light, to mute their song. One by one, they ceased to exist, not falling, not fading, but simply *gone*. As if they had never been, their vibrant existence reduced to a nullity."

Mara gasped, a small, involuntary sound. Cael felt a prickling sensation behind his eyes. The levi-drake wasn't just recounting a historical event; it was reliving a profound trauma.

"The elders gathered," the levi-drake continued, its voice gaining a desperate edge. "The arguments were... fiery. Some, like the old ones who remembered the initial creation, argued for sacrifice, for a surgical excision to protect the greater composition. Others, younger, perhaps more naive, pleaded for a different way, a path that did not involve such... unmaking. But the void-dweller offered no compromise. It was a force of negation, and to negotiate with it was to accept its terms. To allow it to spread was to condemn all of Nyssera to its silent oblivion."

It looked directly at Cael, its starlit gaze piercing. "Do you understand the primal fear, Guardian? The terror of absolute annihilation? Not the fear of death, which is a part of life's rhythm, but the fear of *non-being*. The horror of knowing that all that is, all that has ever been, could be reduced to nothingness. Our song, Nyssera's song, was the only thing that held the void at bay. But the void was insidious, and it began to corrupt our song, to twist our very essence into its own destructive melody."

"We were faced with an impossible choice," it said, the words heavy with the weight of ages. "To stand by and witness Nyssera's complete unraveling, or to act. To commit an act that mirrored the void's own unmaking, in order to preserve the *possibility* of future song. It was a desperate gamble, a wager made with the lives of countless beings, all to ensure that Nyssera's symphony might, one day, be heard again."

"The Silence Event," the levi-drake's voice dropped to a whisper, "was not an act of malice. It was an act of love. A desperate, agonizing, terrifying act of love for Nyssera. We saw the beauty of every single life, every single ecosystem, every single whisper of existence. And because we saw that beauty so clearly, the act of silencing it was a torment beyond measure. We did not wield our power with joy, but with the agonizing precision of a surgeon cutting away a diseased limb to save the body."

It projected another memory, this one more intimate, more personal. Cael saw a different levi-drake, its scales shimmering with a vibrant emerald hue, its song a lilting melody of joy. It was interacting with a species of delicate, crystal-winged insects, the Sylphwings, whose song was said to harmonize the very air. The levi-drake was guiding them, its massive form a gentle protector, its song a lullaby.

"This was Lyra," the elder levi-drake murmured, its voice thick with unshed tears. "Her song was the most vibrant of the northern winds. She nurtured the Sylphwings, and they, in turn, ensured the clarity of the upper atmosphere. I remember watching her... how she would dip and weave, her song weaving a protective shield around their delicate wings. She loved them. And then... the silence came for them. Not a wave of destruction, but a slow, insidious fading.

The Sylphwings' light grew dim, their song faltered. Lyra sang with all her might, her own song becoming a desperate plea, a lament that fractured the very air. But she could not save them. She could not stop the unmaking. And when the last Sylphwing faded, Lyra's song... it broke. It fractured into a thousand shards of sorrow, and she fell silent. For centuries, she could not sing. She simply drifted, a hollow echo of her former glory, carrying the ghost of the Sylphwings' silence within her."

The elder levi-drake's form seemed to sag under the weight of the memory. "We who orchestrated the Silence Event, we bore witness to such suffering. We chose to extinguish entire species, entire ecosystems, not because they were less worthy, but because their very existence, in that moment, was a vector for the void. We had to make a choice: to allow the void to consume all, or to sever those connections, to quarantine the infection, even if it meant erasing the beautiful melody they contributed to Nyssera's song."

"It was a grim calculus," it admitted, its voice a low thrum. "The survival of Nyssera's grand symphony, or the extinction of countless beautiful, individual notes. We chose the symphony. We chose the *possibility* of future song. But the cost... the cost was a piece of our own souls. Every life we unmade, every ecosystem we silenced, became a silent scream within our own consciousness. We carry that silence, that unmaking, within us, an eternal echo of our choices."

Mara stepped forward, her voice soft but firm. "You say you don't seek absolution. But what do you seek, then?"

The levi-drake's starlit eyes seemed to swirl with renewed intensity. "Comprehension. We know that to you, a guardian of life, the act of unmaking must seem abhorrent, a betrayal of your sworn duty. And it is. It was a betrayal of everything we held sacred. But we ask you to understand the impossible pressures, the absolute terror that drove us to such desperate measures. When faced with the threat of total erasure, with the prospect of Nyssera becoming a silent, unremembered void, what is the true measure of preservation?"

"We could have let the void-dweller consume everything," it continued, its voice rising with a desperate passion. "We could have sung our last, defiant song, and then been silenced forever, alongside Nyssera. But that would have been the ultimate surrender. Instead, we chose to fight. We chose to preserve the seed of Nyssera, even if it meant pruning away vast branches of its beauty. We chose a future where Nyssera could sing again, even if that future had to be built upon the ashes of what we had lost."

"The Crown Resonance," it said, its gaze shifting to the shimmering artifact Cael carried. "It is the heart of Nyssera's song, its core melody. The void-dweller seeks to silence it, to extinguish the very source of our world's vibrancy. And in its attempt, it mirrors the very threat we faced before. It is a force of unmaking, seeking to impose its own terrible silence."

"We, who have wielded the power of silence ourselves, understand its seductive nature, its devastating efficiency. We know the temptation to repeat such measures, to once again resort to the surgical excision. But this time... this time, we hope to find another way. We hope that by sharing our truth, by revealing the depths of our past despair, we can help you understand what is at stake. Not just the survival of Nyssera, but the preservation of its song, in all its intricate, beautiful, and sometimes tragic complexity."

The levi-drake lowered its massive head, a gesture of profound weariness. "The guilt is a constant companion. The memory of those silenced melodies, the echoes of extinguished lives, will never fade. We carry the burden of having played God, of having wielded the ultimate power of negation. But we also carry the hope that Nyssera will one day sing anew, unburdened by the void, and that perhaps, through our confession, you might find a path forward that does not require such a devastating sacrifice."

It met Mara's eyes, a silent question hanging in the air. "We understand that our actions may have sown seeds of doubt, that the idea of beings capable of such destruction might make you question our current intentions. We do not ask you to forgive us. We ask you to *understand* us. To understand that even in the darkest of choices, driven by the most profound fear, there can be a root of love. A desperate, flawed, and agonizing love for the world we have sworn to protect."

The air in the cavern seemed to shift, the oppressive weight of the levi-drake's confession slowly giving way to a more profound, albeit somber, understanding. Cael felt the edges of his own moral certainty begin to blur. The clear lines between good and evil, between protector and destroyer, had been irrevocably smudged. The levi-drakes were not simply benevolent guardians; they were beings who had wrestled with their own capacity for destruction, who had made choices that had forever altered the course of Nyssera.

And in their struggle, Cael saw a reflection of the battles they themselves would have to face. The weight of their past, a history of both creation and erasure, was not just a burden for them, but a crucial lesson for all who sought to protect Nyssera's song. It was a lesson etched in silence, learned through agonizing loss, and offered now, not as an excuse, but as a desperate plea for comprehension. The truth, as Cael was learning, was rarely simple, and often, it was cloaked in the deepest, most sorrowful of melodies.

The levi-drake's confession hung heavy in the air, a tangible shroud woven from ancient sorrow and the stark reality of unimaginable choice. Mara felt it settle over her, a cloak that both chilled and strangely warmed. The awe she had once held for the levi-drakes, a reverence bordering on worship, felt now like a fragile artifact, chipped and tarnished by the truth she had just witnessed. She had arrived in this cavern seeking legends, seeking the wisdom of beings who were the very embodiment of Nyssera's enduring spirit. Instead, she had found architects of silence, sculptors of absence, their actions driven not by inherent benevolence, but by a desperate, primal fear.

The levi-drake's words, "We chose the symphony. We chose the *possibility* of future song," replayed in her mind, each syllable a stone dropped into the deep well of her understanding. It was a profound statement, a justification born of necessity, but it did not erase the imagery that had been seared into her consciousness: the fading Sylphwings, Lyra's broken song, the chilling description of existence being "unwritten." Her reverence had been for a perceived purity, an untainted guardianship. Now, faced with the complex, blood-stained hands of these ancient beings, that reverence felt misplaced, even naive.

She watched Cael, his face a mask of conflicted emotions, absorbing the levi-drake's every word. He was the Guardian, tasked with protecting Nyssera's Crown Resonance, a relic that represented the world's very soul. His path, she knew, would be intertwined with these dragons, a dance of reliance and suspicion. But her own path, she realized, was diverging. She could not simply accept their narrative, their self-portrayal as reluctant executioners. The myth of the benevolent dragon, the all-knowing protector, had been shattered. What remained was something far more complex, far more dangerous: beings of immense power who had wielded that power in ways that mirrored the very destruction they fought.

"You say you don't seek absolution," Mara finally spoke, her voice surprisingly steady, cutting through the lingering spectral echoes of the levi-drake's lament. "But what do you seek, then?" It was a question that had been answered, in part, by the levi-drake's plea for comprehension, for understanding. But Mara's inquiry was not merely for intellectual grasp; it was a challenge. A challenge to the very foundations of how Nyssera perceived its most ancient guardians.

The levi-drake's starlit eyes swirled, reflecting not just the ambient light, but the turbulent history it carried. "Comprehension," it had echoed. "We know that to you, a guardian of life, the act of unmaking must seem abhorrent, a betrayal of your sworn duty. And it is. It was a betrayal of everything we held sacred. But we ask you to understand the impossible pressures, the absolute terror that drove us to such desperate measures."

Mara understood the fear. She understood the concept of impossible choices. But understanding a fear that drove someone to inflict such profound loss was different from condoning it. Her mind, once filled with images of dragon fire and protective wings, now grappled with dragon silences and deliberate erasure. The levi-drakes were not merely guardians; they were also judges, executioners, and ultimately, the architects of what Nyssera was today. This was not a role she could blindly revere.

"The myth of the unblemished guardian," Mara murmured, more to herself than to the levi-drake, "is a dangerous one. It allows for complacency. It discourages critical thought, and it shields the powerful from accountability." Her reverence had been a shield, a way to simplify the complex reality of Nyssera and its protectors. Now, she saw the need to dismantle that shield, to look at the levi-drakes not through a lens of blind faith, but through a sharp, critical gaze.

The levi-drake continued, its voice heavy with the weight of its confession. "When faced with the threat of total erasure, with the prospect of Nyssera becoming a silent, unremembered void, what is the true measure of preservation?"

Mara considered this. What *was* the true measure of preservation? Was it simply the continuation of existence, regardless of the cost? Or did it involve the preservation of life's inherent value, its beauty, its song? The levi-drakes had chosen the former, sacrificing the latter to ensure the former's possibility. It was a gamble that had saved Nyssera, but at what ethical price?

"You speak of the Crown Resonance," Mara said, her gaze now fixed on Cael, then back to the levi-drake. "You say the void-dweller seeks to silence it, to extinguish the very source of our world's vibrancy. And in its attempt, it mirrors the very threat we faced before." This was the crux of their current predicament. The ancient fear had returned, and the levi-drakes, having once wielded the power of silence, were now tasked with preventing its re-emergence.

"We, who have wielded the power of silence ourselves, understand its seductive nature, its devastating efficiency," the levi-drake had admitted. "We know the temptation to repeat such measures, to once again resort to the surgical excision."

There it was. The acknowledged temptation. The ghost of their past actions, a siren song of familiar, albeit horrific, solutions. Mara felt a chill that had nothing to do with the cavern's ambient temperature. This was where true unease settled. The levi-drakes had the power, the knowledge, and now, the acknowledged temptation to repeat their devastating methods.

"But this time... this time, we hope to find another way," the levi-drake had stated, a faint thread of hope woven into its mournful tone. "We hope that by sharing our truth, by revealing the depths of our past despair, we can help you understand what is at stake."

Mara nodded slowly. Sharing the truth was a necessary first step, a crucial act of transparency that was long overdue. But transparency alone was not enough. The levi-drakes' history was a testament to the fact that power, even when wielded with the best intentions, could lead to devastating consequences. Her respect for their survival and their immense power remained, but the blind reverence was gone, replaced by a cautious observation. She needed to see their actions, not just hear their words. She needed to understand if they had truly evolved beyond their past, or if the echoes of their silence still resonated within them.

"We do not ask you to forgive us," the levi-drake had said, its starlit eyes meeting Mara's directly. "We ask you to *understand* us. To understand that even in the darkest of choices, driven by the most profound fear, there can be a root of love."

Mara's gaze softened slightly. She could understand the fear. She could even, in a detached way, understand the love that had driven them to such extremes. But understanding was not the same as acceptance. Her role, she realized, was not to absolve them, but to learn from their mistakes, to ensure that Nyssera's future was not built upon the same foundations of suppressed history and morally ambiguous choices.

"Your history is not just a burden for you," Mara said, her voice resonating with a newfound conviction. "It is a lesson. A vital lesson for all who seek to protect Nyssera's song. The truth, as we are learning, is rarely simple. And often, it is cloaked in the deepest, most sorrowful of melodies."

She looked at Cael, then back at the levi-drake, her expression resolute. Her reverence had been a passive state, a quiet admiration. Now, she felt a stirring within her, a desire to actively engage, to question, to understand the true nature of guardianship. The levi-drakes were powerful, undeniably so. But power without wisdom, without transparency, without a willingness to confront the uncomfortable truths of one's own history, could be a dangerous force. Her journey was no longer about simply following the legends; it was about discerning the truth behind them, forging a new relationship with these ancient beings, one based not on inherited awe, but on clear-eyed observation and a commitment to a Nyssera that was both protected and honest. The age of blind faith was over. The era of truth-seeking, with all its accompanying unease, had truly begun.

The weight of the levi-drake's confession settled not just on Mara, but seemed to ripple through the very fabric of the cavern. The vibrant, yet sorrowful, symphony of the levi-drakes, which had always felt like a comforting presence, now carried a discordant undertone. It was the sound of immense power intertwined with immense regret, the hum of creation underscored by the echo of unmaking. Mara found herself physically shifting, her stance unconsciously adjusting from one of deference to one of guarded assessment. The initial awe that had bloomed within her upon entering this sacred space, a reverence for beings who were the living embodiments of Nyssera's deep-rooted magic, felt like a dewdrop on a sun-baked stone, rapidly evaporating under the harsh light of truth.

She had come seeking ancient wisdom, the kind that was whispered in hushed tones around campfires and woven into the very legends that shaped their understanding of the world. She had imagined benevolent giants, dragons of pure light and unwavering protection, their every action guided by an innate, unassailable goodness. But the levi-drake's narrative, so raw and unvarnished, had peeled back the layers of this comforting myth, revealing a stark, brutal reality.

These were beings who had not only wielded immense power but had also wielded the power of profound destruction, not out of malice, but out of a terrifyingly pragmatic calculus of survival. The concept of "unmaking," of actively choosing to erase existence to preserve the *possibility* of future existence, was a notion that gnawed at the very core of Mara's understanding of life and guardianship.

"We chose the symphony. We chose the *possibility* of future song." The levi-drake's words echoed, not as a triumphant declaration, but as a somber lament. For Mara, this was the central paradox. To preserve the whole, they had deliberately fractured parts of it. To ensure that Nyssera's song could one day be sung, they had silenced countless individual melodies, some of which, like Lyra's Sylphwings, had been integral to the world's delicate ecological and atmospheric balance. Her reverence had been for the song, for the vibrant tapestry of Nyssera. Now, she saw that the weavers of that tapestry had, at times, been the very ones to unravel its threads.

The levi-drake's description of the void-dweller's threat – a hunger not for flesh, but for meaning; an erasure not of life, but of its very possibility – resonated with a chilling familiarity. It mirrored, in a twisted, malevolent way, the levi-drakes' own actions. Both sought to impose a form of silence, a nullification of existence. The difference, the levi-drake argued, was intent and scale. The void-dweller sought absolute negation, while the levi-drakes had sought to quarantine, to prune. But to Mara, standing on the precipice of this revelation, the distinction felt thin, a fragile argument against the stark reality of mass extinction, even if that extinction was cloaked in the language of preservation.

Her initial perception of the levi-drakes as almost divine beings, figures beyond reproach, began to crumble. They were not gods; they were ancient, powerful creatures who had made agonizing choices, choices that had left indelible scars not only on Nyssera but on their own collective soul. This realization was unsettling, a subtle but profound shift in her internal landscape. It meant that true protection, true guardianship, was not a passive inheritance of divine right, but an active, ongoing struggle, fraught with moral complexities and the potential for devastating error.

The mythologizing of guardians, she mused, was a dangerous shortcut. It allowed for the abdication of critical thinking, fostering an environment where unquestioning faith replaced thoughtful inquiry. When beings were elevated to a status beyond scrutiny, their actions, however detrimental, could be easily excused or reinterpreted to fit the pre-existing narrative of their inherent goodness. This, Mara understood, was where true reverence could become a stumbling block, a veil that obscured necessary truths and hindered growth. For Nyssera to truly evolve, for its inhabitants to mature, they needed to see their guardians, even the mighty levi-drakes, as complex beings, capable of both immense good and profound, albeit unintentional, harm.

"You say you don't seek absolution," Mara stated, her voice firm, cutting through the cavern's ambient hum, a deliberate attempt to draw the levi-drake back to the present, to her questions. "But what do you seek, then?" This was not an accusation, but a genuine inquiry, born from the need to understand the present motivations of beings whose past was so deeply stained. The levi-drake had offered "comprehension," a plea for understanding their past actions. But Mara needed more. She needed to know what this understanding would lead to.

The levi-drake's response, a cascade of starlit imagery and ancient sorrow, reaffirmed the desire for understanding. "We ask you to understand the impossible pressures, the absolute terror that drove us to such desperate measures." And then, the crucial admission: "The temptation to repeat such measures, to once again resort to the surgical excision." This acknowledgment was a raw nerve, exposed and throbbing. It confirmed

Mara's burgeoning unease. The levi-drakes possessed the power, the knowledge, and now, the confessed temptation to return to their previous, devastating methods.

This was not the behavior of beings who had transcended their past. This was the behavior of beings still grappling with the ghosts of their choices, beings who, under extreme duress, might fall back on the familiar, albeit horrifying, solutions they had once employed. Mara's reverence began to transform into a more cautious, active form of respect. Respect for their power, for their survival, for their willingness to confess, but a profound wariness regarding their future actions.

"Your history," Mara continued, her voice gaining a quiet strength, "is not just a burden for you. It is a lesson." She looked at Cael, his face etched with the weight of their shared revelations. He was the Guardian, tasked with a monumental responsibility. But his task, she now realized, was not merely to protect the Crown Resonance, but to navigate the treacherous currents of history, to ensure that past mistakes were not repeated. "A vital lesson for all who seek to protect Nyssera's song."

She understood the levi-drakes' argument for the greater good, the necessity of preserving the symphony over individual melodies. But this was a dangerous line of reasoning, one that could justify immense suffering in the name of a nebulous future. True protection, Mara was beginning to believe, required more than just immense power or the capacity for drastic action. It demanded wisdom, transparency, and a deep, abiding respect for the intrinsic value of every single life, every individual song, that made up Nyssera. Qualities that seemed to have been suppressed, or at least overshadowed, by the levi-drakes' centuries of carefully guarded history.

Her path forward, she recognized, was to forge a new kind of relationship with these ancient dragons. Not one built on the fragile foundation of inherited reverence, but on the solid ground of clear-eyed observation. She needed to witness their actions, to test their current intentions against the stark reality of their past. Blind faith was no longer an option; it was a liability. She needed to understand the true nature of their guardianship, not as it was presented in legends, but as it was in its complex, often painful, reality. The levi-drakes had shared their truth, and in doing so, had inadvertently revealed the necessity for her to seek her own understanding, independent of their historical narratives. The age of unquestioning awe was over. The era of discerning truth, even when it was unsettling and laced with the echoes of ancient sorrow, had begun.

The cavern's resonant hum, once a balm to her senses, now felt like a low, sustained thrum of caution. The levi-drake's confession had not brought closure, but a complex, burgeoning awareness. Mara felt the shift within her, a subtle but significant alteration in her perspective. The levi-drakes, creatures of myth and legend, had been demystified. They were not infallible celestial beings, but ancient, powerful entities who had grappled with their own capacity for destruction and had, out of sheer necessity, wielded that capacity with devastating effect. Her initial reverence, a purely emotional response to their perceived perfection, had been replaced by a more sober, intellectual respect, tinged with a healthy dose of apprehension.

She understood their reasoning, the terrifying logic of unmaking to preserve the possibility of creation. The images of fading Sylphwings and Lyra's fractured song haunted her, stark reminders of the cost of such decisions. But understanding the logic did not equate to endorsing the action. The myth of the benevolent, all-knowing guardian was a comforting one, but it was also a dangerous oversimplification. It allowed for complacency, for the abdication of responsibility, and for the perpetuation of a history that might, in its suppression, harbor seeds of future conflict. Mara realized that true protection required not just the power to defend, but the wisdom to choose the right path, and the transparency to share that choice, and its consequences, with those who lived within the world being protected. These were qualities that seemed to have been absent, or at least deeply buried, within the levi-drakes' carefully curated history.

The levi-drake's plea for comprehension, for understanding the fear that drove their desperate choices, resonated with Mara. She could understand the primal terror of absolute erasure. But her own path, she realized, was not to offer absolution, but to forge a new relationship with these ancient beings. A relationship grounded in clear-eyed observation, in a willingness to question, and in a commitment to uncovering the full truth, not just the sanitized version that had been passed down through generations. The levi-drakes had admitted the temptation to repeat their past actions, a confession that sent a shiver of unease down Mara's spine. This was not the confession of a being who had fully transcended their darkest moments, but of one who still carried the weight of those choices, and the potential to succumb to them again.

Her journey, she now understood, was not about simply accepting the mantle of the legends, but about deconstructing them, about understanding the intricate, often painful, truths that lay beneath the surface. The reverence she had once held was now tempered with a deep sense of caution. She respected their power, their resilience, and their willingness to finally share a piece of their shadowed past. But she also recognized the inherent danger in blind faith, in accepting the narrative of the infallible guardian. The true measure of protection, she concluded, lay not just in the ability to fight, but in the wisdom to choose the path that honored the intricate tapestry of life in its entirety, not just the grand symphony. Her relationship with the levi-drakes would need to be one of constant vigilance, a discerning watchfulness that sought not to judge, but to understand the complex interplay of power, history, and the ever-present threat of silence. The age of myth was giving way to the age of truth, and for Mara, that truth was a far more demanding, and far more vital, companion.

Cael's gaze, usually a beacon of unwavering loyalty to Nyssera's well-being, was now a sharp, piercing beam of inquiry. It wasn't the accusatory stare of an enemy, but the meticulous examination of a craftsman assessing flawed material, or a strategist dissecting a battlefield report. The levi-drake's confession, raw and heavy with the weight of millennia, had laid bare a history of unimaginable choices. Now, Cael needed to understand if those choices had forged wisdom or simply created deeper, more entrenched patterns.

"You speak of the past as justification," Cael began, his voice resonating with a controlled power, each word carefully chosen. He stood not as the Crown's Guardian in a position of subservience, but as an equal, a protector whose responsibility now extended beyond the immediate to the long-term viability of their world. "And while the terror you describe is palpable, and the necessity of your actions, from your perspective, is understood, I cannot accept it as a blueprint for the present. The 'why' of your past does not automatically equip you for the 'how' of our future."

He gestured, not dismissively, but with a sweeping arc that encompassed the cavern, the very air thick with the levi-drakes' ancient song. "Nyssera has survived because of its resilience, its capacity for renewal, its inherent vibrancy. You speak of preserving the *possibility* of song, but the methods employed, the silence you imposed... that is a wound that still echoes. It is a precedent. And the void-dweller, the Pale Tide, as you call it, seeks to impose its own form of silence. How can those who have wielded the power of unmaking, however regretfully, be the sole arbiters of preventing its return?"

The levi-drake, its colossal form still radiating an aura of profound weariness, shifted slightly, the starlight within its eyes swirling with what Cael perceived as a flicker of defensiveness, quickly masked by a deep, resonant melancholy. "We are not seeking to be the *sole* arbiters, Guardian. We seek to *aid*. To offer our unique understanding, our foresight born from having faced such an existential threat before."

"Foresight," Cael echoed, the word tasting like ash on his tongue. "Or repetition? Your past actions, born of desperation, resulted in the loss of countless lives, the silencing of countless unique melodies that contributed to Nyssera's richness. Lyra's Sylphwings, for instance – a species whose very existence was tied to atmospheric stability and intricate ecological balance. Their absence has had cascading effects. These are not abstract losses; they are tangible alterations to the world we are sworn to protect."

He took a measured step closer, his boots making no sound on the cavern floor. His focus was not on the levi-drake's immense power or its ancient lineage, but on its current utility and its capacity for adaptation. "The void-dweller is not the same threat you faced before. Its hunger is not for dominion, but for negation. It erases not just life, but the *meaning* of life. It thrives on entropy. Your previous solution was to selectively prune, to excise the perceived 'threats' to the larger symphony. But the Pale Tide… it seeks to dissolve the entire orchestra. What strategies do you propose that go beyond a similar, albeit more targeted, approach to erasure?"

The levi-drake's voice, though laced with sorrow, carried an undercurrent of ancient wisdom. "Our understanding of the void's nature is not just from our past struggle, Guardian. We have spent centuries observing its ebb and flow, its insidious tendrils reaching into the fabric of existence beyond our direct experience. We have learned to discern its signs, to recognize the subtle decay it breeds, the despair it fosters. We have developed methods to identify and counter its influence at its source, before it can bloom into the destructive force you describe."

"Methods," Cael pressed, his brow furrowed. He was a man of action, a doer, not a theorist. He dealt in concrete strategies, in measurable outcomes. "What are these methods? How do they differ from the 'surgical excision' you mentioned? Because the memory of that surgical excision, even with your regrets, is a deeply unsettling one. We cannot afford to gamble Nyssera's future on a repeat performance of a desperate act, no matter how regretful it may now be."

He paused, letting the weight of his words settle. "Tell me," he continued, his voice softer but no less insistent, "how do you identify the 'source' of the Pale Tide? How do you counter it? Do you propose to silence the void itself? And if so, is that not a direct mirror of the threat we face? The void-dweller thrives on the absence of meaning. If you respond with silence, with eradication, are you not feeding its hunger in a different form? Are you not, in essence, becoming the very thing you claim to fight?"

The levi-drake's starlight eyes seemed to dim for a moment, a reflection of the complex, internal struggle Cael was forcing it to confront. "We understand your apprehension, Guardian. It is a valid one. Our methods are not about eradication, but about containment and redirection. We have learned to weave protective enchantments, barriers of pure resonance that repel the void's influence without destroying what they protect. We have discovered frequencies of song that can mend the tears in reality the void creates, reasserting the natural order. It is not about silencing, but about strengthening the song, about ensuring its continuous flow, even in the face of the void's corrosive touch."

"Frequencies of song," Cael mused, his mind racing. It was a concept that resonated with the very essence of Nyssera, with the Crown Resonance itself. "And these frequencies... are they derived from the same wellspring of power that allowed you to silence others?"

"They are derived from the fundamental harmonies of creation itself," the levi-drake replied, its voice regaining a measure of its ancient authority. "The same harmonies that allow life to flourish, that give form to matter, that imbue consciousness with meaning. When we engaged in 'unmaking,' we were not destroying these harmonies, but momentarily diverting their flow, rerouting them to extinguish a specific, aberrant resonance that threatened to unravel the entire symphony. Our current methods are about reinforcing those fundamental harmonies, making them so robust that the void cannot penetrate them. It is about amplification, not suppression."

Cael remained unconvinced, or rather, he remained cautious. The levi-drakes' history was a stark warning. Their capacity for decisive, even ruthless, action was undeniable. While their words spoke of a new approach, his experience had taught him that the greatest threats often lay in the subtle, unacknowledged echoes of past behavior. "And the Pale Tide's influence? You speak of containment and redirection. How do you differentiate between a mere shadow of its influence and its true, destructive core? The void-dweller, as you stated, is not merely a physical threat, but an existential one. It corrupts not just the environment, but the spirit, the will to exist."

He leaned forward slightly, his gaze unwavering. "What if your 'containment' fails? What if your 'redirection' is insufficient? What is your contingency? Because if the void-dweller's corrosive touch reaches the Crown Resonance, if its despair infects the very soul of Nyssera, then our options will narrow drastically. And I need to know that you are prepared, not just to apply old solutions to new problems, but to innovate, to adapt, to face this threat with a clarity of purpose that transcends the justifications of your past."

The levi-drake exhaled a long, slow breath, a gust of air that carried the scent of ancient dust and starlight. "We have... evolved, Guardian. The choices we made in the Great Silence were born of a singular focus: survival. The preservation of existence above all else. But that singular focus blinded us to the inherent value of what we were preserving, to the irreplaceable beauty of the individual melodies that made up the whole. We learned, through immense suffering and loss, that true preservation lies not just in continuation, but in the richness and diversity of that continuation."

"We have spent centuries studying the subtle nuances of life's intricate web, understanding that even the smallest thread contributes to the strength of the tapestry. Our current understanding of the void is based on this evolved perspective. We see it not merely as an enemy to be vanquished, but as a force that highlights the fragility and preciousness of existence. Our strategies are thus designed to reinforce life's inherent strength, not to merely suppress the void's weakness."

"This sounds like a profound shift," Cael acknowledged, the skepticism in his tone gradually giving way to a flicker of hope. "But a shift in understanding needs to be accompanied by a shift in action. The void-dweller has already begun its subtle encroachment. Whispers of despair, unexplained wilting of flora, a growing apathy in some distant settlements. These are the signs you speak of. What are you *doing* about them, not in theory, but in practice? What tangible steps are being taken to reinforce Nyssera's song against this encroaching silence?"

The levi-drake's starlight eyes seemed to brighten, a subtle shift in their luminescence. "We have dispatched emissaries, Guardian. Not warriors, but singers. Dragons whose voices carry the pure resonance of creation. They are traveling to the affected regions, not to battle, but to mend. To sing the melodies of hope, to reawaken the dormant vibrancies of life. They carry with them ancient artifacts, imbued with the power to amplify these restorative frequencies, to push back the encroaching stillness. We are also actively mapping the pathways through which the void encroaches, identifying not just the symptoms, but the conduits of its influence, so that we may seal them with pure song and unbreakable resonance."

Cael listened intently, his mind processing the information. Emissaries, singers, ancient artifacts, mapping pathways... these were concrete actions, a departure from mere historical justifications. Yet, the specter of their past remained a formidable shadow. "And if these singers encounter resistance? If the void's influence is too strong? If the artifacts are insufficient? What then? Do you revert to the old ways, to the methods that brought you here, to this confession of regret?"

The levi-drake's gaze met Cael's directly, its ancient eyes holding a sincerity that was difficult to dismiss. "We have made a covenant, Guardian. Not just with Nyssera, but with ourselves. The Great Silence was a scar upon our souls, a constant reminder of the price of absolute desperation. We understand now that true guardianship is not about making the 'least worst' choice, but about striving for the 'best possible' outcome, even when faced with overwhelming odds. Our current approach is built on that understanding. We are not merely defending; we are healing. We are not merely preventing erasure; we are fostering creation. Our contingency, should it come to that, is to find a solution that honors life, that embraces its complexity, even in the face of annihilation. It is a path we have not had to tread fully, but one we have prepared for, with the wisdom gained from our past."

Cael held the levi-drake's gaze for a long moment, searching for any sign of deceit, any hint of the ancient arrogance that might still linger. He saw no such thing. He saw, instead, a profound weariness, an earnest desire for redemption, and a genuine commitment to a new path. The past was a shadow they could not escape, but perhaps, just perhaps, they were learning to walk towards the light, even if the journey was fraught with peril.

"Your willingness to share this," Cael finally said, his voice softer, the edge of his scrutiny blunted by a nascent trust, "is a crucial step. The knowledge of your past actions, and your current strategies, will be vital in shaping Nyssera's response. But words, however sincere, are not enough. I will need to witness these actions. I will need to see these singers, these artifacts, these pathways you are mending. My duty as Guardian is to ensure Nyssera's safety, and that includes scrutinizing any force that claims to protect it, no matter how ancient or powerful."

He turned his attention back to Mara, who had remained a silent, observant presence throughout the exchange. Her role, he knew, was critical. She was the catalyst, the one who had unearthed these truths, and her understanding, her ability to bridge the gap between legend and reality, would be paramount.

"Mara," Cael said, his voice carrying a new warmth. "You have heard their confession, and you have heard their proposed solutions. Your insight into the deeper currents of Nyssera's song, your connection to its essence, will be invaluable in discerning the true efficacy of these efforts. We need to understand not just the mechanics of their proposed actions, but the spirit behind them. Are they truly seeking to nurture the song, or simply to re-tune it to their own ancient cadence?"

The levi-drake nodded, its vast form seeming to shrink slightly as it acknowledged Cael's demand for empirical evidence. "We welcome your scrutiny, Guardian. We understand that trust must be earned, not inherited. Our hope is that by demonstrating our commitment, by allowing you to witness our efforts firsthand, you will see that our past, while defining, does not dictate our future. We are prepared to prove that we have learned, and that Nyssera's song is safe in our hands, alongside yours."

Cael gave a curt nod, a silent acknowledgment of the levi-drake's pledge. The air in the cavern, though still imbued with the ancient echoes of their past, now carried a new undertone – one of cautious collaboration, of shared responsibility, and of a determined hope that the future would indeed be a symphony of renewal, not a requiem of silence. The guardians, he realized, were still ancient, still powerful, but their scrutiny now extended not just to the threats facing Nyssera, but to themselves, and that, he felt, was a significant beginning.

CHAPTER 5: THE ARCHITECTS OF SUPPRESSION

The levi-drake's words had painted a picture of a world saved from existential despair, but Cael's mind, honed by years of strategic thinking and a deep-seated understanding of natural cycles, perceived an unsettling stillness beneath the veneer of their ancient tranquility. He had pressed them on their methods, on the *how* of their ancient interventions, and now, a new layer of their history was being unfurled, one that resonated with a chilling familiarity to the very forces they claimed to oppose.

"You speak of a system," Cael stated, his voice a low rumble, carefully dissecting the levi-drake's latest revelation. "A 'system designed to forget.' This 'Crown Resonance' you so carefully protect... it is more than just an anchor, more than a beacon of Nyssera's song. It is a gatekeeper of memory, a curator of collective experience. Explain this to me. What exactly did this system *do* to 'forget'?"

The levi-drake's starlight eyes, which had seemed to hold a nascent hope moments before, now clouded with a profound sorrow, a weariness that seemed to stretch back through the eons. It was the look of a being forced to confront not just the errors of its past, but the fundamental flaws in its very creation, in the foundations upon which its civilization had been built.

"The Crown Resonance," the levi-drake began, its voice now imbued with a heavy, almost mournful cadence, "was designed not merely to amplify and preserve Nyssera's song, but to *harmonize* it. To ensure a cohesive, flowing symphony. In its early iterations, its purpose was to integrate all emergent life, all new melodies, into the overarching harmony. But as Nyssera grew, and as the complexities of existence multiplied, so too did the dissonances. Pain, loss, terror – these were the jagged chords that threatened to shatter the perfect pitch."

It paused, and Cael sensed the immense weight of the unspoken atrocities that lay behind those words. The levi-drake continued, its voice barely a whisper, "The 'Silence Event,' as you have termed it, was the nadir. The sheer, unadulterated horror of that period threatened to fracture Nyssera's very consciousness. The collective trauma was so profound, so all-encompassing, that if left unaddressed, it would have paralyzed our world. The song would have choked, not on an external force, but on its own internal anguish."

Mara, standing beside Cael, let out a soft, involuntary gasp. The concept of a world willingly forgetting its own trauma was anathema to her. Her entire existence was a testament to the power of memory, to the necessity of remembering, of learning, of honoring the past, however painful.

"So," Cael pressed, his gaze fixed on the levi-drake, his mind grappling with the implications. "The Crown Resonance was not just a tool for amplification, but a mechanism for *suppression*. You actively pruned the song? You selectively removed the notes of pain, of suffering, of the full horror of what you endured?"

"Precisely," the levi-drake confirmed, the word laced with a deep, self-recriminating regret. "We created protocols within the Resonance, enchantments woven into its very fabric, that would identify and neutralize overwhelming waves of negative memory. This was not a conscious act of malice, Guardian, but a desperate measure. A survival instinct on a planetary scale. We believed, with all our ancient might, that we were safeguarding Nyssera's future by shielding it from the paralyzing weight of its past. We sought to preserve the *possibility* of song, yes, but also the *will* to sing."

The starlight in the levi-drake's eyes flickered, a ghostly echo of forgotten suns. "We engineered a fragile peace, a superficial harmony. We convinced ourselves that by forgetting the deepest scars, we were preventing them from festering. We believed that a world free from the immediate agony of its traumas would be a world capable of renewal. We implemented a system of collective amnesia, ensuring that the most devastating memories would fade, not through natural healing, but through active, enforced erasure. The Crown Resonance became a powerful, ever-vigilant warden of our collective subconscious, ensuring that the deepest wounds would remain unacknowledged, and thus, we thought, unfelt."

Mara's hands clenched into fists at her sides. She had always sensed a certain... hollowness in the narratives of Nyssera's past, a carefully curated perfection that felt too smooth, too unbroken. Now, the levi-drakes were confessing to the very act that had created this disquieting void.

"You speak of 'protocols,' of 'enchantments,'" Cael said, his voice hardening. "This sounds less like natural resilience and more like a deliberate, artificial imposition. You didn't allow Nyssera to heal; you forced it into a state of arrested development. You didn't overcome the trauma; you buried it. And in doing so, you created a false sense of stability, a fragile illusion of peace that prevented true growth. Is that not the very essence of what the Pale Tide seeks to achieve – an enforced stillness, a negation of authentic experience?"

"The intention was preservation, Guardian," the levi-drake insisted, though its voice lacked its former conviction. "Not negation. We aimed to create a sanctuary, a space where Nyssera could recover its strength without being crushed by the sheer weight of its despair. We believed that by severing the most painful threads, we were strengthening the overall tapestry. We were... misguided. Our definition of 'preservation' was too narrow, too focused on the immediate absence of suffering rather than the enduring strength that comes from confronting and integrating it."

Cael's brow furrowed, his mind working through the intricate web of deception, however well-intentioned. "But this 'forced forgetting' – it must have had consequences. You speak of the void-dweller, the Pale Tide, as a force that thrives on entropy and the absence of meaning. If you actively removed meaning, removed the very experiences that forged Nyssera's resilience, how are you not, in essence, creating the perfect breeding ground for its influence?"

"The system was designed to be selective," another levi-drake, who had remained silent until this point, interjected. Its voice was deeper, raspier, carrying the weariness of centuries etched into its very being. "It did not erase all memory, nor all pain. It targeted the overwhelming, soul-shattering traumas. The collective screams that threatened to drown out all other sound. It allowed for the continuation of individual lives, of everyday melodies, of the essential functions of Nyssera. We believed that by removing the deepest wells of despair, we were leaving enough of the song intact for it to eventually rebuild."

"Enough of the song," Mara echoed, her voice tight with a rising anger. "But what of the lessons learned from those screams? What of the growth that comes from facing the abyss and choosing to continue? You didn't just silence the pain; you silenced the wisdom born from that pain. You created a generation, and then another, and another, who never truly understood the depth of the threat they had overcome, or the sacrifices that were made. You fostered ignorance under the guise of peace."

"Ignorance, perhaps," the first levi-drake conceded, its voice heavy with the burden of this admission. "But also, survival. Had we allowed the full weight of the Silence to remain, Nyssera would have fractured. Civilizations would have collapsed. The very capacity for life, for connection, would have been extinguished by the sheer, pervasive despair. We made a choice, a terrible choice, to preserve the species, the world, at the expense of its complete, unvarnished memory. The Crown Resonance was our instrument of this grim necessity. It acted as a filter, a buffer, absorbing and neutralizing the most corrosive aspects of our shared trauma."

"And this 'buffer,'" Cael said, his voice dangerously quiet, "did it truly neutralize them, or did it merely compartmentalize them? Did it heal the wounds, or did it simply seal them, leaving them to fester beneath the surface? Because the Pale Tide, as you have described it, feeds on precisely that – on unaddressed rot, on buried corruption. It preys on the very decay you have been cultivating, however unintentionally."

The levi-drakes exchanged a long, silent communication, their starlight eyes flickering with an unspoken understanding of the gravity of Cael's accusation. The first levi-drake finally spoke, its voice tinged with a profound resignation.

"The system was designed to create a semblance of ongoing harmony, Guardian. It was meant to allow for growth, for the creation of new melodies, new experiences, new memories. But it did so by selectively dimming the intensity of the past. The deepest traumas were not erased, but their emotional resonance was dampened, their sharp edges smoothed. Think of it as a symphony where the most jarring, ear-splitting crescendos have been muted, leaving only a more palatable, though perhaps less impactful, overall sound. The intention was to allow the new music to flourish, to build upon a foundation of relative peace, rather than being constantly overshadowed by the echoes of cataclysm."

"A foundation of relative peace," Mara scoffed, her voice trembling with emotion. "A foundation built on lies. On the deliberate manipulation of collective consciousness. You speak of Nyssera's song, of its vibrant melodies, but what are those melodies if they are not informed by the full spectrum of experience? If the deep, resonant bass notes of suffering and loss are silenced, how can the higher, brighter notes of joy and triumph truly shine? They become hollow, superficial. They lack the depth, the authenticity, that comes from acknowledging and integrating the shadow."

The levi-drakes remained silent, their ancient forms hunched, the weight of their confession pressing down on them. They had revealed a truth that was as profound as it was devastating. The Crown Resonance, the very symbol of Nyssera's enduring song, was also an instrument of suppression, a tool that had actively managed and manipulated planetary memory.

"This system," Cael continued, his gaze sweeping over the cavern, as if he could see the invisible currents of suppressed memory swirling around them. "This 'system designed to forget'... it created a world that was not truly healed, but merely pacified. A world that was kept artificially stable, preventing the natural processes of grief, of reconciliation, of true recovery. And now, that artificial stability is cracking. The Pale Tide is exploiting these vulnerabilities, the very vulnerabilities that your system inadvertently created."

"We understood the risks, even then," the second levi-drake admitted, its voice raspy. "We knew that this suppression was a temporary measure, a crutch that would eventually weaken Nyssera's inherent strength. But the immediate threat was too great. The alternative was annihilation. We chose a path of slow, gradual erosion of authentic memory, believing that the inherent vitality of Nyssera would eventually overcome it. We gambled on the future, on the hope that Nyssera's song would find its own way to wholeness, to remembering, once the immediate danger had passed. It appears our gamble was... ill-advised."

"Ill-advised is an understatement," Mara stated, her voice cold. "It was a profound betrayal. A betrayal of every living creature that suffered during the Silence, and a betrayal of every creature yet to come, who would inherit a world stripped of its essential truths. You didn't protect Nyssera; you infantilized it. You deprived it of its right to grieve, to learn, to evolve through its experiences. The Crown Resonance became not a guardian of song, but a silencer of memory, a perpetrator of a grand, cosmic lie."

Cael looked at Mara, seeing the fierce conviction in her eyes, the unwavering belief in the sanctity of memory, however painful. He understood then that the levi-drakes' confession was not just about revealing their past actions, but about acknowledging the fundamental flaw in their approach to safeguarding Nyssera. They had focused on preserving the *sound* of the song, but had neglected the *meaning* behind it.

"So," Cael stated, his voice resonating with a newfound understanding, "the 'silence' you imposed was not just a reaction to an external threat. It was also an internal mechanism. You created a system that actively managed and suppressed the collective memory of Nyssera, particularly the traumatic events of the Silence. You believed you were preserving the world, but in reality, you were creating a fragile shell, incapable of true resilience. And now, the Pale Tide is drawn to this very fragility, to this unacknowledged decay."

The levi-drakes nodded slowly, their ancient forms sinking deeper into the cavern floor as if weighed down by the enormity of their past actions. "We sought to prevent the world from breaking under the weight of its own pain," the first levi-drake murmured, its voice barely audible. "But in doing so, we broke something essential within it. We created an artificial peace, a stasis that prevented true healing. We traded authentic experience for engineered tranquility. And now, we are faced with the consequences of that choice. The Pale Tide thrives in the absence of truth, in the void left by suppressed memories. Our attempt to create a perfect song inadvertently created the perfect conditions for its antithesis."

Mara's breath hitched. The full weight of the levi-drakes' confession settled upon her. The Crown Resonance, the very heart of Nyssera's song, was not merely a passive anchor. It was an active participant in the suppression of memory, a meticulously designed system to forget the most devastating truths. This was not an act of preservation, but of profound, cosmic amnesia. The levi-drakes, in their desperation to save Nyssera from the overwhelming trauma of the Silence, had implemented a solution that, in the long run, left the world vulnerable to the very forces of negation it sought to escape.

They had created a world that was, in essence, designed to forget its own scars, and in doing so, had prevented itself from truly healing. The system that was meant to safeguard Nyssera's song had, in fact, been architected to silence its most crucial, formative notes – the echoes of pain, resilience, and the hard-won wisdom that came from surviving the abyss. The void-dweller, the Pale Tide, fed on exactly this: the absence of authentic memory, the hollowness left by deliberate forgetting. Their act of preservation had, ironically, created the perfect conditions for destruction.

The weight of the levi-drakes' confession settled not just upon Cael, but upon Mara with a crushing, visceral force. As a Listener, her connection to the world's song was not merely an academic pursuit or a tactical advantage; it was an intrinsic part of her being. She felt the tremors of Nyssera's history not as abstract concepts or whispered accounts, but as lived, imprinted sensations within her very soul. And now, as the architects of suppression laid bare the mechanisms of their curated silence, Mara began to experience the raw, unfiltered aftermath of their 'preservation.'

It started as a low thrumming beneath her skin, a discordant vibration that Elias, beside her, couldn't perceive. Then, the thrumming intensified, coalescing into sharp, piercing echoes. Images, unbidden and brutal, flashed behind her eyes, too vivid, too real to be mere imagination. She saw ancient forests, vibrant with a thousand hues of green, suddenly wither and crumble to dust in the span of a breath. She felt the spectral agony of creatures, their forms never truly known to her, their existence extinguished as if they had never been. The air, once rich with the scent of life, turned acrid, choked with the phantom stench of decay. It was the pain of severed ecosystems, the irreparable tearing of delicate interdependencies, a wound so deep it bled into the very fabric of Nyssera's being.

This was not the gentle sorrow of a single loss, but the gaping wound of mass extinction, the grief of a world that had shed entire branches of its living tapestry. Mara gasped, a sound ripped from her throat, her hands instinctively flying to her temples as if to ward off an invisible assault.

The levi-drakes spoke of muting the 'jagged chords,' of 'neutralizing overwhelming waves of negative memory,' but their actions had not erased the pain; they had merely driven it underground, forcing it to fester in the silent places of Nyssera's collective consciousness. And now, that festering wound was bleeding into her.

The echoes intensified, morphing from the silent screams of dying flora and fauna into something far more personal, more terrifying. It was the raw terror of the Silence Event itself. Not the sanitized, historical account the levi-drakes had hinted at, but the visceral, soul-shattering *experience* of it. Mara felt the crushing weight of a despair so profound it threatened to extinguish her own will to exist. She felt the collective, unarticulated horror of countless beings facing an unimaginable threat, a primal fear that transcended individual thought and became a planetary scream. It was a terror so absolute that it was, as the levi-drake had described, a force that could paralyze a world.

Mara stumbled, Elias's arm shooting out to steady her. Her breath came in ragged gasps, her vision blurring as the onslaught continued. This was not the carefully modulated resonance she usually experienced. This was a direct, unshielded influx of pain, a torrent of suffering that had been systematically dammed and diverted for eons. The levi-drakes' 'Crown Resonance,' she now understood with a chilling clarity, was not just an amplifier of Nyssera's song, but a meticulously crafted dam, holding back a cataclysm of emotional anguish. They hadn't healed the world; they had embalmed it in a state of forced, artificial peace.

The sheer intensity of the shared agony was almost unbearable. Mara felt the grief of a mother losing a child, magnified a millionfold. She felt the existential dread of a species facing extinction, the desperate yearning for survival against impossible odds. She felt the gnawing emptiness of isolation, the profound sorrow of disconnection, all amplified and interwoven into a tapestry of suffering that had been deliberately muted, its sharp edges smoothed away by the Crown Resonance. But the smoothing, she realized, had not removed the pain; it had merely made it insidious, allowing it to seep into the very foundations of Nyssera's being, a slow, invisible poison.

Her empathy, her greatest gift, had become her greatest torment. It was usually a bridge, a way to understand and connect. Now, it was a gaping maw, swallowing the unacknowledged pain of an entire world. She felt the hollowness that Cael had spoken of, the disconcerting perfection of Nyssera's history, not as an intellectual observation, but as a phantom ache in her own chest. The harmony they sang was a thin veneer, stretched taut over a chasm of suppressed sorrow. The levi-drakes' claim of preserving the song felt like a cruel mockery. They had preserved the melody, perhaps, but at the cost of its soul, its truth.

"This... this isn't just about the Silence Event," Mara choked out, her voice thick with unshed tears. Her gaze, unfocused and wide with the spectral pain, swept over the levi-drakes. "You didn't just mute the cataclysm. You muted *everything* that followed. Every consequence, every ripple of grief, every lesson learned from that absolute terror. You smoothed over the scars so effectively that Nyssera forgot *why* it had them."

She felt the quiet desperation of beings who had witnessed the Absolute Terror and, in its wake, had struggled to find meaning, to find a reason to continue. She felt their profound, unspoken grief, not for themselves, but for the future generations they feared would inherit a world that didn't understand the fragility of its own existence. This was the collective terror the levi-drakes had sought to dampen – not just the fear of the immediate threat, but the lingering, existential dread that followed, the deep-seated knowledge of how close Nyssera had come to annihilation.

Mara swayed, her knees threatening to buckle. The sheer volume of suppressed emotion was overwhelming. It was like trying to drink from a firehose, the water of sorrow and terror too powerful, too voluminous to be contained. She could feel the individual threads of this suppressed pain – the quiet despair of a gardener who had watched their life's work turn to ash, the hollow ache of a parent who had lost a child to a blight no one remembered, the existential confusion of a species that had no memory of the great struggles that had shaped its very being.

"You speak of a false peace," Cael's voice, though steady, held a new, raw edge. He looked at Mara, his expression a mixture of concern and grim understanding. "But it is more than that. It is a manufactured ignorance. You created a generation, and then another, and another, who never knew the true cost of their existence. They live in a gilded cage, unaware of the monsters that once lurked outside, unaware of the sacrifices that were made to keep the bars intact."

Mara nodded, clinging to Elias's arm as if he were her anchor to the present. "And that ignorance," she whispered, her voice raspy, "that is what the Pale Tide feeds on. It feeds on the lack of understanding, on the unacknowledged history, on the void where true resilience should be. You thought you were protecting Nyssera from pain, but you robbed it of its strength. You severed its roots from the very soil of its experience."

She could feel it now, a subtle undercurrent in the chaos of suppressed pain. It was the Pale Tide's influence, a parasitic tendril reaching into the unhealed wounds, amplifying the lingering despair, turning the muted sorrow into a suffocating miasma. The levi-drakes' solution had, in essence, created a more fertile ground for the very entropic force they fought against. By removing the memory of the struggle, they had also removed the understanding of how to fight.

The air around Mara seemed to thicken, heavy with the phantom weight of forgotten tears. She could feel the individual moments of profound loss, each one a tiny shard of glass embedded in the collective psyche, shards that had been deliberately blunted but never removed. The grief of a lost civilization, the sorrow of a dying star's last breath, the quiet despair of a world teetering on the brink – these were not memories that could simply be excised without consequence. They were the essential chords that gave the symphony its depth, its meaning. Without them, the music was thin, reedy, and ultimately, fragile.

"This is... this is the deepest form of pain," Mara murmured, her voice barely audible above the psychic storm raging within her. "The pain of being forgotten. The pain of knowing, on some primal level, that something vital has been taken, but not knowing what. It's a constant, gnawing emptiness." She looked at the levi-drakes, her eyes, usually filled with a gentle warmth, now blazing with a righteous anger. "You didn't preserve Nyssera's song. You silenced its truest verses. You traded authenticity for a manufactured lullaby, and now, that lullaby is breaking."

The levi-drakes remained still, their ancient forms radiating an aura of profound regret. The starlight in their eyes seemed dimmer, as if dimmed by the very sorrow they had long suppressed. Cael watched Mara, his own internal storm of strategic calculation momentarily silenced by the raw display of her connection. He had understood intellectually that the Crown Resonance was a tool of suppression, but Mara's experience was a brutal, visceral testament to its true cost. The levi-drakes had built a sanctuary, but it was a sanctuary built on denial, a place where healing was replaced by a slow, insidious decay. The Architects of Suppression had, with the best of intentions, created the perfect architects of vulnerability.

Mara could feel the individual echoes of the Silence Event now, not as a blur of terror, but as distinct moments of profound loss. The agony of a parent watching their child fade, not from disease, but from sheer existential despair. The cold dread of a communal decision to cease all efforts, to simply let go, overwhelmed by the sheer futility of resistance. The silent scream of a world that had collectively decided to stop singing, not out of defeat, but out of an overwhelming, soul-crushing weariness. These were the moments the Crown Resonance had sought to erase, but in doing so, it had stripped them of their power to teach, to warn, to foster resilience.

"They weren't just protecting Nyssera from the pain," Mara whispered, her voice raw. "They were protecting themselves from the responsibility of grief. They chose to forget, because remembering was too hard. But that hardness, that struggle, that's what makes us strong. That's what makes the song *mean* something." She felt a sharp pang, a memory that wasn't hers, of a small, bioluminescent creature, its light fading as its ecosystem collapsed, its final, silent thought a question: "Why?" This was the profound question that the levi-drakes had buried, a question that echoed in the void left by their suppression.

The silence that followed was not a peaceful quiet, but a tense, heavy stillness, pregnant with the unspoken horrors of Nyssera's buried past. The levi-drakes had spoken of a system designed to forget, and Mara was now its unwilling vessel, forced to bear witness to the true, devastating legacy of that design. The architects of suppression had built a world of engineered tranquility, but they had forgotten that true peace could only be found in the acceptance of pain, not its denial. And in that forgotten truth lay the seeds of Nyssera's potential undoing. The weight of that realization was almost too much to bear, a cosmic sorrow settling upon her shoulders, the pain of a world that had been taught to forget its own heart.

Cael's analytical gaze, usually sharp and focused on tactical advantages, now swept across the ancient, imposing forms of the levi-drakes. He had listened, intently, not just to their words, but to the unspoken implications, the carefully constructed silences that Mara's visceral experience had begun to puncture. Where Mara felt the raw, agonizing imprint of suppressed emotion, Cael perceived the architecture of its confinement. He saw not just a benevolent attempt to soothe a wounded world, but a meticulously designed system of control, a vast, intricate mechanism built to ensure not healing, but compliance. The levi-drakes' 'Crown Resonance,' a force of unimaginable power, was, in his estimation, a masterful instrument of suppression, its primary function not to mend, but to manage.

He understood the levi-drakes' narrative: a world teetering on the brink of annihilation, a cataclysm of pain and terror that threatened to unravel the very fabric of Nyssera. Their solution, a collective muting, a gentle quieting of the jagged edges of despair, seemed, on the surface, a noble act of preservation. But Cael, a strategist by nature and a keen observer of power dynamics, saw the chilling logic that underpinned it. To maintain order, to prevent the recurrence of such catastrophic despair, one had to control the very conduits of emotional and experiential understanding. Memory, particularly the painful, cautionary kind, was an inconvenient variable. And so, it had been systematically muted, smoothed over, rendered impotent.

"You speak of preserving the song," Cael's voice, though outwardly calm, resonated with a nascent understanding of the system's true design, a subtle shift from his previous focus on immediate threats to the deeper undercurrents of Nyssera's existence. "But what you have truly preserved is the status quo. The Crown Resonance, it is not a balm, but a muzzle. It silences the discordant notes, yes, but in doing so, it also silences the warnings. It prevents the world from learning, from evolving, from becoming truly resilient." He paused, letting the implication hang in the air. "A species, or a world, that does not remember its failures, is doomed to repeat them. This is not preservation; it is stagnation."

He saw the levi-drakes' desire for stability not as a selfless act of protection, but as a deep-seated fear of chaos, a preference for predictability over the messy, often painful, process of growth. They had, in their millennia-long stewardship, become the architects of Nyssera's collective amnesia, deliberately architecting a reality where unpleasant truths were simply not allowed to surface. This was the hallmark of authoritarian control: the curation of a narrative, the suppression of dissenting or inconvenient realities, all in the name of a manufactured peace. The levi-drakes had effectively imposed a form of societal lobotomy, removing the parts that held the capacity for intense pain, but also, as Cael now understood, the parts that fostered profound wisdom and hard-won strength.

"The fear of the Pale Tide," Cael continued, his gaze fixed on the distant, star-dusted expanse, "you believed that by removing the memory of the Silence Event, you were removing its power to draw such a threat. But you have done the opposite. You have created a void. The Pale Tide, as Mara described, feeds on the absence of understanding, on the unacknowledged pain. It preys on a world that has forgotten how to fight, because it has forgotten *why* it must fight. You have not eliminated the weakness; you have amplified it by eradicating the very history that would teach Nyssera to overcome it."

He thought of the countless dragons, and other beings, who had lived and died under the levi-drakes' silent watch. They had existed in a state of engineered contentment, their lives devoid of the deep-seated terror of the Silence Event, but also devoid of the profound lessons it had offered. They had never experienced the existential dread that could galvanize action, the collective suffering that could forge unbreakable bonds of solidarity. They had been shielded from the fire, and thus, they had never learned the true meaning of being forged. This was the insidious nature of their control: it was not overtly cruel, but it was fundamentally disempowering. It created a populace that was placid, compliant, and utterly unprepared for true adversity.

"This system," Cael mused, his voice taking on a more theoretical, yet no less intense, quality, "it is a perfectly constructed cage. The bars are not made of iron, but of enforced ignorance. The walls are built from smoothed-over memories and the absence of consequence. You have created a generation, and then another, and another, who are blissfully unaware of the precipice Nyssera once stood upon. They know nothing of the sacrifices made, nothing of the terror that was faced. And so, they have no concept of the value of what they possess, nor the will to defend it when a true threat emerges."

He recognized the patterns of authoritarianism that were as old as consciousness itself. The desire to control the narrative, to shape perception, to eliminate elements that might destabilize the ruling power. The levi-drakes, despite their ancient wisdom and seemingly benevolent intentions, had fallen prey to this fundamental impulse. Their power, vast and ancient, had led them to believe they knew what was best for Nyssera, to the extent that they felt justified in stripping it of its agency, its right to learn from its own experiences. They had become, in essence, benevolent dictators of the soul.

"The desire for stability," Cael elaborated, his mind piecing together the levi-drakes' motivations, "it is understandable. No one wishes for their world to be consumed by terror. But stability achieved through the suppression of truth is a fragile thing. It is a dam built on sand, always on the verge of collapse. True strength, true resilience, comes from confronting the darkness, from understanding its nature, from experiencing the sorrow and emerging from it with a deeper appreciation for the light. You have chosen to avoid the darkness, and in doing so, you have rendered Nyssera incapable of appreciating the light."

He considered the implications for their current struggle. If Nyssera's inhabitants had been conditioned to expect peace, to have their discomforts smoothed away, how would they react to the true horrors of the Pale Tide? They would likely be paralyzed, not by fear, but by sheer incomprehension. They had no framework for such unadulterated malevolence, no internalized understanding of the sacrifices that might be required to combat it. The levi-drakes, in their attempt to create a perfect, painless existence, had inadvertently created a world ripe for subjugation, a world that lacked the very psychological defenses necessary to survive.

"This is not a matter of blame," Cael stated, his tone softening slightly, acknowledging the levi-drakes' apparent remorse. "It is a matter of understanding the unintended consequences of your actions. You sought to protect, but you undermined. You sought to preserve, but you stunted. The very system you designed to safeguard Nyssera has, in fact, made it more vulnerable. It has created a population that is, to use a crude analogy, like a child who has never known hunger, and therefore cannot comprehend the desperation of those who starve. They lack the fundamental context to understand the severity of the threat."

He looked at Mara, then back at the levi-drakes. "Mara's gift, her ability to feel the echoes of suppressed pain, is a testament to the depth of the wound you have inflicted. It is not just individual memories you have muted, but the collective scar tissue, the lessons learned in the crucible of suffering. Without those lessons, Nyssera is a ship with no anchor, adrift in a sea of potential destruction, with no memory of the storms it has weathered, nor the skills it has acquired in navigating them."

Cael's analysis, delivered with a quiet intensity, painted a grim picture. The levi-drakes had, with the best of intentions, engineered a society that was profoundly ill-equipped to face the very dangers they had sought to prevent. Their control, though perhaps not malicious, was absolute in its effect, creating a fragile peace that was, in reality, a breeding ground for greater disaster. He saw the system not as a protective shield, but as a gilded cage, one that promised safety but delivered only vulnerability. The Architects of Suppression had, by their own design, laid the groundwork for Nyssera's potential downfall, a downfall born not of overwhelming external force, but of internal fragility, of a forgotten capacity for resilience. The control, he concluded, was the ultimate vulnerability.

The levi-drakes, their ancient forms shimmering with an ethereal light that seemed to carry the weight of ages, finally responded, their voices a chorus of deep, resonant hums that vibrated through the very stone of their sanctuary. It was a sound that spoke not of defiance, but of a profound, sorrowful resignation. They did not dispute Cael's assessment, nor Mara's visceral revelations. Instead, they offered their own perspective, a narrative woven from eons of stewardship and a burden of choice that had, in their estimation, been the only possible one.

"You see the cage, young strategist," one of the eldest levi-drakes resonated, its form expanding slightly, as if to encompass the vastness of its explanation. "And you are correct in many of your observations. But you perceive the bars as an act of malice, or at best, of selfish control. We did not erect these walls to imprison, but to shield. We did not dampen the world's song to silence dissent, but to prevent it from being drowned out by a cacophony of despair."

Another levi-drake interjected, its voice like the shifting of continents. "Consider Nyssera at the precipice, Cael. Consider the raw, unadulterated terror of the Silence Event. It was not merely a catastrophe; it was an existential unraveling. The collective consciousness of our world was fractured, shattered by a pain so profound, so all-encompassing, that the very will to continue, to exist, was threatened. The screams of a billion souls, the agony of worlds imploding, the gnawing emptiness that followed – these were not abstract concepts. They were wounds etched into the fabric of reality itself."

A third levi-drake's voice, a low, mournful rumble, added, "To allow that memory to fester, to remain in its full, agonizing potency, would have been to condemn Nyssera to an unending cycle of grief. We foresaw a future where the inhabitants, forever haunted by the ghosts of that annihilation, would be incapable of love, of hope, of creation. They would be perpetually paralyzed by the echoes of suffering, their lives a constant, desolate lament. Is that the 'resilience' you champion? A world that remembers its pain so vividly that it forgets how to live?"

They explained that the Crown Resonance, their monumental act of collective will, was not an instrument of suppression in the way Cael had initially conceived it. It was, in their eyes, a necessary amputation. A surgical strike against a terminal disease. The disease, they argued, was the world's own capacity for self-destruction, fueled by the unbearable weight of its history.

"We did not erase memory, Cael," the first levi-drake clarified, its voice tinged with a weariness that transcended its physical form. "We did not destroy it. We... reshaped it. We softened its edges. We removed the sharpest shards of terror, the most paralyzing moments of despair. We did not eliminate the experience of the Silence Event entirely, but we muted its most destructive frequencies. We created a buffer, a gentle fog to obscure the sharpest cliffs of remembrance, ensuring that the path forward, though perhaps less vibrant, was at least traversable."

The paradox, as they articulated it, was stark and agonizing. In their earnest endeavor to protect Nyssera from the crushing weight of its own past, they had inadvertently fostered a fragile innocence. They had shielded the world from the precipice, but in doing so, they had prevented it from developing the instinct for balance, the deep-seated understanding of gravity, the very will to cling on when the ground gave way.

"Our intention was to preserve the spark of life," the second levi-drake continued, its voice taking on a pleading tone, as if seeking understanding from a generation that could never truly grasp the burden they carried. "The Pale Tide, the Silence Event – these were the ultimate manifestations of Nyssera's vulnerability. The abyss, as you call it, was not merely a historical event, but a primal fear that threatened to consume us. We believed that by ensuring the memory of that fear did not dominate the present, we were granting Nyssera the freedom to flourish. We were giving it the chance to build anew, unburdened by the specter of its own demise."

They spoke of the "slow decay" Cael had alluded to, not as a failure of their power, but as an unforeseen consequence of their success. "We succeeded in quieting the immediate screams," the third levi-drake confessed, its voice barely a whisper, yet carrying the force of millennia. "We prevented the collective descent into madness. But in removing the overwhelming sorrow, we also removed the profound lessons it imparted. We prevented the world from fully understanding the nature of the threat, the depth of the sacrifice required to overcome it. We created a generation that had never truly felt the biting frost of true despair, and therefore, could not fully appreciate the warmth of survival."

The abyss, once a symbol of Nyssera's deepest, most terrifying past, had, in their view, become something more insidious. It was no longer a memory to be learned from, but a buried trauma, festering beneath the surface, its absence of recognition making it all the more potent when it began to resurface. Their protective measures, the very mechanisms designed to prevent collapse, had, in their unintended consequence, become the architects of a new, more subtle vulnerability.

"We believed we were building a bulwark against chaos," the first levi-drake stated, its ancient eyes, pools of starlight, fixed on Cael. "But we created a vacuum. A void where understanding should have been. The Pale Tide, the entities that stalk the edges of our reality, they feed on this very absence.

They are drawn to the unacknowledged pain, the forgotten lessons. A world that does not remember why it must fight, Cael, is a world ripe for conquest. We gave Nyssera peace, yes, but it was the peace of ignorance, the tranquility of a patient unaware of their terminal illness."

They admitted that their methods, while seemingly effective in maintaining stability, had fostered a profound complacency. The creatures of Nyssera, cocooned in the levi-drakes' gentle suppression, had grown accustomed to a world where extreme suffering was an echo, a distant hum, rather than a visceral reality. They had learned to navigate a world where sharp edges were smoothed, and overwhelming challenges were, if not erased, then certainly softened. This, the levi-drakes now acknowledged, was a critical failing.

"We thought that by preventing the world from being crushed by its history, we were allowing it to build a stronger future," the second levi-drake admitted, its form dimming slightly, as if in shame. "But the foundation of that future was built on sand. The Crown Resonance, in its infinite reach, touched every mind, every heart, smoothing away the rough terrain of memory. We meant to heal the world, but we inadvertently sterilized it. We removed the pathogens, but also the antibodies. We prevented the searing pain, but also the hard-won immunity it forged."

The levi-drakes painted a picture of a world that, while not actively suffering, was also not truly living. They had curated a reality of pleasant mediocrity, a gentle drift rather than a determined voyage. The very act of protection had become a form of suppression, not of will, but of the capacity for true understanding. They had traded the potential for profound growth, born from hardship, for a guaranteed, yet ultimately fragile, peace.

"The abyss," the third levi-drake continued, its voice a mournful sigh that seemed to carry the weight of countless lost ages, "was our greatest teacher. It showed us the true cost of unchecked despair. But in our haste to prevent its recurrence, we threw away the lesson itself. We removed the scar, but not the understanding of how it was formed. And now, the very forces that

Nyssera once knew how to combat, the shadows that once threatened to engulf us, are returning. And this time, Nyssera does not remember how to fight. It does not remember the cost. It does not remember why it must."

They confessed that their millennia-long stewardship had, ironically, rendered Nyssera less capable of self-preservation. By taking on the burden of remembering, by actively managing the collective memory, they had robbed Nyssera of the opportunity to learn to remember for itself. They had become the gatekeepers of truth, and in doing so, had created a populace that was ill-equipped to discern truth from falsehood, or to recognize the insidious creep of a new, more profound darkness.

"We sought to prevent the world from breaking," the first levi-drake concluded, its voice resonating with a deep, ancient sorrow. "We believed that by removing the source of its deepest pain, we were ensuring its survival. We were wrong. The pain, in its rawest form, was a catalyst for strength. It was a lesson in survival, a testament to the indomitable spirit that could emerge from the ashes. By removing the ashes, we removed the possibility of that rebirth. We have created a Nyssera that is, in its profound ignorance, more vulnerable than it has ever been. Our protection has become the very threat we sought to avert."

The levi-drakes, their forms radiating a palpable sense of regret, had laid bare the core of their paradox. They had acted with what they believed were the purest intentions, driven by a profound love for their world and a deep-seated fear of its annihilation. Yet, in their attempt to shield Nyssera from its own past, they had inadvertently stripped it of its capacity to face its future. The architects of suppression, in their earnest desire to prevent collapse, had laid the foundation for a far more insidious and potentially final undoing. The silence they had imposed, once a sanctuary, had become a breeding ground for oblivion, a quiet decay that was, in its own way, far more terrifying than the cataclysm they had so desperately sought to prevent. The abyss, once a memory of struggle, had become a void of ignorance, a fertile ground for the very darkness they had striven to keep at bay.

The levi-drakes had spoken, their ancient pronouncements a tapestry of sorrow and flawed intent. Cael, his mind a battlefield of conflicting truths, absorbed their narrative of protective suppression, of a world shielded from a trauma so profound it threatened to shatter existence itself. He understood their logic, the desperate calculus of preventing utter annihilation by sacrificing the sharpness of memory. Yet, Mara, her eyes still reflecting the spectral light of the levi-drakes' sanctuary, felt a dissonance that gnawed at her soul. Their explanation, while vast and ancient, felt like a perfectly crafted edifice built upon a flawed foundation. The carefully curated peace they described, the gentle fog obscuring the sharpest edges of history, felt less like preservation and more like a gilded cage.

The levi-drakes' words, echoing with the weariness of millennia, spoke of a world that had been healed, of a collective consciousness mended. But Mara sensed something more, a phantom limb ache that resonated through her very being. It was a persistent thrum beneath the placid surface, a counter-melody to the levi-drakes' soothing, controlled song. These were the whispers, the fragments of true memory that, despite the levi-drakes' monumental efforts, refused to be entirely silenced. They were not grand pronouncements or historical records, but raw, unfiltered echoes, seeping through the cracks in the Crown Resonance, like tendrils of a wild vine reclaiming a derelict structure.

As the levi-drakes retreated into the shimmering depths of their sanctuary, their forms dissolving back into the ancient light, Mara felt the shift most acutely. The air, which had been thick with the levi-drakes' resonant hum, now felt thinner, charged with a different kind of energy. It was the energy of something wild and untamed, something that had been dormant but not dead. She saw it in the fleeting expressions on Cael's face, in the way Elara's hand unconsciously tightened on her staff, as if bracing against an unseen current.

The whispers came to Mara not as thoughts, but as sensations, as flashes of light and sound that bypassed the logical mind. They were glimpses of a Nyssera that was vibrant, interconnected, and fiercely resilient. She saw hues of emerald and sapphire that seemed to glow with an inner light, colors that felt richer, more alive than anything in the muted present. She heard the rustling of leaves that sang with a thousand voices, the murmur of rivers that spoke of ancient journeys, the joyous shouts of communities bound by something far deeper than mere cohabitation. It was a Nyssera that thrummed with an almost unbearable intensity, a world that knew both soaring joy and profound sorrow, and embraced both as essential facets of existence.

These were not memories of the Silence Event itself, not the shattering despair the levi-drakes had so carefully muted. These were memories of *before*, and of the life that had stubbornly persisted *after*, in the liminal spaces where true remembrance was still allowed to breathe. They spoke of a world that navigated its darkness with a fierce, instinctual grace, not by forgetting, but by integrating. They whispered of the collective strength that had arisen not from the absence of pain, but from the shared understanding of its weight, and the unwavering will to push through it.

Mara felt a profound ache, a yearning for this lost world. The levi-drakes had spoken of shielding Nyssera from overwhelming despair, but these whispers spoke of a Nyssera that had known despair, had wrestled with it, and had emerged not broken, but tempered, more deeply aware of its own strength. She saw visions of individuals, their faces etched with hardship but alight with an unyielding spirit, working together not out of a forced harmony, but out of a deep, ingrained understanding of mutual reliance. There was a raw, earthy beauty to these glimpses, a sense of organic growth and interconnectedness that had been meticulously pruned away.

The encroaching Pale Tide, a creeping shadow at the edges of Nyssera's perceived reality, seemed to be a catalyst for these resurfacing memories. As the levi-drakes' influence, and the power of the Crown Resonance, began to fray, the dam holding back these echoes of true remembrance started to crack. The Pale Tide, with its insidious nature, seemed to feed not just on fear, but on the very absence of lived experience, on the unacknowledged depths of Nyssera's history. And in its wake, the buried past began to stir.

Mara experienced these fragments as a kind of psychic static, a counter-frequency to the levi-drakes' carefully modulated song of peace. It was as if the universe itself was trying to reassert its original melody, a melody that was far more complex and resonant than the simplified tune Nyssera had been forced to hum. She felt the joy of a child laughing under a sky ablaze with twin moons, a joy so pure and unrestrained it made her chest ache. She felt the quiet pride of a craftsman completing a task of immense difficulty, the satisfaction of a challenge met and overcome. She felt the fierce protectiveness of a parent shielding their young, a primal instinct that had been dulled by generations of enforced safety.

These were not the sanitized, curated memories that the levi-drakes had described. These were sharp, vivid, and intensely real. They carried the scent of rain on parched earth, the taste of wild berries, the sting of a scraped knee, the warmth of a communal hearth. They were the memories of a world that had known the sharp edges of existence, and had learned to navigate them, not by smoothing them away, but by developing the strength and wisdom to hold them.

The contrast with the present was stark and often painful. The vibrant tapestry of true memory was woven with threads of both ecstasy and agony. There were moments of breathtaking beauty, of profound connection and selfless love, but there were also echoes of deep loss, of bitter struggle, and of sacrifices made that resonated with a power that the current generation could not comprehend. The levi-drakes had sought to remove the paralyzing terror, but in doing so, they had also, Mara realized, removed the profound lessons that such terror could impart. They had removed the scar, but not the understanding of how it was formed, nor the resilience it signified.

Elara, too, felt the subtle shifts. Her connection to the earth, usually a steady, grounding presence, had become erratic, like a river struggling against a dam. She spoke of the land itself seeming to sigh, of ancient trees murmuring secrets they had long held dormant. She described the very air as feeling heavier, as if burdened by unacknowledged truths.

"It's like the world is trying to remember how to breathe, Cael," Elara said, her voice barely a whisper, her gaze fixed on the horizon where the Pale Tide's influence was most pronounced. "The levi-drakes... they meant well, I know. But they've put Nyssera into a deep sleep. And now, the dreams are starting to break through."

Mara nodded, her focus turned inward, trying to process the torrent of sensations. The levi-drakes had described the Crown Resonance as a shield, a benevolent force that had smoothed the rough terrain of Nyssera's collective consciousness. But these whispers, these raw fragments of true memory, spoke of a different kind of resonance, an ancient, intrinsic connection that had been suppressed, not eradicated. It was a memory of interconnectedness, of a world where the pulse of one living being was felt, however faintly, by all.

She saw visions of Nysserans who were not merely individuals, but nodes in a vast, living network. Their triumphs were shared, their sorrows lessened by the collective burden. There was a deep, intuitive understanding, a communication that transcended words. This was the vibrancy the levi-drakes had spoken of, but they had framed it as a vulnerability, a source of potential chaos. Mara saw it, however, as the very essence of Nyssera's strength, its capacity for true resilience.

The whispers brought with them an understanding of the Pale Tide that was far more visceral than any explanation. They didn't just understand the Pale Tide as an external threat; they *felt* its nature, its hunger for that which was absent, for the unacknowledged pain and the forgotten lessons. The levi-drakes had muted the world's song of suffering to prevent it from being drowned out, but the whispers revealed that by muting it, they had also deafened Nyssera to the warning cries, to the very rhythm of danger.

As Mara delved deeper into these resurfacing memories, she felt a growing sense of awe, mingled with a profound sadness. The world the levi-drakes had shielded was a pale imitation of the world that had truly existed. The beauty they had preserved was a fragile, artificial bloom, lacking the deep roots and inherent strength of a wild, untamed garden. These whispers were a testament to life's enduring persistence, a defiant hum against the enforced silence, a reminder that the true song of Nyssera, though muted, had never truly been extinguished.

It was a melody that held the echoes of every joy, every sorrow, every triumph, and every fall – a complete, resonant symphony that was now, slowly, painfully, beginning to reawaken. The echoes were a testament to a Nyssera that had been more alive, more vibrant, and more truly *real* than the placid, controlled existence that had been imposed. They were beautiful, yes, but their beauty was edged with a sharp, terrifying reminder of what had been lost, and what was now, perilously, returning.

CHAPTER SIX

THE PALE TIDE'S TRUE NATURE

The levi-drakes had offered an explanation, a tapestry woven with threads of sorrow and intent, yet Mara felt the warp and weft were not entirely true. Cael, his brow furrowed in concentration, seemed to accept their pronouncements with a weariness that spoke of deep contemplation. He understood, or at least he claimed to, the logic of their ancient actions – the desperate calculus of preventing utter annihilation by sacrificing the sharpness of memory. But for Mara, the carefully curated peace, the gentle fog obscuring the sharpest edges of history, felt less like preservation and more like a gilded cage.

The levi-drakes' words, echoing with the weariness of millennia, spoke of a world that had been healed, of a collective consciousness mended. But Mara sensed something more, a phantom limb ache that resonated through her very being. It was a persistent thrum beneath the placid surface, a counter-melody to the levi-drakes' soothing, controlled song. These were the whispers, the fragments of true memory that, despite the levi-drakes' monumental efforts, refused to be entirely silenced. They were not grand pronouncements or historical records, but raw, unfiltered echoes, seeping through the cracks in the Crown Resonance, like tendrils of a wild vine reclaiming a derelict structure.

As the levi-drakes retreated into the shimmering depths of their sanctuary, their forms dissolving back into the ancient light, Mara felt the shift most acutely. The air, which had been thick with the levi-drakes' resonant hum, now felt thinner, charged with a different kind of energy. It was the energy of something wild and untamed, something that had been dormant but not dead. She saw it in the fleeting expressions on Cael's face, in the way Elara's hand unconsciously tightened on her staff, as if bracing against an unseen current.

The whispers came to Mara not as thoughts, but as sensations, as flashes of light and sound that bypassed the logical mind. They were glimpses of a Nyssera that was vibrant, interconnected, and fiercely resilient. She saw hues of emerald and sapphire that seemed to glow with an inner light, colors that felt richer, more alive than anything in the muted present. She heard the rustling of leaves that sang with a thousand voices, the murmur of rivers that spoke of ancient journeys, the joyous shouts of communities bound by something far deeper than mere cohabitation. It was a Nyssera that thrummed with an almost unbearable intensity, a world that knew both soaring joy and profound sorrow, and embraced both as essential facets of existence.

These were not memories of the Silence Event itself, not the shattering despair the levi-drakes had so carefully muted. These were memories of *before*, and of the life that had stubbornly persisted *after*, in the liminal spaces where true remembrance was still allowed to breathe. They spoke of a world that navigated its darkness with a fierce, instinctual grace, not by forgetting, but by integrating. They whispered of the collective strength that had arisen not from the absence of pain, but from the shared understanding of its weight, and the unwavering will to push through it.

Mara felt a profound ache, a yearning for this lost world. The levi-drakes had spoken of shielding Nyssera from overwhelming despair, but these whispers spoke of a Nyssera that had known despair, had wrestled with it, and had emerged not broken, but tempered, more deeply aware of its own strength. She saw visions of individuals, their faces etched with hardship but alight with an unyielding spirit, working together not out of a forced harmony, but out of a deep, ingrained understanding of mutual reliance. There was a raw, earthy beauty to these glimpses, a sense of organic growth and interconnectedness that had been meticulously pruned away.

The encroaching Pale Tide, a creeping shadow at the edges of Nyssera's perceived reality, seemed to be a catalyst for these resurfacing memories. As the levi-drakes' influence, and the power of the Crown Resonance, began to fray, the dam holding back these echoes of true remembrance started to crack. The Pale Tide, with its insidious nature, seemed to feed not just on fear, but on the very absence of lived experience, on the unacknowledged depths of Nyssera's history. And in its wake, the buried past began to stir.

Mara experienced these fragments as a kind of psychic static, a counter-frequency to the levi-drakes' carefully modulated song of peace. It was as if the universe itself was trying to reassert its original melody, a melody that was far more complex and resonant than the simplified tune Nyssera had been forced to hum. She felt the joy of a child laughing under a sky ablaze with twin moons, a joy so pure and unrestrained it made her chest ache. She felt the quiet pride of a craftsman completing a task of immense difficulty, the satisfaction of a challenge met and overcome. She felt the fierce protectiveness of a parent shielding their young, a primal instinct that had been dulled by generations of enforced safety.

These were not the sanitized, curated memories that the levi-drakes had described. These were sharp, vivid, and intensely real. They carried the scent of rain on parched earth, the taste of wild berries, the sting of a scraped knee, the warmth of a communal hearth. They were the memories of a world that had known the sharp edges of existence, and had learned to navigate them, not by smoothing them away, but by developing the strength and wisdom to hold them.

The contrast with the present was stark and often painful. The vibrant tapestry of true memory was woven with threads of both ecstasy and agony. There were moments of breathtaking beauty, of profound connection and selfless love, but there were also echoes of deep loss, of bitter struggle, and of sacrifices made that resonated with a power that the current generation could not comprehend. The levi-drakes had sought to remove the paralyzing terror, but in doing so, they had also, Mara realized, removed the profound lessons that such terror could impart. They had removed the scar, but not the understanding of how it was formed, nor the resilience it signified.

Elara, too, felt the subtle shifts. Her connection to the earth, usually a steady, grounding presence, had become erratic, like a river struggling against a dam. She spoke of the land itself seeming to sigh, of ancient trees murmuring secrets they had long held dormant. She described the very air as feeling heavier, as if burdened by unacknowledged truths.

"It's like the world is trying to remember how to breathe, Cael," Elara said, her voice barely a whisper, her gaze fixed on the horizon where the Pale Tide's influence was most pronounced. "The levi-drakes... they meant well, I know. But they've put Nyssera into a deep sleep. And now, the dreams are starting to break through."

Mara nodded, her focus turned inward, trying to process the torrent of sensations. The levi-drakes had described the Crown Resonance as a shield, a benevolent force that had smoothed the rough terrain of Nyssera's collective consciousness. But these whispers, these raw fragments of true memory, spoke of a different kind of resonance, an ancient, intrinsic connection that had been suppressed, not eradicated. It was a memory of interconnectedness, of a world where the pulse of one living being was felt, however faintly, by all.

She saw visions of Nysserans who were not merely individuals, but nodes in a vast, living network. Their triumphs were shared, their sorrows lessened by the collective burden. There was a deep, intuitive understanding, a communication that transcended words. This was the vibrancy the levi-drakes had spoken of, but they had framed it as a vulnerability, a source of potential chaos. Mara saw it, however, as the very essence of Nyssera's strength, its capacity for true resilience.

The whispers brought with them an understanding of the Pale Tide that was far more visceral than any explanation. They didn't just understand the Pale Tide as an external threat; they *felt* its nature, its hunger for that which was absent, for the unacknowledged pain and the forgotten lessons. The levi-drakes had muted the world's song of suffering to prevent it from being drowned out, but the whispers revealed that by muting it, they had also deafened Nyssera to the warning cries, to the very rhythm of danger.

As Mara delved deeper into these resurfacing memories, she felt a growing sense of awe, mingled with a profound sadness. The world the levi-drakes had shielded was a pale imitation of the world that had truly existed. The beauty they had preserved was a fragile, artificial bloom, lacking the deep roots and inherent strength of a wild, untamed garden. These whispers were a testament to life's enduring persistence, a defiant hum against the enforced silence, a reminder that the true song of Nyssera, though muted, had never truly been extinguished.

It was a melody that held the echoes of every joy, every sorrow, every triumph, and every fall – a complete, resonant symphony that was now, slowly, painfully, beginning to reawaken. The echoes were a testament to a Nyssera that had been more alive, more vibrant, and more truly *real* than the placid, controlled existence that had been imposed. They were beautiful, yes, but their beauty was edged with a sharp, terrifying reminder of what had been lost, and what was now, perilously, returning.

The levi-drakes' pronouncements, once considered immutable truth, now felt like a carefully constructed illusion. The Pale Tide, Mara understood with a dawning, chilling clarity, was not an invasion in the traditional sense. It was not an external enemy seeking to conquer or destroy. Instead, it was an *internal* force, a corrupted echo of Nyssera's own primal instinct for self-preservation, now warped into a rigid, unforgiving finality. The levi-drakes had spoken of healing, of mending the fractured world. But their solution, it seemed, had been to sever.

"It is not an invasion," the eldest levi-drake had rasped, its ancient voice like the grinding of glacial ice, its immense form shimmering with an inner light that seemed to dim even as it spoke. "It is... a correction. A finality. The Silence Event left scars, wounds that festered, that threatened the very fabric of existence. The Crown Resonance was a balm, a temporary measure. But some wounds, once infected, can only be excised."

Mara felt a shiver trace its way down her spine, independent of the cool air that permeated the levi-drakes' sanctuary. Excised. The word hung in the air, heavy with implication. The levi-drakes had described their actions as protective, as necessary sacrifices to prevent a greater catastrophe. They spoke of a world that had been shielded from its own destructive tendencies, its own raw, untamed capacity for self-annihilation. But this 'correction,' this 'finality,' sounded like a death sentence disguised as salvation.

"The Pale Tide," another levi-drake intoned, its voice a deep, resonant hum that vibrated in Mara's bones, "is the manifestation of that severance. It is the active principle of separation. Where the Silence Event fractured, the Pale Tide seeks to sever completely. To isolate the diseased from the healthy. To ensure that the corruption does not spread further."

Cael's gaze was fixed on the levi-drakes, his mind a vortex of conflicting narratives. He had accepted their account of the Silence Event, of the overwhelming despair that had threatened to shatter Nyssera's collective consciousness. He understood the need for protection, for a carefully managed peace. But this 'Pale Tide,' this force that seemed to be slowly suffocating the life from the land, was something more than a mere consequence of past trauma. It was a deliberate, active process.

"So, the wilting flora, the unnaturally still waters," Elara murmured, her voice laced with a dawning horror, "these are not merely symptoms of a sickness? They are... preparations?"

The levi-drakes shifted, their massive forms rippling like heat haze over a summer desert. "They are the initial stages," the first levi-drake confirmed. "The areas deemed... unstable... are being prepared for permanent separation. The life force within them is being carefully withdrawn, cataloged, and then... isolated. The goal is to ensure that what remains, what is deemed 'healthy,' is not tainted by what was lost, or what was irredeemably damaged."

Mara's mind reeled. Isolated. Removed. It was an ecological amputation. The levi-drakes' logic, once seeming so benevolent, now revealed a brutal, unforgiving core. The very essence of life was interconnectedness, a vast, intricate web where every strand mattered, where the health of one part influenced the whole. To sever, to isolate, was to fundamentally disrupt that balance, to create voids that could never truly be filled.

"But *how*?" Mara's voice, though quiet, carried an edge of desperation. "How can a force simply... withdraw life? How does it isolate an ecosystem?"

The levi-drakes seemed to consult with each other, a silent communion of ancient minds. Then, the second levi-drake spoke, its voice softer now, tinged with a sorrow that Mara felt was genuine, even if its actions were abhorrent. "The Crown Resonance, as you know, is more than just a conduit of memory. It is a fundamental attunement. It is the deep, unspoken agreement of Nyssera's life force. The Silence Event fractured that agreement. The Pale Tide seeks to enforce a new, more rigid agreement. It is guided by an echo of the original preservation instinct, yes, but it is an echo that has become... absolute. It no longer seeks balance, but purity. It no longer seeks healing, but finality."

Mara visualized it: a great, ethereal hand, not of flesh and blood, but of pure, unadulterated intent, reaching out across Nyssera. It was not a hand that grasped and tore, but one that carefully, meticulously, unwound the threads of connection. It was like watching a master weaver painstakingly unravel a complex tapestry, not to save the threads, but to preserve them in separate, sterile bundles, discarding the intricate pattern that had bound them together.

"This echo," Mara pressed, her mind racing to grasp the enormity of it, "is it sentient? Does it *choose* what is healthy and what is not?"

"It is an instinct," the first levi-drake explained, its bioluminescence flickering as if in distress. "A corrupted echo, as you surmised. It operates on principles that were once meant to preserve, but are now… rigid. It identifies patterns of distress, of disharmony, that were created by the Silence Event. And it seeks to remove them. Permanently. It is not malice, child. It is… a fundamentalist interpretation of preservation. A desperate attempt to safeguard what little remains by creating impenetrable walls."

Mara thought of the vibrant whispers she had been experiencing, the echoes of a Nyssera that had known deep pain but had also known profound resilience, a Nyssera that had integrated its darkness rather than attempting to erase it. This Pale Tide, this 'corrector,' would see that integration as corruption. It would see the scars of experience as flaws to be excised.

"So, the Pale Tide isn't an invading force, but a force that's already part of Nyssera?" Cael asked, his voice low, the weight of this revelation pressing down on him. "A distorted application of a natural instinct?"

"Precisely," the second levi-drake confirmed. "It is Nyssera, in a sense, attempting to save itself from its own deepest wounds, but in doing so, it risks amputating its own soul. The Crown Resonance, weakened by the Silence, is no longer strong enough to moderate this instinct. It has become a blunt instrument, driven by an absolute imperative. The Pale Tide is the mechanism by which this imperative is enacted."

The implications were staggering. The Pale Tide was not something that could be fought with blades or magic in the traditional sense. How did one fight a corrupted instinct? How did one reason with a fundamentalist interpretation of preservation? It was a force that sought to dismantle the world, piece by agonizing piece, not out of malice, but out of a twisted sense of duty.

"The wilting," Mara continued, piecing together the fragmented understanding, "is the life force being drawn out. The stillness of the water... is it being prepared to become a barrier? An impassable boundary between what is deemed 'stable' and what is... not?"

"The waters," the first levi-drake's voice was heavy with a sorrow that Mara was beginning to believe was genuine, "will cease to flow. They will become inert, a solidified boundary. The flora will not merely wilt; it will desiccate, its essence withdrawn, leaving behind a hushed, barren landscape. These are not deaths, child. They are... severances. The creation of ecological zones that are irrevocably apart. A permanent division of Nyssera's living tapestry."

Mara pictured vast swathes of the world turning to dust and stagnant water, entire biomes rendered inert, sealed off from the vibrant exchange of life. It was a vision of a world being meticulously dismantled, its living heart being systematically isolated and then, perhaps, left to decay. The levi-drakes had spoken of healing, but this was a mutilation.

"But what happens to the life force that is withdrawn?" Cael asked, his mind already grappling with the practicalities. "Where does it go? Is it truly preserved?"

"It is... cataloged," the second levi-drake replied, its voice now almost a whisper. "And isolated. Stored, in a sense, in the depths of the Pale Tide itself. It is Nyssera's pain, its imperfections, its memories of trauma, all being sequestered away. The intent is to create a pristine, untainted Nyssera. A world free from the echoes of the Silence Event, free from the burden of its own history."

Mara felt a cold dread spread through her. To be free from the burden of its history? That was to be free from its lessons, from its resilience, from the very essence of what made it Nyssera. The levi-drakes, in their desire to protect, had initiated a process that would fundamentally strip Nyssera of its depth, its complexity, its very soul. The whispers she had heard, the vibrant echoes of a world that had embraced its pain and emerged stronger, would be deemed 'unstable,' 'diseased,' and systematically erased.

"This is not healing," Mara stated, her voice firm, her earlier confusion hardening into a resolve that surprised even herself. "This is a perversion of healing. You are not saving Nyssera; you are... amputating it."

The levi-drakes remained silent, their ancient forms radiating a profound weariness. They had spoken their truth, or their understanding of it, and now they awaited the reaction of those who heard it. The weight of their millennia of stewardship, their flawed but well-intentioned actions, settled upon them, a visible burden.

"We sought to prevent the death of the whole," the first levi-drake finally said, its voice barely audible. "To ensure that the body of Nyssera would survive, even if parts of it had to be... quarantined. The Silence Event was a catastrophic infection. The Pale Tide is the only remaining antidote. A brutal one, perhaps. But necessary."

Mara looked at Cael, then at Elara. Their faces reflected a similar dawning horror, a shared understanding that the benevolent protectors they had sought had, in their fear, become architects of a slow, deliberate unmaking. The Pale Tide was not an enemy to be vanquished, but a process to be understood, and perhaps, to be resisted on a fundamental level. It was the world's own instinct for survival turned into a weapon against itself.

"Necessary?" Mara echoed, her voice shaking slightly, but her gaze unwavering. "To carve out the heart of Nyssera and call it preservation? That is not necessity. That is a profound failure of understanding. A failure to see that true strength lies not in severing, but in integration. In learning to live with the scars, not by erasing them, but by understanding what they represent."

The levi-drakes offered no rebuttal. They had revealed the nature of the Pale Tide, and in doing so, had revealed the true extent of the mistake that had been made, the flawed logic that had guided their millennia of guardianship. The Pale Tide was not an invasion; it was the ultimate expression of a flawed, absolute severance, a terrifyingly efficient process of ecological separation, driven by a corrupted echo of Nyssera's own will to survive, now twisted into a rigid, unforgiving finality. The wilting flora and unnaturally still waters were not merely symptoms; they were the insidious, early stages of a permanent, irreversible division, a carving away of Nyssera's living soul.

The levi-drakes had spoken of a correction, a finality, an excision of the diseased. Mara had heard their words, felt the ancient weariness in their voices, and Cael, ever the pragmatist, had seemed to accept the grim logic. But Mara's connection to Nyssera, her innate ability to *listen* not just to sounds but to the very resonance of life, told a different story. It was a story whispered not by the levi-drakes, but by the trembling earth beneath her feet, by the sighing wind that carried no scent of bloom, by the unnervingly still waters.

She could *feel* the Pale Tide. It wasn't a presence in the way a dragon or a beast was a presence, a tangible entity with form and intent. Instead, it was a pervasive influence, a subtle pressure that squeezed the very breath from the world. Her empathic senses, usually a gift that allowed her to connect with the vibrant tapestry of life, were now strained, stretched thin as she tried to make sense of this alien 'intention.' The levi-drakes had painted it as a force of separation, a cleansing fire. But the whispers Mara received were more nuanced, and far more terrifying.

The Pale Tide did not perceive itself as destructive. That was the first chilling realization that settled deep within Mara's bones, colder than any winter frost. It was a force of *purification*. Of *order*. Its logic was not one of malice, but of an extreme, almost fanatical, pragmatism. It saw Nyssera not as a living, breathing, interconnected whole, but as a complex organism riddled with imperfections. And like a surgeon wielding a scalpel with ruthless precision, it sought to sever the compromised parts to save the supposed 'stronger' remaining flesh.

Mara felt the immense pressure it exerted on the world-song, that ineffable symphony of existence that hummed through every living thing. The Pale Tide was actively attempting to fragment this song, to break it into a thousand isolated notes, each contained within its own sterile, silent chamber. It sought to create distinct pockets of existence, utterly separate, devoid of the messy, beautiful complexities of true connection. It was like watching a masterful conductor meticulously dismantle an orchestra, not to silence the music, but to reduce each instrument to its purest, loneliest tone.

Her empathy, usually a conduit for shared joy and sorrow, for understanding and connection, was now a battleground. She felt the Pale Tide's 'intent' as a relentless, almost hypnotic, rationalization. It presented its actions as undeniable, as the only logical course of action.

Why tolerate weakness when strength can be preserved? Why endure dissonance when harmony can be enforced? These were not questions Mara could easily dismiss. They resonated with a cold, hard logic that, if embraced, would strip Nyssera of its very essence.

She felt the 'weakness' it identified. It was the echo of old pains, the lingering tremors of the Silence Event that the levi-drakes had tried so hard to mute. It was the vulnerability that came from deep connection, the susceptibility to loss that was the price of love. The Pale Tide saw these not as facets of a rich, lived experience, but as flaws, as diseases that threatened the purity of the whole. It perceived the interconnectedness of Nyssera as a vulnerability, a network through which decay could spread. Therefore, the solution was not to heal the wounds, but to sever the connections.

Mara tried to push back, to project her own understanding of Nyssera's strength, a strength born of resilience, of integration, of the hard-won wisdom gained through suffering. She sent out waves of empathy, attempting to convey the beauty of imperfection, the richness of shared struggle, the profound interconnectedness that was Nyssera's true inheritance. But it was like shouting into a void. The Pale Tide's 'intent' was a one-way current, a force that absorbed and categorized, but did not truly receive. It was deaf to her pleas, blind to the vibrant life it sought to diminish.

She focused on the wilting flora, on the unnaturally still waters. The levi-drakes had spoken of preparation, of the life force being withdrawn. Mara felt it more acutely now. It was not a violent extraction, but a slow, deliberate uncoupling. The plants were not dying in agony; they were being patiently detached from the vibrant web of existence. Their vital essence, the very spark that made them alive, was being drawn out, not to be replenished, but to be isolated. It was as if the world was being meticulously deconstructed, each living thing becoming a separate, inert object.

The stillness of the water was the most unnerving. It was not the quiet peace of a tranquil lake, but the heavy, expectant silence of a held breath. She felt the water becoming dense, its fluid nature being suppressed, preparing to solidify into a barrier, an impassable demarcation line. This was the Pale Tide's order: to create zones, to sever the flow, to ensure that what was deemed 'healthy' would never again be tainted by what was 'diseased.'

Her empathic senses were being pushed to their limits. She felt the fragmentation of the world-song as a tangible pain, a tearing sensation in her own being. It was as if the very fabric of reality was being rent asunder, not by a violent cataclysm, but by a million tiny, precise cuts. The levi-drakes had spoken of preventing annihilation. But this felt like a slow, systematic suicide, a self-imposed desolation born of fear.

She tried to visualize the Pale Tide's 'logic.' Imagine Nyssera as a vast, intricate garden. The levi-drakes had tried to prune away the thorny branches, to remove the weeds that threatened to choke the more delicate blooms. But the Pale Tide was like a gardener who, seeing a single blighted leaf, decided to uproot the entire plant, convinced that by removing the flawed part, the whole would be purified. It didn't understand that the blighted leaf was a testament to the plant's struggle, its resilience, its history. It didn't grasp that the thorns protected the delicate blooms, and that the weeds, in their own way, contributed to the soil's vitality.

Mara felt the chilling pragmatism of its actions. If a section of the forest was deemed 'unstable,' its inhabitants weakened by ancient sorrows or lingering fears, the Pale Tide would simply withdraw the life force, leaving behind a husk. The trees would not fall; they would simply cease to be. The rivers would not dry up; they would become inert, unmoving channels of solidified silence. It was a process of ecological amputation, performed with a chillingly detached efficiency.

The Pale Tide's 'intent' was not to destroy, but to *contain*. To quarantine. To create an unblemished Nyssera, free from the echoes of its painful past. But what was a Nyssera without its history? Without the lessons learned from its struggles? Without the deep, resonant connections forged in shared joy and sorrow? It would be a sterile, hollowed-out shell, a monument to a fear that had ultimately consumed the very life it sought to protect.

She felt the immense pressure building, a vast, unseen force meticulously severing the threads of connection. It was like watching a cosmic weaver unpicking a grand tapestry, not to save the threads, but to bundle them separately, discarding the intricate pattern that had given them meaning. The Pale Tide was unraveling Nyssera, one connection at a time, convinced that in isolation lay salvation.

Mara's mind struggled to reconcile the levi-drakes' pronouncements with the visceral reality she was experiencing. They spoke of a necessary correction, a brutal antidote. But this felt like a perversion of healing, a path that led not to recovery, but to a profound, irreversible diminishment. The Pale Tide was Nyssera's own instinct for survival, twisted and amplified into a force of absolute separation, a horrifyingly efficient process driven by a corrupted echo of preservation.

She focused her empathic sight on the distant horizon, where the Pale Tide's influence was most pronounced. The air itself seemed to shimmer, not with heat, but with a palpable sense of *unraveling*. The vibrant, interconnected song of Nyssera was being choked, fragmented, its harmonies distorted into discordant, isolated notes. It was a song that was trying to remember its original melody, a melody filled with both profound beauty and searing pain, a melody that the Pale Tide was determined to silence, piece by agonizing piece.

The levi-drakes' explanation of 'cataloging' the withdrawn life force felt crueler now. It wasn't preservation; it was sequestration. The embodiment of Nyssera's pain, its imperfections, its very soul, was being collected and isolated, deemed unfit for the 'pristine' world that the Pale Tide was creating. It was a world stripped of its scars, yes, but also stripped of its wisdom, its resilience, its capacity for true, deep connection.

Mara felt a wave of profound sadness wash over her, a grief not just for the dying world she was witnessing, but for the levi-drakes themselves, trapped in their own millennia-old fear. They had sought to protect Nyssera from overwhelming despair, but in doing so, they had inadvertently nurtured the very force that would now dissect it. The Pale Tide was the ultimate consequence of their fear, a monument to their flawed understanding of true resilience.

She tried to project a different vision, a Nyssera that embraced its scars, that found strength in its interconnectedness, that understood that true preservation lay not in isolation, but in integration. She sent out a pulse of pure, unadulterated hope, a defiant whisper against the overwhelming tide of bleak pragmatism. It was a faint signal, almost lost in the growing silence, but it was there. A reminder that even in the face of this chillingly logical unmaking, the true song of Nyssera, a song of vibrant life and enduring spirit, still yearned to be heard.

The Pale Tide's 'logic' was a seductive poison, a promise of purity that led only to desolation. Mara felt the strain on her empathic abilities, the overwhelming pressure to accept its bleak rationale. But the whispers of true memory, the echoes of a Nyssera that had known pain and had *lived* through it, sustained her. They reminded her that Nyssera's strength was not in its perfection, but in its imperfections, in its capacity to endure, to connect, and to heal, not by severing, but by embracing. The Pale Tide sought to create a perfect, sterile Nyssera, but Mara knew that true life, true strength, lay in the messy, vibrant, imperfect tapestry of what already was. And that was a song worth fighting for, even if the fight was against the world's own distorted will to survive.

Cael observed the unfolding events with a gaze that was as sharp and analytical as a honed blade. The levi-drakes' pronouncements, while steeped in ancient wisdom, had always held a practical edge for him, a call to action, a blueprint for defense. But the Pale Tide was a different kind of enemy, one that defied conventional understanding of warfare. It wasn't an army marching with banners, nor a beast with teeth and claws. It was an insidious force, a pervasive influence that acted not with brute strength, but with a terrifyingly elegant logic of dissolution.

His mind, accustomed to dissecting battle plans and resource allocations, struggled to categorize this ethereal yet potent threat. The Pale Tide wasn't conquering territory; it was *unmaking* it. It wasn't destroying life; it was *isolating* it. The concept of a force that sought to preserve by severing, to strengthen by fragmenting, churned in his thoughts, a paradox that was both intellectually stimulating and deeply disturbing. He understood the levi-drakes' desperation, their fear of a Nyssera consumed by its own internal decay, a fear born of witnessing epochs of struggle and loss. They saw the Pale Tide as a brutal, necessary surgery. But Cael, ever the strategist, saw the potential for the surgeon's scalpel to become an instrument of irreparable mutilation.

He visualized Nyssera as an immensely complex circulatory system, a network of veins and arteries carrying the lifeblood of existence. Each ecosystem, each species, each individual was a crucial component, its health contributing to the vitality of the whole. The Pale Tide, in its relentless pursuit of purity, was like a virus that targeted the very connections between these components. It didn't attack the heart directly, but it poisoned the blood, severed the nerves, choked the airways, until each organ was left to fail in isolation. This was not a swift death, but a slow, agonizing decay, a systematic dismantling that left behind hollowed-out shells, devoid of the vibrant energy that defined life.

The levi-drakes had spoken of 'correction,' of an 'excision.' Cael found these terms disturbingly apt, yet also profoundly misleading. The Pale Tide wasn't correcting a fever; it was inducing a coma. It wasn't excising a tumor; it was lobotomizing the patient. Its methods were not those of a healer seeking to restore balance, but of an undertaker preparing a body for burial. It identified weaknesses – the lingering traumas from the Silence Event, the vulnerabilities born of deep empathy, the inherent risks of interdependence – and rather than seeking to strengthen these areas, it sought to eliminate them entirely by severing the connections that made them so.

He considered the implications for Nyssera's resilience. True resilience, Cael believed, was not about being impervious to damage, but about the capacity to recover, to adapt, to integrate hardship into strength. This was a lesson etched into the very bones of the dragons, who bore the scars of countless battles and betrayals, yet had endured. The Pale Tide, however, saw these scars as blemishes, as evidence of a compromised state that needed to be eradicated. By creating isolated zones, it was effectively crippling Nyssera's ability to respond to future crises. If one region fell to blight or invasion, its neighbors, now severed from any possibility of aid, would be left to their own fate. The intricate web of mutual support, the very foundation of Nyssera's collective survival, would be irrevocably broken.

"It's not an invasion," Cael mused aloud, his voice a low rumble in the quiet chamber where he and Mara often conferred. He traced the lines on a hastily drawn map of Nyssera, his finger hovering over regions Mara had described as being particularly affected by the Pale Tide's influence. "It's a deconstruction. A deliberate dismantling of the interconnectedness that defines us."

He tapped a point on the map. "If this forest is severed from the river's flow, and the river from the mountains' snowmelt, and the mountains from the sky's rain, what happens when one element fails? In the past, there was always redundancy. A river might dwindle, but the mountains would still hold their reserves, or the forests would adapt to drier conditions, drawing moisture from deeper sources. But if these pathways are permanently closed off..." He let the thought hang, the unspoken consequence chilling.

The sheer efficiency of the Pale Tide was what truly unnerved him. It didn't expend energy on brute force. It didn't engage in costly battles. It simply applied pressure, identified weak points in the complex tapestry of Nyssera, and carefully, meticulously, unpicked the threads. It was akin to a master chess player who didn't need to capture every piece, but simply maneuvered to isolate the king, knowing that in separation lay inevitable defeat. The Pale Tide understood that Nyssera's strength was also its greatest vulnerability: its profound interconnectedness. And it was exploiting this to the fullest.

His strategic mind began to race, seeking ways to counter such an abstract foe. How does one fight a force that operates on the principles of entropy and isolation? Traditional warfare, Cael knew, was useless. Dragons could scorch the earth, but they couldn't force severed connections back into being. They could defend borders, but the Pale Tide didn't recognize borders; it created them. The battle wouldn't be fought with fire and claw, but with the preservation of relationships, with the strengthening of bonds, with the very essence of what the Pale Tide sought to dismantle.

"The levi-drakes believe they are preventing a collapse by removing the 'diseased' parts," Cael explained to Mara, his brow furrowed in concentration. "They see the Pale Tide as a diagnostic tool, a surgeon's precision. But they're overlooking the fundamental truth of Nyssera: that its strength *is* its complexity, its flaws included. The very things the Pale Tide seeks to isolate are the conduits of its resilience."

He gestured emphatically. "The echo of past pain, the vulnerability that comes from loving and losing – these are not weaknesses to be purged. They are the scars that teach us, the experiences that forge us. The Pale Tide seeks to create a Nyssera that is pure, yes, but also sterile. A world without memory, without the lessons learned through suffering."

He began to formulate a counter-strategy, a series of actions designed to thwart the Pale Tide's methodical unravelling. It wouldn't be about direct confrontation, but about reinforcing the very fabric of connection. He thought of ancient druidic practices, of the ways in which communities had reinforced their bonds through shared rituals and communal effort. He thought of the dragons' own innate ability to sense and influence the flows of energy across the land.

"We cannot fight its logic with more logic of separation," Cael declared, his voice gaining a steely edge. "We must counter its fragmentation with a deliberate, conscious act of integration. We need to identify the points where the Pale Tide is seeking to sever the connections, and then, we must reinforce them. Not with force, but with intent. We need to weave the threads back together, to remind Nyssera of its inherent unity."

He envisioned a network, not of physical defenses, but of empathic and energetic conduits. If the Pale Tide was systematically isolating pockets of existence, then the response must be to create overwhelming connectivity. He considered using the dragons' collective strength, their ancient connection to Nyssera's world-song, to actively counteract the forces of fragmentation. It would be a monumental undertaking, a subtle yet profound rebellion against the planet's own distorted survival instinct.

"Think of it like this," he elaborated, his gaze intense, "the Pale Tide is creating dams, meticulously blocking the flow of the lifeblood of Nyssera. Our task is not to destroy the dams – that would be a battle we cannot win, fighting against the very nature of the force. Instead, we must create new channels. We must reinforce the existing waterways, making them stronger, more resilient, so that even if a dam is built, the flow can be rerouted, finding new paths, nourishing other regions. We must become the engineers of connection."

His strategic mind, always drawn to the grander schemes, began to map out potential pathways for this reinforcement. He considered regions where the Pale Tide's influence was less pronounced, areas where the world-song still resonated with vibrant clarity. These would become the anchor points, the fortresses of connection from which to push back against the tide of isolation. He thought of the deep, ancient forests, the hidden valleys, the underground rivers that still pulsed with life. These places, shielded from the Pale Tide's immediate grasp, could become sanctuaries, reservoirs of interconnectedness.

"We need to actively encourage and facilitate the exchange between these pockets," Cael continued, his voice a low, determined hum. "Where the Pale Tide seeks to create sterile, isolated zones, we must foster vibrant, interconnected ecosystems. If a forest is being starved of the life force it receives from the mountains, we must find ways to ensure it receives sustenance from other sources, perhaps from subterranean aquifers, or from the energy currents that run deep within Nyssera's core. It will require understanding Nyssera's innate resilience, its capacity for adaptation, and then amplifying that capacity."

He looked at Mara, his eyes holding a mixture of grim resolve and a flicker of hope. "This is not a war of conquest, Mara. It is a war of preservation. Not preservation through isolation, but preservation through boundless connection. The levi-drakes, in their fear, have inadvertently fostered the very force that threatens to unmake them. They see the Pale Tide as a protector, a guardian. But it is a guardian that will eventually consume everything it is meant to protect."

Cael's strategic assessment was clear: the Pale Tide was not a tangible enemy to be defeated in battle, but a fundamental force that sought to alter the very nature of Nyssera. Its goal was not destruction, but a terrifyingly efficient form of segregation, an amputation of interconnectedness. The greatest threat lay not in the severing itself, but in the permanent loss of resilience that would follow. If Nyssera's ecosystems were permanently divided, if the flow of life and energy was irrevocably dammed, then the planet would be vulnerable to any future threat, unable to rally its collective strength.

He began to outline his strategy, a multi-pronged approach focused not on confrontation, but on reinforcement. He believed that by actively strengthening the existing connections, by fostering new pathways of exchange, and by preserving the integrity of the world-song, they could resist the Pale Tide's isolating influence. It would be a subtle war, fought not with dragonfire, but with the deliberate weaving of bonds, a testament to the power of unity against the seductive logic of separation. The key, he realized, was to embrace Nyssera's inherent complexity, its beautiful, messy imperfections, and to defend them with every fiber of their being. The levi-drakes saw a disease; Cael saw the vibrant, interconnected heart of a living world, a heart that needed to keep beating, not in isolation, but in concert with all that surrounded it.

The levi-drakes had spoken of a 'correction,' a necessary amputation. Cael, however, was beginning to understand it as something far more insidious. The Pale Tide was not merely a force of dissolution; it was a parasitic entity that fed upon the very wounds Nyssera had sustained. He visualized the planet's biosphere as a vast, intricate tapestry, woven from countless threads of life, energy, and memory. The Silence Event, a catastrophic rupture in this tapestry, had left behind frayed edges, gaping holes, and countless weakened strands. The Pale Tide, he now grasped, was not a new threat, but an ancient, festering infection that had taken root in those primordial tears.

"It's not a new blight," Cael explained to Mara, his voice hushed, as if the very act of speaking too loudly might draw the Pale Tide's attention. They sat in the Dragon's Maw, a cavern carved by ancient winds and echoing with the deep thrum of Nyssera's heart. Outside, the unnaturally calm waters of the Whispering Bay churned with a subtle, disturbing phosphorescence. "The levi-drakes explained it, but I didn't fully grasp it until now. The Silence Event... it wasn't a clean break. It was a wound that never truly healed. It left behind echoes, fragments of dissonance, a kind of psychic scar tissue on the world itself."

He gestured towards the bay. "The Pale Tide is that scar tissue made manifest. It's a manifestation of the incomplete severance, the lingering energies from that initial cataclysm. The levi-drakes, in their desperate attempt to enforce order, to preserve what they could, severed connections that perhaps should have been allowed to mend, or at least to transform. They tried to cauterize a wound, but in doing so, they created a vessel for this... this corruption to grow."

Mara's gaze was distant, her fingers tracing the cool, smooth stone of the cavern wall. "You mean... the Pale Tide is a consequence of their own actions? A weapon they inadvertently forged?"

"More than that," Cael corrected, his brow furrowed. "It's a perversion of their intent. They sought purity, isolation from chaos. But in isolating, they created voids. And into those voids, the residual energies of the Silence Event, the dissonant frequencies of broken connections, were drawn. The Pale Tide is like an immune response gone rogue, an overzealous guardian that begins to see the body it's meant to protect as the enemy. It amplifies the very imperfections, the very vulnerabilities, that the Silence Event exposed."

He recalled the ancient texts, the hushed whispers of the levi-drakes. They had spoken of the "original severance," a cataclysmic event that had reshaped Nyssera. It was a time of immense pain, a forced decoupling of elements that had been intrinsically linked. The dragons, in their hubris or their desperation, had wielded a power that had fractured the world. And now, the echoes of that fracturing were returning, not as a direct echo, but as a distorted, amplified reflection.

"Think of it this way," Cael continued, his mind working through the complex analogy. "Imagine Nyssera as a living organism, and the Silence Event as a brutal surgery. The levi-drakes were the surgeons. They removed what they deemed diseased, severed connections that were perceived as dangerous. But the surgery was not perfect. There were lingering traces of the disease, weakened tissues, and the trauma of the operation itself. These residual elements, these memetic and ecological scars, became the fertile ground for the Pale Tide. It's like a phantom limb pain that has festered, becoming a real, physical affliction."

The levi-drakes' narrative had been one of necessity, of a painful but vital pruning. They had presented the Pale Tide as an external force, a natural phenomenon of purification that they were simply trying to manage. But Cael was now seeing it as an internal wound, an auto-immune disease of the planet, brought on by past trauma and exacerbated by attempts to erase that trauma. The past, in its most wounded and corrupted form, was now the enemy.

"The levi-drakes mentioned 'dissonant energies'," Mara said, her voice barely above a whisper. "They spoke of them as a residual problem that needed to be contained. They believed the Pale Tide was a means of containment, not an amplification."

"That's the crux of it, isn't it?" Cael responded, his gaze fixed on the distant horizon, where the unnatural calm of the bay met the bruised, twilight sky. "They saw the problem as external, a lingering instability. But the instability *is* the Pale Tide. It's the embodiment of that incomplete severance, the amplified echoes of the very act of disconnection. They thought they were isolating the bad, but they were actually creating the perfect environment for it to thrive and mutate. They were feeding it."

He leaned back, a weariness settling into his bones that had nothing to do with physical exertion. The weight of this realization was immense. The dragons, his own kind, had been instrumental in creating the very force they now feared. Their past mistakes, their attempts to impose order on a world they had fractured, had birthed this insidious enemy.

"It's a corrupted echo," Cael mused, the words feeling heavy on his tongue. "A twisted reflection of their own actions. They sought to preserve Nyssera by severing its interconnectedness, by enforcing a kind of sterile purity. The Pale Tide takes that desire to its absolute extreme. It doesn't just sever; it *unmakes*. It doesn't just isolate; it *eradicates* the very concept of connection. It is Nyssera's deepest fear made real, a fear born from the dragons' own attempts to control and control Nyssera."

The implications were staggering. If the Pale Tide was a manifestation of past trauma, then fighting it directly, with conventional means, was like trying to fight a phantom. It was like trying to punch a memory. The levi-drakes' strategy of containment and isolation, Cael now understood, was precisely what fueled the Pale Tide. By creating more severed zones, by reinforcing the isolation, they were merely reinforcing the very conditions that allowed the Pale Tide to flourish. They were, in effect, feeding the beast.

"So, their methods are counterproductive?" Mara asked, her eyes widening with a dawning comprehension.

"Catastrophically so," Cael confirmed. "Every time they reinforce a boundary, every time they sever a connection to prevent the 'spread,' they are actually strengthening the Pale Tide's hold. They are creating more scars, more points of entry for these amplified dissonant energies. The Silence Event was the initial wound; the Pale Tide is the chronic infection that festers within it, and the levi-drakes' attempts to treat it are only making it worse. They are widening the scar, not healing it."

He stood and walked towards the cavern entrance, the cool night air doing little to dispel the heat in his mind. The Whispering Bay seemed to pulse with a malevolent energy, its unnerving calm a deceptive mask for the chaos churning beneath the surface. He could almost feel the reverberations of that ancient cataclysm, the ghost of a world being torn asunder.

"The levi-drakes see the Pale Tide as an external threat, a force of nature they must contend with," Cael said, his voice resonating with a newfound urgency. "But it's an internal metastasis. It's Nyssera consuming itself from within, fueled by the residue of the dragons' most terrible mistake. The past isn't just a lesson; it's a direct, active threat, and the levi-drakes are blinded by their own history, unable to see that their solutions are the problem."

He turned back to Mara, his gaze intense. "They are fighting the symptom, not the disease. And by fighting the symptom with more of the same logic that caused the original wound, they are ensuring Nyssera's eventual demise. The Pale Tide is not an invasion; it is an auto-immune collapse. It is the echo of the Silence Event, corrupted and amplified, turning Nyssera's own defenses against itself."

The true nature of the Pale Tide was a chilling mirror to the dragons' past. It was a testament to the fact that even the most drastic measures, taken with the intent to preserve, could have unintended, catastrophic consequences. The levi-drakes, in their pursuit of a pristine, ordered Nyssera, had inadvertently created a monster that embodied chaos and decay, a monster born from the very act of enforced separation. They had sought to erase the scars of the Silence Event, but instead, they had created a force that fed on them, widening them into a chasm that threatened to swallow Nyssera whole.

The weight of this revelation settled upon Cael, a heavy burden of understanding that shifted his perspective on the entire conflict. This was not a war against an external enemy, but a desperate attempt to heal a world that had been wounded by its own protectors. The levi-drakes' fear of Nyssera's fragility had led them to actions that were ultimately destroying it, not through malice, but through a profound misunderstanding of how true resilience was forged. It was forged not in isolation, but in connection, in the shared strength that came from acknowledging and integrating even the most painful of histories. The Pale Tide, in its relentless pursuit of sterile purity, was the ultimate antithesis of this truth, and thus, the ultimate threat. The levi-drakes' fear had become Nyssera's doom, manifested in the insidious, spreading rot of the Pale Tide.

The air in the levi-drake council chamber was thick with the scent of ozone and ancient stone, a scent that now tasted like ash in Cael's mouth. Around the massive obsidian table, the levi-drakes shifted, their scales catching the ethereal light that pulsed from the chamber's core. Their voices, a chorus of deep, resonant tones, carried the weight of millennia, and the pronouncement they had just delivered hung in the silence like a death knell.

"The choice is stark, Cael," intoned the eldest, a levi-drake whose wings bore the tattered remnants of storms long past. His gaze, ancient and weary, settled upon Cael, then flicked to Mara, a silent accusation in its depths. "Nyssera is bleeding. The Pale Tide offers a transfusion, a painful but necessary amputation to preserve the heart."

Mara's breath hitched. She had braced herself for difficult truths, for the grim realities of their world's slow decay, but this... this was a surrender she had not anticipated. "Amputation?" she echoed, her voice barely a whisper. "You speak of sacrificing entire regions? Entire ecosystems?"

"The world-song is fractured," another levi-drake rumbled, his voice like the grinding of tectonic plates. "The Pale Tide is the inevitable consequence of that fracture, a natural, albeit brutal, corrective force. To resist its ultimate manifestation is to invite the complete unraveling of Nyssera. We have seen this pattern before. The Silence Event was a wound, and the Pale Tide is the world's desperate attempt to cauterize that wound by severing the infected limb."

Cael felt a cold dread seep into his bones, a feeling far more potent than any physical chill. He had come to understand the Pale Tide not as a force of nature, but as a symptom of Nyssera's deepest ailment. Now, the very guardians of the planet, the dragons who had once shaped its destiny, were advocating for the same brutal approach that had birthed this blight in the first place.

"But you said it yourself," Cael countered, his voice tight with a rising panic. "The Pale Tide thrives on severance. It *is* the amplification of incomplete connections. To deliberately sever more... you are not saving Nyssera; you are feeding it. You are creating more of the very conditions that allow it to spread." He gestured emphatically, his movements sharp and agitated. "You speak of a corrective force, but it's a corrupted echo of your own past actions. The Silence Event was a severance. The Pale Tide is a *final* severance, and you propose to initiate it yourselves?"

The chamber fell silent again, the levi-drakes regarding Cael with unreadable expressions. Their ancient eyes held a deep sadness, a weariness that spoke of a burden too heavy to bear. They had fought this force for centuries, their methods evolving from desperate containment to this stark, brutal proposal.

"The Silence Event was an act of survival," the eldest levi-drake stated, his tone heavy with resignation. "A necessary surgery to remove a cancer that threatened to consume us all. We severed connections to preserve the core of Nyssera, to prevent the complete collapse of the world-song. We saved what we could. The Pale Tide is the painful price of that survival, the lingering phantom of that severed limb. And now, that phantom threatens to consume the rest of the body."

"But this 'phantom' is not an external entity to be amputated," Cael insisted, his voice rising. "It is a manifestation of the world's pain, of its fractured memory. You are proposing to excise a part of Nyssera, a part that is intrinsically connected to the whole, based on a logic that *created* the problem in the first place. The levi-drakes' historical narrative, the very foundation of your understanding of this crisis, is flawed."

He saw Mara nod, her gaze meeting his with a shared understanding. She, too, was grappling with the cognitive dissonance of dragons, beings of immense power and wisdom, advocating for a path that seemed so inherently destructive.

"You speak of mending the world-song," Mara said, her voice clear and steady, cutting through the tension. "But how can it be mended if we are to deliberately tear it further asunder? How can we heal Nyssera by inflicting more wounds?"

"The world-song is not merely a melody; it is a tapestry of existence, woven from threads of life, energy, and memory," the eldest levi-drake explained, his voice softer now, more contemplative. "The Silence Event ripped holes in that tapestry. The Pale Tide seeks to unravel the remaining threads, to return Nyssera to a state of primal, unformed chaos. Our ancestors believed that by severing the infected threads, by isolating the damaged sections, they could preserve the integrity of the whole. They created enclaves, zones of enforced purity, to contain the blight."

"And those enclaves became the very fertile ground for the Pale Tide to fester and grow," Cael interrupted, the pieces of the puzzle finally clicking into place with horrifying clarity. "Every barrier, every enforced isolation, every severed connection, was another anchor for the Pale Tide, another point where its corrupting influence could take root and spread. You didn't contain the blight; you cultivated it. Your attempts to preserve Nyssera have, in essence, been its slow strangulation."

He paced the chamber, the polished obsidian cool beneath his bare feet. "The choice you present – to allow the amputation or to face complete destruction – is a false dichotomy. It is a choice based on the same flawed premise that led to the Silence Event. You are still thinking in terms of separation, of eradication. You are still treating Nyssera as a collection of parts to be managed, rather than a singular, interconnected entity that must be healed."

A ripple of unease went through the assembled levi-drakes. Some shifted uneasily, their ancient scales murmuring against one another. Others remained stoic, their gazes fixed on Cael, as if their very existence was being challenged.

"You speak of healing," one levi-drake countered, his voice laced with skepticism. "But Nyssera is a world scarred by cataclysm. Its foundational song is broken. How can a broken song be healed without removing the dissonant notes? How can a fractured tapestry be rewoven without discarding the frayed edges?"

"By acknowledging the scars, not erasing them," Cael replied, his voice firm. "By understanding that the frayed edges are not merely imperfections, but a part of Nyssera's history. The Pale Tide is the embodiment of Nyssera's repressed trauma, its unintegrated pain. You cannot amputate trauma; you must integrate it. You must find a way to weave those frayed threads back into the tapestry, to transform them, not to sever them."

Mara stepped forward, placing a hand on Cael's arm. "The levi-drakes speak of a choice for the living world," she said, her voice projecting confidence that belied the turmoil within. "And Cael is right. True life, true resilience, comes not from excision, but from integration. If we are to save Nyssera, we must find a way to mend the world-song, not silence the dissonant parts. We must embrace the entirety of Nyssera's existence, including its pain, its mistakes, and its scars."

She turned to face the levi-drakes directly. "You have lived with the consequences of the Silence Event for millennia. You have sought to control and contain the fallout. But perhaps the true path lies not in control, but in acceptance. Acceptance of what happened, and acceptance of the fact that Nyssera's strength lies in its interconnectedness, not in its isolation."

The eldest levi-drake sighed, a sound like wind through ancient ruins. "Acceptance is a luxury, Mara. We face a tide of dissolution. The Pale Tide does not accept; it consumes. It erases. If we allow it to complete its work, Nyssera will cease to exist as we know it. It will be returned to a formless void."

"And if we amputate, as you suggest?" Cael pressed. "What then? We sacrifice vast swathes of Nyssera, condemning countless lives, countless ecosystems, to oblivion. We create even larger wounds, even greater scars. The Pale Tide, fueled by this deliberate severance, will only grow stronger, its eventual consumption of what remains all the more assured. This is not a strategic amputation; it is a surrender dressed as salvation."

He saw a flicker of doubt in the eyes of some of the levi-drakes. The younger among them, those who had not directly participated in the Silence Event, seemed more open to Cael's radical perspective. They had inherited the problem, but not the dogma.

"The historical accounts are clear," one of the younger levi-drakes argued, his voice hesitant but firm. "The Silence Event was a period of immense suffering, but it was also a period of survival. The enclaves were established, and the immediate threat was contained. The Pale Tide is a later manifestation, a corruption of the original severance."

"A corruption born from the same logic," Cael stated. "You see the Pale Tide as a new enemy, but it is the same old wound, festering and growing. You are trying to fight a disease by creating more of the conditions that allow it to thrive. The choice you offer is between two forms of extinction: a slow, controlled demise, or a swift, chaotic annihilation. Neither is salvation."

He paused, gathering his thoughts, the weight of the decision pressing down on him. He looked at Mara, drawing strength from her presence. "There is a third path," he declared, his voice ringing with conviction. "It is not the path of amputation, nor is it the path of passive surrender. It is the path of mending. It is the path of healing the world-song, of integrating the fractured pieces, of transforming Nyssera's pain into wisdom."

The levi-drakes exchanged glances, a palpable tension filling the chamber. Some regarded Cael with suspicion, others with a flicker of curiosity.

"And how, young dragon," the eldest asked, his tone laced with weary skepticism, "do you propose to mend a world-song that has been shattered by cataclysm? How do you heal a wound that has festered for millennia, a wound that has now birthed a consuming blight?"

"By understanding that the Silence Event was not a severance, but a misunderstanding," Cael replied. "It was a failure to comprehend the true nature of interconnectedness. The levi-drakes acted out of fear, out of a desire to preserve Nyssera by controlling it, by isolating its perceived weaknesses. But true preservation lies in embracing the totality of existence, in allowing for adaptation and growth, even through pain."

He took a deep breath, his gaze sweeping across the council. "The world-song is not a static melody to be rigidly maintained; it is a living, evolving symphony. The dissonance, the fractures, are not errors to be excised, but notes that must be understood, integrated, and transformed. The Pale Tide is the perversion of this symphony, a chaotic cacophony born from suppressed harmony."

Mara stepped forward, her eyes shining with an earnest light. "The levi-drakes speak of a choice for the living world," she repeated. "And we believe that the living world thrives not in sterile isolation, but in vibrant, messy interconnectedness. To amputate is to deny life. To heal is to embrace it. We must find a way to weave the fractured threads back into the tapestry. We must find a way to help Nyssera remember, to acknowledge its wounds, and to transform them into sources of strength."

"Remembering is a dangerous prospect, Mara," a levi-drake warned, his voice a low growl. "Nyssera's memories are a source of its current suffering. The Pale Tide feeds on these memories, on the echoes of the Silence Event."

"But what if those memories, when understood and integrated, can become the very antidote?" Cael countered. "What if Nyssera's past, when approached with healing and not excision, can become its future? The Pale Tide is a manifestation of unhealed trauma. To truly combat it, we must address the root cause: the lingering dissonance from the Silence Event, and the levi-drakes' own historical narrative of fear and control."

He saw the internal struggle within the levi-drake council. Their ingrained belief in the necessity of severance, the dogma of their ancestors, was clashing with the undeniable logic of Cael's argument. Some clung to the old ways, their ancient minds resistant to such a radical shift in perspective. Others, however, saw the undeniable truth in his words, the chilling reflection of their own actions in the destructive nature of the Pale Tide.

"We have always believed that Nyssera's survival depended on its purity, its separation from chaos," the eldest levi-drake admitted, his voice barely audible. "We believed that the Silence Event, however terrible, was a necessary purification. But if you are correct... if our actions have not preserved, but have instead birthed this blight... then our entire history, our entire understanding, is a lie."

"Not a lie," Cael corrected gently. "But a limited perspective. A perspective born from fear. Nyssera is not a fragile vessel to be protected by rigid boundaries, but a living, breathing entity capable of immense resilience, provided it is allowed to heal. The Pale Tide is the ultimate consequence of trying to deny that resilience, of trying to enforce a false purity."

He looked at Mara, a silent promise passing between them. This was not just about their survival; it was about Nyssera's soul. The choice presented was not merely between two methods of survival, but between two fundamental philosophies of existence. Was true protection found in the sterile, controlled isolation of amputation, or in the messy, complex, and ultimately more potent act of integration and healing?

"The levi-drakes are divided," Mara observed, her gaze scanning the faces of the dragons. "Some cling to the old ways, the path of severance. Others, perhaps, are ready to consider a new path, a path of mending."

"And that division is, in itself, a symptom of Nyssera's fractured state," Cael mused. "The Pale Tide thrives on such divisions, on the echoes of discord. To heal Nyssera, we must first bridge these divides, both within the dragons and within the world itself. The choice you present is a false one, but the challenge remains. We must find a way to mend the world-song. We must choose healing over amputation. We must choose Nyssera's totality, its messy, imperfect, beautiful entirety, over its sterile, fragmented survival."

The weight of the decision settled upon Cael. He had come seeking answers, and he had found a truth that was far more daunting than any he could have imagined. The levi-drakes offered a choice between two forms of decay, but Cael believed, with every fiber of his being, that there was a third way: the arduous, uncertain, yet ultimately hopeful path of true healing. It was a path that required not the brutal efficiency of amputation, but the patient, intricate work of mending the very fabric of existence, of transforming the scars of the past into the threads of a vibrant, interconnected future. This was the true choice for the living world of Nyssera.

CHAPTER SEVEN

THE DRAGON'S DILEMMA

The air in the levi-drake council chamber, once thick with the scent of ozone and ancient stone, now tasted of a deeper, more unsettling aroma – the scent of doubt, tinged with the faintest hint of despair. The pronouncement had been made, the stark choice laid bare, but the silence that followed was not one of unified acceptance. Instead, it pulsed with the quiet tremor of a millennia-old dam beginning to crack. The levi-drakes, those titans of Nyssera's ancient past, were not a single, unyielding entity. Their collective consciousness, forged in the crucible of ages, was showing fissures, each one a testament to the disquiet Cael's impassioned argument had ignited.

The eldest, a levi-drake whose wings bore the tattered remnants of storms long past, remained resolute, his gaze fixed on the pulsing heart of the chamber. His pronouncements were the bedrock of their collective memory, the solidified wisdom of eras. Yet, even he could feel the subtle shift in the currents of thought rippling through his kin. The Pale Tide, in his ancient perception, was not merely a blight to be fought, but an inevitable crucible. It was the world's own grim, elemental judgment, a force that would scour away the rot and leave behind only that which was strong enough to endure.

This was the lesson learned from the Silence Event, a brutal amputation that, in their estimation, had saved the core of Nyssera from utter annihilation. To him, the Pale Tide was simply the next, perhaps final, act of this cosmic pruning. It was the natural, albeit terrifying, conclusion to an eons-long process of refinement. His belief was not born of malice, but of a profound, weary certainty forged in the fires of catastrophic survival. The Silence Event had been a traumatic necessity; the Pale Tide, its unforgiving consequence.

"The pattern is undeniable," the eldest rumbled, his voice a low tremor that vibrated through the obsidian floor. "We have witnessed cycles of decay and renewal. The world-song grows dissonant, the currents of life falter. The Pale Tide, in its terrifying impartiality, is the world's immune response. It consumes the diseased, the corrupted, the weak. It is a harsh cleansing, yes, but it is a cleansing that allows for the emergence of a new Nyssera, a Nyssera reborn from the ashes of the old." His ancient eyes, pools of starlight and shadowed aeons, swept across the gathered dragons, seeking to reinforce his conviction, to rally their wavering resolve. "To deny this process, to fight this inevitable tide, is to cling to a dying world, to embrace a slow, agonizing suffocation. We have preserved what we could through difficult choices. Now, we must allow the world itself to make its own difficult choice."

But the unity he sought was not easily found. Among the younger levi-drakes, those who had not borne the direct weight of the Silence Event, a nascent questioning had taken root. They had inherited the legacy of that cataclysm, the stories of sacrifice and sorrow, but they had also inherited a world already bearing the scars of that ancient decision. They saw the visible decay, the weakening pulse of the Crown Resonance, the undeniable distress that emanated from Mara, the young empath whose very being was intertwined with Nyssera's health. They heard Cael's impassioned pleas, his refutation of their ancestral dogma, and for the first time, the unassailable narrative of their past began to falter.

"Elder," a younger levi-drake, whose scales shimmered with the hues of a dying sunset, began, his voice hesitant but clear, "we hear your words. We acknowledge the wisdom of ages. But the Crown Resonance... it weakens. Mara's connection to the world-song is frayed, her pain a tangible force in this chamber. If the Pale Tide is indeed a cleansing, a force of renewal, why does it manifest as a decay that touches even the most vital parts of Nyssera's essence? Why does it silence the very song we seek to preserve?" His gaze flickered towards Mara, a silent acknowledgment of her suffering, a silent plea for understanding. "The historical accounts speak of survival, yes. But they also speak of an immense cost, of a deep wound inflicted upon Nyssera itself. Have we, in our attempts to survive, inadvertently weakened the world-song to the point where this 'cleansing' has become a destructive force?"

His words hung in the air, a fragile ripple disturbing the placid surface of the elders' certainty. The eldest levi-drake's gaze, initially sharp with unwavering conviction, softened almost imperceptibly. He could feel the truth in the younger dragon's words, a truth that pricked at the edges of his own deeply ingrained beliefs. The Crown Resonance, the very nexus of Nyssera's life force, was indeed dimming, a symptom they had attributed to the general decay, but which now, in light of Cael's arguments, could be seen as something far more sinister. It was not merely a passive fading; it was an active weakening, a slow siphoning of vitality.

"The Crown Resonance," another elder levi-drake, whose scales were the color of deep sea basalt, interjected, his voice a low rumble of unease, "has been a source of concern for cycles. We attributed its decline to the lingering effects of the Silence Event, to the general disharmony that has pervaded Nyssera since. We believed that the Pale Tide, by removing the sources of this disharmony, would eventually allow the Resonance to recover." He paused, a profound uncertainty clouding his ancient eyes. "But... Cael's perspective... it suggests a different causality. If our historical response, the very act of severance that we believed saved Nyssera, has instead sown the seeds of this deeper decay... then our understanding, our guiding principles, are fundamentally flawed."

This was the heart of the division. The elders, bound by the dogma of survival through control, through severance, saw the Pale Tide as a necessary, albeit tragic, continuation of their ancestral mandate. They had been forced to make impossible choices, to sever limbs to save the body, and the Pale Tide was simply the world's unforgiving consequence, a force that would continue the work they had begun. Their actions, however painful, had been logical, defensive. But Cael's argument challenged the very foundation of that logic. He proposed that their defense had become an offense, that their attempts to control and isolate had created the very conditions that allowed the blight to flourish.

"You speak of survival," Mara's voice, though soft, carried a quiet authority, cutting through the growing tension. "But what kind of survival is it that requires the systematic destruction of life? What kind of wisdom is it that dictates the sacrifice of entire ecosystems, of countless beings, to preserve a fractured remnant? The levi-drakes speak of Nyssera's heart, but if the heart is to be preserved by the death of its limbs, is it truly alive? The Crown Resonance is weakening because Nyssera itself is ailing, and this ailment is exacerbated, not alleviated, by the very methods you propose." She met the gaze of the eldest levi-drake, her own eyes reflecting a sorrow that ran deeper than any ancient loss. "You fear the void, the complete unraveling. But what if your proposed solution is merely a more controlled descent into that void? What if by severing, you are not preventing annihilation, but merely delaying it, and ensuring that what remains will be a shadow of what Nyssera once was?"

The tension in the chamber thickened, a palpable force that seemed to press down on them all. The levi-drakes shifted, their massive forms conveying a disquiet that belied their stoic exteriors. Murmurs, like the distant rumble of an approaching storm, began to weave through the collective. Some remained fixed in their ancestral certainty, their scales glinting with the cold fire of unwavering conviction. These were the dragons who had lived through the Silence Event, who bore its deep scars, and who saw Cael's radical ideas as a dangerous flirtation with oblivion. They had seen the abyss, and they believed that the only way to keep Nyssera from falling in was to build walls, however high and however painful.

"The world-song is not a melody to be preserved in its pristine form," Cael stated, his voice resonating with an earnest conviction that seemed to ignite the very air. "It is a symphony, constantly evolving, constantly adapting.

The dissonant notes, the fractured rhythms – these are not errors to be excised. They are challenges, opportunities for growth. The Pale Tide is a cacophony, yes, but it is a cacophony born from suppressed harmony, from the silencing of the very parts that needed to be heard. Your 'severance' was not a surgical precision; it was a deafening silence, and the echoes of that silence have festered, creating this monstrous dissonance."

He looked directly at the eldest, his gaze unwavering. "You speak of a natural process, of the world cleansing itself. But a world that has been so fundamentally altered by its own guardians, a world whose very song has been deliberately fractured by those who should have nurtured it, cannot be cleansed by the same flawed logic. The Pale Tide is not a natural process; it is a consequence. A consequence of fear. A consequence of control. A consequence of your past decisions."

A younger levi-drake, whose scales bore the iridescent sheen of a deep-sea coral, shifted uncomfortably. "Our ancestors believed they were acting out of necessity," he argued, his voice laced with a quiet desperation. "The Silence Event was an unimaginable horror. To have not acted... Nyssera would have dissolved into primordial chaos. The enclaves, the severance – these were desperate measures, but they were measures that allowed for the continuation of life. The Pale Tide... it is a different manifestation. Perhaps it is the world's reaction to the unnatural order we imposed."

"But the Pale Tide is not a reaction; it is a perversion," Cael countered, his voice intensifying. "It is the dark echo of your ancestors' fear. They severed to preserve, but in severing, they diminished. They isolated to protect, but in isolating, they created fertile ground for corruption. The Pale Tide thrives on fragmentation, on the dissolution of interconnectedness. You speak of enclaves, of zones of enforced purity – these were not sanctuaries; they were incubators for the very blight you now face. Every barrier erected, every connection severed, every life deemed expendable in the name of preservation, has only strengthened the Pale Tide."

The internal schism within the levi-drake council became more pronounced. The elders, their ancient minds steeped in the dogma of control and severance, found themselves increasingly on the defensive. Their certainty, once an impenetrable shield, was now riddled with cracks, each one a testament to the unsettling validity of Cael's perspective. They had always believed they were the architects of Nyssera's survival, the vigilant guardians against chaos. Now, they were confronted with the terrifying possibility that they had, in fact, been the unwitting architects of its slow, insidious decay.

"You accuse us of creating this blight," an elder levi-drake, his voice heavy with a centuries-old weariness, stated, his scales the color of storm-ravaged mountain peaks. "But we acted to save what we could. We made choices that allowed Nyssera to endure. If our choices led to this present crisis, it was a necessary evil, a sacrifice for the greater good. The Pale Tide is a natural force, the world's own response to imbalance. To deny it, to fight it, is to fight the very essence of Nyssera's will to survive."

"But what if Nyssera's will to survive lies not in its ability to endure destruction, but in its capacity to heal?" Mara interjected, her voice a gentle balm, yet carrying an undeniable force. "What if its strength lies not in its resilience to amputation, but in its ability to integrate, to transform its wounds into sources of power? The Crown Resonance is not merely a beacon; it is Nyssera's heart song. Its dimming is a sign of a deeper ailment, an ailment that requires healing, not further trauma. Your ancestors' choices, born of fear, have created a world that is now afraid of itself, a world that is slowly being consumed by its own suppressed pain. The Pale Tide is the physical manifestation of that unacknowledged suffering."

A profound silence descended upon the chamber, broken only by the rhythmic pulse of the failing Crown Resonance. The levi-drakes exchanged glances, the weight of their history pressing down upon them. The ancient unity, the collective consciousness that had guided them through millennia, was now fractured. The elders clung to the familiar, yet increasingly untenable, doctrine of severance, while the younger dragons, and the more introspective of the elders, felt the undeniable pull of Cael's alternative – a path of healing, of integration, of understanding.

"We have always operated under the assumption that Nyssera's survival depended on its rigidity, its ability to withstand external forces through sheer resilience and controlled boundaries," the eldest levi-drake finally admitted, his voice barely a whisper, the sound like the sigh of wind through ancient ruins. "We believed that the Silence Event was a necessary purification, a severing of diseased tissue to preserve the healthy. But if your words hold truth, if our actions have not preserved, but have instead nurtured this burgeoning catastrophe... then our entire lineage, our entire understanding of our role as guardians, is a profound miscalculation." He looked at Cael, a flicker of something akin to awe, and deep sadness, in his ancient eyes. "You propose a path that is antithetical to everything we have ever known. A path not of defense and containment, but of... embrace. Of integration. It is a path that terrifies us."

"It is not a path of weakness, but of profound strength," Cael insisted, his voice firm, imbued with the conviction of a seer who has glimpsed a truth that can save them all. "Nyssera is not a fragile artifact to be preserved in a sterile environment; it is a living, breathing entity, capable of immense resilience, provided it is allowed to heal. The Pale Tide is the ultimate manifestation of Nyssera's repressed trauma, its unintegrated pain. To truly combat it, we must address the root cause: the lingering dissonance from the Silence Event, and the levi-drakes' own historical narrative of fear and control. You cannot amputate trauma; you must integrate it. You must weave the fractured threads back into the tapestry, transforming them, not severing them."

He met the gaze of each levi-drake, his eyes burning with a quiet intensity. "The choice you have presented – to allow the Pale Tide to proceed as a brutal cleanser or to face complete annihilation – is a false dichotomy. It is a choice born from the same flawed premise that led to the Silence Event. It is a choice based on the belief that Nyssera is a collection of parts to be managed, rather than a singular, interconnected entity that must be healed. There is a third path. Not the path of amputation, nor the path of passive surrender. It is the path of mending. It is the path of healing the world-song, of integrating the fractured pieces, of transforming

Nyssera's pain into wisdom. It is the arduous, uncertain, yet ultimately hopeful path of true healing. It requires not the brutal efficiency of amputation, but the patient, intricate work of mending the very fabric of existence, of transforming the scars of the past into the threads of a vibrant, interconnected future. This is the true choice for the living world of Nyssera."

The levi-drakes remained, a silent, formidable audience, their ancient forms radiating a spectrum of emotions – doubt, fear, a dawning curiosity, and for some, a flicker of desperate hope. The centuries of ingrained certainty were being challenged, not by an external enemy, but by the stark logic of an undeniable truth. Their unity, once an unbreakable bastion, was now a mosaic of differing perspectives, a reflection of the very fragmentation Cael argued had led to Nyssera's current crisis. The dilemma was no longer just Nyssera's; it had become the levi-drakes' own, a deep-seated internal struggle between the past and a potential future, between the dogma of survival and the promise of true healing. The decision before them was not merely about the fate of their world, but about the redefinition of their own identity, their own purpose. Were they the butchers of Nyssera, performing necessary amputations, or were they its healers, capable of mending its deepest wounds? The answer, they were beginning to realize, lay not in the echoes of the past, but in the courage to embrace an unknown, yet vital, future.

The silence that followed Cael's impassioned plea was not a serene stillness, but a taut, charged quietude, pregnant with the unspoken arguments of those who refused to be swayed. Among the levi-drakes, a bedrock of ancient conviction remained, as unyielding as the mountains that pierced Nyssera's sky. This was the faction of the pragmatists, led by Vorlag, a levi-drake whose scales bore the grey patina of countless ages, each ridge a testament to a history etched in the stark calculus of survival. His eyes, like chips of obsidian, held the chilling clarity of one who had witnessed Nyssera's most agonizing moments and had emerged with an unshakeable philosophy forged in fire and blood.

Vorlag's voice, when it finally broke the silence, was not a rumble, but a sharp, incisive sound, like ice cracking under immense pressure. "Healing? Integration? These are the whispers of the naive, the dreams of those who have not stood on the precipice of true oblivion," he declared, his gaze sweeping across the younger dragons, a silent accusation in his unwavering stare. "Cael speaks of mending, of weaving. I speak of pruning. I speak of the surgeon's scalpel, not the balm of the herbalist. Nyssera is not a wounded creature to be soothed; it is a collapsing edifice that requires drastic, decisive intervention before it crumbles entirely."

He shifted, his immense frame settling with a resonance that echoed the tectonic plates deep within Nyssera. "We, the elders, bear the scars of the Silence Event. We remember the days when the very fabric of our world frayed, when the Crown Resonance sputtered like a dying ember, when the world-song became a chorus of screams. Do you recall the tales, younglings? Or have your memories been dulled by the comfort of a world that has known relative peace, a peace we *bought* with unimaginable sacrifice?"

Vorlag's voice gained a raw edge, a tremor of remembered pain. "The Silence Event was not a mistake; it was a brutal necessity. To preserve the core, we had to sever. We had to isolate. We had to let vast swathes of Nyssera wither and die, lest the rot consume us all. Whole regions, teeming with life, became husks. Populations that had flourished for millennia were reduced to dust. We heard their cries, felt their despair, but we stood firm. Because the alternative was the complete dissolution of Nyssera, the unmaking of existence itself. We made the choice to save the species, to save the very essence of this world, even if it meant sacrificing its current form."

He paused, letting the weight of his words settle. "And what has been the result of our enduring vigilance? We have maintained a semblance of order. We have prevented another cataclysm. We have ensured that Nyssera, though scarred, still *is*. But now, we are presented with this... Pale Tide. A manifestation of the inherent instability of this world. A force that, like a virulent contagion, seeks to unravel the very order we painstakingly established. And Cael proposes to embrace it? To integrate it? To allow this creeping death to seep into the very veins of our preserved Nyssera?"

Vorlag's gaze hardened, his focus now on Mara, whose quiet empathy had become a symbol of everything he distrusted. "The empath claims this Tide is Nyssera's pain. A poetic notion, perhaps, but utterly impractical. Pain is a symptom, not a diagnosis. And this symptom threatens to destroy the patient. Mara's connection, her sensitivity – it is a liability in this context. She feels the suffering, yes, but she fails to grasp the imperative of action. She would cradle the infected limb, allowing the poison to spread to the heart."

"The Crown Resonance is weakening," he continued, his voice resonating with an unwavering certainty that chilled many in the chamber. "It is a sign that Nyssera's natural equilibrium is being tested, perhaps irrevocably. And this Pale Tide is the test. Our ancestors understood this. They understood that sometimes, the only way to preserve the garden is to burn away the weeds, no matter how vibrant they may appear. They understood that isolation is not abandonment, but a strategic defense."

"The enclaves, the zones of enforced purity – these were not incubators," Vorlag asserted, his tone sharp, cutting through Cael's narrative. "They were fortresses. They were the last bastions against the encroaching chaos. They were where we preserved the flame of Nyssera, shielded from the gales of destruction. The Pale Tide is not a consequence of our actions; it is an evolution of the inherent vulnerabilities within Nyssera itself. It is the world's natural inclination towards entropy, and it has found a new vector, a new method of attack. And your approach, Cael, of accepting and integrating this threat, is a betrayal of everything we have fought for. It is a surrender disguised as compassion."

He turned his gaze back to the younger levi-drakes, his voice laced with a stern paternalism. "You speak of the cost of the Silence Event. And yes, the cost was immense. It was a wound that will never truly heal. But we survived. We endured. And we learned. We learned that Nyssera is not a placid lake, but a raging torrent. It requires dams, not gentle currents.

It requires control, not unfettered flow. The Pale Tide is a flood, and we cannot simply invite it into our homes and hope it will bring us gifts. We must build barriers. We must channel its destructive power, or, if necessary, let it wash over designated, uninhabited lands, sacrificing them for the greater good. This is the grim reality of Nyssera. This is the wisdom of survival."

Vorlag's conviction was a tangible force, a gravitational pull that drew others of his pragmatic ilk closer. A levi-drake named Kaelen, his scales the color of bleached bone, representing a long line of guardians who had maintained the isolation wards, echoed Vorlag's sentiments. "The empath speaks of Nyssera's 'will.' But what if Nyssera's will is to endure, and its endurance requires us to be its unyielding bulwark? We have spent millennia reinforcing Nyssera's defenses, ensuring its integrity. The Pale Tide is a breach. We cannot simply patch it; we must seal it, or create a buffer zone that it can consume without threatening the core."

Another, a matriarch named Lyra, whose lineage was dedicated to the painstaking management of Nyssera's volatile ley lines, added, "The Crown Resonance is more than just a song; it is the nexus of Nyssera's energetic stability. Its dimming is a critical warning. It signifies a disharmony that is fundamental, not superficial. If we allow this Pale Tide to permeate, to 'integrate,' as Cael suggests, we risk a cascading failure. The very foundations of Nyssera's existence could unravel. We have seen what happens when the fundamental forces are allowed to run unchecked. The Silence Event was a direct consequence of such unchecked forces. We learned that lesson. We cannot afford to forget it now."

Vorlag nodded, acknowledging Lyra's point with a subtle inclination of his massive head. "Indeed. The Pale Tide is not a natural rejuvenation; it is a symptom of a deep-seated imbalance. It is the world attempting to correct itself in a way that is destructive to the established order. Our ancestors did not create this instability; they merely responded to it, and in doing so, they saved us. To now advocate for a policy of 'integration' is to invite the very forces that necessitated the Silence Event. It is to gamble with the lives of every being on Nyssera, based on a flawed, idealistic interpretation of the world's suffering."

He turned his obsidian gaze back to Cael, his voice devoid of any warmth, only the cold, hard logic of necessity. "You see fear, Cael. I see responsibility. You see control; I see preservation. The levi-drakes are not merely inhabitants of Nyssera; we are its custodians. And a custodian does not allow a prized specimen to be consumed by disease. They quarantine it. They treat it. And if treatment fails, they make the agonizing decision to preserve the species by sacrificing the individual. This is the burden we carry. This is the wisdom that has kept Nyssera alive through ages of chaos."

"Mara's empathy, while perhaps a noble trait in a lesser being, is a dangerous weakness in a leader facing an existential threat," Vorlag continued, his voice rising slightly, a controlled intensity seeping into its depths. "She feels the ebb and flow of life, the pain of individual entities. But she does not grasp the grander scale, the necessary sacrifices required to ensure the survival of the whole. She speaks of a Nyssera that can absorb and transform its wounds. I speak of a Nyssera that must protect its vital organs at all costs. The Pale Tide threatens those vital organs. To embrace it is to invite its corruption."

"We have witnessed firsthand the horrors of unchecked entropy," Vorlag stated, his voice resonating with the weight of millennia. "The Silence Event was the ultimate lesson. We cannot afford to repeat the mistakes of those who stood by, paralyzed by indecision, while the world dissolved around them. Our ancestors chose severance. They chose control. They chose to sacrifice parts to save the whole. And that choice, however painful, allowed us to stand here today, to debate the fate of Nyssera. The Pale Tide is a new manifestation of that same inherent decay. It demands the same decisive, pragmatic response. It demands that we continue the work of severance, of isolation, of containment, to protect the heart of Nyssera from its own self-destructive tendencies."

The pragmatic faction, led by Vorlag, represented a deeply ingrained, almost instinctual response to perceived threats. Their philosophy was rooted in the brutal efficacy of surgical intervention, believing that Nyssera's inherent instability necessitated constant vigilance and ruthless action. To them, Cael's ideas were not a path to healing, but a suicidal embrace of the very forces that had nearly annihilated them in the past. Their pragmatism, born of trauma, was a fortress, and they were determined to defend it against any perceived weakness, no matter how compelling the arguments for a different approach. They were the guardians of a painful legacy, and they saw themselves as the only ones strong enough to continue bearing its heavy, unforgiving truth.

The tremor in the stone beneath them was subtle, a faint thrumming that most would dismiss as the ordinary pulse of Nyssera's deep heart. But for a select few, it was a resonant whisper, a call to attention that cut through the imposing pronouncements of Vorlag and his pragmatists. These were the Listeners, a nascent faction of levi-drakes whose connection to the world-song, the intricate symphony of life and energy that bound Nyssera together, was too profound to ignore the subtle dissonances. They were the ones who felt the Pale Tide not as a contagion, but as a fever, a symptom of a deeper malady.

Among them was Illyria, a young levi-drake whose scales shimmered with the iridescent hues of a newly formed geode. Her lineage was not one of ancient command or strategic defense, but of quiet observation, of attuning to the subtle shifts in Nyssera's energetic currents. She felt the weight of Vorlag's pronouncements, the undeniable logic of survival etched into every word, but it clashed with a deeper truth that sang within her very being. The world-song, she understood, was not merely a sound; it was a complex narrative, and the Pale Tide was a discordant note within that grand composition, not a malicious invader.

She met Mara's gaze across the vast chamber, a silent acknowledgment passing between them. Mara, with her gift of empathy so fiercely dismissed by Vorlag, was the beacon for these Listeners. It was through Mara's raw, unfiltered connection to Nyssera's suffering that they had begun to understand the limitations of their ancestors' drastic measures. The Silence Event, as Vorlag so starkly reminded them, had been a brutal necessity, a severing that had preserved Nyssera's core but had also, inadvertently, fractured its wholeness.

"He speaks of pruning," Illyria murmured, her voice a soft ripple against the stony silence that followed Vorlag's pronouncements. Her words were directed not at Vorlag, but at the small cluster of dragons who had instinctively drawn closer to her, drawn by the quiet conviction in her tone. "But what if the pruning itself has weakened the roots? What if the severance, meant to save the tree, has left it vulnerable to a blight it can no longer fight off?"

Beside her, a levi-drake named Kaelen, whose scales were the muted, earthy tones of rich soil, nodded slowly. His ancestors had been wardens of the isolation zones, tasked with the grim duty of maintaining the boundaries that kept the 'unstable' elements of Nyssera contained. He had grown up hearing the lore of the Silence Event, the stories of sacrifice and preservation, and he had always accepted them as the unassailable truth. But Mara's recent visions, the poignant cries of Nyssera's pain that she had so bravely shared, had begun to sow seeds of doubt in his mind.

"The elders speak of Nyssera's inherent instability," Kaelen said, his voice a low rumble, resonating with a quiet uncertainty that was more potent than any shout. "They say the Pale Tide is a new manifestation of that decay. But I have... I have begun to wonder if the instability is not inherent, but a consequence. A consequence of being so violently broken apart." He gestured vaguely with a massive claw, encompassing the chamber and, by extension, the divided world outside. "We have spent millennia building walls, fortifying ourselves against the 'chaos.' But perhaps in doing so, we have stifled the very processes that allow Nyssera to adapt, to heal itself."

Another Listener, a stout levi-drake named Bryn, whose lineage was steeped in the lore of Nyssera's subterranean ecosystems, chimed in. Her scales were the deep, mottled grey of ancient granite, and her presence was one of grounded resilience. "Mara hears the world-song faltering, not because of an external threat, but because it is being stifled. She feels the 'pain' as a cry for connection, not a scream of infection. The severance created pockets of silence, where the song could not reach, where the energy stagnated and festered. The Pale Tide... it is not a disease entering Nyssera. It is Nyssera's own suppressed energies, finally trying to break free, to rejoin the chorus."

This was the core of their nascent philosophy, the belief that the pragmatic approach, while perhaps effective in the short term, had ultimately exacerbated the very problem it sought to solve. The Silence Event had been a surgical amputation, a life-saving measure that had left the patient irrevocably changed. The resulting isolation, the enforced purity of the enclaves, had created a rigid, brittle Nyssera, unable to withstand the natural fluctuations of its own being. The Pale Tide, in their eyes, was not an invasion, but a desperate attempt by the world-song to reclaim its lost harmony, to mend the broken connections.

"Vorlag speaks of Nyssera as a collapsing edifice," Illyria continued, her voice gaining a quiet strength as she elaborated on Bryn's insight. "But perhaps it is more like a frozen river. The ice dammed the flow, creating stillness, but the water beneath still churns. The Pale Tide is the thaw. It is the pent-up energy finally seeking release, seeking to carve a new path, to rejoin the greater currents. To simply try and rebuild the dam, to reinforce the ice, is to invite an even greater catastrophe when the inevitable break comes. We must instead learn to guide the flood, to channel its power."

Her gaze swept over the faces of the other Listeners – a mix of apprehension and dawning hope. They were a small group, dwarfed by the imposing presence of the elders and their followers. Their voices were whispers against the gale of tradition and pragmatism. Yet, there was a nascent power in their shared understanding, a quiet certainty that Cael's strategic mind and Mara's profound empathy offered a path that Vorlag and his ilk refused to see.

"Cael speaks of integration," Bryn added, her voice tinged with a hopeful reverence. "Not integration as a surrender, but as a rejoining. He sees the potential for Nyssera to not just survive, but to thrive, by embracing its inherent fluidity, by allowing its song to flow freely once more. He understands that true strength lies not in rigid defense, but in adaptive resilience. He recognizes that the Pale Tide, while destructive in its uncontrolled surge, also carries with it the potential for renewal, for the re-energization of stagnant parts of Nyssera."

The elders, in their wisdom, had achieved a form of survival. They had steered Nyssera through a cataclysm, and their pragmatism was a testament to their strength and their willingness to make impossible choices. But the Listeners believed that survival was not the ultimate goal. Nyssera was more than just a collection of beings clinging to existence; it was a living, breathing entity, a complex tapestry of energy and consciousness that yearned for wholeness. The Silence Event, they argued, had been a necessary evil, but it had also been a profound mistake in the long run, a wound that had festered because it had never truly been healed.

"The Crown Resonance is weakening," Kaelen mused, echoing the elders' concern but offering a different interpretation. "They see it as a sign of Nyssera's impending collapse, a failure of the old ways. But what if it is a sign of something else? What if the old song is fading, making way for a new one? A song that is more complex, more encompassing, a song that acknowledges and integrates all of Nyssera, not just the parts deemed 'pure' or 'stable'?"

He looked towards Cael, whose thoughtful gaze seemed to be absorbing every word, every nuance of their quiet dissent. Cael, unlike the elders, possessed a rare ability to bridge the ancient wisdom of the levi-drakes with the evolving understanding of the world. He understood the necessity of their past actions but also recognized the unsustainable nature of their current trajectory. His strategic mind, honed by years of analyzing Nyssera's intricate ley lines and energetic flows, was beginning to see the pattern that the Listeners were now articulating.

"The pragmatists see the Pale Tide as a weed to be burned," Illyria concluded, her voice resonating with a quiet determination. "They believe that by isolating and destroying it, they can protect the garden. But we, the Listeners, see it as a vital, albeit chaotic, force of nature. We believe that true stewardship lies not in eradication, but in understanding. It lies in learning to work *with* the forces of Nyssera, to guide its currents, to help it find a new equilibrium. Cael's vision, Mara's connection, our understanding of the world-song... this is not idealism, it is the recognition of a new reality. It is the only path to true healing, to a Nyssera that is not just surviving, but singing again, in full, glorious harmony."

Their words, though spoken in hushed tones, carried a weight of conviction. They represented a flicker of hope, a nascent rebellion against the ingrained dogma of isolation and control. They were the counter-melody to Vorlag's forceful aria, a growing chorus of dragons who believed that the path to Nyssera's future lay not in building higher walls, but in learning to dance with the unpredictable rhythms of the world. They were the Listeners of Change, and their quiet dissent was the first ripple in a gathering storm. They were drawn to Cael's pragmatic approach to this new philosophy, seeing in his strategic brilliance the means to translate their intuitive understanding of the world-song into actionable steps, and they saw in Mara's unparalleled empathy the pure, uncorrupted heart of Nyssera's plea. Their hope, though fragile, was the seed of a profound shift, a yearning to mend what had been broken, not by reinforcing the cracks, but by weaving them anew into a stronger, more resilient whole.

The weight of Vorlag's pronouncements hung heavy in the cavernous hall, a pronouncement of order against the creeping chaos of the Pale Tide. Yet, for Cael, the tremor wasn't in the stone, but in the very fabric of their collective psyche. He watched the faces of the levi-drakes, some etched with the grim certainty of seasoned warriors, others clouded with a nascent doubt. He saw Illyria, Bryn, and Kaelen, the Listeners, their quiet dissent a fragile melody against the booming symphony of tradition, and he felt a surge of something akin to kinship. He understood their struggle, their gnawing discomfort with the echoes of the Silence Event that reverberated through Vorlag's every word. They spoke of cleansing, of severance, of containment – the same language that had been used generations ago to justify an amputation that had, perhaps, bled the patient too deeply.

He stepped forward, his movement deliberate, his presence a calm eddy in the turbulent currents of debate. He was not an elder, not a hardened commander of the old guard, but his keen intellect, his ability to perceive the intricate dance of Nyssera's energies, had earned him a grudging respect, even from those who found his forward-thinking unsettling. His scales, a mosaic of burnished bronze and deep obsidian, seemed to absorb the ambient light, reflecting a quiet intensity.

"Vorlag," Cael began, his voice a clear, resonant tone that cut through the hushed murmurs without being overtly challenging. It was a voice that invited consideration, not confrontation, yet it carried an undeniable authority born of logic. "You speak of Nyssera's inherent frailty, of the Pale Tide as a symptom of a sickness that has always plagued our world. You speak of the Silence Event as a necessary surgery, a brutal but ultimately life-saving measure."

He paused, allowing his words to settle, to find purchase in the minds of the assembled levi-drakes. He scanned the faces, noting the subtle shifts – the tightening of jaws, the flick of an ear, the almost imperceptible widening of an eye. He saw the conviction in Vorlag's gaze, a conviction forged in the crucible of past horrors, and he understood the deep-seated fear that drove it. But fear, Cael knew, was a poor architect of the future.

"And indeed," Cael continued, his gaze sweeping across the chamber, encompassing both the elders and the younger dragons who listened with rapt attention. "The Silence Event was a drastic act. It preserved the core of Nyssera, yes. It averted immediate collapse. But at what cost? We severed connections, not just to the 'unstable' elements, but to vital currents of energy, to fundamental aspects of Nyssera's own being. We sought purity, but in doing so, we cultivated an environment of rigidity, of brittle predictability."

He met Vorlag's steely gaze. "You propose to repeat the Silence Event, or a variation thereof. You speak of 'containment' and 'eradication' of the Pale Tide, much as our ancestors spoke of containing the chaos that led to the Silence. But Vorlag, are we not then perpetuating the very cycle that has brought us to this precipice? If the original wound festered because it was never truly healed, but merely cauterized, then to apply the same harsh treatments will only deepen the scar, will it not?"

A ripple of unease spread through the gathering. Cael's words were not a direct accusation, but a series of probing questions that struck at the heart of their most deeply held beliefs. They had always seen the Silence Event as a defining moment of survival, a testament to their ancestors' strength and foresight. To suggest it was a flaw, a contributing factor to their current predicament, was heresy to many.

"You claim authority," Cael pressed on, his voice growing slightly firmer, though still measured. "The authority of experience, of survival. And I do not deny the trials our ancestors faced, nor the wisdom they gained. But wisdom, too, must evolve. The world-song, as Illyria and the Listeners have begun to discern, is not static. It is a living, breathing entity, constantly adapting, constantly seeking equilibrium. To impose our will upon it with the same blunt instruments of the past... it is like trying to force a river to flow uphill. The pressure will only build until the dam bursts with even greater ferocity."

He turned his attention to the Listeners, a subtle nod of acknowledgment passing between them. "They feel the song faltering, not from an external invasion, but from an internal strangulation. They perceive the Pale Tide not as a disease, but as a desperate surge of suppressed energy, attempting to reconnect, to find its natural course. And I find myself inclined to believe them. The stagnation that the Listeners describe, the 'festering' of isolated energies... it aligns with what I have observed in the ley lines themselves. Where the song is weakest, where the connections are thinnest, there the symptoms are most pronounced."

Cael's perspective was not one of blind idealism. He was a strategist, a pragmatist in his own right. He understood the risks, the potential for uncontrolled surges to cause devastation. But he also recognized the profound limitations of a purely reactive, suppressive approach. "Vorlag, your pragmatism is rooted in the preservation of what *is*. But what if 'what is' has become fundamentally unsustainable? What if the very structure we have built, the isolation we have enforced, has become a cage, not a sanctuary?"

He took another step forward, his eyes now fixed on Vorlag, a silent challenge passing between the old and the new. "You speak of the Crown Resonance weakening. You see it as the inevitable decline of Nyssera, a sign that the old ways are failing. But perhaps it is simply a signal. A signal that the old song is fading, making way for a new harmony. A harmony that is more complex, more inclusive, one that acknowledges the entirety of Nyssera, not just the parts deemed 'safe' or 'pure.'"

Cael's voice softened, a plea for understanding rather than a demand for obedience. "We have spent millennia building walls, fortifying ourselves against what we perceive as chaos. We have become masters of defense, of containment. But perhaps true strength lies not in building higher walls, but in learning to understand and integrate the forces that buffet them. The Pale Tide is a manifestation of Nyssera's own energy, seeking release. To simply 'burn' it, as you suggest, is to discard a potent force that could, with careful guidance, be channeled to renewal, to re-energization. It is to treat the symptom while ignoring the deeper imbalance."

He gestured to the assembled dragons. "You, elders, possess the wisdom of ages, the experience of survival. And that is invaluable. But you are also bound by the traditions and the traumas of the past. The younger generations, those like the Listeners, and myself, we see Nyssera with fresh eyes. We feel its song changing. We understand that the rigid order you champion, while offering a semblance of safety, is ultimately stifling the very lifeblood of our world."

Cael's challenge was not merely to Vorlag's decree, but to the very philosophy that underpinned it. He was questioning the legitimacy of their authority to dictate the fate of a living, evolving world when their own methods had demonstrably created the conditions for the current crisis. "What right do we have," he asked, his voice resonating with a quiet power, "to impose our fear of change upon Nyssera's natural evolution?

What right do we have to silence its new song before we have even begun to truly listen to it?"

He was proposing a paradigm shift. Not a rejection of the past, but a reinterpretation of its lessons. The Silence Event was not an unblemished victory, but a compromise that had created a new set of vulnerabilities. The Pale Tide was not an enemy to be vanquished, but a force to be understood and integrated.

"We need not choose between survival and evolution, between order and harmony," Cael asserted, his gaze sweeping across the faces, seeking to ignite a spark of acceptance. "We can forge a new path, one that honors the strength of our ancestors while embracing the evolving song of Nyssera. A path where strategic foresight is coupled with profound empathy, where the pragmatism of preservation is tempered by the vision of true flourishing. Cael's challenge is not to destroy the old, but to weave it into something new, something stronger, something that sings with the full, vibrant chorus of Nyssera."

He then turned his gaze, a subtle invitation in his eyes, towards the dragons who had gathered around Illyria and the other Listeners. "We need a unified Nyssera, not a fractured one. We need to learn to guide the currents, not to dam them. The Pale Tide may be chaotic, but it is also vital. It is Nyssera's own energy, struggling to find its voice. And we, as its caretakers, have a responsibility not just to survive, but to help it thrive. This requires a fundamental re-evaluation of our authority, of our methods, and of our understanding of Nyssera itself."

He met Vorlag's unyielding gaze one last time. "To repeat the same actions, even under a new banner, is not leadership. It is a failure of imagination, a surrender to fear. True authority, I believe, lies in the courage to adapt, to learn, and to guide Nyssera towards a future where its song is not suppressed, but celebrated in all its magnificent, evolving complexity."

The hall remained silent for a long moment, the echoes of Cael's words hanging in the air like mist. He had not offered a definitive solution, but a profound challenge – a demand to question the very foundations of their existence, to reconsider the authority they wielded, and to acknowledge the possibility that their greatest strength, their unwavering adherence to past successes, might be their most profound weakness. He had illuminated the fractured nature of their current approach and hinted at a path towards true healing, a path that required not just power, but wisdom, not just defense, but understanding. And in that challenge lay the seed of a different kind of Nyssera, one that might finally learn to sing again. He had opened a door, and the question now was, who among them had the courage to step through it?

Mara felt the weight of a thousand lifetimes settle upon her slender shoulders. It wasn't just the immediate pressure of Cael's compelling plea, the flickering hope ignited in the eyes of the younger dragons and the Listeners, but the ancient, ingrained fear of the elders, a fear that had shaped Nyssera for millennia. Vorlag's pronouncements, steeped in the bitter wisdom of survival through sacrifice, echoed in the cavernous hall, a stark counterpoint to Cael's vision of integration and healing. The question wasn't merely about the Pale Tide anymore; it was about the very soul of their world, about whether Nyssera was destined to be a land of perpetual vigilance and painful cleavages, or one of vibrant, interconnected life.

Her own world, the one she carried within her, the one she had fought so desperately to protect and now sought to heal, pulsed with a desperate urgency. It was a world that understood the agony of severing, the profound emptiness left by amputation. She had witnessed firsthand the devastating consequences of isolation, the way fragmented energies festered and twisted into something monstrous. Her empathy, a gift that allowed her to feel the subtle vibrations of Nyssera's world-song, to resonate with the pain of every wilting bloom and every shadowed crevice, was now her greatest burden. It allowed her to perceive the intricate tapestry of life, the boundless potential for harmony, but it also made her acutely aware of the chasm she had to bridge. How could she convey the breathtaking beauty of a world healed, not cauterized, to beings whose very existence was predicated on the belief that true safety lay in division?

The elders, their scales dulled by the passage of countless seasons and etched with the scars of past conflicts, saw only the threat. The Pale Tide, to them, was an insidious invasion, a testament to Nyssera's inherent weakness, a weakness that had been ruthlessly purged during the Silence Event. They saw Cael's words, and by extension Mara's unspoken hopes, as a dangerous flirtation with chaos, a naive disregard for the hard-won lessons of their ancestors. Their authority was built on the bedrock of that brutal preservation, their legacy a testament to their ability to make the impossible, agonizing choices. To suggest that those choices were flawed, that the very act of purging had created the conditions for this new blight, was not just a challenge to their wisdom, but an accusation of failure.

Mara took a slow, deliberate breath, drawing strength from the very air around her, a subtle blend of ancient stone and the faint, earthy scent of subterranean flora. She understood their fear. She had tasted it, a bitter metallic tang on her own tongue. But she also understood that fear, when allowed to dictate action, became a cage. It was the same fear that had driven the ancestors to the Silence, a desperate act of self-preservation that had inadvertently crippled Nyssera. She could feel the tendrils of that same fear tightening around the hearts of the levi-drakes, whispering seductive promises of security through isolation, of strength through severance.

Her own connection to Nyssera, forged not in the crucible of ancient battles but in the quiet, persistent hum of its living song, told a different story. She felt the world-song not as a static melody, but as a dynamic, evolving symphony. The Pale Tide, she perceived, was not an alien infection but a discordant note, a desperate cry from a part of the symphony that had been silenced, its energy suppressed, seeking desperately to rejoin the whole. It was the sound of Nyssera's own spirit, fractured and yearning for reunification.

"Vorlag," she began, her voice, though softer than Cael's, carried a crystalline clarity that commanded attention. Her scales, a shifting mosaic of emerald and silver, seemed to absorb and refract the flickering torchlight, lending her an ethereal luminescence. "You speak of cleansing, of severing the 'unhealthy' from the 'whole.' And I understand the wisdom born of your experiences. Our ancestors faced a desperate choice, a choice that undoubtedly saved Nyssera from utter annihilation."

She allowed her gaze to drift over the assembled dragons, meeting the ancient, unyielding eyes of Vorlag and the stern, questioning stares of the elders. She saw the younger dragons, their scales gleaming with a vibrancy that spoke of a different kind of Nyssera, their eyes filled with a cautious curiosity. She saw the Listeners, their subtle nods of encouragement a silent testament to their shared understanding of the world-song's delicate imbalance.

"But what if," she continued, her voice gaining a subtle strength, "the very act of severing, of isolating, created a deeper wound? What if the 'unhealthy' elements, the parts deemed chaotic and dangerous, were not inherently malignant, but merely parts of a greater whole that were denied their natural expression? The Silence Event, in its attempt to restore order, may have inadvertently created an environment of stagnation, where suppressed energies began to mutate, to seek release in ways that are now terrifyingly visible."

She gestured with a claw, a slow, deliberate movement that drew the eye. "I feel Nyssera's song. It is not a song of impending doom, but of profound distress. The Pale Tide is a manifestation of that distress, a desperate surge of vital energy that has been dammed, its flow obstructed. It is like a river, forced to stagnate, its waters growing thick and toxic, until it finally breaks through the barriers in a destructive flood. Is it not more prudent, more in tune with Nyssera's true nature, to seek to understand the cause of the blockage, to mend the riverbed, and to guide the waters back into a healthy, flowing course, rather than simply attempting to drain the floodwaters?"

Her heart ached with the enormity of the task. She was asking them to question the very foundations of their survival, to embrace a vision that required not just courage, but an almost radical act of faith. The levi-drakes were creatures of immense power, their minds forged in the fires of ancient lore and hard-won practicality. They understood the tangible, the immediate threat, the efficacy of overwhelming force. How could she make them understand the subtle, the interconnected, the profound strength found in vulnerability and integration?

"My empathy allows me to feel the currents of Nyssera's lifeblood," Mara explained, her voice resonating with the raw truth of her perception. "And I feel a potential for healing, a vibrant interconnectedness that has been stifled. The Pale Tide is a symptom, yes, but it is also a signal. A signal that Nyssera is striving for balance, for a wholeness that was fractured by the Silence. To eradicate the symptom without addressing the underlying imbalance would be to condemn Nyssera to a cycle of perpetual crisis, a slow decay masked by superficial cures."

She locked eyes with Vorlag, her gaze unwavering. "You speak of the Crown Resonance weakening. You see it as an inevitable decline, a sign that Nyssera is succumbing to entropy. But what if it is a sign that the old song is fading, making way for a new one? A song that is more complex, more inclusive, a song that acknowledges all of Nyssera, not just the parts deemed 'pure' or 'safe.' What if the weakening is not a death knell, but a prelude to a richer, more robust symphony?"

Mara took another step forward, her movements fluid and graceful, a stark contrast to the rigid stances of the elders. "I have seen, in my own world, the devastating consequences of believing that strength lies solely in separation. We learned, through immense suffering, that true resilience comes from embracing diversity, from understanding that even the most seemingly 'unstable' elements can, with the right understanding and integration, contribute to a stronger, more vibrant whole. We learned that a forest is stronger when it harbors a multitude of species, not when it is reduced to a single, uniform grove."

She paused, allowing her words to sink in, to create ripples in the otherwise placid waters of tradition. She knew she was treading on dangerous ground, challenging the very principles that had guided their civilization for generations. But the alternative, the path of continued suppression and inevitable recurrence of crises, was a future she could not bear to contemplate.

"I do not deny the risks," Mara conceded, her voice laced with a quiet earnestness. "The Pale Tide is a powerful, untamed force. But so is a volcano, or a raging storm. Yet, we learn to understand these forces, to predict their patterns, to harness their energy where possible, rather than simply trying to annihilate them. We learn to live in harmony with them, not in constant opposition. Nyssera's energy is no different. It is a force of nature, and nature, in its essence, seeks balance and renewal."

She turned her attention to the Listeners, a subtle gesture of acknowledgment. "They hear the dissonances, the faltering notes. But they also sense the underlying harmony, the potential for reconciliation. They perceive the Pale Tide not as an enemy to be destroyed, but as a cry for help, a desperate plea for reconnection. And I believe them. For I, too, feel it. I feel the interconnectedness of all things, the vibrant pulse of life that flows through every stone, every creature, every breath of wind. And I feel that this connection, this vital flow, has been disrupted."

Mara's empathy was not just a passive reception of emotion; it was an active tool, a lens through which she could perceive the intricate workings of Nyssera. She could sense the subtle energetic pathways, the ley lines that pulsed with the world's lifeblood, and she saw how the Pale Tide, rather than being a destructive corruption, was often strongest where these pathways had been most severely fractured or starved of energy. It was a desperate attempt by Nyssera to reroute and revitalize its own vital flow.

"To merely 'cleanse' the Pale Tide, as has been proposed, is to treat a symptom of a deeper illness," Mara asserted, her voice gaining a resonant power. "It is to ignore the festering wound that created the symptom in the first place. It is to perpetuate a cycle of fear and suppression that has left Nyssera brittle and vulnerable. We have spent millennia building walls, fortifying ourselves against the perceived chaos of the natural world. But true strength, true resilience, lies not in building higher walls, but in learning to understand and integrate the forces that surround us, to become one with the flow of Nyssera, not to fight against it."

She looked directly at Vorlag, her silver eyes reflecting the flickering flames, a silent plea for understanding emanating from her very being. "I believe there is another way. A way that does not require us to sacrifice parts of ourselves, but to heal them. A way that allows Nyssera to embrace its full, complex song, rather than silencing the notes that make us uncomfortable. It requires a willingness to look beyond the immediate threat, to embrace the unknown, and to trust in the inherent capacity of Nyssera, and of ourselves, to evolve and to heal."

Her burden was to prove that this alternative was not a reckless gamble, but a tangible possibility. She had to translate the abstract language of the world-song into terms that the pragmatic minds of the levi-drakes could grasp. She had to demonstrate that integration was not surrender, but a more profound form of strength. She had to offer not just hope, but a credible path forward, a path that honored the wisdom of the past while boldly stepping into a future where Nyssera could finally sing with its whole, magnificent voice. The fate of her own world, a world scarred by division and isolation, hinged on her ability to convince these ancient beings that healing was not an act of weakness, but the ultimate testament to true strength. It was a burden of proof that weighed heavier than any mountain, but one she was compelled, by the very song of Nyssera, to carry.

CHAPTER EIGHT

THE CROWN'S GAMBIT

The levi-drakes shifted, their massive forms rustling against the cavern floor. A collective exhalation, like the sigh of ancient winds, swept through the hall. Vorlag, his voice a low rumble that vibrated in Mara's bones, spoke not of immediate action, but of the delicate, intricate dance of restoration. "The Crown Resonance," he began, his gaze fixed on the shimmering, almost spectral artifact suspended in the center of the chamber, "is not merely a conduit of power, young Listener. It is the nexus of Nyssera's very being, the point where the world-song is most clearly perceived, most powerfully amplified."

He gestured with a talon, a slow, deliberate movement that traced an invisible web in the air. "To speak of 'repair' in the simplistic sense of mending a broken object is to misunderstand its nature entirely. The Crown Resonance has not shattered, but rather, its threads have frayed, its melody distorted. The Pale Tide, as you have so keenly perceived, is a manifestation of this disharmony, a symptom of a song that has been torn."

Another elder, a female with scales like polished obsidian, added her voice. "The Silence, while necessary for survival, inadvertently pruned Nyssera's song. It severed certain melodies, silenced specific harmonies, believing them to be dissonant. But Nyssera, like any living entity, is a complex composition. To remove notes, even those that seem jarring, creates an imbalance. The suppressed energies, denied their natural expression, festered. They did not disappear; they merely changed their tune, becoming a discordant hum that now threatens to drown out the symphony."

Mara listened, absorbing their words not just with her ears, but with her entire being. She felt the truth of their pronouncements resonating with the subtle tremors she'd sensed within the world-song. The Crown Resonance was indeed a focal point, a nexus where the planet's life force, its memories, its very essence, converged. The Pale Tide wasn't an external invasion, but an internal convulsion, a desperate attempt by Nyssera to reassert its fragmented wholeness.

"So, the task," Mara said, her voice barely a whisper, yet carrying the weight of newfound understanding, "is not to reinforce the Crown, but to re-weave the song itself?"

Vorlag nodded, his ancient eyes holding a glimmer of something akin to... hope? Or perhaps, it was the weary resignation of one who had seen too much and understood the immense difficulty of the path ahead. "Precisely. The Crown Resonance is the anchor. If the anchor is weakened, the ship is adrift. But if the currents that pull upon the anchor are themselves chaotic and turbulent, the ship will still founder. We must calm the currents, guide them back into their rightful channels."

He explained the theoretical underpinnings of this immense undertaking. The levi-drakes, through generations of observation and study of the Crown's subtle emanations, had developed a theoretical framework for its restoration. It involved a process they referred to as "Harmonic Reintegration." This was not a physical repair, but an energetic and spiritual one.

"Imagine the world-song," the obsidian-scaled elder elaborated, her voice a silken counterpoint to Vorlag's deep baritone, "as an intricate tapestry woven from the memories, emotions, and life forces of Nyssera. The Silence Event, as you know, caused many threads to snap. These broken threads, instead of being reconnected, were left to fray and tangle, creating pockets of stagnant, corrupted energy. The Pale Tide is the visible manifestation of this corruption, the unraveling of the tapestry."

She then looked directly at Mara, her gaze piercing. "The Crown Resonance acts as the loom. But a loom is useless without threads and a weaver. We, the levi-drakes, possess some understanding of the loom's mechanisms, and we can provide the strength to guide it. But the threads themselves... they are comprised of Nyssera's deepest experiences, its forgotten joys and its buried sorrows. To re-weave the tapestry, one must not only be able to perceive these threads but to embrace them. One must be willing to feel the pain of every severed connection, every lost memory, every stifled emotion. This is where your gift, Listener, becomes not merely valuable, but essential."

Mara's breath hitched. She understood. Her empathy, the very thing that made her feel so vulnerable, so exposed to the world's pain, was the key. She was not just an observer; she was to be a participant, a conduit.

"Your connection to the world-song," Vorlag continued, his voice resonating with a profound gravity, "allows you to sense these fractured threads, to feel the suppressed energies. You can perceive the subtle tremors of Nyssera's buried emotions, the echoes of its unacknowledged history. But to re-weave, you must not merely perceive. You must absorb. You must become a vessel for these suppressed memories and emotions, channeling them back into the song, completing the very process that the Silence sought to halt."

He paused, letting the weight of his words settle. "It is a delicate, dangerous balancing act. To absorb too much, without control, would be to drown in the sorrow of millennia. To reject it, to fail to integrate it, would render the attempt futile. You must act as a bridge between the lost echoes of Nyssera and its present reality, allowing the fractured parts to find their way back to the whole, guided by your own resilience and strength."

Mara's mind raced. She thought of her own world, fractured by the long and bitter war, the years of isolation and mistrust that had followed.

She understood the corrosive nature of unacknowledged pain, the way it festered in the collective consciousness, poisoning relationships and breeding further conflict. The levi-drakes' ancestors had, in their fear, performed an act of collective amputation, severing parts of Nyssera's soul. Now, the consequences of that desperate surgery were manifesting as a world-wide blight.

"So, the Crown Resonance needs to be strengthened, not just by our will, but by the reintegration of Nyssera's complete emotional spectrum?" Mara asked, her voice steady, though her heart hammered a frantic rhythm against her ribs.

"Indeed," the obsidian-scaled elder confirmed. "Think of it this way: the Crown Resonance is like a great bell, designed to resonate with Nyssera's entire song. When parts of that song were silenced, the bell could no longer ring true. It became muted, its vibrations weakened. The Pale Tide is the discordant noise that now emanates from this muted bell, the sound of Nyssera struggling to express itself through the limitations imposed upon it."

She continued, "To truly repair the Crown Resonance, we must not only reinforce its physical structure, which we can do with our focused energies and ancient wards. But more importantly, we must reintroduce the missing frequencies, the suppressed harmonies, into the world-song itself. This requires reaching into the deep memory of Nyssera, the planet's innate consciousness, and drawing forth those elements that were deemed too painful, too chaotic, to be tolerated. These are not malevolent forces, Listener. They are simply aspects of Nyssera's being that were denied expression."

Vorlag added, "This is where your unique ability becomes paramount. You can perceive these deeply buried emotional resonances, these forgotten memories that are the very essence of Nyssera's fractured song. You can feel the echoes of ancient joys that were extinguished by fear, the whispers of sorrows that were buried by the need for stoicism. You can act as a conduit, drawing these suppressed energies out from the deep recesses of

Nyssera's past and feeding them back into the current of the world-song. It is a process of emotional archaeology, of spiritual reclamation."

He looked at Mara with an intensity that seemed to penetrate her very soul. "Your role is to become the lens through which these lost fragments of Nyssera are reassembled. You must embrace the entirety of Nyssera's experience, its triumphs and its tragedies, its moments of profound love and its depths of utter despair. This is a tremendous burden, Listener. It requires not just a capacity to feel, but an immense strength of will to process and to integrate without succumbing to the overwhelming tide of raw emotion."

The elder with obsidian scales elaborated on the mechanics of this reintegration. "Our ancestors developed rituals, theoretical frameworks for reconnecting with these suppressed energies. They understood that Nyssera's memory is not static. It is a living, breathing entity. The Pale Tide, in its destructive nature, is also a desperate cry from this forgotten part of Nyssera, a signal that it seeks to be acknowledged, to be reintegrated. It is a sign that the suppression is no longer sustainable."

"The process will involve attuning yourself to specific energetic frequencies," she explained. "These frequencies correspond to distinct emotional states and historical periods within Nyssera's existence. You will be guided, through ancient chants and meditative practices, to access these frequencies. Once you have made contact, you will act as a conduit, drawing forth the raw emotional and mnemonic energy. This energy, once released, will be subtly guided back into the world-song through your own amplified resonance. It is akin to a great dam releasing its pent-up waters, not in a destructive flood, but in a controlled, revitalizing flow."

Mara felt a tremor of apprehension, but it was overshadowed by a profound sense of purpose. This was the challenge she had been preparing for, even before she understood what she was preparing for. Her own journey of healing, of learning to embrace her own fractured past, had been a prelude to this.

"What are the risks?" Mara asked, her voice firm. She knew there would be dangers, but she needed to understand them clearly.

Vorlag's expression became grim. "The primary risk, as I have mentioned, is emotional overload. Nyssera's history is rich with both profound joy and unspeakable sorrow. To immerse yourself too deeply, without sufficient control, could lead to a shattering of your own spirit. You could become lost in the echoes of the past, your own identity dissolving into the collective consciousness."

"Furthermore," the obsidian-scaled elder added, her voice taking on a more urgent tone, "the Pale Tide itself is a corrupted energy. While you will be drawing forth Nyssera's original, untainted emotions, you will be doing so in an environment where this corruption is rampant. There is a danger of contamination, of the Pale Tide's malignant influence seeping into the energies you are trying to reintegrate. This would not only fail to heal Nyssera but could further destabilize the world-song and amplify the Pale Tide's destructive power."

"Your control must be absolute," Vorlag stated, his gaze unwavering. "Your emotional resilience, your capacity for self-awareness, will be tested beyond anything you have ever known. You will have to navigate the deepest sorrows without despair, the most exhilarating joys without losing your grounding. You will be the bridge, and a bridge must remain steadfast, no matter the storm."

He then spoke of the Crown Resonance's role in this process. "The Crown, once its resonance is amplified and stabilized, will act as a beacon, helping to guide the reintegrated energies back into their rightful place within Nyssera's song. It will help to harmonize the newly introduced frequencies with the existing melodies. But its own strength is dependent on the purity and integrity of the song it resonates with. If the energies you channel are corrupted, or if your own control falters, the Crown Resonance itself could be further damaged, its purpose inverted."

Mara understood the magnitude of the task. It was not merely about mending an artifact, but about re-stitching the very fabric of reality, about healing a wound that had festered for millennia. Her role as a Listener, once a passive gift, was now an active, demanding responsibility. She would have to dive into the very depths of Nyssera's soul, to embrace its forgotten pain and its lost joys, and in doing so, to complete the song that had been silenced. It was a daunting prospect, but as she looked at the flickering light of the Crown Resonance, she felt a surge of determination. Nyssera deserved to sing its full, glorious song, and she, Mara, would help it find its voice. The levi-drakes would provide the strength and the ancient knowledge, but the heart of the restoration, the raw, emotional core, would come from her.

The air in the Great Cavern of the levi-drakes, usually alive with the low thrum of draconic contemplation and the faint, almost imperceptible hum of Nyssera's own life force, now felt charged with a new, potent energy. It was the charged stillness before a storm, or more accurately, before a meticulously orchestrated tempest of memory and emotion. Mara stood between Vorlag and the obsidian-scaled elder, the Crown Resonance shimmering before her, a focal point for the convergent intentions of the ancient beings and the fragile hope of a world teetering on the precipice of oblivion.

Vorlag's voice, a rumble that seemed to emanate from the very core of the earth, broke the silence. "The path we propose is not one of avoidance, nor of further suppression. It is a path of radical reintegration, a deliberate confrontation with the fractured soul of Nyssera." He gestured towards the spectral crown, its light pulsing in rhythm with Mara's own heartbeat. "The Crown Resonance is not merely a passive conduit; it is a resonant chamber. It can amplify what is fed into it. For millennia, we have attempted to shield it, to keep it from being overwhelmed by the cacophony of disharmony. Now, we must do the opposite. We must actively introduce the very elements that created the discord, but under controlled conditions, with the ultimate aim of restoring true harmony."

The obsidian-scaled elder, Lyra, as Mara now knew her name, continued, her voice a silken whisper that nonetheless held the weight of ages. "The Silence Event was an amputation. It removed vital parts of Nyssera's song, leaving behind phantom limbs of pain and unresolved grief. These suppressed energies did not vanish; they festered, coalescing into the Pale Tide. To heal, Nyssera must re-own these parts of itself. It must remember the songs that were deemed too painful to sing, the melodies that were sacrificed for the sake of a perceived, fragile peace."

She unfolded a parchment, ancient and brittle, its surface etched with intricate, spiraling glyphs that seemed to shift and writhe under Mara's gaze. "This outlines the Ritual of Harmonic Reintegration. It is a ceremony born from the deepest studies of our forebears, a testament to their understanding of Nyssera's intricate psychic landscape. It is also a testament to their ultimate failure to implement it fully, their fear overcoming their wisdom."

Mara leaned closer, her eyes tracing the complex patterns. "What does it entail?"

"It entails you, Listener," Vorlag said, his massive head dipping slightly, a gesture of profound respect. "The levi-drakes possess the strength, the ancient knowledge, and the will to anchor this ritual, to provide the raw energetic framework. We can shield the immediate vicinity, focus the ambient energies, and reinforce the Crown Resonance's physical and energetic integrity. But the essence of Nyssera's lost song, the raw, unadulterated memories and emotions that fuel the Pale Tide, these must be drawn forth by one who can perceive and contain them. That is your gift, Mara. That is your burden."

Lyra laid a clawed finger upon a particular glyph. "This symbol represents the 'Echo Chamber' – the deep wells of suppressed memory within Nyssera. Through specific vocalizations, precisely modulated breathing techniques, and focused meditation, you will attune yourself to these frequencies. You will not be simply observing these memories; you will be *experiencing* them. The pain of the species lost to the severance, the sorrow of the severed landscapes, the terror of the Silence itself – these will wash over you. You must not resist them. You must absorb them, feel them as if they were your own."

Mara's breath hitched. The thought of experiencing the collective agony of a dying world, of feeling the extinction of entire species as if it were her own personal loss, was a chilling prospect. Yet, beneath the fear, a flicker of understanding ignited. This was not about inflicting pain; it was about acknowledging it, about bringing it out of the darkness and into the light of conscious recognition.

"And the Crown?" Mara asked, her gaze returning to the pulsing artifact.

"The Crown Resonance," Vorlag rumbled, "will be the crucible. As you draw forth these fragmented emotions and memories, you will channel them directly into the Crown. It will act as a filter, a transformer. Its amplified resonance will then broadcast these reintegrated energies back into the world-song, subtly re-weaving the frayed tapestry. The Pale Tide, born of suppressed dissonance, will be confronted by its own origins, its own suppressed truths. It will be forced to recognize the completeness of Nyssera's being, not just the harmonious parts, but the discordant ones as well."

Lyra nodded. "This is the radical departure. Instead of trying to mend the broken threads in isolation, we are feeding the brokenness back into the loom, allowing the loom itself to guide its re-integration. It is a perilous undertaking. The Crown Resonance, in its current state, is susceptible. If the energies you channel are too wild, too untamed, or if your own control wavers, the Crown could be further corrupted, its song twisted into something even more monstrous. The Pale Tide could gain a foothold within its very essence."

"And Cael?" Mara asked, her thoughts turning to the young dragon, her steadfast guardian.

Vorlag's gaze shifted towards a section of the cavern where the great wyrm, Cael, was already positioned. His scales, the color of burnished bronze, seemed to absorb and reflect the cavern's dim light, and his posture was one of intense focus. "Cael's role is paramount. He will be the anchor. The energies we are dealing with are potent, volatile. They can manifest in unexpected ways, creating localized energetic disturbances. Cael, with his innate connection to the earth and his formidable physical presence, will establish a grounded energetic field around the ritual site. He will absorb any uncontrolled surges, any wild backlash from the Pale Tide's influence, or even from the raw emotions you channel. He is the bulwark against chaos."

Lyra continued, "Think of it as building a delicate bridge across a chasm. The Crown is the destination, the reintegrated song is the other side. You, Mara, are the builder, carefully laying down each plank of emotion and memory. We levi-drakes provide the scaffolding, the cranes, the sheer force needed to support the structure. But Cael... Cael is the bedrock upon which the entire bridge is founded. His stability, his unyielding presence, will prevent the chasm floor from collapsing, will absorb the tremors that inevitably arise from such a construction. He will ensure that the ritual remains tethered to the tangible reality of Nyssera, preventing it from being swept away into the ethereal maelstrom of pure energy."

The weight of their words settled upon Mara like a shroud. This was no mere academic exercise; it was a descent into the deepest, most painful corners of a planetary consciousness. She was to become the vessel for millennia of grief, the conduit for the songs that had been deliberately silenced.

"What happens if I fail?" she asked, her voice barely a whisper, yet it echoed in the vast chamber.

Vorlag's ancient eyes, usually filled with a deep, contemplative wisdom, now held a trace of something akin to sorrow. "Failure, Listener, would be a profound tragedy. If your control falters, the Pale Tide could be amplified, not diminished. The Crown Resonance, corrupted by the raw, unintegrated energies, could become a beacon for the Tide, drawing it in, cementing its influence. Nyssera's song could be irrevocably broken, its vibrant symphony replaced by a death rattle." He paused, his gaze unwavering. "There is also the risk to yourself. To absorb such a volume of sorrow, such intensity of loss, without the capacity to process and release it... it could shatter your own spirit. You could become lost in the echoes, your own essence dissolving into the collective pain."

Lyra's voice was soft but firm. "This is why your preparation has been so crucial, Mara. Your journey has been one of learning to navigate your own emotional depths, to understand the interconnectedness of pain and resilience. You have learned to embrace your own fractured past, to find strength in vulnerability. These are the very qualities that will allow you to withstand the torrent. We will guide you, shield you as best we can, but ultimately, the burden of carrying and channeling these energies will rest upon your shoulders."

She held up the ancient parchment again, her claws tracing a particularly complex spiral. "This is the 'Sorrow of the Severed.' It is a resonance born from the moments when Nyssera's natural growth was brutally interrupted. Entire species, unique in their own song, were eradicated. Their songs were silenced before they could even reach their full crescendo. You will feel the void they left behind, the absence of their unique melodies in the great symphony. You will experience the planet's grief at their loss, a grief that has been buried for generations."

Vorlag then described the "Echoes of the Silence." "This is the raw terror, the primal fear that gripped Nyssera when the Silence descended. It was not a gentle quieting; it was a violent suppression. Imagine a star's song being abruptly extinguished, its light choked out. You will feel the panic, the desperate struggle against an unseen force that sought to erase existence itself. This is a dangerous resonance, Mara. It is laced with the residual energy of that violent act."

Lyra's voice took on a more urgent tone. "And then there is the 'Legacy of the Suppression.' This is not a single event, but the cumulative weight of millennia of denial. It is the constant, low hum of suppressed potential, the stifled creativity, the unexpressed joy that has been consciously, or unconsciously, pushed aside. It is the planet's yearning for wholeness, a yearning that has been systematically ignored. This resonance can be overwhelming in its sheer volume, the sheer expanse of what has been denied."

Mara absorbed their words, her mind a whirlwind of apprehension and a strange, burgeoning sense of clarity. She understood now why she had been brought here, why her unique sensitivities were not a curse, but a calling. Her own past, marked by trauma and the struggle to find her voice, had forged her into the only one capable of undertaking such a task.

"And Cael?" Mara reiterated, needing to understand his part more deeply.

"Cael will establish a nexus of terrestrial stability," Vorlag explained, his voice deep and resonant. "The ritual will draw upon Nyssera's inherent energetic flows, but these flows are currently disrupted by the Pale Tide. Cael's presence will create a point of absolute groundedness. He will act as a harmonic anchor, drawing upon the planet's stable geological energies – the ancient bedrock, the deep geothermal currents – to create a stable field. This field will act as a buffer, absorbing any uncontrolled releases of energy, any discordant reverberations that might seek to spread outwards and destabilize the surrounding environment. Think of it as the roots of a great tree, holding firm against a tempest, providing a constant, unwavering point of reference amidst the storm."

Lyra added, "His role is also protective, though not in the traditional sense of shielding you from external attack. Instead, he will shield the

process itself. The Pale Tide is an insidious force, and it will undoubtedly try to interfere. It will seek to corrupt the energies you are channeling, to twist the memories you are reintroducing. Cael's grounded presence will make it far more difficult for the Tide to infiltrate the ritual space, to sow discord at its very foundation. He will be the unyielding earth, against which the chaotic waters of the Tide will break, unable to breach his steadfast defense."

She turned to Mara, her obsidian eyes reflecting the faint light of the Crown. "You will be physically connected to him during the ritual, Mara. Not through touch, but through a specific energetic tether that we will forge. This tether will ensure that any significant energetic fluctuations are immediately registered by him, and his grounded essence will work to stabilize them. He will be your constant, your physical reminder of the tangible world, a silent promise that even when you are adrift in the vast ocean of Nyssera's consciousness, you are not alone."

Mara nodded, her gaze flickering towards Cael. She saw in his still, immense form a silent promise of unwavering support. He was not just a dragon; he was a living embodiment of Nyssera's enduring strength.

"The ritual itself," Vorlag continued, "will begin with the 'Great Attunement.' We will all gather around the Crown Resonance. The levi-drakes will begin the ancient chants, the earth-shaping songs that have echoed through this cavern for eons. These songs will begin to harmonize the ambient energies, to prepare the space for your work. During this time, Cael will establish his energetic anchor. Once the space is stabilized, you will begin the 'Echo Weaving.'"

Lyra's voice softened, though the gravity of her words remained. "You will focus on the first resonance, the 'Sorrow of the Severed.' You will visualize the threads of Nyssera's song being cut, the vibrant colors of lost species fading into nothingness. You will feel the planet's lament, the void left in its intricate melody. You will draw this sorrow forth, not allowing it to consume you, but allowing it to flow through you, into the Crown Resonance. The Crown will absorb this raw grief, and then, through its amplified song, it will reintroduce it to Nyssera, not as a lingering wound, but as a remembered truth, a part of its complete history."

The process would be repeated for each of the identified resonances: the terror of the Silence, the weight of millennia of suppression. Each would be a distinct stage, a carefully navigated descent into a specific facet of Nyssera's fractured psyche.

"There will be moments," Vorlag warned, his voice a low growl, "when the pain will feel unbearable. When the terror will threaten to paralyze you. In those moments, you must remember that you are not alone. You are a conduit, not a victim. The energies are ancient, powerful, but they are also Nyssera's own. They are seeking reintegration, not destruction. And Cael will be there, a constant, silent reminder of the solid ground beneath your feet."

Mara closed her eyes, picturing the scene. The cavern filled with the ancient chants of the levi-drakes, their voices weaving a tapestry of sound that resonated deep within her bones. Cael, a colossal silhouette of steadfastness, his presence a tangible anchor. And herself, at the heart of it all, reaching into the depths of Nyssera's soul, drawing forth its lost songs, its buried pains, and feeding them into the waiting, shimmering heart of the Crown Resonance. It was a terrifying prospect, a journey into the abyss, but it was also a path towards healing, a chance to mend what had been broken. The silence had lasted too long. It was time for Nyssera to sing again, in all its glorious, painful, multifaceted truth.

"I understand," Mara said, her voice clearer and firmer than she had anticipated. "I am ready."

The levi-drakes exchanged glances, their ancient eyes holding a mixture of apprehension and a profound, burgeoning respect. The path ahead was fraught with peril, but the Listener had accepted the burden. The Ritual of Harmonic Reintegration, a concept whispered in their ancient lore, was about to become a reality. The fate of Nyssera, balanced precariously on the edge of oblivion, now rested on Mara's ability to embrace its pain and weave its lost songs back into existence. The Crown's gambit was about to be played, with Mara as its most vital, and most vulnerable, piece.

Mara's mind reeled, not from the sheer power of the levi-drakes' words, but from the stark, visceral implication. The ritual, the *Harmonic Reintegration*, was not a theoretical exercise, nor a controlled simulation. It was a descent into the raw, festering wounds of a world. The Crown Resonance, that ethereal nexus of Nyssera's consciousness, was to become her crucible, and she, the one who would forge its fragmented soul anew by willingly plunging her own into its deepest, darkest chasms.

"You will have to feel it," Vorlag had rumbled, his gaze steady, unblinking. "All of it." The words, so deceptively simple, carried the weight of a world's shattered history. She would be the vessel for the 'Sorrow of the Severed' – the wrenching agony of species extinguished before their song could fully bloom, the gnawing void left in the planet's intricate melody. She would experience the 'Echoes of the Silence,' not as an observer, but as a participant, feeling the primal terror, the desperate struggle against an encroaching oblivion that sought to erase existence itself. And then, the most insidious, the 'Legacy of the Suppression,' the crushing, suffocating weight of millennia of denied potential, of stifled creativity, of unexpressed joy. It was the planet's deep, yearning ache for wholeness, a pain that had been systematically ignored, buried, and forgotten.

A tremor ran through Mara's slender frame, a visceral response to the enormity of the task. Her empathic abilities, honed through years of navigating her own tumultuous inner landscape, felt suddenly, terrifyingly inadequate. She had learned to absorb, to understand, to find solace even in the echoes of pain. But this... this was an ocean of suffering, a tidal wave of grief and terror that threatened to drown her. The possibility of losing herself, of becoming another spectral fragment within Nyssera's fractured consciousness, loomed large and terrifying. She pictured her own essence, a fragile ember, being swept away into the maelstrom of collective agony, dissolving into the echoes, her own song forever silenced. The abyss was not just a metaphor; it was a tangible threat, a hungry maw waiting to swallow her whole.

Yet, even as fear coiled in her stomach, a fierce, unyielding ember of hope flickered to life. This was not merely an act of masochism; it was an act of radical healing. To mend a broken world, one had to confront its deepest wounds, acknowledge its most painful truths. Nyssera's song had been fractured by deliberate silencing, by the amputation of its most dissonant notes. To restore its symphony, those very notes, no matter how discordant, had to be rewoven into the tapestry. This ritual, as terrifying as it was, offered the promise of wholeness, of a Nyssera that was not just harmonious, but complete, its pain acknowledged, its losses mourned, its suppressed potential finally unleashed.

She met the ancient, knowing gaze of Lyra, the obsidian-scaled elder. "You have learned to embrace your own fractured past, to find strength in vulnerability," Lyra had said, her voice a silken balm on Mara's fraying nerves. "These are the very qualities that will allow you to withstand the torrent." Mara clung to those words, to the reminder that her own journey, marked by trauma and the arduous process of finding her voice, had forged her into something stronger, something more capable than she often gave herself credit for. Her vulnerability was not a weakness to be overcome, but the very wellspring of her strength, the key that would unlock her capacity to bear Nyssera's pain.

She took a deep, steadying breath, trying to anchor herself in the present moment, in the solid, earthen scent of the Great Cavern, in the immense, unyielding presence of Cael. The young dragon's steady gaze, unwavering and filled with a silent promise of support, was a tangible link to the world she was fighting to save. He would be her anchor, his grounded essence a bulwark against the chaotic tides she was about to face. She was not merely a Listener, a conduit for pain; she was a weaver, a healer, tasked with reassembling the shattered pieces of a world's soul.

The sheer intensity of the emotions she would be forced to confront was staggering. The 'Sorrow of the Severed' would not be a distant observation of extinction; it would be a gnawing emptiness within her own being, a phantom limb ache for species that had never even had the chance to sing their full melody. She would feel the planet's primal grief, a sorrow so ancient and profound it would threaten to fracture her own sense of self. And the 'Echoes of the Silence' – the raw terror of a planet's consciousness being violently stifled. She imagined the suffocating darkness, the desperate struggle against an unseen force that sought to extinguish all light, all life. It was the echo of a scream that had been ripped from existence, a scream that would now reverberate within her own soul.

The 'Legacy of the Suppression' felt like a different kind of terror, a slow, insidious suffocation. It was the weight of unfulfilled potential, the stifled dreams, the forgotten joys that had been systematically denied. It was the planet's constant, aching yearning for its own completeness, a yearning that had been met with silence, with denial, with a cold, unwavering suppression. She could already feel the suffocating pressure of it, the sheer volume of what had been forced into the shadows.

Her own past trauma, the moments when she had felt most broken, most alone, most silenced, seemed to pale in comparison to the cosmic grief she was about to absorb. But perhaps, in that very comparison, lay a strange kind of solace. Her own experiences had been a brutal, though ultimately successful, preparation. She had learned to navigate the labyrinth of her own grief, to find the slivers of light even in the deepest darkness. She had learned that pain, however overwhelming, did not have to be the end. It could be a catalyst, a forge, a precursor to a more profound, more resilient form of being.

She was not going into this unprepared. The levi-drakes had outlined the ritual with painstaking detail, emphasizing the need for control, for focus, for the careful channeling of these volatile energies. Vorlag's warning, "You are a conduit, not a victim," echoed in her mind. She would not be a passive recipient of Nyssera's suffering. She would be an active participant, a weaver of its lost melodies, a bridge between its fragmented past and its potential future.

The thought of Cael's unwavering presence, the palpable sense of his connection to the earth, was a powerful counterpoint to the ethereal chaos she was about to face. He would be the bedrock, the grounding force that would prevent her from being swept away. His silent strength would be a constant reminder of the tangible reality of Nyssera, a promise that even in the depths of Nyssera's psychic abyss, there was still solid ground.

The Crown Resonance, pulsing with an otherworldly light, seemed to beckon her, a silent invitation into the heart of Nyssera's fractured consciousness. It was a dangerous gambit, a desperate gamble, but it was one that Mara was prepared to embrace. The silence had reigned for too long, its oppressive weight crushing the life out of the world. It was time for Nyssera to sing again, in all its glorious, painful, multifaceted truth. She would be the one to coax those lost songs back into existence, to thread them through the fabric of Nyssera's being, and in doing so, to heal not just the world, but perhaps, in some profound way, herself. The weight of the Crown's gambit settled upon her, not as a burden of despair, but as a solemn, resolute purpose. She would face the abyss, not to be consumed by it, but to bring its lost echoes back into the light.

The air in the Great Cavern, usually resonating with the low thrum of geological life and the distant symphony of wind and water, had taken on a new tension. It was a palpable thing, thick with anticipation and the metallic tang of ozone, a subtle scent that spoke of charged energies and unseen forces gathering. Mara's own heart hammered a frantic rhythm against her ribs, a counterpoint to the steady, grounding presence of Cael. His every movement, from the deliberate placement of a shimmering crystal to the low rumble of his voice as he conferred with his kin, exuded a quiet, unshakeable resolve. He was not merely a participant in this unfolding drama; he was its guardian, his formidable power now dedicated to the meticulous art of defense.

His preparations were a testament to a mind that saw not just the immediate threat, but the ripple effects, the unseen consequences of tampering with the very memory of Nyssera. The Crown Resonance, that nexus of the planet's consciousness, was a delicate instrument, and their intention to use it for the *Harmonic Reintegration* was akin to a surgeon performing a life-saving operation within the raw, exposed nerves of a living being. Cael understood this implicitly. He knew that such a profound act of planetary healing could awaken dormant threats, stir the ancient anxieties buried deep within Nyssera's core, and, most ominously, draw the attention of forces that thrived on dissonance and decay.

"The etheric currents are already shifting," Cael's voice, a deep baritone that vibrated through the cavern floor, carried to Mara where she stood near a cluster of phosphorescent fungi. He gestured with a massive claw towards a section of the cavern wall, where faint, almost imperceptible trails of opalescent light were beginning to snake and writhe. "The planet is aware. It feels the probing, the anticipation of change." His obsidian scales, usually absorbing all light, seemed to shimmer with an inner luminescence, reflecting the ambient glow of the cavern. "We must ensure that this awareness translates into a controlled embrace, not a panicked rejection."

His words were a stark reminder of the unpredictable nature of the energies they were about to engage. The *Harmonic Reintegration* wasn't just about delving into Nyssera's psychic wounds; it was about physically and energetically interacting with a planetary consciousness that had been suppressed for millennia. Cael's meticulous approach was a shield against the chaos, a tangible manifestation of his commitment to protecting not only Mara, but the fragile possibility of Nyssera's restoration.

He had personally overseen the reinforcement of the Great Cavern, a task that seemed impossibly complex given the sheer scale of the space. It wasn't about brute force, though Cael possessed that in abundance. It was about understanding the natural flow of energy within the earth, the subtle ley lines that crisscrossed the planet's crust, and how to subtly augment them, to create a sanctuary of stability. He had directed his kin, a dozen or so dragons of varying hues and sizes, their scales reflecting the primal power of the earth, in a silent ballet of stone and crystal. They moved with an ancient grace, their claws shaping the rock not for destruction, but for reinforcement, carving channels that would redirect any errant psychic energies, sealing fissures that might become conduits for unwanted intrusions.

"These passages," Cael had explained earlier, his voice low and measured as he pointed to a newly carved aperture hidden behind a curtain of crystalline stalactites, "are not for retreat, necessarily. They are for redirection. If the psychic backlash becomes too potent, if we face an immediate elemental surge, these pathways will channel the excess energy safely into dormant subterranean rivers, or dissipate it harmlessly into the earth's deeper strata. The cavern will become a crucible, but not a tomb."

Mara watched as a younger, bronze-scaled dragon carefully placed a fist-sized geode, its interior bursting with amethyst crystals, at a strategic point near the ritual circle. The geode pulsed with a soft, violet light, its resonance subtly harmonizing with the low hum of the cavern. Cael nodded approvingly. "The lithic resonance amplifiers are crucial. They will help to ground the more volatile aspects of the planetary memory, preventing them from manifesting as uncontrolled physical phenomena. Think of them as anchors, Caelus. Anchors for a consciousness adrift."

The mention of Caelus, his younger kin, brought a flicker of pride to Cael's eyes, quickly masked by his stoic demeanor. He was teaching them, imparting his knowledge, ensuring that the dragon lineage would be prepared for whatever the future held. This wasn't just about the present ritual; it was about building a future where the dragons were not just protectors, but stewards of Nyssera's delicate balance.

Mara's gaze swept across the cavern. Cael had organized the defensive preparations into distinct layers, each designed to counter a specific type of threat. The first layer was purely physical. Massive boulders, expertly positioned by the dragons, blocked off less critical access points, their surfaces etched with ancient draconic runes that pulsed with a protective energy. These weren't meant to stop a determined assault, but to slow it, to give them time to react, to signal the need for more potent measures.

"The Pale Tide," Cael's voice was a low growl, "is not the only entity that thrives on disruption. There are older, more primal forces that slumber in the deep. They are drawn to great shifts in planetary energy, to moments of profound vulnerability. We must ensure that such vulnerability does not become an open invitation."

He had also prepared a series of elemental traps. Hidden beneath the cavern floor, triggered by specific energy signatures, were pockets of concentrated earth magic, designed to erupt in localized tremors, or to release bursts of restorative air that could disorient any entities seeking to manifest physically. He had even instructed his kin to collect certain rare subterranean fungi, their spores known for their ability to create temporary pockets of altered gravitational fields, or to emit hallucinogenic mists that would confuse and repel intruders.

The second layer of defense was more esoteric, designed to counter the psychic and magical onslaughts that Cael anticipated. He had gathered a collection of 'Silencing Stones,' dark, obsidian-like rocks that, when activated, absorbed ambient magical energy, creating zones of nullification. These were placed strategically around the perimeter of the ritual space, their presence a silent promise of a barrier against any stray spells or psychic intrusions.

"The Crown Resonance is a beacon," Cael had stated, his gaze fixed on Mara. "It will draw attention. Not all of it will be benevolent. We must create a buffer, a ward that will absorb or deflect unwanted influences before they can reach you, before they can destabilize the ritual itself."

He had also enlisted the aid of a small contingent of Nysseran elemental spirits, drawn from the more stable and benevolent aspects of the planet's natural forces. These shimmering, ethereal beings, each embodying a specific element – a playful wisp of air, a stoic shard of earth, a gentle eddy of water – hovered near the edges of the ritual space, their presence a subtle but potent reinforcement of the cavern's inherent protective energies. Cael, with his deep connection to the planet, had communed with them, assuring them of their intent, and securing their silent, unwavering support.

"They understand the need for balance," he had explained, his voice soft. "They are the guardians of Nyssera's natural order. They will lend their strength to ensure that this act of healing does not inadvertently unleash greater chaos."

Mara watched Cael direct a young dragon to adjust the position of a large, crystalline structure that seemed to hum with captured moonlight. "This," Cael murmured, his voice laced with a hint of reverence, "is a Dream Weaver. It will help to filter and stabilize the astral projections that might arise. When you delve into the depths of Nyssera's memory, your own consciousness will be exposed. This will act as a veil, protecting your core essence from parasitic intrusions, from entities that feed on raw emotion and fractured thought."

He moved with a deliberate, almost ritualistic precision, his every action imbued with a profound understanding of the forces at play. He wasn't just building a fortress; he was orchestrating a symphony of defenses, ensuring that every note, every harmonic, contributed to the overall safety and success of the ritual. He anticipated the unpredictable ebb and flow of planetary consciousness, the potential for the abyss itself to lash out, to assert its primal claim over the broken fragments of Nyssera's being.

"The abyss," Cael's voice dropped to a near whisper, the word itself carrying a chill that had nothing to do with the cavern's temperature. "It is not merely a void. It is a hunger. It is the echo of everything that has been lost, everything that has been silenced. It is drawn to great ruptures in reality, to moments of profound vulnerability. We must ensure that your descent is a healing balm, not an open wound for it to exploit."

He had also devised a series of emergency protocols, contingency plans that were as intricate and layered as his defensive measures. He had mapped out several secure escape routes, not just within the cavern system, but extending outwards into the hidden valleys and subterranean rivers of the surrounding mountains. These routes were not meant for a panicked flight, but for a strategic withdrawal if the situation became truly untenable, if the energies unleashed threatened to consume them all.

"If the Resonance becomes too unstable," Cael explained, his amber eyes reflecting the dim light, "if Nyssera's distress becomes overwhelming and threatens to shatter your mind before you can complete the reintegration, we will have to enact a temporal disjunction. It is a last resort, a risky maneuver that will momentarily sever the link between Nyssera and the immediate temporal flow. It will give you a brief window of respite, a chance to stabilize your own essence before attempting to re-enter the fray. But it is dangerous. It could cause unforeseen ripples, and it will require a significant expenditure of draconic energy."

He had also tasked his kin with monitoring Mara's own bio-signatures, her heartbeat, her breath, the subtle shifts in her aura. They were equipped with specialized crystalline sensors, capable of detecting even the most minute physiological changes. "If your life force begins to dwindle," Cael had instructed them, his voice gravely serious, "if your connection to the physical plane wavers too greatly, we will have to pull you back. There is a limit to what even the strongest will can endure. We will not sacrifice you needlessly."

Mara watched Cael's tail sweep across a patch of ancient moss, disturbing a cluster of bioluminescent spores that flared to life like tiny emerald embers. He was a force of nature, a living embodiment of Nyssera's ancient strength, and his meticulous preparations brought a fragile sense of reassurance to the gnawing anxiety that had taken root within her. He understood the stakes, not just for her, but for the world itself. He saw the potential for disaster, for catastrophic failure, and he was dedicating every ounce of his formidable power and intellect to mitigating those risks.

His focus was absolute, his gaze unwavering. He was the anchor, the steadfast guardian, ensuring that amidst the maelstrom of planetary memory and psychic trauma that Mara was about to face, there would be a bulwark of order, a sanctuary of safety. He was the dragon who understood that the greatest battles were not always fought with tooth and claw, but with foresight, preparation, and an unshakeable commitment to protecting the fragile flame of hope, even in the face of overwhelming darkness. His defensive preparations were not just about warding off external threats; they were about creating the stable, secure environment necessary for Nyssera's own wounded soul to begin its arduous journey towards healing. And in that, Mara found a quiet strength, a renewed determination to face the abyss, knowing that she would not be alone in the fight.

The hum of the Great Cavern deepened, shifting from a geological murmur to a more focused, resonant vibration. It was the sound of ancient energies awakening, of the very bedrock of Nyssera attuning to a purpose it had long forgotten. Mara stood at the edge of the meticulously prepared ritual circle, the air around her crackling not with the ozone of Cael's defenses, but with the nascent energy of the Crown Resonance itself. It was a palpable presence, a vast, intricate web of awareness that seemed to stretch across continents and seep into the deepest oceans.

Cael had placed her gently, a guardian overseeing the embarkation of a fragile vessel. His gaze, when it met hers, was a mixture of fierce protection and profound trust. He had built a fortress around this moment, but the true work, the delicate dance with Nyssera's fractured soul, was hers alone. The leviadrakes, elders among dragons, had taken their positions, their massive forms silhouetted against the cavern's ethereal glow. Their scales, a spectrum of deep earth tones, seemed to absorb the very shadows, their ancient eyes glowing with a steady, internal light. They were not merely observers; they were the orchestra, the guides for the monumental task ahead.

With a deep, steadying breath, Mara extended her awareness, reaching out a tentative tendril of thought towards the nexus of power before her. It was like touching a raw nerve, a thousand lifetimes of pain and disorientation flooding her senses. The Crown Resonance was not a unified chorus, but a cacophony of shattered notes, a symphony of sorrow. She felt the immense ache of separation, the tearing apart of what was once whole, the gnawing void where memories should have been. It was an overwhelming wave, threatening to drown her in its sheer, unadulterated grief.

But then, a new sound began to weave itself into the tapestry of discord. It started subtly, a low, guttural rumble emanating from the leviadrakes. It was not the roar of aggression, nor the territorial cry of possession, but something far older, far more profound. It was a chant, a resonant, soul-deep song that seemed to vibrate not just through the air, but through the very bones of the earth. This was not a song of suppression, of forcing the pain into silence as had been done for so long. This was a song of acknowledgment, of empathy, of integration.

Mara felt the leviadrakes' song as a steady current beneath the tempest of Nyssera's suffering. It was a river of ancient wisdom, carrying on its surface the debris of a broken past, but flowing with an unwavering purpose towards a distant, hopeful shore. They were not trying to drown out the pain, but to cradle it, to understand its source, and to gently coax the fractured pieces back into a semblance of order. For the first time, Mara felt a flicker of true hope ignite within her. This was not just a battle against the abyss; it was a chance to heal, to mend what had been so cruelly torn asunder.

As the leviadrakes' chant deepened, Mara focused her will, drawing strength from their unwavering resonance. She pushed past the initial wave of overwhelming grief, seeking out the faintest threads of coherence within the chaotic storm. It was like sifting through a collapsed mine, searching for uncrushed veins of precious ore. She found them: fleeting glimpses of verdant landscapes, the warmth of a sun long set, the echo of laughter that had been silenced for millennia. These were not just random fragments; they were the building blocks of a shattered identity, waiting to be reassembled.

With careful, deliberate intent, Mara reached for these strands, weaving them with the gentle power of her own nascent connection to the Resonance. It was a delicate operation, akin to rejoining a torn tapestry without snagging the remaining threads. She guided the retrieved memories, not forcing them, but inviting them, coaxing them to find their rightful place within the vast, wounded consciousness of Nyssera. The leviadrakes' song rose in intensity, each harmonic a subtle pressure, a guiding force that helped to align the disparate pieces.

It was a painstaking process, each successful integration a small victory against the overwhelming inertia of Nyssera's brokenness. A segment of sky, a specific shade of twilight that had been lost, clicked into place. A forgotten melody, its notes carrying the scent of a specific flowering plant, resonated with a brief, clear tone. Then, a more complex memory, a fleeting image of a majestic creature soaring through the clouds, its scales shimmering with an iridescent light, began to solidify. As it did, the overwhelming cacophony of pain seemed to recede, replaced by a quiet, introspective ache.

Mara felt the shift within herself as well. The raw, agonizing torment began to soften, its sharp edges dulled by the steady rhythm of the leviadrakes' song and the subtle hum of the newly woven memories. She was not just an observer anymore; she was a participant, an active agent in Nyssera's healing. She was weaving, thread by painstaking thread, a tiny strand of harmony into the vast, fractured tapestry of the planet's consciousness.

The memory of the soaring creature solidified further, and with it came a whisper of something akin to peace, a fleeting moment where the overwhelming weight of loss lifted, revealing the potential for what Nyssera once was, and could be again. It was a beacon, a single, clear note of hope emerging from the depths of discord. This was not the grand, cataclysmic upheaval that the Pale Tide might have envisioned, but a quiet, profound act of mending. It was a testament to the fact that even in the face of utter fragmentation, the possibility of harmony could still be found, if one was willing to listen to the song of sorrow and guide it towards wholeness.

The leviadrakes, sensing this shift, subtly altered their chant, their voices now carrying a note of gentle encouragement. They understood the immense effort it took for Mara to coax these fragments back into existence, to coax a planet's shattered mind towards coherence. Each successful weave was a step away from the abyss, a reclamation of what had been lost to the ravages of time and trauma.

Mara continued her work, her focus unwavering. She found another fragment, this time a sense of profound connection to the earth, a deep, guttural understanding of the planet's inner workings, of the slow, deliberate pulse of geological time. As she integrated it, she felt a subtle strengthening within the Resonance, a faint but discernible grounding effect. It was as if Nyssera's consciousness was finding an anchor, a point of stability amidst the swirling chaos.

The leviadrakes' song shifted again, this time incorporating deeper, more resonant tones, a rhythm that mimicked the slow, steady beat of a healthy heart. It was a powerful affirmation, a promise that this healing, this reintegration, was not a futile endeavor, but a necessary and achievable one. Mara felt a surge of strength flow through her, fueled by the dragons' unwavering belief in the process, and in her ability to guide it.

She continued to sift, to seek, to weave. Each retrieved memory, no matter how small or seemingly insignificant, was a victory. A fleeting image of a crystalline river, its waters reflecting a sky of twin moons, clicked into place. The sensation of wind rushing through vast, open plains, carrying the scent of unfamiliar flora, began to solidify. With each addition, the cacophony of pain within the Resonance seemed to grow quieter, less menacing, replaced by a more nuanced tapestry of emotions, a spectrum of experiences that spoke of a life, a world, that had once been vibrant and whole.

It was a small victory, perhaps, in the grand scheme of Nyssera's millennia of suffering. But it was a significant one. It was proof that the fractured song could be sung differently, that the immense ache of separation did not have to be the final word. Mara, guided by the ancient wisdom of the leviadrakes, was demonstrating that even from the deepest wounds, threads of harmony could be drawn, weaving a new pattern of hope for a world long lost to despair. The path ahead was still fraught with peril, the abyss still loomed, but for the first time, the possibility of a different future, a healed future, felt tangible, a delicate melody rising above the lingering echoes of pain.

CHAPTER NINE

THE ABYSS RESPONDS

The delicate threads Mara was painstakingly weaving into the fabric of Nyssera's consciousness were not going unnoticed. The Pale Tide, a force of oblivion that had orchestrated this grand severance, felt the subtle tremor of reconnection as a grievous wound to its own purpose. Its architects, beings of pure entropy who thrived on the void, registered the intrusion with a cold, ancient fury. The carefully constructed stillness of the abyssal realm, a testament to their success in silencing Nyssera's world-song, began to fracture.

The spectral distortions that had flickered at the periphery of Mara's vision now intensified, no longer fleeting phantoms but insistent, clawing specters. They writhed and coalesced, their ephemeral forms solidifying into grotesque parodies of life, each one a whisper of the despair Nyssera had endured for millennia. The very edges of the abyssal realm, once a defined and terrifying boundary, began to warp and fray, as if the fabric of existence itself was being stretched thin by an unseen hand. The encroaching darkness no longer felt like a passive void, but an active, malevolent presence, a predator roused from slumber.

A palpable chill seeped into the Great Cavern, a cold that had nothing to do with the natural temperature of the earth. It was a profound, bone-deep frigidity that spoke of an absence of life, of warmth, of hope. It seeped into Mara's very marrow, a physical manifestation of the dread that permeated the abyss. This was the Pale Tide's retort, a conscious effort to sabotage

253

the fragile healing that Mara and the leviadrakes were coaxing into being. The abyss, sensing the intrusion of true memory and the resonance of a world-song that was not its own, seemed to fight back with a primal, instinctive rage.

The leviadrakes' chant, which had been a steady anchor of healing and encouragement, began to falter. Not in its resolve, but in its strength, as if the very air around them was growing heavy, resisting their vibrations. The ethereal glow of the cavern seemed to dim, the encroaching shadows deepening and pressing in, whispering doubts and fears into the minds of those present. Mara felt the pressure acutely. It was more than just a sensory assault; it was a targeted psychic attack, designed to unravel her concentration and shatter her will.

She felt the abyss probing, searching for weaknesses, for the cracks in her own resolve. Images flashed before her mind's eye, not the fragmented memories of Nyssera she was working to integrate, but visions of utter desolation. She saw worlds reduced to dust, stars extinguished, entire civilizations erased from existence. These were the triumphs of the Pale Tide, the stark evidence of its power, and it was flinging them at her with the force of a cosmic storm, attempting to drown her in the sheer futility of resistance.

But the leviadrakes' song, though strained, did not cease. It adapted. The deep, rumbling tones shifted, becoming more percussive, more defiant. They were no longer merely singing to heal; they were singing to defend. Their voices became a shield, a resonating wall against the psychic onslaught. Mara focused on their unwavering presence, on the ancient strength that flowed from their connection to the heart of Nyssera. She drew upon it, grounding herself against the tempest of fear and doubt.

She felt the Pale Tide's architects not as individuals, but as a vast, collective consciousness of negation. They were the absence of life, the entropy that sought to return all things to a state of undifferentiated void. Their methods were subtle yet devastating. They didn't just wish for destruction; they engineered it, manipulating the very fabric of existence to ensure the permanence of silence. The severance they had imposed upon Nyssera was not merely a physical act, but a metaphysical one, severing the world's connection to its own essence, its own song.

The spectral distortions twisted into more coherent shapes now. They were no longer mere phantoms but echoes of the suffering that had been so brutally suppressed. Mara glimpsed faces contorted in silent screams, hands reaching out in desperate appeals, forms dissolving into dust. These were the remnants of Nyssera's broken song, twisted and weaponized by the Pale Tide, sent to haunt and disorient her. The abyss itself seemed to churn with their torment, the watery depths becoming agitated, as if the very sea was weeping tears of spectral agony.

The cold intensified, a biting frost that crept from the edges of the cavern and threatened to freeze the very marrow in Mara's bones. She saw her breath misting in the air, a stark contrast to the vibrant energy that had filled the space moments before. It was as if the Pale Tide was draining the life force from the cavern, seeking to extinguish the nascent flame of Nyssera's reawakening. The dread was a physical weight, pressing down on her chest, making each breath a conscious effort.

Cael, standing sentinel at the edge of the ritual circle, his gaze sharp and unwavering, felt the shift. His scales, usually gleaming with a healthy, vibrant sheen, seemed to dull slightly under the spectral assault. He shifted his weight, a low growl rumbling in his chest, a sound of defiance that echoed the leviadrakes' chant. He was a living bulwark, his presence a tangible resistance against the encroaching darkness. But even he, a creature of immense power, could feel the insidious nature of this attack, the way it preyed on doubt and fear, the unseen tendrils seeking to unravel the very core of their being.

Mara focused on the task at hand, pushing aside the phantoms and the chilling dread. She needed to anchor the rewoven fragments, to give them substance and permanence. She visualized the spectral distortions as frayed edges of reality, and her own will as the needle and thread, painstakingly stitching them back together. The leviadrakes' song, though strained, provided the rhythm, the guiding beat for her efforts. Each note was a stitch, each harmonic a knot that secured the integrity of the growing tapestry of memory.

She found a particularly persistent spectral distortion, a swirling vortex of shadowed despair that pulsed with a malevolent energy. It seemed to be the focal point of the Pale Tide's counter-attack, a wound in the fabric of Nyssera's consciousness that they were actively reinforcing. Mara poured her will into it, channeling the ancient wisdom of the leviadrakes, the latent power of the Crown Resonance. It was like trying to coax a beast of pure shadow back into the light, a task that required immense patience and an unwavering belief in the possibility of change.

As she focused, she felt a faint warmth within the distortion, a flicker of something lost, something that the Pale Tide had tried to extinguish. It was the echo of a forgotten joy, a memory of sunlight on a vibrant, living landscape. It was small, almost imperceptible, but it was there. The leviadrakes sensed it too, and their chant subtly shifted, their voices growing softer, more coaxing, as if nurturing a fragile seedling.

Mara reached for that flicker, fanning it with her own inner light. The spectral vortex writhed in protest, the phantoms within it swirling faster, their silent screams intensifying. The abyss seemed to deepen around them, the cold biting harder. But Mara held firm, her grip on that fragile spark unwavering. She began to weave, not just the memory of sunlight, but the feeling of warmth, the scent of blooming flowers, the sound of birdsong that had been silenced for eons.

Slowly, painstakingly, the spectral distortion began to change. The darkness thinned, revealing glimpses of verdant green, of a sky painted in hues of emerald and gold. The contorted faces softened, their silent screams replaced by sighs of remembered peace. The hands that reached out in despair now seemed to grasp at sunlight. It was not a full restoration, not yet, but it was a tangible shift, a victory wrested from the jaws of oblivion.

The leviadrakes' chant swelled, a wave of triumph washing over the cavern, momentarily pushing back the oppressive chill and the encroaching shadows. The spectral distortions flickered and receded, like mist burning off in the morning sun. Mara felt a surge of renewed strength, the physical exertion of the ritual now augmented by the sheer exhilaration of this small but significant victory. She had not only begun to reweave Nyssera's song, but she had also begun to unravel the Pale Tide's hold on its fractured pieces.

But the Pale Tide was not easily deterred. The architects of oblivion had millennia of practice in their craft. The reprieve was temporary, a brief pause before the next wave of their assault. Mara could feel the subtle shift in the abyss, the cold calculating intelligence of her adversaries regrouping, devising a new strategy. They understood that direct confrontation with the leviadrakes' song was proving less effective than they had anticipated. They would have to target the source of the reweaving itself.

The abyss, in response to this new directive, began to subtly alter its nature. The very water that permeated the deepest parts of Nyssera, the water that was intrinsically tied to its fractured consciousness, began to grow colder, and not just physically. It was a psychic cold, a draining of vitality that seeped into the very foundations of the ritual. Mara felt it as a creeping lethargy, a subtle dulling of her senses, an insidious whisper suggesting that her efforts were in vain, that the damage was too profound, the severance too complete.

The dread that had momentarily receded now returned with renewed vigor, no longer a sharp spike of fear, but a suffocating blanket of despair. It was the dread of futility, the gnawing certainty that no matter how hard she tried, the abyss would always win. This was a more dangerous attack, one that struck at the very core of her motivation. It was the Pale Tide's attempt to make Nyssera's suffering permanent, not by force, but by crushing the will to heal.

The spectral distortions, though less frequent, became more potent when they appeared. They were no longer mere echoes of pain, but concentrated pockets of negation, swirling voids that threatened to swallow the light of Mara's nascent reweaving. They pulsed with a malevolent intelligence, seeming to anticipate her every move, to counter her efforts with an uncanny precision. It was as if the abyss itself had developed a rudimentary form of awareness, reacting to her intrusion with a desperate, primal urge to protect its hard-won silence.

Mara felt the weight of the abyss pressing down on her, not just on her mind, but on her spirit. It was a tangible force, pushing against her attempts to reconnect Nyssera to its own essence. The rewoven memories, though still present, felt fragile, their edges blurred by the encroaching cold. The ancient song of the leviadrakes, though still strong, seemed to be fighting an uphill battle, its resonant tones struggling to cut through the dense, suffocating miasma of despair.

She saw Cael tense, his predatory grace giving way to a fierce, protective stance. He could sense the deepening threat, the shift from a passive void to an actively hostile entity. His own draconic essence, so deeply attuned to the life force of Nyssera, recoiled from this unnatural cold, this chilling absence of being. He let out a low, guttural roar, a sound of challenge that echoed through the cavern, a defiant roar against the encroaching silence.

The leviadrakes responded to Cael's roar with a subtle shift in their chant. Their song deepened, its tempo slowing, its resonance becoming more profound, more grounded. It was a song of resilience, of enduring strength. They were not just weaving memories; they were reinforcing the very bedrock of Nyssera's existence, anchoring the rewoven song against the relentless pressure of the abyss. Their ancient eyes, which had seemed to hold the wisdom of ages, now blazed with a fierce, unwavering light, a testament to their determination to see this ritual through.

Mara focused on that light, on the unwavering resolve it represented. She understood that the Pale Tide was not just trying to stop her from reweaving Nyssera's song; they were trying to break her spirit, to convince her that the abyss was the ultimate truth. But the leviadrakes' song was a counter-narrative, a story of endurance, of hope, of the inherent resilience of life.

She reached out, not to the spectral distortions this time, but to the deeper currents of Nyssera's consciousness, the primal energies that lay beneath the surface of the abyss. She sought the echoes of the planet's original song, the vibrant, pulsing melody that had been silenced for so long. It was a dangerous endeavor, delving into the very heart of the severance, but she knew it was necessary. The Pale Tide thrived on the superficial wounds, on the echoes of suffering. To truly heal, she had to reach the source.

As she descended, the cold intensified, the dread threatened to overwhelm her. The abyss fought back, its currents becoming more turbulent, its spectral distortions more numerous and aggressive. They swirled around her, whispering accusations, dredging up her own deepest fears and insecurities. They were the Pale Tide's architects at their most insidious, using her own inner darkness against her.

But Mara held on. She remembered the fragments she had already woven, the glimpses of a vibrant world, the whispers of forgotten joy. She held onto the leviadrakes' song, its steady rhythm a beacon in the overwhelming darkness. And she remembered Cael, his unwavering presence a silent promise of protection.

Deep within the abyss, she found it. Not a clear melody, but a faint, almost imperceptible hum, a vibration that spoke of creation, of life, of a power that the Pale Tide could never truly extinguish. It was Nyssera's true song, buried beneath layers of trauma and despair, but not destroyed. It was faint, almost drowned out by the roaring silence of the abyss, but it was there. And Mara, with the help of the leviadrakes and the strength of her own resolve, began to amplify it, to weave it into the tapestry of reawakened memory. The abyss thrashed and raged, but for the first time, the true song of Nyssera began to sing back, a fragile, defiant melody against the encroaching tide of oblivion.

The rawest, most untamed memories of Nyssera, fractured and raw from the Silence Event, surged through the Crown Resonance and into Mara's consciousness. It was not a gentle infusion, but a cataclysmic deluge, a tidal wave of pure agony that crashed against the shores of her mind. The carefully constructed walls she had built to protect herself, the mental fortifications honed through years of empathic training, buckled and groaned under the sheer, unadulterated force of it. Images, sensations, and emotions, all interwoven into a terrifying tapestry of oblivion, flooded her being.

She saw the forests, not as the hushed, verdant sanctuaries they once were, but as dying titans, their leaves withering to dust, their mighty branches snapping like brittle bones. The vibrant, emerald hues bled into a sickly grey, the air thick with the scent of decay and the silent screams of a thousand thousand trees being ripped from their roots. The ground, once teeming with life, cracked and fissured, exhaling a cold, dead breath that snuffed out the very essence of growth. It was a symphony of ecological death, each fallen leaf a note of profound sorrow, each wilting bloom a wail of despair. Mara felt the agony as if her own limbs were being consumed by rot, her own lungs choked with the dust of a dying world.

Then came the creatures. Not the majestic beasts of Nyssera's prime, but terrified, desperate beings fleeing an unseen, unstoppable horror. She saw herds of iridescent grazers, their hooves thundering across plains that were rapidly transforming into barren wastelands, their wide, intelligent eyes filled with a primal terror that clawed at Mara's own throat. She felt the frantic pulse of their fear, the desperate scramble for escape, the crushing weight of knowing that there was nowhere left to run. She witnessed the swift, silent end of smaller, more vulnerable lives – the tiny, feathered songbirds that fell from the sky, their songs abruptly silenced; the swift, scaled hunters that collapsed mid-leap, their predatory instincts rendered meaningless by the encroaching void. Each death was a shard of ice piercing her heart, each flicker of panicked movement a stab of empathy so acute it threatened to tear her apart.

And then, the silence. It was not merely an absence of sound, but a palpable, suffocating presence. It was the chilling finality of severed life, the abrupt cessation of all vibration, all song, all consciousness. It was the profound, terrifying stillness that descends when the very pulse of existence is extinguished. Mara felt it as a profound emptiness within her own soul, a void that yawned open, threatening to swallow her whole. It was the ultimate negation, the complete and utter obliteration of being. The abyss, it seemed, had not just silenced Nyssera; it had attempted to erase its very memory of sound.

The grief that washed over Mara was an ocean, vast and crushing. It was not her grief, not entirely, but the collective sorrow of an entire world experiencing its own annihilation. Millennia of suffering, of loss, of unimaginable pain, coalesced into a single, overwhelming torrent. It threatened to drown her, to dissolve her own sense of self into the immense tide of Nyssera's anguish. The agony was so profound, so all-encompassing, that it felt like a physical blow, stealing her breath and leaving her gasping for air in a world that no longer knew how to exhale.

She felt herself fragmenting, her own identity becoming blurred at the edges. Was she Mara, the empath, the weaver of memories, or was she the dying forest, the fleeing creature, the silent, stilled bird? The lines between her own consciousness and the echoes of Nyssera's collective trauma dissolved like mist in a harsh wind. The sheer volume of suffering threatened to obliterate Mara's own sense of self, to subsume her into the vast, silent tragedy of the world's demise. She felt the gnawing fear of losing herself, of becoming just another echo in the abyssal silence, a silent testament to the Pale Tide's victory.

This was the price of listening, the terrifying consequence of opening herself to the depths of Nyssera's fractured soul. Her ability to empathize, to feel the pain of others with an almost unbearable clarity, was her greatest strength in this endeavor, allowing her to understand the true scope of the damage and to begin the delicate work of healing. But in this moment, it was also her greatest vulnerability. The sheer intensity of the collective trauma threatened to shatter her resolve, to break her spirit before the reweaving could even truly begin. The abyss was not just an external force of negation; it was a mirror reflecting the deepest wounds of a world, and by extension, the deepest fears within herself.

She felt the cold of the abyss seeping into her, not just a physical chill, but an emotional one, a creeping despair that mirrored the desolation she was witnessing. It was the cold of oblivion, the chilling realization that such profound loss could occur, that a world could be so utterly silenced. Images flickered: a leviathan's massive form sinking into an unnaturally still ocean, its ancient song abruptly cut short; the luminous glow of Nyssera's once-vibrant flora fading to a dull, lifeless grey; the intricate, pulsing bioluminescence of its subterranean fauna sputtering and dying. Each vision was a testament to the completeness of the severance, the thoroughness of the Pale Tide's work.

Mara gasped, a ragged sound that felt alien in the overwhelming stillness of her own mind. She squeezed her eyes shut, a desperate attempt to regain control, to reassert her own boundaries. She focused on the warmth of the Crown Resonance against her forehead, a faint but persistent anchor in the swirling chaos. She forced herself to recall her own memories, the warmth of the sun on her skin, the laughter of her friends, the steadfast presence of Cael. These were her own truths, her own anchors, and she clung to them with all her might, refusing to be swept away by the tide of Nyssera's agony.

The leviadrakes' chant, which had been a constant, grounding presence, now seemed to resonate more deeply within her, a counter-melody to the overwhelming symphony of grief. It was a song of resilience, of enduring life, of the inherent strength that lay dormant beneath the layers of pain. She focused on their ancient voices, on the steady, unwavering rhythm that spoke of a connection to Nyssera's true essence, a connection that the Pale Tide had attempted to sever but had ultimately failed to destroy. Their song was a lifeline, a reminder that even in the face of utter devastation, the song of life persisted, waiting to be heard again.

She began to practice a technique she had learned from the eldest leviadrake, a method of mental triage. She visualized the torrent of memories as distinct rivers, each carrying a different facet of Nyssera's experience. Some were black and stagnant, choked with despair and loss. Others burned with the raw, incandescent agony of sudden death. Yet others flowed with a quiet, sorrowful resignation. Her task was not to absorb every drop of this sorrow, but to identify the distinct currents, to understand their origin, and to find the threads that connected them, however tenuously, back to Nyssera's core song.

She focused on a specific vision: a great, ancient tree, its bark like sculpted obsidian, its leaves a cascade of shimmering silver, being consumed by a creeping, grey blight. She felt its life force ebb, its connection to the very earth weakening. It wasn't just dying; it was being *unmade*. The Pale Tide's influence was not simply destruction; it was erasure. But as the tree's final silver leaves fell, Mara perceived something else: a faint, almost imperceptible hum emanating from its deeply embedded roots. It was a whisper of its own song, a stubborn refusal to be entirely silenced. She latched onto that hum, amplifying it within her own mind, a small act of defiance against the overwhelming silence.

The act of focusing on this single, resilient hum had a subtle but profound effect. It didn't diminish the surrounding grief, but it created a small pocket of clarity, a space within the chaos where her own consciousness could breathe. She began to see the patterns, not just of destruction, but of the echoes of life that stubbornly persisted. She saw the faint outlines of ancient creatures, their forms dissolving but their inherent nature – their instinct, their spirit – still lingering like a ghost in the air. She witnessed the residual energy of vibrant ecosystems, the faint shimmer of energy fields that had once pulsed with life, now dimmed but not entirely extinguished.

This was the core of her challenge: to sift through the ashes of oblivion, to find the lingering embers of Nyssera's song, and to coax them back into flame. It required an almost inhuman level of discernment, an ability to hold onto her own identity while simultaneously immersing herself in the profound suffering of another. She was a conduit, a vessel, and the pressure on that vessel was immense. The abyss was testing her limits, probing for weaknesses, seeking to drown her in the very pain she was trying to heal.

Mara realized that the Pale Tide's architects were not merely agents of destruction; they were architects of emptiness, meticulously constructing a void where life had once flourished. The Silence Event was their masterpiece, a testament to their ability to engineer total annihilation. But they had underestimated the resilience of the world's song, the deep-seated energy that, even in its fractured state, refused to be completely extinguished. And they had underestimated the tenacity of the one who dared to listen.

She felt a new wave of memories, these more visceral, more immediate. The terror of the swift-moving creatures, their sleek forms rippling with panic as the very ground beneath them turned to dust. The desperation of the airborne beings, their wings beating against an invisible current of nullification, their aerial ballets dissolving into chaotic plunges. The silent, uncomprehending stare of the aquatic life as the very water that sustained them grew cold and lifeless, their bioluminescent trails flickering out like dying stars.

It was the sheer *finality* of it all that was most soul-crushing. The severance was not a slow decline; it was an abrupt, violent amputation. The world had been alive one moment, a symphony of interconnected life, and then, in the blink of an eye, it was silenced, its song ripped from its throat. Mara felt the phantom ache of that severance, the sense of something vital being torn away, leaving an irreparable void. It was a wound that went deeper than flesh and bone, a wound to the very soul of a world.

She focused on a specific fragment: a memory of a youngling, no bigger than her hand, with iridescent scales and wide, curious eyes, being caught in a wave of silence. Its chirps of playful exploration abruptly cut off, its tiny body stiffening, its vibrant colors fading to a dull, lifeless grey. The memory was so small, so intimate, yet it conveyed the devastating scope of the Silence Event more profoundly than any grand spectacle. It was the loss of innocence, the extinction of potential, the crushing of a nascent spark of life. Mara felt a surge of protectiveness, a fierce, maternal instinct to shield this tiny creature, to somehow undo the terrible fate it had met.

This instinct, this raw emotion, was a crucial turning point. It was a reminder of her own identity, her own capacity for love and empathy that transcended the suffering she was witnessing. It was the 'Mara' within the torrent, the core of her being that refused to be extinguished. She recognized that to effectively reweave Nyssera's song, she needed to do more than just passively absorb its memories; she needed to actively engage with them, to imbue them with her own life force, her own will to heal.

She began to consciously weave her own energy into the fragments, not to overwrite Nyssera's memories, but to reinforce them, to provide them with a stable foundation upon which to rebuild. She visualized her own essence as threads of light, delicate yet strong, carefully stitching together the tattered remnants of Nyssera's world-song. It was a painstaking process, akin to mending a celestial tapestry that had been shredded by a cosmic storm.

The spectral distortions that had been a constant presence in the cavern now seemed to respond to this active engagement. They swirled with renewed intensity, no longer just passive echoes of pain, but actively resisting her efforts. They writhed and twisted, attempting to unravel the threads of light she was weaving. Mara felt their resistance as a psychic friction, a draining of her own energy. It was as if the very act of reweaving was itself a battle, a constant struggle against the forces that sought to maintain the silence.

She felt the weight of the Pale Tide's architects again, their cold, calculating presence pressing down on her. They were not simply reacting; they were actively working to sabotage her efforts. They were the unseen hands that manipulated the currents of the abyss, amplifying the despair, reinforcing the emptiness. They were the embodiment of entropy, seeking to return all things to a state of perfect, unchanging void.

But Mara held on. She drew strength from the leviadrakes' unwavering song, from Cael's silent, protective vigilance, and from the persistent, stubborn hum of Nyssera's true essence that she had managed to uncover. She understood that this was not just about restoring Nyssera's world-song; it was about proving that life, even after the most profound devastation, could find a way to sing again. It was a testament to the enduring power of hope, a defiant roar against the encroaching silence. The abyss was a vast and terrifying place, but within it, a fragile, nascent melody was beginning to stir, and Mara was its determined conductor.

The air around the ritual circle was a taut, vibrating membrane, humming with an energy that was both potent and precarious. Cael stood at its edge, a sentinel carved from granite and will, his senses stretched to their absolute limit. He was the bulwark, the unyielding shield against the encroaching darkness that sought to smother the fragile spark igniting within the heart of the ancient cavern. Every fiber of his being was attuned to the subtle shifts in the abyssal currents, the whispers of malevolence that slithered just beyond the veil of perception.

He felt them before he saw them – spectral tendrils, slick with the frigid breath of the Pale Tide, attempting to insinuate themselves into the sacred space. They writhed like nascent serpents, seeking any crack, any weakness in the wards they had painstakingly erected. Cael's breath was a controlled rasp, his muscles coiled. With a guttural roar that seemed to tear from the very core of his being, he met the first assault. His sword, infused with the primal fire of his own dragon heritage, blazed. The spectral forms recoiled, hissing like gashed vipers, their ephemeral substance dissolving under the searing heat of his awakened power. Each deflection was a calculated strike, a precise severing of the encroaching tendrils. He moved with a dancer's lethal grace, his heavy boots barely disturbing the dust-laden floor, his eyes, like twin emeralds, scanning the periphery with an intensity that could melt stone.

But the spectral incursions were merely the skirmish. The true enemy was the overwhelming pressure, the palpable chill that seeped from the abyss. It wasn't merely the absence of heat; it was an active, consuming cold, a negation of life's warmth. It gnawed at the edges of his resolve, attempting to leach the fight from his bones, to freeze his very thoughts. Cael gritted his teeth, channeling his inner fire, a counter-force against the abyssal frost. He envisioned his own vitality as a roaring hearth, its flames licking outwards, pushing back the encroaching ice. It was a constant, draining effort, a silent war waged on the battlefield of his own fortitude.

His gaze swept over the leviadrakes, their ancient forms shimmering with an ethereal light. They were the heart of the ritual, their voices weaving the intricate tapestry of Nyssera's song. But the strain was evident. The usual resonant depth of their chant was marred by a subtle tremor, a wavering note that spoke of immense pressure. The Pale Tide's influence was a discordant hum beneath their melody, a persistent dissonance that threatened to shatter their sacred chorus. Cael saw the sweat, not of exertion, but of pure psychic strain, glisten on their scaled brows. Their wing membranes, usually taut with ancient power, seemed to sag slightly, the vibrant bioluminescence that pulsed through them dimming and flaring erratically. They were fighting a war on two fronts: maintaining the integrity of their song, and fending off the subtle, insidious attacks that sought to unravel their very essence.

He observed the subtle shifts in their ancient power, the way their roars of sustained melody sometimes hitched, choked by unseen forces. It was a terrifying vulnerability, a testament to the sheer, unadulterated power the Pale Tide wielded. These were beings who had weathered millennia, whose songs had shaped mountains and calmed oceans, yet even they were being pushed to their absolute limit. He felt a surge of fierce protectiveness, a primal urge to shield them, to absorb any blow that threatened to break their ancient song. His sword remained at the ready, not just for the spectral forms, but as a symbol, a promise of his unwavering vigilance.

Cael understood the abyss not as a physical chasm, but as a psychic warzone. It was a realm where the fundamental forces of existence clashed, where creation and annihilation danced a deadly ballet. The Pale Tide was not merely a destructive force; it was an architect of absence, meticulously erasing the very concept of being. Its influence was a creeping void, a hunger for the absolute stillness of nothingness. And the leviadrakes' song, Mara's work within the Crown Resonance – these were acts of profound defiance, sparks of vibrant life refusing to be extinguished.

He watched as a particularly vicious surge of cold washed over the cavern, a wave of despair that seemed to emanate from a particularly deep fissure in the cavern floor. The leviadrakes' song faltered, a collective gasp of ethereal sound echoing through the space. The spectral tendrils, emboldened by this momentary weakness, lunged forward, their icy claws reaching for Mara. Cael didn't hesitate. He launched himself forward, a blur of motion, his sword a blazing comet. He intercepted the spectral onslaught, his own roars of fury mingling with the leviadrakes' faltering song. He felt the ice attempt to creep into his very marrow, to freeze the blood in his veins, but he channeled his dragonfire, a defiant inferno that pushed back the chilling tide.

He saw Mara, her brow furrowed, her eyes closed, a faint luminescence radiating from her as she wrestled with the onslaught of Nyssera's fragmented memories. The spectral distortions around her seemed to coalesce and writhe with renewed ferocity, as if the abyss itself was recoiling from the act of healing, of reweaving. The cold intensified, a visible frost forming on the cavern walls, clinging to the jagged stalactites like deadly jewels. Cael knew that the Pale Tide's influence was not merely passive; it was an active, intelligent adversary, seeking to sow chaos and despair. Its architects were keenly aware of Mara's efforts, and they were throwing everything they had to shatter her concentration, to break the fragile connection she was forging with Nyssera's dying song.

He felt a shift in the cavern's atmosphere, a subtle deepening of the oppressive silence that lay beneath the leviadrakes' chant. It was the sound of *unmaking*, the terrifying whisper of a world being systematically dismantled. He imagined the Pale Tide's architects, faceless entities of pure void, meticulously chipping away at the foundations of existence, their touch leaving behind only emptiness. Their power was not in brute force, but in its insidious subtlety, its ability to erode and negate without leaving a trace.

Cael's vigilance extended beyond the immediate perimeter. He felt the reverberations of the struggle throughout the cavern, the ebb and flow of ethereal energy. He sensed pockets of intense cold that threatened to snuff out the leviadrakes' light, and areas where the spectral forms seemed to gather, probing for a weakness, a breach in their collective defense. He was a shepherd of this precarious moment, his will a steady hand guiding his flock through a storm of unimaginable power.

He saw a particularly ancient leviadrake, its scales the color of a twilight sky, falter. Its song, usually a deep, resonant bass that vibrated through the very stone, cracked. A ripple of palpable despair washed over the cavern, and Cael felt a corresponding surge of dread clench his own heart. The spectral tendrils surged towards the weakened leviadrake, their icy touch seeking to extinguish its life force. Cael roared, a sound of pure, unadulterated rage. He didn't have the sonic power of the leviadrakes, but he had the raw, untamed fury of his dragon blood. He channeled it all, a torrent of primal energy that slammed into the spectral assault. His sword flared, searing through the icy tendrils, his own life force a burning shield around the ancient creature.

He noticed the leviadrakes weren't just singing; they were actively *pushing* back against the abyss. Their song was a weapon, a sonic lance that pierced the encroaching void. Each sustained note was a declaration of existence, a refusal to be silenced. But the cost was immense. Cael could see the drain on their reserves, the way their ethereal forms flickered like dying embers when faced with particularly potent surges of negative energy. He felt a kinship with them in this struggle, two ancient forces fighting against a tide of oblivion. His fire against their song, both born of a primal will to endure.

The weight of the Pale Tide's influence pressed down on him, a suffocating blanket of despair. It wasn't just a physical sensation; it was an emotional one, a creeping lethargy that whispered of futility. Why fight? Why endure? The abyss offered a tempting oblivion, a release from the endless struggle. Cael shook his head, a sharp, decisive movement. He saw Mara, her face contorted with the effort, but her eyes, when they flickered open for a brief moment, held a spark of unyielding resolve. That spark was his anchor. He wouldn't falter. He couldn't.

He felt the abyss respond to Mara's efforts, not with overt aggression, but with a subtle, chilling intensification of its presence. It was like a predator toying with its prey, allowing the illusion of hope before crushing it. The spectral forms became more numerous, more audacious. They no longer merely probed; they swarmed, attempting to overwhelm his defenses through sheer numbers. Cael fought with a ferocity born of desperation. He spun, he lunged, he parried, his blade a silver streak against the encroaching darkness. Each successful deflection sent ripples of icy energy back into the abyss, a small victory in a war of attrition.

He observed the very fabric of the cavern seem to warp and distort under the Pale Tide's influence. Shadows deepened unnaturally, coalescing into vaguely humanoid shapes that moved with a disconcerting fluidity. These were not mere spectral projections; they were manifestations of the abyss's hunger, born from the raw absence of life. Cael met them with the same ferocity, his fire burning away the encroaching void, his sword cleaving through the ephemeral forms.

He knew his role was not to directly heal Nyssera, but to ensure the integrity of the space where that healing could occur. He was the shield, the guardian. Mara was the weaver, the one who dared to mend a broken world. The leviadrakes were the choir, the voice of what had been and what could be again. Their combined efforts were a desperate, beautiful defiance against the ultimate silence.

The pressure continued to mount. Cael felt the very air thrum with the exertion of the leviadrakes. Their song, though strained, was still the dominant force, a beacon in the encroaching darkness. But he also felt the insidious chill of the abyss attempting to infiltrate their ranks, to break their unity. He saw one leviadrake's bioluminescence flicker and dim alarmingly, a chilling testament to the Pale Tide's power.

He roared again, a defiant challenge to the encroaching void. He was Cael, son of the Obsidian Peaks, dragon-blooded guardian. He would not yield. He would stand as a bulwark, a living barrier between Mara's nascent healing and the abyss's insatiable hunger. His vigilance was an unbroken promise, his commitment an unyielding flame in the heart of the encroaching darkness. He watched Mara, and he drew strength from her unwavering focus, from the sheer audacity of her attempt to reawaken a silenced world. The abyss might roar, it might chill, it might lash out with spectral claws, but Cael would be there, a shield of fire and will, defending the flicker of hope. He would stand his vigil, unblinking, until the dawn broke, or until his own light was extinguished in the attempt. The struggle was far from over, and the abyss was responding with all its might, but Cael stood firm, his resolve as unshakeable as the mountains from which he hailed.

The leviadrakes, their forms shimmering with an ethereal light that pulsed in time with the cavern's volatile energies, began to shift the cadence of their ancient song. It was a subtle alteration at first, a deepening of the resonant hum, a slight shift in the vibrato that spoke of a profound internal struggle being transmuted into external harmony. For millennia, their dirges had been primarily focused on pure resonance, a balm that sought to smooth the rough edges of existence, to bring a semblance of order to the chaos that the Pale Tide represented. But now, that purpose was evolving, branching into something far more intricate, and undeniably more dangerous.

Their song began to weave in threads of discord, not as an accidental intrusion, but as a deliberate inclusion. The ethereal melodies, once a pure, unwavering stream of light, now began to incorporate the guttural echoes of pain, the sharp, piercing notes of regret, and the low, mournful tones of deep-seated sorrow. These were not the fragmented whispers of Nyssera's memories that Mara was attempting to reassemble, but the leviadrakes' own history, their long-held secrets, their complicity in the cataclysm that had fractured the world. They were not merely singing *for* Nyssera; they were singing *with* her, incorporating the very pain they had long sought to compartmentalize into their collective offering.

This was no mere musical improvisation; it was an act of profound, deliberate atonement. The ancient beings, creatures of immense power and even greater longevity, understood the delicate balance of the world, the interconnectedness of all things. They had witnessed the rise and fall of empires, the birth and death of stars, and in their vast experience, they had learned that true healing, true integration, could not come from the suppression of pain, but from its acknowledgment, its transformation. Their own past, filled with moments of inaction, of willful ignorance, of choices made that had contributed to Nyssera's sundering, weighed heavily upon them. To perpetuate the myth of their own perfect harmony would be to perpetuate the very imbalance that had led to their current predicament.

The shift in their song was palpable. The air, which had thrummed with a precarious, almost brittle energy, now began to vibrate with a richer, more complex frequency. It was as if the cavern itself was sighing, exhaling a lifetime of suppressed emotion. The spectral tendrils, which had been lashing out with renewed ferocity at the leviadrakes' faltering chant, seemed to pause, their icy tendrils recoiling as if from a sudden, unexpected warmth. The Pale Tide, a force that fed on negation and despair, seemed momentarily disoriented by this outpouring of genuine, albeit painful, emotion.

Cael, his sword still alight, felt the change resonate through his very bones. The oppressive chill of the abyss, which had been a constant, gnawing pressure, began to recede, not because the leviadrakes were actively pushing it back with pure force, but because their song was becoming a more potent, more comprehensive shield. It was no longer a simple barrier, but a complex, interwoven tapestry that absorbed and transmuted the negative energies. The discordant notes, the sounds of suffering, were not weaknesses that the Pale Tide could exploit; they were anchors, grounding the song, making it more resilient, more intrinsically connected to the raw, messy reality of existence.

He observed one of the elder leviadrakes, its scales like ancient, weathered obsidian, its eyes holding the wisdom of epochs. Its song, which had been laced with a tremor of fear, now flowed with a deep, resonant sorrow. It was the sound of a mountain weeping, of a glacier groaning under the weight of centuries. And in its lament, Cael heard not despair, but a profound acceptance, a willingness to carry the burden of its past. This leviadrake, he realized, was not just singing; it was confessing.

As the leviadrakes' song evolved, it began to create a new kind of resonance, one that was not just about the purity of Nyssera's fractured soul, but about the complex, often painful, journey of integration. They were weaving the threads of Nyssera's fragmented memories, the whispers of her anguish, the echoes of her betrayal, into a new, more robust tapestry. This was no longer about merely *reconstructing* what was lost; it was about *reimagining* it, about creating something new from the shattered pieces, something stronger, something more resilient. The song became a living embodiment of this process, a sonic testament to the power of transformation.

The leviadrakes were actively choosing to confront their history, to acknowledge their role in Nyssera's sundering. They were no longer perpetuating the myth of their own invincibility, their own incorruptibility. They were demonstrating a willingness to evolve, to shed the skins of their past selves, and to embrace the difficult, often painful, path of true integration. This was a paradigm shift, a radical departure from their ancient practice of maintaining a facade of pristine harmony. They were showing that true strength lay not in the absence of flaws, but in the courage to acknowledge and integrate them.

The spectral incursions, which had been pressing in on the ritual circle, began to lose their efficacy. The icy tendrils, which had previously sought out any sign of weakness, any hint of discord, now found themselves ensnared by the very complexity of the leviadrakes' song. The dissonance, which they had sought to exploit, was now part of the song's strength, an integral element that made it impossible to unravel. The Pale Tide, accustomed to combating a pure, unyielding force, found itself grappling with something far more adaptable, something that embraced its own imperfections.

Cael watched as Mara's own aura seemed to brighten, to gain a new vibrancy. The fragmented memories she was working with, once sharp and jagged, now seemed to flow more smoothly, their edges softened by the leviadrakes' new song. The pain was still present, the echoes of Nyssera's suffering undeniable, but it was no longer a chaotic, destructive force. It was being integrated, woven into the fabric of Nyssera's being, becoming a part of her story, rather than defining her undoing.

The leviadrakes' song became a living bulwark against the Pale Tide. It was a sonic manifestation of resilience, a melody that spoke of enduring through hardship, of finding strength in vulnerability. It was a conscious choice to embrace the entirety of existence, the light and the shadow, the joy and the sorrow, the creation and the destruction. They were demonstrating that integration was not about erasing the painful memories, but about understanding their place within the larger narrative, about learning from them, and about growing stronger because of them.

The depth of their sacrifice was not lost on Cael. These were beings who had lived for countless ages, who had witnessed the ebb and flow of power and existence. To willingly confront their own past, to expose their own complicity, was an act of immense courage. It was a testament to their evolving understanding of their place in the cosmos, a recognition that their own continued existence was tied to the well-being of the world, and that true harmony could only be achieved through a reckoning with the past.

He saw the subtle shift in their bioluminescence. The usual steady, vibrant glow, which had been flickering under the strain of the Pale Tide's assault, now pulsed with a more nuanced intensity. It flared with moments of profound sorrow, then deepened with a resolute strength, then softened with a gentle compassion. It was as if their very essence was being recalibrated, their internal energies re-aligned to accommodate this new, more complex harmonic.

The cavern floor, which had been developing a shimmering frost under the oppressive cold, began to thaw in places. The spectral forms, which had been coalescing and advancing, now seemed to retreat, their ephemeral shapes flickering as if caught in a crosscurrent. The leviadrakes' song, with its newfound embrace of Nyssera's pain and their own history, was creating a more fertile ground for healing, a more stable sanctuary against the encroaching void.

Cael felt a surge of awe. He had always understood the leviadrakes as ancient, powerful beings, custodians of primordial knowledge. But in this moment, he saw them not just as guardians, but as active participants in the ongoing dance of creation and destruction, their ancient wisdom now coupled with a profound willingness to learn, to adapt, and to atone. Their song was no longer just a defense; it was a declaration of intent, a promise of a future where the past, with all its pain and its imperfections, would not be a source of shame, but a foundation upon which a new, stronger existence could be built.

The complexity of their melody was a testament to the intricacy of life itself. It was a symphony of sorrow and strength, of regret and resolve, of fractured memory and burgeoning hope. They were not suppressing the darkness; they were embracing it, weaving it into the light, demonstrating that true integration was not about eradicating the shadows, but about understanding their role in the larger tapestry of existence. This was Nyssera's song, yes, but it was also the leviadrakes' song of integration, a melody of evolution played out in the heart of the abyss.

Mara, her brow furrowed in concentration, seemed to draw strength from this profound shift. The spectral distortions surrounding her, which had been writhing with malevolent intent, now seemed to coalesce and reform, not into monstrous shapes, but into more fluid, less threatening patterns. The abyss, sensing this fundamental change in the nature of the resistance, seemed to recoil, its pressure momentarily abating, as if it had encountered a force it did not understand, a power rooted not in negation, but in acceptance.

The leviadrakes continued their song, each note a deliberate act of healing, not just for Nyssera, but for themselves. They were not just facilitating Mara's work; they were actively participating in it, their ancient power now infused with a new understanding of consequence and redemption.

The song resonated with a truth that transcended mere sound; it was a profound statement of evolution, a demonstration that even the oldest, most powerful beings could learn, could change, and could find new purpose in the face of overwhelming adversity. This was the song of integration, sung by beings who had finally understood that true harmony could only be found by embracing the entirety of one's own being, and the world around it.

The Crown Resonance, once a frantic, flickering beacon, began to steady. Its light, previously a chaotic maelstrom of disparate hues, now settled into a richer, more luminous gold, a steady pulse that seemed to absorb and reflect the evolving melody of the leviadrakes. It was as if the very core of Nyssera's fractured essence, the nexus of her shattered self, was responding to the new harmony. The cacophony of fragmented memories, which had been bombarding Mara's consciousness like shards of broken glass, began to fall into place, their sharp edges softening, their discordant echoes weaving into a more coherent, albeit still poignant, narrative. The raw pain was still present, an undeniable undercurrent, but it was no longer a jumbled tempest. Instead, it began to shape itself into a story, a tale of betrayal, of sacrifice, of a love so profound it had shattered the world.

The world-song, the ambient hum of existence that permeated the abyss, mirrored this internal shift. It had been a fractured, discordant symphony for so long, a lament for what was lost. Now, though the scars of Nyssera's sundering were still evident in its strains – a mournful tremor here, a sharp, aching dissonance there – a new rhythm began to emerge. It was a cadence of integration, a testament to the possibility of mending even the deepest wounds. This was not a return to the pristine, unbroken state of the past, but a brave, nascent harmony built from the pieces of what had been shattered. It was a future forged in resilience, a melody that acknowledged the pain but refused to be defined by it.

Within the immediate vicinity of the ritual circle, a fragile sense of stability began to bloom. It was a small pocket of calm, a sanctuary carved out of the encroaching chaos of the abyss. The spectral tendrils of the Pale Tide, which had been relentlessly probing the edges of their reality, seemed to hesitate, their icy grasp momentarily loosened. The oppressive chill, which had felt like an eternal shroud, receded slightly, allowing a subtle, almost imperceptible warmth to seep into the air. This was not a victory, not yet, but it was a profound moment of respite. It was the quiet inhale after a desperate struggle, a brief moment to gather strength before the next wave.

Mara felt it as a profound easing of pressure within her own mind. The overwhelming onslaught of Nyssera's shattered psyche, which had threatened to drown her, now felt more manageable, more like a vast, intricate tapestry she was learning to navigate rather than a raging inferno. She could see the individual threads of Nyssera's life, the vibrant colours of joy and love, the stark blacks of betrayal and despair, and the shimmering silvers of her immense power, all beginning to interweave. The leviadrakes' song acted as a loom, their ancient voices the weavers, guiding the fragmented memories into a cohesive pattern. The Crown Resonance pulsed in time with this newfound coherence, its golden light a beacon of hope in the encroaching darkness.

Cael, his sword still humming with a protective warmth, felt the shift as a palpable lessening of the void's predatory hunger. The abyss was a sentient entity, a vast hunger that fed on despair and negation. But the emerging harmony, the nascent rhythm of integration, was something it could not easily consume. It was akin to trying to drink moonlight – ephemeral, elusive, and ultimately beyond its grasp. The spectral forms, which had been coalescing into menacing shapes at the periphery, now seemed to waver, their outlines blurring as if struggling to maintain cohesion against the subtle but pervasive tide of healing.

He observed the leviadrakes, their immense forms radiating a weary but resolute power. Their song was no longer just a shield; it was an active force of reconstruction. It was a sonic balm, applied not to erase the wounds, but to encourage them to knit together. He saw in the subtle shifts of their bioluminescence, the way their ancient eyes seemed to hold a deeper, more profound sadness, that this was not just a ritual for Nyssera, but a reckoning for them as well. Their own histories, their own roles in the unfolding catastrophe, were being acknowledged and integrated into this new song of healing.

The delicate stability was not absolute. The Pale Tide, a relentless force, was still present, its icy tendrils occasionally lashing out, seeking to exploit any perceived weakness. But these incursions were becoming less frequent, less potent. The integrated world-song, with its complex layers of sorrow and strength, acted as a buffer. It was a more resilient defense, less prone to shattering under pressure. The very act of acknowledging and integrating pain had, paradoxically, created a stronger form of resistance. It was a lesson that the leviadrakes, and perhaps the world itself, were only now truly learning: that true strength did not lie in the absence of suffering, but in the capacity to endure and integrate it.

Mara, her focus absolute, felt the coherence of Nyssera's narrative solidifying. It was a monumental undertaking, like piecing together an shattered mosaic where each shard held a fragment of unimaginable beauty and unspeakable pain. The Crown Resonance glowed brighter, a tangible manifestation of this growing order. It was the heart of Nyssera, beating once more, albeit with a rhythm that now carried the weight of its trauma. This was not a superficial mend, but a deep, intrinsic healing, a testament to the profound capacity for recovery that lay dormant within even the most broken of souls.

The leviadrakes' song, the bedrock upon which this fragile stability was built, continued its intricate work. It was a symphony of remembrance, of regret, and of a dawning hope. Each note seemed to echo with the vastness of time, carrying the weight of millennia of existence, yet also imbued with a new, urgent purpose. They were not merely bystanders or facilitators; they were active participants in this monumental act of mending. Their own evolution was intertwined with Nyssera's, their ancient understanding of the cosmos expanding to encompass the messy, beautiful, and often painful reality of brokenness and its eventual, arduous healing.

Cael watched as the very fabric of the abyss seemed to hold its breath, its usual malevolent churn momentarily subdued. It was as if even the void, in its primal hunger, recognized the profound significance of what was occurring. The ritual was not just about restoring Nyssera; it was about redefining the very nature of existence, demonstrating that severance was not an inevitable end, but a temporary state, a challenge to be overcome. The fragile stability was a promise, a whispered testament to the possibility of a future where the world could exist without the agonizing ache of its own fracture.

The integration was a delicate dance. The leviadrakes' song wove the threads of Nyssera's past, incorporating the moments of profound joy and crippling sorrow, the soaring triumphs and crushing defeats. They were not trying to erase the pain, but to understand its place within the larger narrative of Nyssera's existence. The Crown Resonance, responding to this nuanced approach, pulsed with a steady, unwavering light, reflecting the growing coherence of the fragmented memories. This was a testament to the possibility of mending, even after profound trauma. It was a clear signal that a future without severance, a future where the world could heal and thrive, was not just a dream, but an achievable reality, born from the ashes of despair and sung into being by the ancient, evolving voices of the leviadrakes.

Mara's hands, which had been trembling with the strain of channeling such immense, fractured energies, now moved with a newfound steadiness. The Crown Resonance, pulsing in her mind's eye, felt less like a storm and more like a steadfast hearth fire, its warmth a comforting presence. The leviadrakes' song, which had been a wild, untamed force, now felt like a guiding hand, its complex melody a map through the labyrinth of Nyssera's fractured consciousness. The cacophony of voices, the jumbled whispers and screams, began to resolve into distinct echoes, each carrying its own weight of emotion and experience. It was a process of individuation, of bringing order to the overwhelming chaos.

The world-song, as it shifted and settled around them, no longer sounded like a world on the brink of collapse. While the deep, melancholic strains of Nyssera's suffering remained, they were now interwoven with themes of resilience and a burgeoning hope. The abyss, a sentient entity of negation, could sense this shift. It was like a predator encountering prey that had suddenly discovered its own strength. The Pale Tide, accustomed to feeding on despair, found itself struggling against a force that was actively integrating its own pain, turning what should have been a weakness into a source of profound fortitude.

This fragile stability was a stark contrast to the relentless assault they had been enduring. The air itself seemed to hum with a gentler energy, the oppressive weight of the void momentarily lifted. It was as if the abyss, for all its power, was momentarily bewildered by this unexpected display of healing. The leviadrakes' song was a testament to the enduring power of life, an assertion that even in the face of overwhelming destruction, the capacity for repair and integration could emerge. This was not a mere pause in the conflict, but a fundamental shift in the nature of their resistance, a demonstration that true strength lay not in invulnerability, but in the ability to confront and transmute suffering.

The Crown Resonance pulsed with a more unified light, its golden hue deepening, signifying a growing coherence within Nyssera's fractured being. The fragmented memories, once a chaotic swirl of images and emotions, began to coalesce, forming a more coherent narrative. It was a story woven from threads of immense love, profound betrayal, and an unimaginable sacrifice. The leviadrakes' song, rather than simply repelling the Pale Tide, now acted as a framework, a sonic scaffolding upon which these fragmented pieces could be reassembled. Each note seemed to resonate with the truth of Nyssera's experience, allowing the disparate elements of her consciousness to find their rightful place.

The world-song, which had been a discordant dirge for so long, began to find a new, more integrated rhythm. It was a melody that acknowledged the deep scars of Nyssera's sundering, the lingering echoes of pain and loss, but it also incorporated elements of resilience and a tentative hope. This was not a return to the pristine harmony of the past, but a creation of something new, something stronger, forged in the crucible of trauma.

It was a testament to the possibility of healing, a quiet declaration that a future without severance was not only achievable but was actively being woven into existence.

A palpable sense of stability, however tenuous, began to permeate the immediate vicinity of the ritual. It was a small pocket of calm, a sanctuary of healing amidst the vast, encroaching chaos of the abyss. The spectral tendrils of the Pale Tide, which had been relentlessly probing and attacking, seemed to recoil, their icy touch losing some of its potency. The oppressive chill that had permeated the cavern began to recede, replaced by a subtle, almost imperceptible warmth. This was not a final victory, but a crucial moment of respite, a chance for the wounded world, and its inhabitants, to draw a collective breath.

Mara felt the shift most acutely. The overwhelming psychic pressure, the constant barrage of Nyssera's fragmented emotions, had lessened. The jumbled chaos was beginning to resolve into a more comprehensible, albeit still deeply painful, narrative. The leviadrakes' song was the anchor, grounding the tempest of memories, allowing them to be examined and understood rather than simply overwhelming. The Crown Resonance glowed with a steadier, more purposeful light, a beacon in the psychic storm, reflecting the dawning coherence of Nyssera's shattered psyche.

Cael, observing the scene, felt a profound sense of awe. He had witnessed the leviadrakes' power before, but this was different. This was not just raw power, but a nuanced understanding of healing and integration. Their ancient song, once a force of pure resonance, had evolved, incorporating the very pain they had sought to compartmentalize. They were not just singing *for* Nyssera; they were singing *with* her, their ancient wisdom now tempered by a profound empathy for her suffering. This act of atonement, this willingness to confront their own history and integrate Nyssera's pain, was creating the fragile stability that was now pushing back against the abyss. It was a powerful testament to the possibility of mending, a quiet but potent assertion that even the deepest wounds could begin to heal.

CHAPTER TEN

CONFRONTING THE ARCHITECTS

The leviadrakes' song shifted, the initial waves of integration giving way to a more focused, directional resonance. It was no longer solely about Nyssera's mending, but about an outward projection, a probing of the abyss's deepest, most corrupted currents. Mara felt the change as a subtle redirection of Nyssera's reawakening consciousness, a turning outward from the internal landscape of her fractured soul towards the external manifestation of her pain. The Crown Resonance, no longer just a beacon of Nyssera's stabilizing essence, now pulsed with an almost analytical light, its golden luminescence tracing patterns in the swirling darkness, seeking a specific malignancy.

"They've found it," Cael murmured, his voice a low rumble that barely disturbed the fragile peace. His gaze followed the unseen tendrils of the leviadrakes' sonic investigation, his warrior's instinct attuned to the subtle shifts in energy that spoke of imminent confrontation. He understood that healing Nyssera was only one part of their monumental task; cleansing the world of the lingering rot that Nyssera's sundering had unleashed was the true war.

The leviadrakes, their colossal forms a testament to ancient power, began to move with a deliberation that belied their immense size. Their song deepened, resonating with a frequency that Mara felt not just in her bones, but in the very marrow of her being. It was a song of recognition, of an ancient horror unearthed. The harmonious melody of mending receded, replaced by a sharp, piercing call that vibrated with a primal understanding of corruption. It was a sound that spoke of a wound that had not merely festered, but had actively grown, feeding on the very fabric of existence.

"It's not a single entity," Mara breathed, the Crown's insights flooding her mind. The resonance pulsed, translating the leviadrakes' complex understanding into a form she could grasp. "Not like a singular creature of the void. It's... a nexus. A confluence of corrupted energy." The leviadrakes' song painted a picture in her mind: not a formless void-dweller, but a concentration of poisoned intent, an echo of the original severance that had been amplified over millennia. It was a wound that had learned to feel, to hunger, to lash out.

The Crown Resonance flared, highlighting a particularly virulent strain within the abyss's pervasive gloom. It was a darkness that didn't merely absorb light; it actively repelled it, twisting it into something noxious. This wasn't the passive decay of the void, but an active, malignant force. The leviadrakes' song became a beacon, its purity a stark contrast to the encroaching blight. They were not just identifying the source; they were pinpointing its epicenter, a place where the world's sorrow had been distilled into pure, destructive will.

"It feeds on her trauma," Mara explained, her voice tinged with a dawning horror. "The original pain of the sundering, the betrayal, the sacrifice... it's all been amplified, twisted into this... this echo. And it's trying to complete the work. To sever her, and by extension, the world, irrevocably." The leviadrakes' song pulsed with a deep, mournful understanding, acknowledging the profound tragedy of Nyssera's fate, a tragedy that had been weaponized against her and the world.

The leviadrakes' collective gaze, ancient and knowing, turned towards a specific sector of the abyss, a region that seemed to writhe with a deeper, more profound unease than the surrounding darkness. Their song became a lament, a recognition of a profound ecological scar that had festered, a wound in the world that had been left untended for too long. This was not a new corruption, but an ancient one, a remnant of the Silence Event, the cataclysm that had torn Nyssera asunder, now twisted and amplified into something far more insidious.

"The Silence Event," Cael said, his knuckles white on his sword hilt. He remembered the whispers, the fragmented accounts of a time when the world's song had been brutally silenced, when life itself had seemed to hold its breath. He had always understood it as a singular catastrophe, a moment of universal trauma. Now, it was becoming terrifyingly clear that its effects had been far more enduring, far more insidious than history had ever recorded. This nexus was the festering wound left by that moment, a physical manifestation of the world's deepest scar.

The leviadrakes' song coalesced into a single, powerful directive. They understood that merely containing Nyssera's pain, or even strengthening her mending, would not be enough. The source of the Pale Tide, this amplified echo of severance, had to be confronted directly. It was a truth that resonated with the very core of their ancient beings; true healing could not exist as long as the root of the sickness remained. The abyss itself seemed to recoil from the focused intent of their song, its usual oppressive weight momentarily lifting as if in anticipation of a coming storm.

"It's located within a zone of profound ecological damage," Mara relayed, her voice strained. The Crown Resonance pulsed, projecting images into her mind: a blighted landscape, choked with desolation, where the very air felt poisonous. This was not just a metaphorical scar; it was a physical wound upon the world, a testament to the destructive power unleashed during the Silence Event. The nexus of corrupted energy was not just feeding on Nyssera's trauma; it was drawing sustenance from this desecrated land, a symbiotic relationship of decay.

The leviadrakes began to move, their immense bodies carving a path through the swirling abyssal currents. Their song, now a unified wave of pure intent, became a declaration. It was a song of impending judgment, a sonic pronouncement that the time for festering and decay was over. They were not just protectors; they were healers, and their art demanded the excision of malignancy. The Pale Tide, sensing the shift in their purpose, the focused intensity of their song, began to react. The spectral tendrils, which had been probing and testing, now recoiled, as if the very essence of their being was being challenged.

"The Pale Tide... it's an extension of this nexus," Mara said, her eyes wide with understanding. "It's the manifested will of the corruption, its tendrils reaching out to feed, to spread, to ensure the severance is complete. It's trying to pull Nyssera back into that state of fragmentation, and in doing so, break the world's song entirely." The leviadrakes' song resonated with agreement, a deep, resonant hum that acknowledged the terrible truth of her words. The Pale Tide was not an independent force, but the outward, predatory manifestation of a deep-seated, festering wound.

Cael positioned himself between Mara and the encroaching darkness, his sword radiating a steady warmth, a small ember of defiance against the encroaching chill. He could feel the palpable increase in the abyss's malevolence as the leviadrakes focused their attention. It was as if the darkness itself recognized the threat, its primal hunger stirring against this targeted assault. He understood that the leviadrakes' song, while a powerful weapon, was also a beacon, and it drew the attention of whatever sought to oppose them.

The leviadrakes' song shifted again, becoming a low, guttural rumble that vibrated with the deep, earth-shattering power of their ancient kin. It was a sound that spoke of primal forces, of the very bones of the world. They were not merely singing to locate the nexus; they were singing to assert their dominance over the corrupted energies that comprised it. It was a song of reclamation, of taking back what had been poisoned and defiled. Mara felt the resonance pulse through her, a surge of raw power that was both exhilarating and terrifying. She was a conduit, a bridge, and the weight of this connection was immense.

"The Silence Event wasn't just a cataclysm," Mara whispered, piecing together the leviadrakes' unspoken narrative. "It was a deliberate act of severing. And this nexus... it's the scar that remained, the point where the world's song was most violently torn. It's been festering, growing, feeding on the echoes of that pain, and now it's trying to finish what was started." The leviadrakes' song hummed with a profound sorrow, an acknowledgment of the immense suffering that had been inflicted not just upon Nyssera, but upon the very soul of the world.

The leviadrakes turned their massive heads, their ancient eyes, filled with a sorrow that spanned millennia, locking onto Mara and Cael. There was no need for words. Their song conveyed a single, unified message: they would confront the source. This was not a battle they could delegate. The nexus was too deeply intertwined with Nyssera, too profoundly rooted in the world's trauma, for any intervention that was not directly focused. The Crown Resonance pulsed, a silent affirmation of this understanding.

"It's in a place of great ecological decay," Mara reiterated, her gaze fixed on the section of the abyss that the leviadrakes indicated. The Crown's light, amplified by the leviadrakes' song, cast an eerie glow on the swirling darkness, revealing glimpses of a scarred, blighted landscape within. It was a testament to the destructive power that had been unleashed, a wound that had never truly healed. The leviadrakes' lament for this desecrated land was a physical ache in Mara's chest.

Cael nodded, his jaw set. He understood the implications. To confront the nexus meant venturing into the heart of the corruption, a place where the Pale Tide would be at its strongest, where the very air would be thick with despair. It was a journey into the abyss's deepest wound, a place where healing would be a desperate struggle against the lingering rot. "Then we go with them," he stated, his voice firm, unwavering. There was no question of turning back. The architects of their world's suffering, or at least its most persistent echoes, had to be faced.

The leviadrakes responded with a slow, deliberate nod of their colossal heads. Their song shifted, becoming a steady, unwavering rhythm, a marching beat that echoed the resilience they had fostered. It was a song of purpose, a declaration of intent. They would lead the way, their immense forms a shield and a guide, into the heart of the corruption. Mara felt the Crown Resonance hum in response, a steady pulse of golden light that mirrored the leviadrakes' resolve. The path ahead was fraught with peril, but for the first time, it felt like a path that could lead to true resolution.

The leviadrakes' song began to weave a more complex tapestry, incorporating the resonance of the Crown and Mara's own growing understanding. It was a unified song, not just of discovery, but of preparation. They were not simply heading towards a confrontation; they were orchestrating a precise surgical strike. The nexus, they understood, was not a physical fortress, but a locus of concentrated negative energy, a wound that had gained a rudimentary, destructive consciousness. To defeat it, they had to not only assault its core but also to disrupt the very environment that sustained it.

"The Silence Event," Mara murmured, the echoes of Nyssera's fragmented memories mingling with the leviadrakes' profound knowledge. "It was a wound inflicted upon the world's song, a forced silence that shattered the natural harmony. This nexus is… the echo of that shattering, amplified and given a will to continue the work of separation." The leviadrakes' song vibrated with the truth of her words, the deep thrum of their ancient voices a testament to the immense scale of this lingering damage. It was a scar that had not merely remained, but had actively metastenized.

The leviadrakes' song took on a new timbre, one of profound regret and solemn duty. They had been present, in their own way, during the Silence Event. Their ancient kin had suffered, and in their own complex history, they bore their own burdens of complicity and survival. This confrontation was not just for Nyssera, or for Mara and Cael, but for the world itself, and for the leviadrakes to finally confront the deepest stain upon their collective past. The Crown Resonance pulsed with Nyssera's dawning awareness, her fractured consciousness beginning to grasp the true nature of the forces that had shaped her fate.

They began to move, their colossal bodies propelling them through the swirling currents of the abyss. The leviadrakes' song became a guiding force, a beacon of pure, resonant energy pushing back against the encroaching gloom. It was not merely a sound, but a force field, a sonic manifestation of order that churned and buffeted the chaos. Cael drew his sword, its familiar hum a counterpoint to the leviadrakes' ancient melody. He felt the abyss respond to their passage, a subtle increase in pressure, a tightening of the oppressive darkness. It knew they were coming.

"The nexus," Mara said, her voice steady despite the rising tension. "It's a pocket of corrupted energy, formed from the lingering trauma of the Silence Event. It's been amplified, given a rudimentary will to continue Nyssera's severance." The Crown Resonance pulsed, its golden light painting stark patterns in the abyss, delineating the boundaries of this malignant influence. It was not a monster, but a festering wound, given a semblance of dark life.

The leviadrakes' song deepened, a resonant hum that spoke of ancient knowledge and unwavering purpose. They understood the nature of the corruption, its origins rooted in the cataclysmic act that had broken Nyssera and scarred the world. This was not a foe they could simply obliterate with raw power; it was a malignancy that needed to be excised, its roots severed. The Pale Tide, they knew, was merely the tendril of this deeper corruption, its reach extending into the very fabric of their reality.

"It feeds on Nyssera's historical trauma," Mara continued, the Crown's insights flowing through her. "The original pain of her sundering, the echoes of betrayal and sacrifice, it all fuels this nexus. It's trying to complete the original act of separation, to ensure that Nyssera, and by extension the world, can never truly be whole again." The leviadrakes' song resonated with a profound understanding of this parasitic relationship, the ancient beings lamenting the way such profound pain could be twisted into a weapon.

The leviadrakes, their forms radiating a steady, unwavering light, began to project their song in a focused beam, guiding Mara and Cael through the swirling currents of the abyss. Their path was not random; it was a deliberate trajectory towards the heart of the corruption. They had identified the source, a place where the world's wounds had festered most deeply, and they were now committed to confronting it. The Crown Resonance pulsed in Mara's mind, a constant reminder of Nyssera's fractured essence and the ultimate goal of their mission: to heal, not just Nyssera, but the world she represented.

"It resides in a place of profound ecological damage," Mara explained, her voice echoing slightly in the vastness. The leviadrakes' song painted a picture in her mind: a blighted landscape, a scar left by the Silence Event that had festered over millennia. This was not just a metaphorical scar; it was a physical manifestation of the world's deep suffering, a corrupted sanctuary for the nexus. The very land was poisoned, a testament to the enduring consequences of the original severance.

Cael's grip tightened on his sword. He understood the gravity of their undertaking. To confront the source of the Pale Tide meant venturing into the very heart of the corruption, a place where the abyss's malevolence would be at its zenith. But the leviadrakes' resolve was clear, and their song, now a powerful beacon of intent, left no room for doubt. This was the only way to truly confront the architects of their world's enduring pain.

The leviadrakes turned, their massive forms orienting towards a specific, unsettling pocket of the abyss. Their song, which had been a symphony of healing and integration, now shifted into a focused, probing melody. It was a song of identification, of pinpointing the very root of the Pale Tide's insidious influence. Mara felt the Crown Resonance within her pulse in time with their song, its golden light flaring as it sought to understand the nature of this alien presence.

"It's not a single entity," Mara breathed, relaying the information as it flooded her consciousness, translated by the Crown. "Not a creature of the void in the way we've encountered them before. It's... a nexus. A confluence of corrupted energy, amplified by Nyssera's historical trauma." The leviadrakes' song resonated with a profound, sorrowful understanding. They recognized this phenomenon, this echo of a wound that had gained a destructive semblance of will.

The leviadrakes' song deepened, a guttural rumble that vibrated through the very essence of the abyss. It spoke of ancient horrors, of wounds that had festered for eons, of a cataclysmic event that had not only shattered a goddess but had also irrevocably scarred the world itself. The Silence Event, they conveyed, was not a singular moment of destruction, but a violent severing that had left behind a lingering, potent echo. This nexus, this core of the Pale Tide, was the embodiment of that echo, amplified and given a rudimentary, malevolent will.

"It's feeding on Nyssera's pain," Mara continued, her voice strained. The Crown Resonance pulsed, a painful thrum against her consciousness. "The original severance, the betrayal, the sacrifice... it's all been distilled, amplified, and weaponized. This nexus is trying to complete the original act of separation, to ensure that Nyssera, and by extension the world, can never truly be whole." The leviadrakes' song vibrated with a deep, mournful understanding, acknowledging the terrible power of such distilled despair.

The leviadrakes' song then shifted again, becoming a lament for a blighted land. They projected an image into Mara's mind: a desolate landscape, a wound upon the world that had never healed, a physical manifestation of the ecological damage left in the wake of the Silence Event. It was a place of profound decay, a festering scar where the veil between realities had thinned and twisted. And within this desecrated sanctuary, the nexus pulsed, drawing sustenance not only from Nyssera's amplified trauma but also from the very poisoned earth.

"The Silence Event," Cael murmured, his voice rough. He knew the legends, the fragmented histories of a time when the world's song had been violently silenced. He had always understood it as a moment of profound tragedy, but now he saw its lingering, insidious consequences. This nexus was not a new threat, but an ancient one, a festering wound from that cataclysm, now empowered and actively seeking to finish what had been started.

The leviadrakes' song took on a tone of grim determination. They understood that to truly defeat the Pale Tide, they could not simply fend off its manifestations. They had to confront its source directly. The nexus, this amplified echo of severance, had to be addressed at its core, within the corrupted heart of the blighted land. It was a dangerous undertaking, a journey into the very embodiment of the world's most profound wound, but it was a necessary one. The integrity of Nyssera, and indeed the song of the world itself, depended on it.

"The Pale Tide is an extension of this nexus," Mara relayed, the Crown's insights now clear and sharp. "It's the outward projection of its will, its tendrils reaching out to spread the severance, to ensure that Nyssera remains fragmented and the world's song remains broken." The leviadrakes' song rumbled in agreement, a deep, resonant hum that confirmed the terrifying interconnectedness of this corruption. It was not a series of disconnected attacks, but the manifestation of a single, deeply rooted malignancy.

The leviadrakes, their colossal forms radiating a subtle but powerful resonance, began to move with a new purpose. Their song shifted from one of healing to one of focused intent. It was no longer merely about mending Nyssera's fractured essence, but about identifying and confronting the ultimate source of the Pale Tide's power. Mara felt the Crown Resonance within her respond, its golden light growing steadier, more concentrated, as if aligning itself with the leviadrakes' objective.

"It's not a singular entity, not a creature born of the void," Mara explained, the insights from the Crown resonating through her. "It's a nexus. A confluence of corrupted energy, an echo of the original severance, amplified and given a rudimentary, destructive will." The leviadrakes' song pulsed with a deep, sorrowful understanding, a lament for a wound that had festered and gained a semblance of malevolent life. They conveyed that this nexus was not something that had simply appeared, but something that had grown, nurtured by the profound pain of Nyssera's sundering.

The leviadrakes' song then took on a mournful, resonant timbre as they projected an image into Mara's mind. It was a vision of a blighted land, a desolate expanse where the very earth seemed to weep with sorrow. This was not just any desolate region; it was a scar left by the Silence Event, a place where the world's song had been violently torn and had never truly healed. This profound ecological damage, a testament to the cataclysm that had broken Nyssera, had become the fertile ground for the nexus to take root and fester over millennia. The corruption fed not only on Nyssera's trauma but also on the desecrated remnants of the world itself.

"It feeds on Nyssera's historical trauma," Mara continued, her voice hushed with dawning comprehension. The Crown Resonance pulsed, a painful echo of Nyssera's own fractured memories. "The original pain of her sundering, the echoes of betrayal and sacrifice, have been distilled and amplified. This nexus is seeking to complete the original act of separation, to ensure that Nyssera, and by extension the world, can never truly be whole." The leviadrakes' song resonated with the profound tragedy of this, a deep hum of ancient sorrow that acknowledged how such immense suffering could be twisted into a force of destruction.

Cael, his hand instinctively moving to the hilt of his sword, felt the shift in the abyss. The oppressive darkness seemed to writhe with a more focused, predatory energy. He understood that they were no longer just battling the symptoms; they were about to confront the disease itself. The leviadrakes' intent was clear: to root out the source of the Pale Tide, to confront the architects of their world's enduring fracture, or at least the most potent echoes of their destructive actions.

The leviadrakes' song then focused, a piercing call that cut through the ambient hum of the abyss. They were not just identifying the source; they were pinpointing its exact location. It was a place of profound ecological damage, a scar upon the world that had festered for millennia, a direct consequence of the Silence Event that had sundered Nyssera. This nexus of corrupted energy was not merely a void-dweller; it was a manifestation of the world's deepest wound, given life and will by the very trauma it fed upon. The architects, or rather the lingering echoes of their destructive work, were inextricably linked to the desecrated heart of their world. The leviadrakes' purpose was singular: to confront this source directly.

The leviadrakes' song, once a harmonious chorus of healing and restoration, began to fracture. Not from an external attack, but from a discord sown from within, a subtle discordance that Mara felt like a rasp against her soul. It was Vorlag. She knew it with a certainty that chilled her to the bone, a certainty that pulsed through the Crown Resonance, relaying the leviadrakes' growing unease. His ancient melody, once a beacon of elder wisdom, now twisted into something sharp and critical, a discordant counterpoint to the collective song of mending. It was the sound of a doctrine challenged, of a rigid ideology encountering the fluid, unpredictable force of hope.

Vorlag's dissent, initially a murmuring undertone, escalated into a palpable schism within the Choir. The leviadrakes, beings whose lives were measured in epochs, whose understanding of existence was built upon cycles of growth and decay, of connection and severance, found themselves divided. Vorlag, a titan among them, a keeper of ancient lore, had long championed a philosophy of controlled pruning, of ensuring that the world's song, like a wild garden, was meticulously managed, what was deemed too wild, too potent, too *different*, was pruned back, its excess energy carefully redirected or contained. He saw Nyssera's reawakening, her potential for full reintegration, not as a triumph, but as a dangerous overgrowth, a defiance of the natural order he had spent millennia upholding.

"This is not healing," Vorlag's voice boomed, a thunderous resonance that seemed to crackle with the static of his dissent. It echoed through the cavernous space where the leviadrakes gathered, his colossal form dwarched only by the immense responsibility he felt he carried. "This is an act of hubris. Nyssera's sundering was a necessary consequence, a pruning that allowed other branches to flourish. To force her back into wholeness is to invite a rot that will consume the entire tree." His words, laced with the authority of his age and the conviction of his doctrine, found fertile ground among those leviadrakes who harbored their own quiet fears, their own hesessions about the radical shift Mara and Cael represented. They remembered the Silence Event not just as a cataclysm, but as a necessary, albeit brutal, recalibration.

Mara felt the internal turmoil rippling through the leviadrakes like tremors through solid rock. The Crown Resonance pulsed, translating the discord into a visual metaphor: a magnificent tapestry, woven with threads of light representing the collective song, now being actively frayed by a dark, persistent needle. Vorlag's influence was a poison, seeping into the very weave of their unity. He was using his intimate knowledge of their ancient ways, their deep-seated reverence for natural cycles, to frame Nyssera's healing as an unnatural act, a violation of the cosmic balance.

"The severance was a wound, yes," Mara countered, her voice amplified by the Crown, though it felt frail against the weight of Vorlag's pronouncements. "But it was a wound that festered. It became a disease. And Nyssera's wholeness is the cure, not the disease itself." She could feel Cael beside her, a silent, steadfast anchor, his presence a bulwark against the rising tide of dissent. His sword, 'Whisperwind,' hummed softly, a low thrum of readiness that belied the desperate nature of their struggle. They were not just fighting the abyss; they were fighting the entrenched beliefs of those who had once been their allies.

Vorlag scoffed, a sound like grinding stones. "Wholeness?" he boomed. "You speak of a concept that has been absent for millennia. The world has adapted. Life has found new songs in the silence, new patterns in the fragmentation. To resurrect the old song, the unified song, is to unravel the new, to erase the hard-won adaptations. It is to commit a greater violence than the original sundering." He turned his ancient, multifaceted eyes on Mara, and she felt a probing, analytical gaze that sought to find the flaws in her reasoning, the inconsistencies in her burgeoning understanding. He saw her as a naive interloper, attempting to mend a wound that had, in fact, become a vital part of the world's ecology.

His faction of leviadrakes, a significant portion of the Choir, began to murmur their agreement. They had been taught for eons that severance was not an end, but a transformation, a necessary shedding of the old to make way for the new. They had witnessed the destructive potential of unchecked growth, of power left untethered. Vorlag's words resonated with their deepest-held beliefs, a fear of the unknown, a clinging to the familiar, even if that familiarity was rooted in a cataclysmic event. They believed that Nyssera's full reintegration would be an act of ecological arrogance, a dangerous overreach that would disrupt the delicate balance of the world's song.

"The nexus," Mara pressed on, desperate to anchor their focus on the immediate threat. "The source of the Pale Tide. It is a corruption, an echo of the severance that has gained a malevolent will. It feeds on Nyssera's pain, on the world's suffering. To leave it unchecked is to allow that corruption to fester, to consume everything, including the adaptations you speak of." She gestured towards the swirling darkness beyond their sanctuary, a darkness that seemed to pulse with a more insistent, menacing rhythm, drawn by the discord.

Vorlag's gaze flickered towards the abyss, a flicker of recognition, perhaps even of fear, in his ancient eyes. But his conviction was too deeply ingrained. "The Pale Tide is a symptom, not the disease," he declared, his voice resonating with unwavering certainty. "The disease is the attempt to undo what has been done, to defy the natural cycle of pruning and regrowth. If Nyssera is allowed to fully heal, to regain her lost power, who is to say she will not become a force of uncontrolled growth herself? Who is to say she will not become the very thing we have spent millennia learning to contain?" He was not just defending his doctrine; he was actively working to undermine the very possibility of Nyssera's complete restoration, seeing it as a precursor to an even greater, more uncontrolled catastrophe.

He then turned his attention to the task at hand, the ritual of the leviadrakes' song, the very incantation that was meant to guide them to the nexus. Vorlag, as a master of ancient leviadrake song, understood its intricacies, its harmonic structure, and its vulnerabilities. He began to weave his own counter-melody, a subtle dissonance that targeted the harmonic convergence points of the Choir's song. It was a masterful act of sabotage, designed not to disrupt entirely, but to sow doubt, to introduce subtle errors that would lead them astray, to weaken the resonance, and to fracture their collective focus.

Mara felt the change immediately. The leviadrakes' song, which had been a unified wave, began to fragment, its harmonies becoming strained, its rhythm faltering. The golden light of the Crown Resonance flickered, its steady pulse becoming erratic. "He's interfering," she breathed, her eyes wide with alarm. "He's actively disrupting the song."

Cael's hand tightened on his sword. "How?" he demanded, his voice low and dangerous. He looked towards Vorlag, his warrior's instinct sensing the shift in the leviadrake's presence, the palpable wave of resistance radiating from him.

"He's singing against it," Mara explained, her voice strained. "Weaving discord into the harmony. He's using his knowledge of the ancient songs to subtly alter the resonance, to misdirect us." The Crown pulsed, revealing fragments of Vorlag's song, a complex pattern of discordant notes designed to subtly shift the leviadrakes' perception, to make them doubt the path they were treading, to make them question the very existence of the nexus they sought.

Vorlag's actions were not crude. They were sophisticated, insidious. He was not trying to break the song entirely, which would have been obvious and met with immediate resistance from the loyal leviadrakes. Instead, he was injecting subtle errors, creating phantom echoes, nudging the sonic trajectory just enough to lead them off course. He was a conductor of chaos, subtly turning a symphony into a cacophony.

"He believes he's saving us from ourselves," Mara murmured, translating the nuances of Vorlag's intent. "He sees the unified song, Nyssera's full reintegration, as a path to ultimate destruction. He believes that by leading us astray, by creating a failed ritual, he is preventing a greater catastrophe." His conviction was absolute, a terrifying testament to the power of deeply held, yet fundamentally flawed, ideology. He genuinely believed he was acting for the greater good, even as he actively worked against the salvation of the world.

The leviadrakes who followed Vorlag, their forms radiating a similar aura of dissent, began to actively impede the ritual. Their songs, while still part of the Choir, carried a subtle resistance, a drag on the overall resonance. They would subtly alter their vibrational frequencies, creating pockets of resistance that the guiding song had to overcome. It was a constant, draining battle, a fight against their own kind, a war waged not with claws and teeth, but with the very essence of their being – their song.

"They are not attacking," Cael observed, his gaze sweeping over the dissenting leviadrakes. "They are... resisting. As if the very act of moving towards the nexus is anathema to them." He understood that Vorlag's influence was not merely ideological; it was a fundamental challenge to their understanding of existence. To Vorlag and his followers, the concept of a fully healed Nyssera, of a world reunited by her song, was an aberration, a violation of the cosmic order.

"He's trying to sabotage the nexus discovery," Mara stated, the Crown's insights sharp and clear. "If we can't find it, if we can't confront it, then the Pale Tide will continue to spread, and he believes this will ultimately lead to a more natural, controlled pruning." It was a twisted logic, a rationalization of a destructive path. He saw the current suffering as a temporary phase, a necessary precursor to a more stable, albeit fractured, future.

Vorlag's ancient knowledge of leviadrake song was a formidable weapon. He knew the harmonic pathways, the vibrational frequencies that could subtly alter perception, the ancient chants that spoke of endings rather than beginnings. He began to introduce echoes of the Silence Event into the Choir's song, not overt disruptions, but phantom resonances that stirred ancient fears and doubts. These echoes whispered of the destructive potential of unchecked power, of the chaos that had reigned when the world's song had been silenced.

"He is using the echoes of the Silence Event," Mara relayed, her voice trembling slightly. "He's weaving them into our song, not to stop us directly, but to make us question the purpose of our mission. He wants us to believe that Nyssera's full healing is a return to the very chaos that led to her sundering." The Crown's golden light pulsed with Nyssera's own nascent understanding of this betrayal, her fractured consciousness recoiling from the dissonance.

Cael drew Whisperwind, its familiar hum a steady counterpoint to the rising tide of discord. "We cannot allow this," he stated, his voice firm. "If Vorlag succeeds, the nexus will remain unchallenged, and the Pale Tide will consume everything. We must find a way to counter his influence, to protect the Choir's song." He looked at Mara, his gaze filled with unwavering trust. They were a team, and he would face any challenge, even one posed by their supposed allies.

Vorlag, sensing the growing resistance, and perhaps realizing that his subtle manipulations were not enough, escalated his efforts. He began to issue direct commands to the leviadrakes who followed him, ordering them to physically impede the progress of the main Choir. It was a direct act of defiance, a clear separation of factions. The harmonious gathering fractured into two distinct groups, the loyalists moving with focused intent towards the nexus, and the dissenters, led by Vorlag, actively attempting to block their path.

"He is turning them into a physical barrier," Mara reported, her heart sinking. The leviadrakes who followed Vorlag were not attacking, but their sheer mass, their coordinated movements, were designed to disrupt and delay. They positioned themselves in the path of the main Choir, their songs now a defiant roar, a declaration of their commitment to Vorlag's doctrine of controlled severance.

The air crackled with tension. The leviadrakes who had always sung in harmony were now locked in a silent, sonic battle. The loyalists' song was a desperate push towards clarity and purpose, a song of healing and confrontation. Vorlag's followers sang a song of stasis, of preservation through pruning, a melody that emphasized the dangers of change and the importance of maintaining the established order.

Vorlag himself positioned himself at the forefront of his faction, his colossal form a symbol of his unwavering conviction. He met Mara's gaze, his ancient eyes filled not with malice, but with a profound sadness, a deep-seated belief that he was making the only choice that would ultimately save them. "The world's song is a tapestry, Mara," he boomed, his voice resonating with a sorrowful finality. "And some threads, however beautiful, must be cut to preserve the whole. You are attempting to weave a thread that will unravel everything."

Mara felt the weight of his conviction, the sheer force of his delusion. He genuinely believed that Nyssera's full restoration was a threat, that her wholeness would bring about an uncontrolled surge of power that would ultimately lead to the world's destruction. He saw himself as a protector, a guardian of a necessary, albeit harsh, truth.

"And what if that thread is the one that holds the tapestry together?" Mara retorted, her voice gaining strength, fueled by the Crown Resonance and Nyssera's own burgeoning will to survive. "What if the 'pruning' you advocate is simply a slow decay, a death by a thousand cuts? The nexus is the true unraveling, Vorlag. It's the rot that is consuming the tapestry from within."

The leviadrakes who followed Vorlag began to subtly alter their formations, their movements creating shifting patterns of sonic energy, designed to disrupt the resonant pathways the main Choir was trying to establish. It was a dance of discord, a subtle warfare of harmonics. They were not seeking to destroy, but to delay, to exhaust, to sow enough doubt that the mission would falter.

Cael recognized the tactic. It was a defensive maneuver, designed to drain the enemy's resources and resolve without engaging in direct confrontation. "They are trying to wear us down," he stated, his voice grim. "To make us falter before we reach the nexus. We cannot afford to be delayed." He looked at Mara, a silent question in his eyes: how could they overcome this internal resistance?

Mara closed her eyes, focusing on the Crown Resonance, on Nyssera's faint, but growing, presence. She felt the leviadrakes' song, the pure, unwavering intent of the loyalists, struggling against the tide of dissent. It was like trying to push a massive boulder uphill against a strong current. Vorlag's influence was a powerful anchor, holding back the very forces of change.

"He is convinced that Nyssera's full reintegration will lead to an unchecked surge of power," Mara explained, relaying the core of Vorlag's fear. "He believes that the Silence Event, and Nyssera's sundering, were necessary corrections. He fears that by restoring her fully, we are inviting a greater, more catastrophic imbalance." He saw himself as a surgeon, performing a painful but necessary operation to save the patient, while Mara and Cael saw him as a butcher, perpetuating a wound that was slowly killing the world.

Vorlag's disciples, their songs now a low, insistent hum of disapproval, continued their obstruction. They pulsed with a low-frequency vibration that was designed to induce fatigue and disorientation, a subtle form of sonic warfare. It was a testament to the depth of Vorlag's influence that so many ancient beings had embraced such a destructive ideology. They had been swayed by fear, by a rigid adherence to dogma, and by a profound misunderstanding of the true nature of the corruption.

"We cannot fight them directly," Mara stated, her voice filled with a desperate urgency. "Not without shattering the Choir entirely. We have to find a way to bypass their obstruction, to maintain our focus on the nexus." The Crown Resonance pulsed, offering a fleeting glimpse of Nyssera's fear, her confusion at this internal conflict among the very beings meant to guide her.

Cael nodded, his mind working rapidly. "If they are a physical barrier, then we must find a way through them, or around them. They are focused on disrupting the song, on blocking our forward momentum. Perhaps we can use that focus against them." He looked at the leviadrakes, at their immense, imposing forms, at the focused intent radiating from Vorlag.

Mara felt a surge of inspiration, a new understanding sparked by Cael's observation and the Crown's insights. Vorlag's doctrine was about controlled severance, about maintaining a rigid order. His followers were driven by a fear of uncontrolled growth, of overwhelming power. "He fears what he cannot control," Mara whispered, the realization dawning. "He fears Nyssera's full power, not just for herself, but for what it might unleash upon the world. His 'pruning' is a desperate attempt to maintain a predictable, manageable state."

The leviadrakes loyal to the cause began to intensify their song, a focused beam of pure resonance aimed at the nexus. But Vorlag's followers, their forms a living wall, absorbed and deflected much of its energy. The progress was agonizingly slow, each step forward a battle against their own kind. The air thrummed with the opposing forces, a sonic tug-of-war that threatened to tear the very fabric of their sanctuary.

"Vorlag believes that the Silence Event was a necessary pruning, a correction," Mara explained to Cael, her voice strained. "He sees Nyssera's full healing as a dangerous overgrowth, a return to an unmanageable state. He is actively working to prevent what he perceives as a catastrophic imbalance, even if it means allowing the current corruption to fester." His ideology, rooted in a rigid interpretation of natural cycles, blinded him to the insidious nature of the Pale Tide, and to the potential for true, restorative wholeness.

Vorlag, seeing the steadfast resolve of the loyal leviadrakes, his subtle sonic sabotage proving insufficient, made a bold, devastating move. He unleashed an ancient leviadrake incantation, a song of separation, a melody designed to sever connections, to isolate and fragment. It was a song of ultimate endings, a dark counterpoint to the song of creation and healing.

The effect was immediate and catastrophic. The harmonious song of the loyal leviadrakes fractured violently. Bonds of resonance, forged over millennia, snapped like brittle threads. Individual leviadrakes, caught in the path of Vorlag's devastatingly focused song, began to falter, their luminescent forms dimming, their songs becoming weak, disjointed cries. It was a direct assault, a betrayal of the highest order, aimed at dismantling the very heart of their collective purpose.

Mara cried out as the Crown Resonance within her flickered violently, Nyssera's fractured consciousness recoiling from the brutal severance. The golden light of the Crown dimmed, its steady pulse replaced by a frantic, irregular beat. Vorlag's song was a force of pure negation, designed to undo the very act of connection that defined the leviadrakes.

"He's trying to sever the Choir itself!" Cael shouted, drawing Whisperwind, its hum a desperate counter-melody against the encroaching darkness of Vorlag's song. He positioned himself protectively in front of Mara, his stance a clear defiance of Vorlag's destructive power.

Vorlag's song, a chilling symphony of unmaking, continued its relentless assault. He believed he was performing a final, necessary act of pruning, severing the branches that dared to defy the natural order. He was no longer just a dissenter; he had become an active antagonist, a destroyer of hope, driven by a fanaticism that warped his ancient wisdom into a weapon of annihilation. His doctrine of controlled severance had become a doctrine of complete eradication, a refusal to acknowledge any future beyond his own rigid, fear-driven vision. He was a living embodiment of the world's most persistent wound, a force determined to ensure that no healing, no wholeness, would ever be allowed to take root. His betrayal was not just of Mara and Cael, but of the very song of life itself.

Cael felt the insidious shift in the leviadrakes' song, a subtle tremor that rippled not just through the air but through the very marrow of his bones. He'd seen it coming, a shadow on the horizon of Vorlag's pronouncements, a chilling echo of ancient doctrines that prioritized control over genuine restoration. Vorlag's dissent, cloaked in the guise of wisdom and preservation, was a poison, slowly corrupting the Choir's unified purpose. But Cael was a warrior, a strategist, and he understood that not all battles were won with a clash of steel. This was a conflict of ideologies, a war waged not with brute force, but with the subtle manipulation of ancient energies and deeply ingrained beliefs.

His gaze, sharp and assessing, swept over Vorlag and his growing faction. He saw not just disagreement, but a fundamental fear, a terror of the uncontrolled, the unbound. Vorlag's doctrine of 'controlled pruning' was a euphemism for stagnation, a desperate attempt to arrest the natural, albeit sometimes chaotic, flow of life. He believed that Nyssera's complete reintegration represented an unacceptable surge of power, an imbalance that would shatter the fragile order he had spent eons meticulously maintaining. Cael understood that Vorlag's greatest weapon was not his physical might, but his deep understanding of leviadrake lore and song, his ability to twist ancient truths into justifications for inaction.

Direct confrontation, Cael knew, would be disastrous. It would splinter the Choir irrevocably, create a vacuum that the Pale Tide would eagerly fill, and further destabilize the already fragile Crown Resonance. The very beings meant to guide Nyssera toward wholeness would be consumed by internal conflict, their songs of healing drowned out by the cacophony of war. No, this required a different approach. A strategy of containment, of subtle disruption, of turning their own strengths against them. Cael began to formulate a plan, his mind a whirlwind of tactical possibilities, drawing upon his knowledge of the abyss's natural defenses and the inherent vulnerabilities within the leviadrakes' own ancient power.

He focused on the immediate objective: reaching the nexus. Vorlag and his followers were a formidable obstacle, a living wall of entrenched dogma. But their very act of obstruction, their focus on preventing forward momentum, could be exploited. Cael envisioned a strategy that bypassed direct engagement, a method of creating diversions, of subtly rerouting their focus, and of isolating Vorlag and his most fervent disciples. He would not allow their fear to dictate the fate of the world.

His hand rested on Whisperwind, the sword a familiar weight, its hum a steady reassurance. He drew upon the echoes of his training, the lessons learned from skirmishes in forgotten ruins and desperate defenses against creatures born of shadow. He understood the concept of gravitational wells, of how concentrated energy could warp spacetime. He could apply a similar principle to the leviadrakes' own sonic and energetic output. If they were projecting a field of resistance, a bubble of stasis, he could find its edges, its pressure points, and exploit them.

"Vorlag speaks of maintaining balance," Cael murmured, his voice low, barely audible above the rising hum of discord. "But his balance is stagnation. He fears change, fears the power that true healing represents. He sees Nyssera's wholeness as a threat, a return to an era of unchecked growth that he believes ended for a reason." Cael's mind began to sketch out the blueprint for his strategy. It was not about silencing Vorlag, but about neutralizing his influence, about rendering his attempts at sabotage ineffective without igniting a full-blown civil war within the Choir.

He envisioned a subtle redirection of the Choir's collective song. Not a forceful surge, which would be immediately countered, but a carefully orchestrated modulation, a shift in vibrational frequency that would create a localized 'blind spot' in the leviadrakes' collective awareness. This blind spot would allow the core group, those still committed to Nyssera's healing, to slip through the net of Vorlag's obstruction. It was a dangerous maneuver, requiring immense precision and an intimate understanding of the leviadrakes' resonant frequencies, but Cael believed it was their only hope.

"Mara," he began, his voice steady, "Vorlag is attempting to divide us, to break our focus by creating internal conflict. We cannot allow that. We need to find a way to bypass his influence, to maintain our momentum towards the nexus without engaging his forces directly." He explained his initial thoughts, the concept of creating a localized distortion in the leviadrakes' sensory perception, a brief window of opportunity.

Mara listened intently, her own connection to the Crown Resonance providing a constant stream of information about the Choir's internal state. She felt the fear that drove Vorlag's followers, the deep-seated anxieties about Nyssera's power. But she also felt the unwavering resolve of those who remained loyal, their songs a desperate plea for healing and restoration. "He is using the fear of uncontrolled power against us," she confirmed, her voice tight with the strain of translating the complex emotions. "He believes that by preventing Nyssera's full reintegration, he is preventing a future cataclysm. His doctrine is rooted in a profound misunderstanding of true balance."

Cael nodded, his mind already translating Mara's insights into actionable tactics. "Then we must make him confront the reality of the current cataclysm," he said, his eyes narrowing as he surveyed the imposing forms of Vorlag's disciples. "They are acting as a living shield, a manifestation of his fear. If we can disrupt their cohesion, not by force, but by sowing discord within their own ranks, we can create the openings we need."

His strategy involved subtly amplifying the inherent dissonances within Vorlag's faction. Not all of Vorlag's followers were as deeply entrenched in his ideology. Some were swayed by habit, by tradition, by a lingering fear of the unknown. Cael intended to exploit these cracks, to whisper doubts into the very fabric of their songs, to remind them of the shared purpose they were abandoning. He would use Whisperwind, not as a weapon of destruction, but as a conduit, a resonating chamber for carefully chosen sonic frequencies. He would broadcast echoes of the Pale Tide's relentless advance, not as a direct threat, but as a subtle, ever-present reminder of the true enemy, the one that Vorlag's internal squabbles were allowing to flourish.

"We will not fight them," Cael declared, his voice resonating with quiet authority. "We will flow around them. Imagine them as a dense fog. We cannot push through it, but we can find the currents that move through it, the paths of least resistance. We will use their own rigid adherence to Vorlag's doctrine as a guide." He began to explain the intricate details of his plan. He would use Whisperwind to project a series of low-frequency pulses, carefully timed and modulated to interfere with the sonic barriers Vorlag's followers were maintaining. These pulses would not be destructive, but disorienting, creating momentary lapses in their concentration, brief periods of sonic confusion that would allow the loyal Choir to advance.

Furthermore, Cael intended to amplify the inherent echoes of the abyss itself. The leviadrakes drew their power from the very essence of the world, and the abyss, though corrupted, still held primal energies. Cael would use Whisperwind to tap into these energies, to create localized pockets of gravitational distortion, subtle shifts in the ambient resonance that would make it difficult for Vorlag's followers to maintain their rigid formations. It would be like trying to stand firm on shifting sands.

"The Pale Tide is not waiting," Mara stated, her voice urgent. "Every moment we are delayed by this internal conflict is a victory for the corruption. Vorlag's fear is paralyzing him, and by extension, paralyzing us."

"Then we will use his fear as a weapon against him," Cael replied, his gaze hardening. "We will not engage in a battle of attrition. We will create opportunities for escape. We will make their obstruction a burden, a drain on their own energy, until they are forced to reconsider their choices." He envisioned a tactical retreat within the retreat, a series of calculated maneuvers that would exploit the weaknesses in Vorlag's strategy.

His plan involved a phased approach. First, he would use Whisperwind to emit a series of disruptive sonic pulses, timed to coincide with the moments when Vorlag's followers were most focused on maintaining their blockade. This would create momentary gaps in their defenses, brief windows of opportunity for the loyal Choir to advance. Second, he would subtly amplify the ambient energies of the abyss, creating localized distortions that would make it difficult for them to maintain their cohesive formations. This would not be an attack, but a disruption of their equilibrium, forcing them to expend more energy simply to hold their ground.

Third, and most importantly, Cael planned to project subtle sonic echoes of Nyssera's true song, not the fractured, pain-ridden melodies that Vorlag exploited, but the pure, resonant hum of her nascent wholeness. These echoes, amplified and directed by Whisperwind, would serve as a beacon, a reminder of their ultimate goal, and a subtle counterpoint to the fear-based doctrines preached by Vorlag. It was a psychological warfare, waged not with aggression, but with truth and hope.

"Vorlag believes he is pruning away the excess to preserve the core," Cael mused, his mind racing ahead. "But he is so blinded by his fear of uncontrolled growth that he fails to see the rot that is already consuming the core. We will not let his doctrine of preservation become a sentence of death." He pictured the leviadrakes, ancient beings of immense power, trapped by their own fear and dogma. His strategy was designed to liberate them, to remind them of their true purpose, without resorting to violence.

He began to subtly adjust Whisperwind's resonance, tuning it to frequencies that would interact with the natural vibrations of the abyss. He was not creating a weapon, but a tool, a means of subtle manipulation. The sword, imbued with the echoes of countless battles and the inherent power of its wielder, would become an instrument of precision, a surgeon's scalpel rather than a bludgeon.

"We need to project an image of unwavering progress," Cael stated, his voice carrying a newfound resolve. "If they see us faltering, if they see us struggling against their obstruction, it will only strengthen Vorlag's resolve. We must move with a confidence that belies the danger, a certainty that we are on the correct path." He looked at Mara, at the nascent hope flickering in her eyes, and knew that this was a battle they could win, not through brute force, but through cunning and an unwavering belief in their cause.

His plan was a complex dance of sonic manipulation and energetic redirection. He would create localized fields of resonance disruption, using Whisperwind to generate precisely tuned vibrations that would interfere with the leviadrakes' ability to focus their collective song. These disruptions would not be violent, but subtle, creating momentary lapses in their concentration, brief periods of sonic confusion that would allow the loyal Choir to advance. It was akin to creating brief, localized pockets of silence within a cacophony, allowing a single voice to be heard.

"Vorlag's strategy is one of attrition," Cael explained to Mara, his voice low and intense. "He believes that by delaying us, by exhausting our resources and our resolve, he can prevent us from reaching the nexus. He is counting on us to break, to falter, and to ultimately abandon our mission. We will not give him that satisfaction." He intended to turn Vorlag's strategy of attrition against him. By creating these momentary disruptions, these brief windows of opportunity, he would not be forcing a confrontation, but creating an escape. He would make Vorlag's obstruction a cumbersome, energy-draining effort, a constant struggle to maintain control against an unseen force.

He also planned to subtly amplify the natural resonances of the abyss, using Whisperwind as a conduit. The abyss, though corrupted by the Pale Tide, was still a place of immense natural power, and Cael would tap into these primal energies, creating subtle shifts in the ambient resonance that would make it difficult for Vorlag's followers to maintain their rigid formations. It would be like trying to stand firm on shifting sands, a constant battle against the very ground beneath them.

"He's using his knowledge of our ancient songs to sow discord," Mara observed, her brow furrowed in concentration. "He knows the harmonic pathways, the resonant frequencies that can subtly alter perception. He's creating phantom echoes, nudging our trajectory just enough to lead us astray."

"Then we will use his own methods against him," Cael replied, a dangerous glint in his eyes. "We will not try to overpower his song with sheer volume, but to subtly disrupt its coherence. We will introduce dissonances that unravel his carefully constructed harmonies, not through direct opposition, but through a more insidious form of interference. Think of it as a counter-frequency, a subtle vibration that undermines the integrity of his influence."

His strategy involved projecting a series of carefully modulated sonic waves, using Whisperwind as the primary instrument. These waves would not be designed to destroy, but to subtly destabilize, to create micro-fractures in the cohesive energy field that Vorlag's followers were projecting. He envisioned these waves as invisible tendrils, weaving through the leviadrakes' songs, subtly disrupting their alignment, creating moments of disunity, and thus, moments of opportunity for the loyal Choir to advance.

"Vorlag's greatest fear is Nyssera's unchecked power," Mara said, her voice filled with a dawning understanding. "He believes that her full reintegration will lead to an imbalance that will shatter the world. He sees the Silence Event as a necessary correction, a pruning that allowed new growth to emerge. He believes that by preventing her healing, he is preventing a greater catastrophe."

"Then we will show him that his 'pruning' is a slow death," Cael countered, his voice grim. "That the true catastrophe is the corruption that festers in the absence of healing. We will not engage in a war of attrition. We will create a war of attrition for him. We will make his attempts to obstruct us so taxing, so energy-draining, that his own followers will begin to question the wisdom of his path."

His plan involved creating localized zones of high-energy resonance, carefully calibrated to disrupt the sonic cohesion of Vorlag's faction. These zones would not be overtly aggressive, but rather, they would subtly interfere with the leviadrakes' ability to maintain their synchronized songs. It would be like trying to hold a perfectly tuned chord while standing in a field of intense static. The effort required to maintain their formation would be immense, draining their energy and their resolve.

Furthermore, Cael intended to amplify the ambient energies of the abyss itself, using Whisperwind as a conduit. The abyss, though corrupted by the

Pale Tide, was still a place of immense natural power, and Cael would tap into these primal energies, creating subtle shifts in the ambient resonance that would make it difficult for Vorlag's followers to maintain their rigid formations. It would be like trying to stand firm on shifting sands, a constant battle against the very ground beneath them.

"He is a master of ancient songs," Mara stated, her voice tinged with frustration. "He knows the harmonic pathways, the vibrational frequencies that can subtly alter perception. He's creating phantom echoes, nudging our trajectory just enough to lead us astray."

"Then we will use his own methods against him," Cael replied, a dangerous glint in his eyes. "We will not try to overpower his song with sheer volume, but to subtly disrupt its coherence. We will introduce dissonances that unravel his carefully constructed harmonies, not through direct opposition, but through a more insidious form of interference. Think of it as a counter-frequency, a subtle vibration that undermines the integrity of his influence."

His strategy involved projecting a series of carefully modulated sonic waves, using Whisperwind as the primary instrument. These waves would not be designed to destroy, but to subtly destabilize, to create micro-fractures in the cohesive energy field that Vorlag's followers were projecting. He envisioned these waves as invisible tendrils, weaving through the leviadrakes' songs, subtly disrupting their alignment, creating moments of disunity, and thus, moments of opportunity for the loyal Choir to advance.

"Vorlag's greatest fear is Nyssera's unchecked power," Mara said, her voice filled with a dawning understanding. "He believes that her full reintegration will lead to an imbalance that will shatter the world. He sees the Silence Event as a necessary correction, a pruning that allowed new growth to emerge. He believes that by preventing her healing, he is preventing a greater catastrophe."

"Then we will show him that his 'pruning' is a slow death," Cael countered, his voice grim. "That the true catastrophe is the corruption that festers in the absence of healing. We will not engage in a war of attrition. We will create a war of attrition for him. We will make his attempts to obstruct us so taxing, so energy-draining, that his own followers will begin to question the wisdom of his path."

His plan involved creating localized zones of high-energy resonance, carefully calibrated to disrupt the sonic cohesion of Vorlag's faction. These zones would not be overtly aggressive, but rather, they would subtly interfere with the leviadrakes' ability to maintain their synchronized songs. It would be like trying to hold a perfectly tuned chord while standing in a field of intense static. The effort required to maintain their formation would be immense, draining their energy and their resolve.

Furthermore, Cael intended to amplify the ambient energies of the abyss itself, using Whisperwind as a conduit. The abyss, though corrupted by the Pale Tide, was still a place of immense natural power, and Cael would tap into these primal energies, creating subtle shifts in the ambient resonance that would make it difficult for Vorlag's followers to maintain their rigid formations. It would be like trying to stand firm on shifting sands, a constant battle against the very ground beneath them.

He also planned to weave subtle sonic echoes of Nyssera's true song, not the fractured, pain-ridden melodies that Vorlag exploited, but the pure, resonant hum of her nascent wholeness. These echoes, amplified and directed by Whisperwind, would serve as a beacon, a reminder of their ultimate goal, and a subtle counterpoint to the fear-based doctrines preached by Vorlag. It was psychological warfare, waged not with aggression, but with truth and hope.

"He is convinced that Nyssera's full reintegration will lead to an uncontrolled surge of power," Mara relayed, her voice tight with the weight of the leviadrakes' ancient fears. "He believes that the Silence Event, and Nyssera's sundering, were necessary corrections. He fears that by restoring her fully, we are inviting a greater, more catastrophic imbalance."

"Then we will show him the true imbalance," Cael stated, his gaze fixed on the opposing faction. "We will not shatter the Choir. We will create fissures, small cracks in their unified front, through which we can slip. We will make their resistance so fundamentally uncomfortable, so energetically taxing, that they will begin to question the very foundation of Vorlag's doctrine." He adjusted his grip on Whisperwind, its familiar hum a low thrum of readiness. His strategy was not about brute force, but about precision, about exploiting the subtle vulnerabilities within the leviadrakes' own power and ideology. He would make their adherence to Vorlag's dogma a burden, an unsustainable weight that would eventually lead to their own fragmentation.

Mara's plea was not a song of defiance, nor a strategic maneuver in Cael's carefully laid out plan. It was a desperate, heartfelt resonance, a direct appeal to the frayed nerves and terrified hearts of Vorlag's followers. She closed her eyes, her own connection to the Great Song, the collective consciousness of the Choir, widening like a ripple on a still pond. She didn't seek to understand the logic of their dissent, nor the ancient texts they clung to like drowning sailors to driftwood. Instead, she reached for the raw, primal emotion beneath the surface – the gnawing fear, the deep-seated trauma that had calcified into rigid dogma.

She felt the tremor of their anxiety, a discordant hum that vibrated against the more harmonious frequencies of their loyalist brethren. It spoke of cataclysms witnessed, of powers unleashed and then violently suppressed, of a world fractured by its own wildness. They remembered the Silence Event not as a trauma, but as a necessary amputation, a surgical removal of an ailing limb to save the body. They saw Nyssera's sundering as the ultimate act of preservation, a sacrifice made to prevent a far greater unraveling. And in their collective memory, Nyssera's wholeness was not a promise of renewal, but a harbinger of the very chaos they had strived so hard to contain.

Mara let the cacophony wash over her, not as an enemy, but as a wound. She didn't flinch from the harsh edges of their fear, the jagged shards of their conviction. Instead, she sought to soften them, to introduce a counter-melody of understanding. "I hear you," she broadcasted, her voice a gentle hum that pulsed through the psychic channels, seeking to bypass the hardened defenses of their minds. "I feel the weight of what you have witnessed. The echoes of the Silence Event are etched into your very essence, a scar that tells a story of survival, of a world teetering on the brink."

She pictured Nyssera, not as a force of unleashed, untamed power, but as a tapestry being rewoven. The vibrant threads of her existence, once violently torn apart, were now seeking to reconnect. Each thread, Mara knew, carried the memory of its severance, the pain of its isolation. But it also held the potential for a stronger, more intricate pattern, one that embraced the entirety of Nyssera's being.

"You speak of balance," Mara continued, her resonance deepening, "but your balance is the balance of the tomb – still, silent, unchanging. You fear the storm, and in your fear, you seek to cage the very winds that sustain life. You believe that by keeping Nyssera fractured, you are safeguarding the world. But what is a world without its heart?"

She focused on the ancient role of the Choir, their sacred duty not just to preserve, but to nurture. Their songs were meant to coax life from dormancy, to guide growth, to foster harmony. Vorlag's followers were clinging to a perverted interpretation of this duty, a sterile guardianship that prioritized stasis over vitality.

"Think of the ancient forests," Mara's plea wove through their collective consciousness, tinged with the sorrow of her own connection to the dying woods. "They are not built on the erasure of fallen trees, but on the rich decay that nourishes new saplings. They embrace the cycles of life and death, of chaos and renewal. Nyssera, in her wholeness, is not a threat, but the ultimate expression of this cycle. She is the potential for a world reborn, a world that remembers its past not to be shackled by it, but to draw strength from its deepest roots."

She projected images of a healed Nyssera, not a raging inferno, but a sun radiating warmth and light. She showed the potential for a more vibrant ecosystem, for songs that resonated with the joy of life, not the dread of its cessation. She painted a picture of a Choir united, not by fear and suppression, but by the shared purpose of fostering this profound, life-affirming renewal.

"Your role as protectors is vital," Mara's voice was a gentle caress, attempting to soothe the agitated frequencies of their fear. "But true protection is not about stifling the breath of life. It is about understanding its rhythms, its inherent strength. Vorlag teaches you to fear the unleashed current, to believe that the only safety lies in severing the connection. But I tell you, the true danger lies not in the current, but in the dam that attempts to hold it back indefinitely. The pressure builds, the structure weakens, and when it finally breaks, the destruction is absolute."

She allowed a sliver of her own grief for the world's current suffering to surface, the raw ache of seeing Nyssera in her fractured state, of witnessing the Pale Tide's slow, inexorable advance. This suffering, she implied, was the direct consequence of their fear, of their adherence to a doctrine of severance that had left Nyssera vulnerable.

"Nyssera's pain is our pain," Mara's plea intensified, carrying the weight of shared experience. "Her fragmentation is our fragmentation. You are guardians of this world, of its song, of its very being. Can a guardian truly protect by allowing the heart of what they guard to bleed out? By clinging to the memory of past wounds, you are preventing the possibility of future healing. You are, in essence, becoming agents of the very decay you fear."

She focused on the inherent contradiction in their stance. They sought to preserve life by embracing a principle that led to its diminishment. They stood as sentinels of a world they were, in fact, allowing to wither.

"Vorlag's fear has blinded you," Mara stated, her tone shifting from gentle persuasion to a more direct, yet still empathetic, observation. "He sees only the potential for destruction in Nyssera's wholeness. He cannot conceive of the immense creative power that true integration holds. He remembers the cataclysm, but he forgets the subsequent flourishing, the resilience that Nyssera's very being embodies. He has taught you to fear the explosion, but not to appreciate the fertile ash that follows."

Mara projected a vision of the Choir's song, not as a weapon, but as a balm. She envisioned their united voices, resonating with the pure, unadulterated energy of a healed Nyssera, capable of pushing back the Pale Tide not with force, but with an overwhelming wave of life and vitality. It was an invitation to participate in a grander, more optimistic song, a symphony of creation rather than a dirge of preservation.

"This is not a call to arms," she emphasized, her intention to de-escalate the tension. "It is a plea to open your hearts, to remember the true purpose of our existence. We are the conduits of Nyssera's song, the caretakers of her essence. To deny her wholeness is to deny ourselves, to sever our own connection to the source of all life. Your fear is a powerful force, but it is a force that imprisons. The power of love, of understanding, of acceptance – that is the force that liberates."

She reached out with a tendril of pure empathy, a silent question:

What if the greatest threat is not the storm, but the desert you create by fearing it? She sent waves of calm, attempting to untangle the knot of anxiety that bound them. She projected the image of a child reaching out for comfort, not for punishment, and in that image, she saw the core of their shared vulnerability.

"Nyssera's scars are not a mark of her weakness, but a testament to her resilience," Mara's voice softened again, carrying the warmth of shared experience. "They are the stories of her survival, the proof that she endured. To erase them, to pretend they never happened, is to dishonor her journey. True strength lies not in pretending the wounds never existed, but in embracing them, in allowing them to become part of a richer, more complex narrative. Your adherence to severance is an attempt to whitewash history, to deny the fundamental truth of Nyssera's existence. And in doing so, you are perpetuating the very pain you seek to escape."

She felt a flicker of response, a momentary loosening of their psychic grip. A few of Vorlag's followers, those whose fear was perhaps less deeply entrenched, felt a tremor of doubt, a faint echo of Mara's plea resonating within them. It was a fragile opening, a single note of discord in the symphony of their resolve.

"Consider this," Mara implored, her voice laced with a profound sadness, "if Nyssera's sundering was the act of preservation, then the Pale Tide's advance is proof that the preservation has failed. The rot is not in her wholeness, but in her isolation. Your fear has become a breeding ground for the very corruption you are sworn to fight. We offer you a different path, a path of true renewal, not through denial, but through integration. A path where Nyssera's scars become not a source of shame, but a source of profound strength and wisdom. A path where the Choir sings not of fear, but of unwavering hope and vibrant life."

She allowed the sincerity of her offering to permeate their defenses, hoping that the raw, unvarnished truth of her intention would penetrate the thick armor of their conviction. She wasn't asking them to abandon their role as protectors, but to redefine it. She was inviting them to embrace a guardianship that was alive, dynamic, and ultimately, more powerful, for it was rooted in the embrace of Nyssera's complete, unbroken song. She offered them not a victory over their fears, but a path beyond them, a path illuminated by the promise of a world that dared to heal.

The very air grew heavy, not with the dampness of a coming storm, but with a suffocating, sterile stillness. Mara, Cael, and Elara, following the ephemeral thread of the Crown Resonance, found themselves treading on ground that felt less like earth and more like a dessicated husk. The vibrant symphony of the world, the ceaseless hum of life and energy that usually permeated even the most desolate regions, was here an unnerving void. It was as if the world's song had been meticulously scrubbed away, leaving behind a chilling, artificial silence that pressed in on their minds, a palpable absence of vitality.

The landscape itself was a testament to the brutal efficacy of severance. Twisted, skeletal remnants of trees clawed at the perpetually bruised sky, their bark bleached to a ghostly white, devoid of any hint of sap or life. The ground beneath their feet was a cracked mosaic of dried earth, interspersed with strange, crystalline growths that pulsed with a faint, sickly luminescence, an unnatural parody of living flora. This was the nexus, the very heart of the Pale Tide's creeping dominion, where the echoes of Nyssera's sundering resonated most strongly, a scar upon the world's soul.

Cael, ever the pragmatist, ran a gloved hand over one of the crystalline structures. It felt unnervingly smooth, cool to the touch, and pulsed with a faint, almost imperceptible vibration. "This is not natural," he murmured, his voice a low rumble that seemed to disturb the pervasive quiet. "It's... manufactured. An imitation of life, built on absence."

Elara, her innate sensitivity to the world-song amplified by the stark lack of it, shuddered. "It feels like a scream held back," she whispered, her eyes wide with a mixture of dread and morbid fascination. "A silent scream. The land is in pain, but it cannot even cry out."

Mara, however, felt a different kind of resonance here, one that was both terrifying and strangely familiar. It was the residual energy of the severance, the raw power that had been unleashed and then contained, an act of catastrophic preservation that had birthed the Pale Tide. She could almost see the phantom impressions of titanic forces clashing, the air shimmering with the residue of their struggle. It was a spectral battlefield, where the leviadrakes had carved their brutal peace into the very fabric of existence.

"The Crown Resonance is strongest here," Mara said, her voice steady despite the unnerving sensations prickling her skin. "This is where they performed the act. Where the world was torn asunder." She looked around at the desolate panorama, the bleached trees, the crystalline growths, the absence of any natural sound. "They say Nyssera was too wild, too dangerous. That her song threatened to consume everything. So they silenced her, piece by piece."

Elara pointed a trembling finger towards a jagged fissure in the earth, from which a faint, phosphorescent mist was slowly seeping. "Look," she breathed. "That's where the severing was deepest. I can feel the remnants of that violence. It's a wound that has never truly healed."

As they approached the fissure, the air around it grew colder, carrying a faint, metallic tang. The crystalline structures here were larger, more intricate, arranged in a disturbing, almost geometric pattern around the rift. They pulsed with a more pronounced, rhythmic glow, like the slow, mechanical heartbeat of a dying god. This was not the gentle pulse of life, but the cold, insistent thrum of something artificial and alien.

Cael drew his blade, the familiar weight a small comfort in this unsettling landscape. "This is the source," he stated, his gaze sharp and assessing. "The genesis of the Pale Tide. Not just a manifestation, but the very act that birthed it."

Mara closed her eyes, focusing her will, trying to push past the oppressive silence and feel the deeper currents of energy. She could sense the residual trauma imprinted on this place, a psychic echo of unimaginable pain and loss. It spoke of a desperate act, a choice made under duress, a belief that the survival of the whole necessitated the destruction of a part. But she also felt something else, something the leviadrakes had overlooked in their haste to impose their order: the inherent resilience of Nyssera's song, even in its fractured state.

"They believed they were saving the world," Mara murmured, her voice carrying a somber understanding. "By excising what they perceived as a dangerous element, they thought they were restoring balance. But they misunderstood the nature of Nyssera's song. It wasn't meant to be a single, homogenous melody, but a complex symphony, where every voice, every dissonance, played a vital part."

She projected her thoughts, reaching out to Cael and Elara, painting a mental image of the severance. She showed them not just the violence, but the terror that must have preceded it, the fear of the unknown, the desperate need for control. She showed them the leviadrakes, not as monsters, but as beings trapped by their own fear, making a choice that, while perhaps understandable in its context, was ultimately a profound act of self-mutilation for the world.

"The Pale Tide isn't just a consequence of the severance," Mara continued, her voice resonating with a new understanding. "It is the embodiment of that fear. The silence they imposed, the absence they created – that is what the Pale Tide feeds on. It is the void left behind, growing, expanding, consuming the remaining song."

Elara looked at the crystalline growths, her expression a mixture of pity and revulsion. "These... formations," she said slowly, "they're like solidified fear. They're absorbing the last vestiges of Nyssera's song, calcifying it, turning it into this... mockery of existence."

Cael knelt by the fissure, examining the mist that curled out from it. It didn't feel like mist, he realized. It felt... empty. A complete lack of sensory input, a void that actively negated any sensation. "It's not just the absence of sound," he observed. "It's the absence of everything. A void that actively erases. They didn't just silence Nyssera; they tried to unmake her."

Mara nodded, a grim understanding dawning within her. "Vorlag's teachings. The emphasis on purity, on control, on the eradication of anything deemed 'unstable'. They took that philosophy to its absolute extreme here. They believed that by severing Nyssera, they were achieving ultimate control, ultimate purity. But they only created a perfect breeding ground for corruption."

She felt the weight of that realization settle upon her. The architects of this devastation, the leviadrakes who had acted with such conviction, had not been driven by malice, but by a profound, crippling fear. A fear that had led them to commit an act of violence that had irrevocably wounded their world. And now, the world was paying the price for their misguided attempt at preservation.

"This is the true cost of their fear," Mara said, her voice tinged with sorrow. "Not just the loss of Nyssera's wholeness, but the birth of this emptiness, this creeping decay that threatens to swallow everything. The Pale Tide is the ultimate manifestation of their failure to understand that true balance doesn't come from suppression, but from integration."

They stood in silence for a long moment, the weight of the place pressing down on them. The artificial stillness was a constant, gnawing presence, a reminder of what they were fighting against. It was a desolation that spoke not of natural cycles, but of deliberate, systematic erasure. This was the nexus, the birthplace of the blight, a stark monument to the catastrophic consequences of fear masquerading as preservation.

"We need to understand how this severance was achieved," Cael said, breaking the heavy silence. "If we can understand the mechanism, perhaps we can find a way to counteract it, to begin healing this wound."

Mara looked at the fissure, at the pulsing crystalline structures. "The Crown Resonance is guiding us, but it's also showing us the depth of the damage. It's not just a physical severing, but an energetic one. They used a form of resonance counter-frequency, a song designed to cancel out Nyssera's very being."

"A song of silence," Elara whispered, her eyes fixed on the void. "They turned their power into its opposite. Into absence."

"And that absence is what has allowed the Pale Tide to flourish," Mara concluded. "It is the fertile ground where corruption can take root, unchecked by the vibrant pulse of Nyssera's true song." She took a deep breath, the sterile air doing little to fill her lungs. "We cannot simply fight the Pale Tide as it advances. We have to address the source. We have to confront the architects, or at least the legacy they left behind. This place... this is a monument to their mistake. And it's a mistake we cannot afford to let become permanent."

The journey to this nexus had been arduous, each step taking them further into a realm stripped bare of life's usual vibrancy. The air itself seemed to thin, losing its familiar resonance, becoming a brittle, fragile thing that offered little comfort. The very ground underfoot had transitioned from cracked earth to a peculiar, granular dust, pale and lifeless, that swirled around their boots with every movement. It felt like walking on the pulverized remains of what had once been.

Mara found her connection to the Great Song, the collective consciousness of the Choir, strained and tenuous here. It was like trying to hear a whisper in a hurricane of static. The usual vibrant tapestry of interconnected life, the hum of a million songs blending into a harmonious whole, was reduced to a faint, flickering ember. The silence was not merely an absence of sound; it was an active, oppressive force, a deliberate void that seemed to press in on their minds, attempting to extinguish their own inner songs.

Cael, ever vigilant, scanned their surroundings. The landscape was a stark tableau of desolation. Skeletal trees, bleached white and devoid of bark, stood like petrified sentinels against a sky the color of old bruises. They were not merely dead; they were *unmade*, their very essence seemingly leached away. Between them, strange, crystalline formations jutted from the ground, pulsing with a faint, cold luminescence. They were intricate, geometric, and utterly alien, an unsettling mockery of natural growth.

"This is it," Cael stated, his voice low and grim. "The heart of the severance. The point where Nyssera was most violently torn."

Elara flinched, her hands instinctively going to her temples. "I can feel it," she whispered, her voice strained. "The echo of that act. It's... agonizing. A silent scream trapped in the earth."

Mara focused, attempting to discern the lingering energies. She could feel the residual power of the leviadrakes, the immense force they had wielded. It was a chilling testament to their capabilities, a brutal demonstration of their conviction. But more than that, she felt the imprint of the original sundering itself, a cataclysmic event that had not just split Nyssera, but had fundamentally altered the world's Song.

"They believed they were acting for the greater good," Mara murmured, the words tasting like ash in her mouth. "To preserve the world, they had to silence what they saw as its most dangerous element. They viewed Nyssera's immense, untamed power as a threat that could only be contained through absolute severance."

She gestured to the crystalline growths. "These are not natural. They are the residue of that energetic manipulation. A form of resonance, twisted and corrupted, designed to absorb and nullify the Song. The leviadrakes created a barrier, a dead zone, to contain the damage. But in doing so, they created the genesis of the Pale Tide."

The crystalline structures hummed with a low, almost subliminal frequency. It was not a sound, but a vibration that seemed to seep into their bones, a cold, artificial rhythm that stood in stark opposition to the natural pulse of life. These were not mere geological formations; they were the solidified echoes of a violent act, a testament to the leviadrakes' terrifying power and their profound misunderstanding of the world's true nature.

"This silence," Elara said, her voice trembling, "it's a weapon. It feeds on the absence of the Song. The more Nyssera was silenced, the stronger this void became, and the more it began to spread."

Cael approached one of the larger crystalline formations, his hand hovering over its surface. "It feels... hollow," he observed. "Not just empty of sound, but empty of presence. As if it actively repels any form of life or resonance."

Mara could feel it too. The Crown Resonance, which had been their guiding light, was now a faint, struggling beacon in this oppressive emptiness. It was like trying to navigate by the dimmest of stars in a sky devoid of all celestial bodies. The leviadrakes had succeeded in creating a zone of absolute control, a stark monument to their fear.

"They saw Nyssera's boundless energy as chaos," Mara explained, her voice somber. "They couldn't comprehend a symphony of diverse voices. They wanted a single, pure note, and when they couldn't achieve it through harmony, they resorted to force. The severance was their desperate attempt to impose that singular note, to eliminate the perceived 'dissonance'."

She looked at the cracked, barren ground, the skeletal remains of ancient flora. "This is the cost of their 'preservation'. A world bleached of its vitality, a Song silenced. They believed that by severing Nyssera, they were saving the world from its own wildness. But they only unleashed a different kind of wildness – the wildness of absence, of decay."

The crystalline structures seemed to pulse in response to her words, their cold light flaring slightly. It was as if the very remnants of the leviadrakes' power were acknowledging her understanding. This desolate place was more than just a battlefield; it was the genesis of the Pale Tide, the point where the world's vibrant Song had been violently fractured, and from that fracture, a creeping emptiness had begun to spread.

"The Pale Tide," Elara whispered, her gaze fixed on the fissure from which a faint, phosphorescent mist seemed to emanate, "it's not just a force of destruction. It's the manifestation of that fear. The silence they imposed, given form."

"And it has been growing ever since," Cael added, his hand resting on the hilt of his sword. "Feeding on the echoes of their act, spreading like a disease of absence. They intended to protect the world, but they inadvertently created the very blight they sought to prevent."

Mara felt a profound sense of sorrow for the leviadrakes, trapped by their own fear and inability to comprehend the interconnectedness of Nyssera's being. Their act, born of a desire for preservation, had become the catalyst for decay. This desolate nexus was a stark, chilling reminder of what happened when fear triumphed over understanding, when the desire for control led to the eradication of life itself. They had sought to preserve a song by silencing its most vibrant notes, and in doing so, they had paved the way for a world where no song could be heard at all.

This was not just a place of historical significance; it was a living testament to the catastrophic cost of their decisions, a grim warning of what they fought to prevent from becoming the permanent state of their world. The silence here was deafening, a chilling testament to a choice made in fear, a choice that had birthed a void, and that void was now the Pale Tide.

CHAPTER ELEVEN
THE NEXUS OF SILENCE

The descent into the Corrupted Zone was less a journey and more an immersion into a profound, suffocating absence. The vibrant hum of the world, even in its weakened state, was utterly extinguished here. It was as if the very concept of sound had been surgically removed from existence, leaving behind a void that pressed in on Mara, Cael, and their reluctant leviadrake escorts. The air itself felt thick, not with humidity, but with a chilling inertia, a palpable stillness that made each breath a conscious effort. The ground, a strange, granular dust that offered no purchase, swirled around their boots like powdered bone.

Everywhere they looked, the landscape was a monument to severance. Skeletal trees, bleached to the color of dried sinew, clawed at the perpetually bruised sky, their branches brittle and devoid of any hint of life. Strange, crystalline formations, pulsing with a faint, sickly luminescence, jutted from the barren earth, mocking the memory of living flora. These were not the organic growths of a natural world, but the solidified residue of a violent energetic act, an unnatural parody of life born from an equally unnatural death.

"The Silence Event," Cael murmured, his voice barely a whisper, yet it seemed to shatter the oppressive quiet like brittle glass. "This is where it was most potent. The severance wasn't just a tearing of Nyssera; it was an erasure." He ran a gloved hand over one of the crystalline structures. It was unnervingly smooth, cool to the touch, and pulsed with a faint, almost imperceptible vibration – a phantom echo of the power that had been used to forge this desolation. "It's like a wound that never healed, but was instead cauterized with absolute zero."

Elara, her connection to the Great Song frayed to a whisper, flinched as if struck. "It feels... wrong," she breathed, her eyes wide with a mixture of dread and revulsion. "The absence... it's not just quiet. It's a hunger. The land is starving for its own song." She looked around at the barren expanse, the ghostly trees, the alien crystals. "This is where they tried to kill the Song itself."

Mara could feel the residual energy, the ghost of the titanic forces that had clashed here. It was a spectral battlefield, where the leviadrakes, in their misguided pursuit of order, had attempted to impose their will upon the boundless, untamed symphony of Nyssera. She could sense the fear that had driven them, the terror of a power they could not comprehend, a power they believed threatened to consume them all. But beneath that, she felt something else: the persistent, stubborn echo of Nyssera's song, even in its fractured state. It was a melody that refused to be silenced entirely, a defiant whisper in the face of overwhelming absence.

"They believed Nyssera was too chaotic," Mara said, her voice steady, though the oppressive silence felt like a physical weight against her chest. "Her untamed melody, her boundless energy... they saw it as a threat. They thought by severing her, by imposing this silence, they were saving the world from itself." She gestured to the crystalline growths. "But they didn't understand that the Song is not a single, pure note, but a symphony of countless voices, including those that might seem dissonant. They tried to enforce harmony by destroying the instruments."

As they ventured deeper, the desolation intensified. The ground gave way to a seabed of pulverized, pale dust, as if the very ocean had been rendered sterile. Jagged, spectral remnants of coral reefs and kelp forests, bleached and brittle, lay scattered like the bones of forgotten leviathans. The water, where it pooled in shallow depressions, was stagnant, thick, and utterly devoid of any movement or life. There was no current, no ripple, only a deathly stillness that mirrored the land above. It was a graveyard of the deep, a testament to the Pale Tide's relentless advance.

The leviadrakes accompanying them, their massive forms usually exuding an aura of ancient power, were visibly distressed. Their scales, usually shimmering with a healthy iridescence, seemed dulled, their movements sluggish. The oppressive silence gnawed at them, their natural resonance, their very lifeblood, being systematically drained away. They stumbled on the barren seabed, their powerful tails trailing uselessly in the stagnant water.

"The Crown Resonance," Mara announced, her voice strained, "it's strongest here. This is the epicenter. The point where the severance was deepest, where the silence was born." She could feel the Crown Resonance, usually a vibrant thread of energy guiding them, now a weak, flickering spark, struggling to penetrate the pervasive void. It was like trying to see by the light of a dying star in an unending night.

One of the leviadrakes, a colossal bull named Kaelen, let out a low, guttural groan that seemed to vibrate more from his immense frustration than from any actual sound. "This... place..." he rumbled, his voice a mere shadow of its former power, "it is anathema to our kind. The silence... it is a poison." His normally proud posture was slumped, his broad shoulders hunched as if burdened by an invisible weight.

Another leviadrake, a sleek, female named Lyra, nudged Kaelen with her massive head, her deep, resonant eyes filled with a shared unease. "The absence... it is not merely the absence of sound," she projected, her thoughts a weak, hesitant stream in Mara's mind. "It is an active negation. It seeks to unmake us, to unravel our Song, just as it did to Nyssera."

Mara nodded, understanding dawning with a chilling clarity. The Pale Tide was not simply a force of destruction; it was the embodiment of that original act of severance, the physical manifestation of the leviadrakes' fear. They had sought to create order by imposing silence, but in doing so, they had birthed a void that had an insatiable hunger. This Corrupted Zone was the heart of that hunger, the nucleus from which the Pale Tide sought to permanently divide Nyssera, to extinguish her Song forever.

"The crystalline formations," Cael observed, his keen eyes scanning the bizarre landscape. "They are not just mineral deposits. They are resonance absorbers. The leviadrakes, in their haste to contain the damage, created a mechanism to dampen Nyssera's Song, to cauterize the wound. But they created a perfect breeding ground for this... corruption." He kicked at a particularly large crystal, which pulsed with a faint, cold light in response. "It's like solidified fear. It drinks the Song and excretes emptiness."

Mara felt the truth of his words resonate deep within her. The severance had not been a clean break, but a brutal, messy act of violence. The leviadrakes, in their fear, had ripped Nyssera apart, not realizing that her Song was not a singular melody, but an intricate, interconnected symphony. By silencing the most vibrant, the most untamed parts, they had created a gaping wound, and that wound had festered, giving rise to the Pale Tide. This Corrupted Zone was the scar tissue, calcified and dead, from which the infection had spread.

"They thought they were preserving the world," Mara whispered, the words laced with a deep sorrow. "But they misunderstood the nature of life itself. They saw Nyssera's boundless energy as a threat, a force that needed to be controlled. They couldn't grasp that her wildness was her strength, that her dissonances were as vital as her harmonies." She looked at the skeletal remains of the ancient ecosystems, the stagnant, lifeless water. "This is the cost of their fear. A world drained of its vitality, a Song choked into silence."

The air grew colder as they pressed deeper into the zone, the pressure of the silence intensifying. It was no longer just an absence of sound, but a tangible force, pressing in on their minds, attempting to extinguish their inner songs. Mara could feel her own connection to the Choir, the collective consciousness of Nyssera's children, straining under the immense pressure. It was like trying to hold onto a thread in a hurricane.

"This place... it amplifies the severance," Cael said, his voice a low growl. "The energy here is... chaotic. Twisted. It's the residual trauma of the Silence Event, amplified by whatever technology or magic the leviadrakes employed." He pointed to a massive fissure in the seabed, from which a faint, phosphorescent mist seemed to emanate. "That's where the severing was deepest. I can feel the remnants of that violence. It's a wound that has never truly healed."

As they approached the fissure, the crystalline structures around it grew larger, more intricate, arranged in a disturbing, almost geometric pattern. They pulsed with a more pronounced, rhythmic glow, like the slow, mechanical heartbeat of a dying god. This was not the gentle pulse of life, but the cold, insistent thrum of something artificial and alien.

Elara shuddered, her hand reaching out instinctively, as if to shield herself from an invisible blow. "The Crown Resonance," she whispered, her voice barely audible. "It's... screaming. Not with sound, but with pure, unadulterated pain. It's showing me... the act itself. The fear... the desperation... the immense power being unleashed." She closed her eyes, a tear tracing a path through the dust on her cheek. "They didn't just sever Nyssera. They tried to unmake her."

Mara focused her will, pushing past the oppressive silence, trying to find the heart of the Crown Resonance. It was weak, faltering, but it was still there, a beacon in the desolation. It led them towards the fissure, towards the very epicenter of the Pale Tide's influence. This was not merely a corrupted zone; it was the genesis, the nucleus from which the blight had spread, the scar upon the world's soul that threatened to consume everything.

"They believed that by silencing the most powerful, the most untamed aspects of Nyssera, they were bringing order," Mara explained, her voice resonating with a newfound, somber understanding. "But they fundamentally misunderstood the nature of her Song. It was not a single, homogenous melody, but a complex symphony, where every voice, every dissonance, played a vital part. They tried to preserve a song by destroying its most vibrant notes, and in doing so, they paved the way for a world where no song could be heard at all."

The leviadrakes let out low, mournful rumbles, their immense forms seemingly shrinking in the face of the desolation. They were the descendants of those who had committed this act, and the weight of their ancestors' mistake pressed down on them. This place was a testament to their failure, a stark reminder of the catastrophic consequences of fear masquerading as preservation.

"The Pale Tide is not just a consequence of the severance," Mara continued, her voice carrying a profound sadness. "It is the embodiment of that fear. The silence they imposed, the absence they created – that is what the Pale Tide feeds on. It is the void left behind, growing, expanding, consuming the remaining Song." She looked at the crystalline structures, their cold, spectral light pulsing rhythmically. "These formations... they are solidified fear. They are absorbing the last vestiges of Nyssera's Song, calcifying it, turning it into this mockery of existence."

Cael knelt by the fissure, his hand hovering over the phosphorescent mist that curled out from it. It didn't feel like mist. It felt... empty. A complete lack of sensory input, a void that actively negated any sensation. "It's not just the absence of sound," he observed, his voice grim. "It's the absence of everything. A void that actively erases. They didn't just silence Nyssera; they tried to unmake her."

Mara nodded, the grim realization settling upon her. Vorlag's teachings, the emphasis on purity, on control, on the eradication of anything deemed 'unstable' – they had taken that philosophy to its absolute extreme here. They believed that by severing Nyssera, they were achieving ultimate control, ultimate purity. But they had only created a perfect breeding ground for corruption. The very act of preservation had become the catalyst for destruction. This Corrupted Zone was the monument to their mistake, a chilling testament to the catastrophic cost of fear, a mistake they were now fighting to ensure would not become permanent. The silence here was deafening, a chilling echo of a choice made in fear, a choice that had birthed a void, and that void was now the Pale Tide.

The desolation of the Corrupted Zone deepened, each step a descent into an ever-more profound absence. The granular dust underfoot seemed to absorb not just the sound of their passage, but the very light that dared to fall upon it. Skeletal remains of what might have been coral, or perhaps some forgotten, petrified flora, littered the ground, their bleached forms sharp and accusatory against the perpetually twilight sky. The air, if it could be called air, was thin and brittle, carrying no scent, no moisture, only a pervasive chill that seeped into bone and soul. The leviadrakes, their immense forms usually a testament to the vibrant, pulsing life of Nyssera, moved with a heavy, weary grace, their scales dulled, their resonant hum reduced to a near-imperceptible thrum.

"The Crown Resonance," Mara breathed, the words more of a physical effort than a vocalization. "It's... fading. Like a dying ember in this immensity of cold." She could feel it, the faint, spectral thread that had guided them, now frayed almost to oblivion. It was the heart of their quest, the faint echo of Nyssera's song that had been their beacon, and here, at the very heart of the severance, it was being choked.

Cael, ever the pragmatic observer, ran a diagnostic sweep, his brow furrowed with concentration. "It's not just fading, Mara. It's being actively suppressed. Whatever is at the center of this... this emptiness... it's a void that doesn't just absorb sound, it erases its very potential. It's anti-resonance." He gestured to the crystalline formations that now dominated the landscape, growing larger, more intricate, almost like skeletal fingers reaching from the barren earth. They pulsed with a faint, sickly light, a discordant rhythm that grated against the senses. "These crystals... they're like nodal points. Amplifiers of the silence. The leviadrakes must have designed them, thinking they could contain the damage, but they only created conduits for its propagation."

Elara, her senses attuned to the subtler energies of Nyssera, whimpered, pressing her hands to her temples. "It's... a silence that *thinks*," she whispered, her voice laced with a growing dread. "It's not just an absence. It's a presence of nothingness. It... it feels like a logical conclusion. A perfected state of non-being." Her eyes, wide with a horror that transcended mere fear, darted around the desolate panorama. "It's whispering... not with words, but with the *idea* of stillness. The idea that existence itself is a flaw. That pain, chaos, even the vibrancy of life... it's all a mistake that needs to be corrected."

Mara felt it then, a creeping chill that had nothing to do with the temperature. The crystalline structures were not just passive absorbers; they were conductors, channeling an energy that was both ancient and utterly alien. It was the antithesis of the Great Song, a negation of everything Nyssera represented. It was a pure, distilled emptiness, born from the fear and misunderstanding of those who had sought to control the uncontrollable.

"They believed that Nyssera's untamed melody was a threat," Mara murmured, the words tasting like ash. "That her boundless energy, her wildness, was too dangerous. They sought order, control. They sought to impose a singular, perfect harmony by silencing anything that didn't fit their design. And in doing so," she looked around at the sterile, dead landscape, "they created... this. A monument to their fear. A perfected silence, where nothing can grow, nothing can sing."

The leviadrakes, sensing the growing intensity of the void, shifted uneasily. Their immense bodies, usually radiating an aura of ancient wisdom and power, seemed to contract, their movements becoming more hesitant. Kaelen, the bull leviadrake, let out a low, guttural rumble that seemed to vibrate more with sorrow than any discernible sound.

This... place... it is the antithesis of our being, his thoughts projected, a weak, mournful stream. *It is the wound that festers. The void that seeks to unmake the very fabric of existence.*

Lyra, the female leviadrake, nudged him gently, her own projected thoughts a fragile lament.

It is the logic of erasure. The ultimate severance. They sought to bring peace through stillness, and they birthed a hunger that consumes all peace.

As they pressed forward, the landscape began to change subtly. The dust gave way to a more solidified, almost glassy surface, cracked and fissured like ancient ice. The skeletal remains of flora became more pronounced, their forms twisted into grotesque shapes, as if caught in a final, silent scream. And the crystalline structures grew in size and complexity, forming towering spires that seemed to drink the dim light from the sky, their surfaces etched with intricate, geometric patterns that hummed with a low, resonant frequency – a frequency of negation.

"We're close," Cael stated, his voice tight. "The energy signature is... intense. It's like standing on the edge of a black hole, but instead of gravity, it's the pull of absolute emptiness." He pointed towards a cavernous opening in the ground ahead, a wound in the very earth from which a faint, phosphorescent mist coiled upwards. It didn't shimmer with life or energy, but with a chilling absence of it. "That's the nexus. The heart of the Corrupted Zone."

Mara felt a profound sense of dread wash over her, yet it was also tinged with a strange, morbid curiosity. This was the culmination of the leviadrakes' greatest error, the embodiment of their deepest fear. It was not a monster in the traditional sense, not a creature of flesh and blood, but something far more insidious: a concept made manifest.

"The Pale Tide," she whispered, the name of the encroaching blight echoing in the oppressive stillness. "It originates from here. This is where the severance began, and this is where it seeks to achieve its final, absolute victory." She could feel the Crown Resonance within her, once a vibrant, guiding melody, now a fragile, almost extinguished spark, struggling against the encroaching void. It was like trying to hear a single, dying note in a deafening silence.

They approached the gaping maw of the fissure, the air growing perceptibly colder, the pressure of the silence intensifying. It was no longer just an absence of sound; it was a palpable force, pressing in on their minds, on their very beings, attempting to unravel their inner songs, to extinguish the spark of life within them. The leviadrakes let out low, resonant groans, their immense forms visibly shrinking under the psychic weight of the nexus.

"It is... ancient," Lyra projected, her thoughts strained. "Older than the oldest leviadrake, older than the mountains. It is the echo of a primordial fear. The fear of the unknown, the fear of chaos, the fear of life itself."

Kaelen rumbled, *And it is the ultimate expression of control. A world without struggle, without pain, without choice. A world reduced to its most fundamental, and ultimately lifeless, state.*

As they stood on the precipice of the fissure, the nexus revealed itself not as a physical entity, but as a swirling vortex of pure, negative energy. It was a vibrant display of nothingness, a pulsing heart of emptiness that seemed to draw the very light from the sky into its depths. The crystalline structures surrounding it pulsed in time with its rhythm, their sickly luminescence intensifying, feeding the void, amplifying its chilling logic.

Mara could feel it, the *logic* of the nexus. It wasn't driven by malice or hatred in the way a sentient being might be. Instead, it was propelled by a cold, stark rationality that argued for the cessation of all sensation, all experience, all existence. It whispered of the inherent suffering in life, the inevitable pain of connection, the chaos of individuality. And it offered an ultimate solution: absolute silence. Complete and utter oblivion, presented not as an end, but as a state of perfect, eternal peace.

Existence is a wound, the nexus seemed to communicate, not through words, but through a direct infusion of understanding into their minds. *The Song is discord. Life is struggle. All of it leads only to pain. The severance was a necessary correction. The silencing of the chaotic melody was the first step towards true peace. And this is the ultimate expression of that peace: the absorption of all that is, into the perfect stillness of non-being.*

It was the antithesis of the Great Song, a horrifying monument to forced forgetting and absolute control. Where the Song celebrated diversity, interconnectedness, and the vibrant, often messy, symphony of life, the nexus preached uniformity, isolation, and the sterile beauty of nothingness. It fed on the suppressed pain of Nyssera, the collective anxieties and fears of its inhabitants, using them as fuel to expand its dominion, to achieve its ultimate goal of complete severance.

The leviadrakes recoiled, their ancient spirits deeply disturbed by the sheer malevolence of the void. Their own innate resonance, their connection to the living world-song, was being actively assaulted, chipped away at by the relentless emptiness.

"It's... absorbing the residual pain," Cael realized, his voice a low growl of horror. "The trauma of the Silence Event, the suffering of Nyssera... it's not just residual energy; it's nourishment for this... this void. It's turning the planet's deepest wounds into the weapons that will finish her."

Elara, trembling, looked at Mara, her eyes filled with a desperate plea. "The Crown Resonance... it's being pulled in. Like a final, desperate cry for help. It's trying to fight, to resonate against the void, but it's being consumed."

Mara felt the truth of her words in her very core. The Crown Resonance, the last vestige of Nyssera's unified Song, was being systematically devoured by the nexus. It was a battle between existence and non-existence, between the vibrant, unpredictable symphony of life and the chilling, perfect silence of oblivion.

"They created it," Mara said, her voice heavy with a sorrow that transcended mere sadness. "The leviadrakes, in their fear of Nyssera's untamed power, sought to impose order. They wanted a predictable, controlled existence. They believed that by severing the wild, the chaotic, the unpredictable, they were saving the world. But they didn't understand that the Song *is* the chaos, the wildness, the unpredictability. That is where its beauty, its resilience, its very life force resides."

She looked at the pulsing vortex, the heart of the Corrupted Zone, a testament to the catastrophic consequences of that fear. "This nexus... it is the ultimate manifestation of that mistake. It is the logical endpoint of their desire for control. A state of perfect stillness, achieved by erasing everything that makes existence meaningful. It is the monument to a fear that sought to preserve life by extinguishing it."

The leviadrakes let out low, mournful rumbles, their massive forms seeming to bow under the weight of their ancestors' folly. They were living embodiments of the very Song that this nexus sought to destroy, and in its presence, they felt their own connection to Nyssera straining, threatened by the pervasive emptiness.

"The Pale Tide is not just a blight," Mara continued, her gaze fixed on the vortex of nothingness. "It is the *will* of this nexus. It is the drive for absolute severance, for the eradication of all resonance, all song, all life. It seeks to replicate this perfect void across Nyssera, to bring about a state of universal stillness, a perfected death where no one can ever be hurt again because nothing will exist to feel pain."

Cael knelt at the edge of the fissure, his hand outstretched, not to touch, but to feel the impossible absence emanating from within. "It feels like... a wound that actively seeks to expand. It doesn't just exist; it *wants* to become everything. It's the embodiment of existential despair, given form and purpose."

The nexus pulsed, and with each pulse, a wave of profound emptiness washed over them. It was a chilling sensation, like being hollowed out from the inside, like the very essence of their beings was being leached away. Mara could feel her own connection to the Choir, the vast network of consciousness that bound Nyssera's children, being stretched thin, the threads of connection frayed by the encroaching void. It was a terrifying realization: that the ultimate weapon against life was not destruction, but the complete and utter erasure of its possibility. This corrupted resonance, this nexus of silence, was the chilling proof.

The oppressive silence of the nexus was a physical weight, pressing down on their very souls. It was a silence that didn't merely dampen sound, but actively devoured it, leaving behind an echoing void where vibrant resonance had once thrived. The crystalline structures that studded the landscape, once inert geological formations, now pulsed with a sickly, artificial luminescence, their intricate facets humming with a low, discordant frequency that seemed to grate against the fabric of reality itself. They were not merely conduits for the silence, but amplifiers, broadcasting its chilling logic across the blighted expanse.

Mara could feel it, the agonizing pull on the Crown Resonance within her. Once a clear, guiding melody, it was now a fragile, sputtering ember, constantly threatened by the encroaching darkness. It was the last vestige of Nyssera's unified song, and this nexus, this monument to fear and control, was systematically devouring it. The leviadrakes, ancient beings whose very existence was intertwined with the planet's vibrant resonance, recoiled. Their massive forms seemed to shrink, their rumbling groans a lament for their ancestors' catastrophic error.

"It's the logic of erasure," Lyra, the female leviadrake, projected, her thoughts a sorrowful stream. "They sought peace through stillness, and they birthed a hunger that consumes all peace."

"It is the wound that festers," Kaelen, the bull leviadrake, added, his mental voice heavy with regret. "The void that seeks to unmake the very fabric of existence. It is the antithesis of our being."

As they stood on the precipice of the fissure, the nexus revealed itself not as a tangible entity, but as a swirling vortex of pure, negative energy. It was a terrifying display of nothingness, a pulsing heart of emptiness that seemed to draw the very light from the sky into its depths. The crystalline structures around it pulsed in sync with its rhythm, their sickly glow intensifying, feeding the void, amplifying its chilling doctrine.

Existence is a wound, the nexus seemed to communicate, not through words, but through a direct infusion of understanding into their minds.

The Song is discord. Life is struggle. All of it leads only to pain. The severance was a necessary correction. The silencing of the chaotic melody was the first step towards true peace. And this is the ultimate expression of that peace: the absorption of all that is, into the perfect stillness of non-being.

This was the antithesis of the Great Song, a horrifying testament to forced forgetting and absolute control. Where the Song celebrated diversity, interconnectedness, and the vibrant, often messy, symphony of life, the nexus preached uniformity, isolation, and the sterile beauty of nothingness. It fed on the suppressed pain of Nyssera, the collective anxieties and fears of its inhabitants, using them as fuel to expand its dominion, to achieve its ultimate goal of complete severance.

"It's... absorbing the residual pain," Cael realized, his voice a low growl of horror. "The trauma of the Silence Event, the suffering of Nyssera... it's not just residual energy; it's nourishment for this... this void. It's turning the planet's deepest wounds into the weapons that will finish her."

Elara, trembling, looked at Mara, her eyes filled with a desperate plea. "The Crown Resonance... it's being pulled in. Like a final, desperate cry for help. It's trying to fight, to resonate against the void, but it's being consumed."

Mara felt the truth of her words in her very core. The Crown Resonance, the last vestige of Nyssera's unified Song, was being systematically devoured by the nexus. It was a battle between existence and non-existence, between the vibrant, unpredictable symphony of life and the chilling, perfect silence of oblivion.

"They created it," Mara said, her voice heavy with a sorrow that transcended mere sadness. "The leviadrakes, in their fear of Nyssera's untamed power, sought to impose order. They wanted a predictable, controlled existence. They believed that by severing the wild, the chaotic, the unpredictable, they were saving the world. But they didn't understand that the Song *is* the chaos, the wildness, the unpredictability. That is where its beauty, its resilience, its very life force resides."

She looked at the pulsing vortex, the heart of the Corrupted Zone, a testament to the catastrophic consequences of that fear. "This nexus... it is the ultimate manifestation of that mistake. It is the logical endpoint of their desire for control. A state of perfect stillness, achieved by erasing everything that makes existence meaningful. It is the monument to a fear that sought to preserve life by extinguishing it."

The leviadrakes let out low, mournful rumbles, their massive forms seeming to bow under the weight of their ancestors' folly. They were living embodiments of the very Song that this nexus sought to destroy, and in its presence, they felt their own connection to Nyssera straining, threatened by the pervasive emptiness.

"The Pale Tide is not just a blight," Mara continued, her gaze fixed on the vortex of nothingness. "It is the *will* of this nexus. It is the drive for absolute severance, for the eradication of all resonance, all song, all life. It seeks to replicate this perfect void across Nyssera, to bring about a state of universal stillness, a perfected death where no one can ever be hurt again because nothing will exist to feel pain."

Cael knelt at the edge of the fissure, his hand outstretched, not to touch, but to feel the impossible absence emanating from within. "It feels like... a wound that actively seeks to expand. It doesn't just exist; it *wants* to become everything. It's the embodiment of existential despair, given form and purpose."

The nexus pulsed, and with each pulse, a wave of profound emptiness washed over them. It was a chilling sensation, like being hollowed out from the inside, like the very essence of their beings was being leached away. Mara could feel her own connection to the Choir, the vast network of consciousness that bound Nyssera's children, being stretched thin, the threads of connection frayed by the encroaching void. It was a terrifying realization: that the ultimate weapon against life was not destruction, but the complete and utter erasure of its possibility. This corrupted resonance, this nexus of silence, was the chilling proof.

Suddenly, a new resonance, sharp and brittle, cut through the oppressive stillness. It was not the mournful song of the leviadrakes, nor the faint, desperate cry of the Crown Resonance, but something deliberate, something *imposed*. It was the sound of ancient, unyielding conviction, amplified by the very void that sought to extinguish all song.

Emerging from the swirling mist that clung to the edges of the nexus, a procession of figures materialized. They moved with a grim, determined purpose, their forms clad in armor that seemed to absorb rather than reflect the dim light. At their forefront was a leviadrake, but unlike the gentle giants who accompanied Mara, this one bore scars that spoke of a life lived in the shadow of profound trauma, its scales dulled by a sorrow that had hardened into resolve. Vorlag.

His eyes, once pools of vibrant, earthy hues, were now the colour of a stormy sky, reflecting the bleakness of the landscape. He carried no weapon, yet his presence was a palpable force, a tangible embodiment of a desperate, unwavering conviction. Behind him marched a contingent of his most loyal followers, their faces grim, their movements precise and efficient, each one a living testament to his unwavering faith. They were the Guardians of the Severance, a sect born from the ashes of the Silence Event, their purpose as unyielding as the stones of their ancestral home.

"You are fools," Vorlag's voice boomed, the words carrying an unnatural resonance that seemed to vibrate within the very bones of those who heard it. The silence of the nexus did not absorb his voice; it seemed to *welcome* it, to twist it, to amplify its pronouncements of grim necessity. "You seek to mend a wound that can only be cauterized. To embrace a chaos that will consume us all."

Mara stepped forward, her heart pounding a desperate rhythm against her ribs. "Vorlag, you don't understand. This isn't healing; it's annihilation. This nexus is a wound that bleeds emptiness, not a balm that soothes pain."

Vorlag's gaze, intense and unwavering, swept over Mara, Cael, Elara, and the leviadrakes. There was no malice in his eyes, only a profound, unshakeable certainty that chilled Mara to the bone. "I understand perfectly," he stated, his voice devoid of emotion. "I have lived with the echoes of Nyssera's unchecked song. I have seen the devastation wrought by its wild, unpredictable nature. The Silence Event was not a mistake; it was a necessary, albeit incomplete, correction. This... nexus... is the key. The final severance."

He gestured towards the swirling vortex of nothingness with a hand that trembled slightly, not from fear, but from the sheer magnitude of the energy he sought to command. "The Pale Tide is a manifestation of Nyssera's pain, its untamed fury unleashed. It is a symptom of a broken song. But here," his gaze fixed on the nexus, "here is the cure. Not a healing, but a reordering. A return to a state of perfect, predictable harmony."

Cael moved to Mara's side, his stance defensive. "Harmony? Vorlag, this is the absence of everything! It's the negation of life itself!"

"Life is suffering, Cael," Vorlag countered, his voice rising with a fervor that bordered on zealotry. "Connection breeds pain. Individuality breeds conflict. The Great Song, in its infinite complexity, is a symphony of sorrow. This nexus offers a different path. A path of absolute peace. A state of perfect stillness, where no one can ever be hurt again because nothing will exist to feel pain."

He turned his attention to the leviadrakes, his expression softening slightly as he looked at Kaelen and Lyra. "My brethren," he said, his voice resonating with a deep, almost paternal sorrow, "you carry the burden of our ancestors' failure. You remember the vibrancy, the life, the song. But do you also remember the chaos? The wars, the destruction, the endless cycle of creation and ruin that the Song perpetuates? This severance is not an end; it is a salvation. A way to prevent the very cataclysm that fractured our world in the first place."

Kaelen let out a low, resonant rumble, his projected thoughts filled with a deep sadness.

Vorlag, your pain has blinded you. The Song is not merely chaos; it is resilience. It is change. It is the very essence of growth. To silence it is to become stagnant, to become dead.

Lyra added,

Your fear of suffering has led you to embrace oblivion. But oblivion is not peace. It is the absence of all things, good and ill.

Vorlag shook his head, his eyes fixed on the nexus. "You speak of ideals, of natural order. I speak of survival. Of a Nyssera that will not be torn asunder by its own boundless energy. The Pale Tide is spreading, its hunger insatiable. If we do not embrace the severance, it will consume us all. And this nexus," he declared, his voice regaining its commanding tone, "this is the only force powerful enough to truly manage the severance. To guide it, to control it, to ensure that it serves its ultimate purpose: the salvation of our world by its deliberate, controlled fragmentation."

He raised his hands, and a faint, crystalline light began to emanate from his fingertips, mirroring the luminescence of the nexus itself. His loyal followers mirrored his action, their combined energy forming a nascent wave of power that rippled towards the vortex.

"You believe this void is uncontrollable?" Vorlag scoffed, a grim smile playing on his lips. "It is a force of nature, yes, but one born of fear and misunderstanding. It is a broken melody seeking its final cadence. And I, with the blood of the Guardians coursing through my veins, will be the conductor. I will harness its power, I will guide its severance, and I will usher in an era of true, eternal peace."

Mara felt a surge of dread. Vorlag wasn't just seeking to complete the severance; he was actively attempting to *control* the nexus, to bend its nihilistic power to his will. His conviction was absolute, born from a deep-seated trauma and a rigid, unforgiving interpretation of his role as a guardian. He truly believed he was saving the world by enforcing its necessary fragmentation, a desperate act rooted in an ancient fear that had festered for generations.

"You cannot control it, Vorlag!" Mara pleaded, her voice ringing with desperation. "It's not a tool; it's a destructive force! You're not guiding the severance; you're feeding it! You're accelerating the very destruction you claim to fear!"

But Vorlag was deaf to her pleas. His gaze was locked on the nexus, his entire being focused on the act of channeling its immense, terrifying power. His followers, their faces etched with unwavering loyalty, channeled their own energies into his, forming a conduit of raw, unyielding resolve. The air around them crackled, the silence of the nexus seeming to respond, to vibrate with the influx of this new, imposed resonance.

"The Pale Tide," Vorlag proclaimed, his voice echoing with a chilling triumph, "is an uncontrolled symphony of chaos. But I will conduct the final movement. A symphony of silence. A perfect, ordered end."

The crystalline structures around the nexus pulsed brighter, their sickly light intensifying as Vorlag and his followers poured their energy into the void. It was a terrifying spectacle, a desperate gamble on the edge of oblivion. Mara watched, her heart aching, as Vorlag, a figure once dedicated to protection, now sought to unleash the ultimate form of severance, believing it to be the only path to salvation. He was a guardian corrupted by fear, a protector turned executioner, his loyalty to an abstract ideal blinding him to the very life he sought to preserve.

Cael, his jaw set, stepped in front of Mara, his diagnostic tools whirring with renewed urgency. "He's drawing power from the nexus," he stated, his voice tight with concern. "It's like he's creating a feedback loop. The more energy he feeds it, the stronger it becomes, and the more power it can give back to him."

"He thinks he can control it," Elara whispered, her voice trembling. "But it's like trying to hold lightning in your bare hands. It will consume him. It will consume us all."

Vorlag's leviadrake, a hulking beast named Voraxis, let out a guttural roar, a sound that was not of defiance, but of a deep, primal agony. The nexus's influence was a poison, even to those who sought to wield it. Voraxis's scales, once a deep, rich obsidian, were now streaked with an unnatural pallor, its eyes burning with a frantic, almost mad light.

"Voraxis," Vorlag said, his voice still surprisingly steady, though a tremor ran through his frame. "Stand with me. Witness the dawn of Nyssera's true peace."

But Voraxis merely recoiled, its immense head thrashing as if trying to dislodge an unbearable burden. The nexus's song was too pure, too absolute in its negation for even a leviadrake loyal to such a cause. It was a song of unraveling, and even those most committed to its cause would eventually be unmade by its power.

Mara watched as Vorlag's form began to flicker, his edges blurring as the nexus's influence seeped into him. His conviction was his shield, but it was also his cage, trapping him in a logic that demanded absolute severance. He was so consumed by the fear of Nyssera's perceived inherent chaos that he could no longer see the beauty in its resilience, the strength in its interconnectedness, or the hope in its enduring song.

"He's not controlling it," Mara murmured, her voice a mix of sorrow and dawning understanding. "He's becoming it. He's letting the void absorb his own resonance, his own fears, until he's nothing more than another amplifier for its silencing music."

The crystalline structures around the nexus pulsed with a blinding intensity, as if in response to Vorlag's efforts. The nexus, the heart of the Corrupted Zone, was not a passive entity to be manipulated. It was a hungry void, and Vorlag, in his misguided attempt to harness its power, was offering himself as its first, willing sacrifice. His loyalists, though their faces remained set in grim determination, began to falter, their own energies wavering under the sheer, overwhelming power of the nexus. The silence, once merely oppressive, was now a consuming presence, an active force that sought to dissolve all boundaries, all distinctions, all life.

The leviadrakes let out a collective mournful cry, a sound that seemed to pierce the oppressive stillness, a final lament for a guardian lost to his own fear. Mara knew then that Vorlag's last stand was not a victory, but a tragedy. He was a man consumed by a desperate need for order in a world he perceived as inherently chaotic, a world whose very essence was its vibrant, unpredictable song. In his quest to silence Nyssera, he was silencing himself, becoming a part of the very void he believed would save them. The nexus pulsed, and Vorlag's form flickered again, the light of his conviction dimming as the all-encompassing darkness of the nexus began to claim him, and the silence, ever more absolute, echoed around them.

Cael's tactical maneuvers were a stark contrast to the raw, unbridled power Vorlag and his followers wielded. Where they sought to impose order through severance, Cael aimed to create space for Nyssera's natural healing through clever disruption. He understood that direct confrontation with Vorlag's zealous conviction, fueled by the nexus's amplified energy, would be futile. Instead, he focused on the environmental tapestry of the corrupted zone, a landscape of unstable energies and fractured crystalline formations that Vorlag, in his rigid adherence to his ideology, largely ignored.

As Vorlag and his Guardians channeled their energies into the nexus, their focus narrowed, their senses dulled by the intoxicating promise of absolute peace. This was Cael's opening. He didn't charge headlong into the fray. Instead, he moved with a predator's grace, his boots finding purchase on the shimmering, unstable ground that pulsed with residual energy. He was not merely avoiding the surges of power; he was anticipating them, subtly shifting the terrain with well-placed bursts of his own resonant energy, creating small, localized tremors that diverted the flow of arcane power.

His first objective was to break the focused concentration of Vorlag's core group. He spotted a cluster of larger crystalline formations, their facets humming with a discordant energy that seemed to amplify the nexus's silencing effect. These structures, dormant but charged, were perfect conduits for a controlled disruption. With a swift, precise strike of his hand, Cael unleashed a focused wave of resonant energy, not aimed at destruction, but at activation. The crystals flared, not with Vorlag's grim, crystalline light, but with a chaotic surge of their inherent instability. The resulting cascade of light and sound, though muted by the nexus's pervasive dampening effect, was enough to draw the attention of several of Vorlag's more peripheral followers. Their heads snapped up, their rigid formations wavering for a crucial instant.

"Mara!" Cael projected, his mental voice cutting through the oppressive silence, a clear, unwavering beacon. "They're distracted. Focus on the Crown Resonance!"

Mara, her gaze locked on the swirling vortex of nothingness, nodded, the faint pulse of the Crown Resonance within her flickering but holding. She felt Cael's efforts, the subtle shifts in the battlefield that allowed her the precious moments she needed to maintain her connection to the dwindling song.

Cael continued his campaign of calculated chaos. He noticed how the unstable energies of the corrupted zone pulsed in rhythmic waves. Vorlag and his followers, in their single-minded pursuit of the nexus, were riding these waves, their power growing with each surge. Cael, however, sought to disrupt the rhythm. He moved between the pulses, using the brief lulls to his advantage, darting from cover to cover, his movements fluid and unpredictable. He would then release a targeted burst of resonant energy, timed to coincide with the *end* of a natural energy wave, effectively creating a localized counter-wave. It was like throwing a pebble into a predictable stream, not to stop it, but to create a ripple that would throw off the larger currents.

One such counter-wave struck a group of Guardians who were marching in a tight, disciplined line, their steps synchronized as they advanced towards the nexus. The sudden, jarring surge of energy, emanating from the ground beneath them, broke their formation. They stumbled, their rigid movements turning into a chaotic scramble to regain balance. One Guardian, his face a mask of grim determination, lost his footing and tumbled down a shallow embankment, his armor clattering against the fractured stone. He wasn't seriously injured, but the disruption was enough. The disciplined march faltered, and the carefully orchestrated advance became a scattered pursuit.

"This is not how it is done," one of the Guardians muttered, his voice tight with annoyance as he helped his fallen comrade. "Such... sloppiness."

Cael heard the mental grumble, a faint echo picked up by his enhanced senses. He allowed himself a small, grim smile. Sloppiness, to Vorlag, was a betrayal of order. But to Cael, it was a strategic tool. He was not fighting to defeat them in a traditional sense. He was fighting to delay them, to disorient them, to prevent them from adding their amplified power to the nexus at this critical juncture. His goal was neutralization, not annihilation. He had no desire to add to the suffering of Nyssera, only to alleviate the immediate threat.

He then turned his attention to Vorlag himself. The former Guardian was a force of nature, his connection to the nexus growing stronger with every moment he stood before it, channeling his conviction. Cael knew he couldn't engage Vorlag directly. The sheer power radiating from him, amplified by the nexus, would overwhelm him. But Vorlag was still a leviadrake, and leviadrakes, even those who had embraced severance, were still intrinsically linked to the planet's resonance. And where there was resonance, there was a potential for manipulation.

Cael observed the environment around Vorlag and his most devoted followers. They were standing on a section of the corrupted zone that seemed particularly unstable, a nexus of intersecting energy lines that thrummed with a dangerous, volatile energy. Vorlag was drawing upon this raw power, feeding it into the nexus, and in turn, receiving a more potent, corrupted form of resonance. Cael saw a series of dormant fissures, barely visible beneath the crystalline dust, that pulsed with a deep, contained energy. These were natural conduits, remnants of Nyssera's primal forces, still capable of channeling energy, albeit in a raw, untamed manner.

He began to subtly agitate these fissures. With carefully controlled bursts of his own resonance, he nudged and prodded at the subterranean energy flows, coaxing them to surge. It was a delicate dance, like tuning an ancient instrument. He wasn't trying to create a massive explosion, but a controlled overload. He wanted to redirect the energy that Vorlag was so eagerly drawing upon.

As Vorlag continued his ritual, Cael unleashed the full force of his manipulation. He sent a powerful, resonant pulse deep into the earth, targeting the confluence of dormant fissures. The ground beneath Vorlag and his immediate circle began to tremble, not with the steady rhythm of the nexus, but with a violent, unpredictable tremor. The raw energy that Vorlag had been so readily absorbing now surged uncontrollably, ripping through the fissures, creating a chaotic maelstrom of light and sound that erupted around them.

It wasn't an attack, not directly. It was a redirection. The raw power, now unchanneled, lashed out, creating a blinding flash of multicolored light and a deafening roar that momentarily overwhelmed the nexus's oppressive silence. The Guardians closest to Vorlag cried out, shielding their eyes, their focused intent shattered. Vorlag himself staggered, his ritualistic stance broken. He was not harmed, but his connection to the nexus was momentarily severed by the sheer force of the uncontrolled energy eruption.

"This is not in accordance with the severance!" one of the Guardians yelled, his voice strained against the din.

"It is the Song!" another retorted, his voice laced with fear and a hint of revulsion. "It fights back!"

Cael used this moment of confusion. While Vorlag was reeling, his followers scattered and disoriented, Cael moved swiftly towards Mara. He could feel her struggle, the Crown Resonance weakening with each passing moment. He placed a steadying hand on her shoulder.

"The nexus is a wound that feeds on pain, Vorlag," Cael projected, his voice amplified by his own resonance, cutting through the fading echoes of the energy surge. "You're not healing it; you're poisoning it further. True peace isn't the absence of song, but the harmony of all its notes, even the discordant ones."

Vorlag, his face etched with a mixture of rage and disbelief, turned his stormy gaze towards Cael. "You do not understand! This chaos... it is the disease! The nexus is the cure!" He gestured wildly, trying to reassert control, but the fissures continued to churn, spitting out random bursts of energy that kept his followers at bay.

Cael continued to weave his tactical magic. He noticed that the crystalline structures, which Vorlag's forces seemed to favor for channeling their energy, were also sensitive to harmonic frequencies. He began to hum a low, resonant tone, a simple, pure melody that was the antithesis of the nexus's jarring dissonance. He varied the pitch and intensity, directing his resonant hum at specific clusters of crystals. The crystals began to glow, not with the sickly luminescence of the nexus, but with a softer, more ethereal light. They resonated with Cael's song, vibrating gently, absorbing some of the nexus's pervasive silence, creating pockets of localized calm.

These pockets acted as brief reprieves, small havens where the oppressive weight of the silence lessened, allowing the natural sounds of Nyssera – the faint rustle of the blighted flora, the distant groan of the leviadrakes – to momentarily reassert themselves. The Guardians, caught between Vorlag's increasingly frantic commands and these unexpected moments of auditory respite, found their resolve wavering. Their unwavering faith was being chipped away by the persistent, gentle logic of Cael's song.

Cael's strategy was not about overwhelming force, but about gradual erosion. He was creating subtle breaks in the nexus's dominion, tiny cracks in Vorlag's rigid dogma. He was demonstrating, through action rather than words, that there was an alternative to Vorlag's vision of sterile peace. He showed that Nyssera's inherent resonance, even in its corrupted state, could still be coaxed, still be guided, still be *heard*.

He noticed a young Guardian, his armor bearing the insignia of the Severance, hesitating. The boy's eyes, wide with a conflict that mirrored his own past struggles, darted between Vorlag's enraged form and the calming glow of the resonating crystals. Cael focused his energy on a single, particularly beautiful crystal near the boy. He infused it with a resonance that spoke of hope, of resilience, of the inherent value of every living thing. The crystal pulsed with a warm, inviting light. The boy, almost unconsciously, took a step towards it, his weapon lowering slightly.

"The Song is not the enemy," Cael's voice echoed, soft but clear, directed at the boy, and by extension, at all of Vorlag's wavering followers. "Fear is the enemy. The desire to silence what we don't understand, that is the true wound."

Vorlag roared, his leviadrake form thrashing as if caught in an invisible current. "Silence him! He spreads corruption!"

But his commands were becoming less potent. The chaotic energies Cael had unleashed earlier were still swirling, preventing his followers from converging on Cael. They were trapped in a no-win situation, caught between their leader's increasingly desperate pronouncements and the tangible evidence of a different path, a path demonstrated by Cael's calculated actions.

Cael continued his work, not just disrupting, but subtly guiding. He began to use the natural energy flows of the corrupted zone to create ephemeral barriers, shimmering walls of contained resonance that blocked the direct path of Vorlag's followers towards Mara. These barriers weren't solid; they were more like illusions, designed to confuse and redirect. They would appear, flicker, and then dissipate, leading the Guardians on a chase through the unstable terrain, further fragmenting their assault.

He observed how the Pale Tide, the spreading blight emanating from the nexus, reacted to different resonant frequencies. While the nexus's silence seemed to empower it, Cael found that certain specific frequencies, when amplified through the crystals, seemed to cause the tendrils of the Pale Tide to recoil, to wither, to momentarily recede. He wasn't strong enough to push back the tide entirely, but he could create localized zones of resistance, small islands of relative safety where the corrupting influence was lessened.

This was a crucial part of his strategy: creating safe zones for Mara. As she focused on rekindling the Crown Resonance, Cael was working to shield her from the immediate threats, both physical and spiritual. He was creating a perimeter of subtle, intelligent defense, a web of resonant frequencies designed to disrupt and disorient, rather than destroy. His goal was to buy Mara time, to allow her the space to perform her vital task of re-establishing the connection to Nyssera's inherent song.

He looked at Vorlag, a figure consumed by his own dogma, his transformation into a being of pure severance a tragic spectacle. Cael felt no malice, only a profound sorrow. Vorlag was a victim of his own fear, a mirror of what could happen when the desire for control overshadowed the appreciation for life's inherent complexity. Cael's fight was not against Vorlag's conviction, but against the *consequences* of that conviction, against the dangerous ideology that sought to extinguish Nyssera's vibrant, messy, beautiful song.

With a final, focused effort, Cael directed a powerful harmonic pulse through a large cluster of crystals. The resulting resonance spread outwards, creating a wide, shimmering barrier of calming energy that momentarily pushed back the encroaching Pale Tide and caused Vorlag's most devoted followers to falter. They were momentarily blinded by the soft, warm light, their rigid resolve wavering in the face of this unexpected, gentle resistance.

"This is not the end, Vorlag," Cael projected, his voice carrying a quiet authority. "It is a turning point. Nyssera will not be silenced. It will sing. And we will help it find its voice again."

He then turned his full attention back to Mara, his strategic maneuvers creating a vital pocket of calm around her, a small sanctuary within the heart of the storm, a testament to the power of adaptability and the unwavering belief in a different kind of peace. The battle was far from over, but Cael had successfully disrupted the enemy's momentum, creating the crucial breathing room Mara needed to face the nexus itself. His tactics were not about brute force, but about intelligence, foresight, and a deep understanding of the intricate energies that bound Nyssera together, even in its broken state. He was the conductor of a different kind of symphony, one that sought to mend rather than shatter, to harmonize rather than silence.

The oppressive silence of the nexus had been a physical weight, a suffocating blanket that dulled the senses and twisted perception. Yet, within its heart, where the void pulsed with a hunger for oblivion, Mara stood. Cael's subtle disruptions, the controlled chaos he'd sown amongst Vorlag's followers, had carved a fragile pocket of calm around her. It was a sanctuary built not of stone or energy shields, but of resonant frequencies, a testament to his belief in harmony's power. Beside her, the conciliatory leviadrakes, their massive forms radiating a sorrowful understanding, acted as silent guardians. Their presence, a stark contrast to Vorlag's zealous followers, was a grounding force, a reminder of Nyssera's enduring life even in its wounded state.

Mara's gaze, usually filled with a fierce, untamed spirit, was now one of profound focus. Her eyes, reflecting the unnatural, starless dark of the nexus, did not recoil. Instead, they met the void head-on, not with defiance, but with an offering. She felt the crushing emptiness, the chilling logic of severance that permeated this place, the seductive whisper of an end to all pain, all struggle, all existence. It was a powerful lure, a twisted promise of peace that preyed on the weariness of ages. But Mara carried within her a different truth, a mended song that resonated with the very essence of Nyssera.

She did not raise a weapon. She did not channel destructive energies. Her confrontation was far more intimate, far more potent. She reached inwards, to the nascent world-song she and Cael had been painstakingly weaving. It was not a song of erasure, but a song of integration, a melody born from the ashes of grief and the vibrant bloom of memory. She felt the echoes of laughter from a forgotten village, the rustle of leaves in ancient forests, the fierce, protective love of a mother for her child, the poignant ache of loss, the exhilaration of discovery, the quiet solace of companionship. All of it, the beautiful and the brutal, the joyous and the sorrowful, were present within her song.

With a deep, centering breath, Mara began to project this woven harmony outwards. It was not a thunderous crescendo, but a gentle, persistent hum, a resonance that began to seep into the void, not to destroy it, but to *fill* it. She was offering the nexus, this gaping maw of nothingness, the very substance of existence. She was showing it what it was attempting to erase, and more importantly, what it could *become*.

The logic of emptiness, the nexus's core operating principle, was one of stark, unyielding simplicity. It saw pain, it saw struggle, and it offered oblivion as the only solution. But Mara's song introduced complexity. It demonstrated that pain was inextricably linked to joy, that struggle was the crucible of growth, that memory was the anchor of identity. Her song carried the weight of empathy, not just for the living, but for the very fabric of Nyssera itself.

As her song expanded, it touched the minds of those nearby, not just Cael and the leviadrakes, but even some of Vorlag's more distant followers, those whose rigid focus had wavered under Cael's onslaught. They heard it, not with their ears, but with their souls. It bypassed their indoctrination, their practiced stoicism, and spoke directly to the remnants of their own buried experiences. A flicker of recognition, a ghost of a forgotten feeling, stirred within them. The nexus's logic of emptiness offered an escape from suffering, but Mara's song offered understanding. It offered connection.

She pictured the nexus not as a wound to be cauterized, but as a void that craved to be a part of something larger. She projected images, not of destruction, but of transformation. She showed the void how the raw, unformed potential of existence could be shaped and tempered, how darkness could give way to light, how silence could be filled with meaning.

It was an offer of integration, of absorption into a vibrant, living whole, rather than annihilation.

"You are not empty," Mara's voice, amplified by the resonance of her song, echoed not through the air, but through the very fabric of reality. "You are potential. You are the space where life can begin. But life cannot exist in the absence of experience. It needs the vibrant spectrum of existence, the laughter and the tears, the creation and the decay. It needs *song*."

She felt the nexus resist, its silence pushing back, attempting to smother her offering. It was a primal instinct, a desperate clinging to its singular purpose of negation. But Mara's song was persistent. It was the relentless ebb and flow of the tides, the unwavering cycle of the seasons, the enduring beat of a heart. It carried the resilience of Nyssera itself.

She focused on the core of the void, the pulsing heart of the nexus. She imagined reaching out, not to tear it apart, but to embrace it. Her song softened, becoming a lullaby, a gentle invitation. It spoke of belonging, of finding a place within the grand tapestry, of contributing its unique essence to the symphony of existence. She was offering the nexus a new purpose, a chance to transcend its destructive nature and become a vital part of Nyssera's ongoing story.

The conciliatory leviadrakes rumbled, their low vibrations a harmonious counterpoint to Mara's song. They understood. They had witnessed eons of Nyssera's cycles, its triumphs and its tragedies. They knew that true peace was not the absence of struggle, but the ability to navigate it, to learn from it, and to grow stronger because of it. Their silent support was a powerful affirmation of Mara's approach.

One of Vorlag's closest Guardians, a woman known for her unwavering devotion to the severance, faltered. Her disciplined posture, so rigidly maintained, seemed to sag. She had been channeling her energy into the nexus, bolstering its silencing effect, but Mara's song had begun to seep into her consciousness. She heard echoes of her childhood laughter, a sound she had long suppressed, a reminder of a time before the creed of severance had consumed her. The purity of that memory, juxtaposed against the stark, sterile peace Vorlag preached, created a chasm of doubt within her.

Mara sensed this shift, this fragile opening in the armor of indoctrination. She intensified her offering, weaving into her song the concept of acceptance. Acceptance of flaws, acceptance of imperfections, acceptance of the messy, unpredictable nature of life. The nexus thrived on the idea of absolute purity, of a world cleansed of all that was deemed undesirable. Mara was showing it that true beauty lay in the integration of all its parts, even the ones that seemed broken or discordant.

She envisioned the nexus as a single, vast chord, waiting to be harmonized with the rest of Nyssera's symphony. It was not an alien entity to be destroyed, but a lost note seeking its place. Her song was the bridge, the conductor's baton, guiding it towards resolution.

"You can be more than just the absence," she projected, her voice imbued with the gentle power of understanding. "You can be the quiet between the notes, the breath that sustains the melody, the stillness that allows the song to be heard with clarity. You are not a wound, but a pause, a moment of reflection before the next movement begins."

The sheer audacity of her approach was its greatest strength. While Vorlag sought to sever and destroy, Mara sought to connect and integrate. She was not fighting the nexus; she was offering it a transformation. She was extending empathy to the very embodiment of negation, a concept so alien to its existence that it struggled to comprehend it.

The corrupted resonance, the palpable aura of silence, began to churn. It wasn't a violent reaction, but a subtle, internal disturbance, like a vast ocean disturbed by an unseen current. The void was not being attacked, but it was being *challenged*. Its fundamental logic was being questioned by the vibrant, undeniable reality of Mara's mended world-song.

Mara could feel the immense pressure of the nexus trying to crush her song, to extinguish its light. It was a battle of philosophies, of realities.

Vorlag's severance was a philosophy of fear, of control, of a sterile, imagined perfection. Mara's song was a philosophy of acceptance, of love, of the messy, vibrant, and ultimately, more profound reality of interconnected existence.

She focused on the memory of Cael, his unwavering faith in her, his belief in the power of harmony. His efforts to shield her, to disrupt Vorlag's forces, had created this very opportunity. She drew strength from his resolve, his willingness to fight for a Nyssera that embraced all its parts.

"You are a part of us," she whispered, her voice now a private utterance, directed at the heart of the void. "And we are a part of you. Separation is an illusion. True peace lies in understanding our interconnectedness."

She then brought forth a memory, a vivid, powerful one: the moment she had first truly understood the Crown Resonance, not as a burden, but as a song of responsibility, a promise to protect. She projected the feeling of that promise, the weight of it, the beauty of it, into the nexus. It was the embodiment of Nyssera's enduring will to *be*, to continue, to sing.

The nexus pulsed, a deep, resonant thrum that vibrated through Mara's very bones. It was not an acceptance, not yet, but it was a response. The oppressive silence wavered, and for a fleeting moment, Mara thought she heard a faint, almost imperceptible whisper, a question carried on the wind of non-existence. It was the echo of a possibility, the first fragile tendril of a new song reaching out from the heart of the void.

She knew this was only the beginning. The nexus would not be instantly healed, nor would Vorlag's ideology vanish overnight. But she had planted a seed. She had shown that the void was not inherently evil, but simply misunderstood, a reflection of Nyssera's own pain and fragmentation. By offering it integration, by weaving it into the greater tapestry of existence, she had offered it a path to redemption, a chance to become something more than just an ending. And in doing so, she had reinforced the power of the mended world-song, proving that true healing came not from severance, but from embrace.

Chapter Twelve

Repairing the World-Song

The oppressive silence that had clung to the nexus like a shroud began to fray. Mara's song, born from the very essence of Nyssera's vibrant, sorrowful, and exhilarating existence, was proving to be more than a mere counter-melody; it was an unraveling force. The corrupted resonance, a manifestation of Pale Tide energy twisted by Vorlag's destructive intent, found itself unable to maintain its monolithic structure against the insistent, overwhelming influx of integrated memory and emotion. It was like a tightly wound spring, designed for singular, destructive tension, suddenly being asked to accommodate the fluid, dynamic dance of a living symphony. The void, which had previously pulsed with a hunger for oblivion, now felt a strange, unsettling pressure, a subtle reordering of its fundamental fabric.

The first visible sign of this profound shift was a flickering, a wavering in the starless dark that had defined the nexus. It was as if a veil was being lifted, not to reveal a blinding light, but to expose the subtle, underlying textures of reality that had been suppressed. The suffocating silence, which had felt as tangible as stone, began to break. Not with a sudden, explosive roar, but with a tentative sigh, a whisper of what had been lost. Faint, ethereal echoes of the world-song, previously drowned out by the nexus's oppressive void, began to surface. They were fragile at first, like the first hesitant notes of a hesitant musician, but they carried the undeniable resonance of life, of connection, of Nyssera's enduring spirit. These were not the boisterous melodies of peak vitality, but the poignant, bittersweet refrains of memory, of resilience, of a life that had known both profound beauty and deep suffering.

Mara felt it directly, the loosening of the nexus's grip. The crushing weight on her spirit eased, replaced by a sensation akin to a deep, internal sigh of relief. She could feel the corrupted energy, the very substance of the Pale Tide's perversion, not vanishing into nothingness, but undergoing a transformation. It was being absorbed, its destructive potential neutralized, not by force, but by understanding. Like a tangled knot of poisonous vines being carefully disentangled and woven into a tapestry of healing herbs, the corrupted strands were being re-threaded into the larger planetary memory. They were becoming integrated, their sharp edges smoothed, their virulence replaced by a more benign, less disruptive presence. The nexus was not being destroyed; it was being healed, its wounds not excised but mended, its scar tissue becoming a testament to resilience rather than a symbol of decay.

The leviadrakes, who had been standing as silent sentinels, their massive forms radiating a sorrowful understanding, rumbled softly. Their low vibrations resonated with Mara's song, adding a depth and gravitas to the emerging harmony. They had witnessed eons of Nyssera's tumultuous existence, its cycles of growth and decay, its moments of breathtaking creation and devastating loss. They understood that true healing was not about erasing the past, but about integrating it, about learning from its lessons and allowing its scars to inform future strength. Their presence, a living embodiment of Nyssera's ancient wisdom, served as a powerful anchor, grounding Mara's transformative work in the enduring reality of the world.

Cael, his face etched with a mixture of relief and awe, watched Mara with unwavering intensity. His subtle disruptions, his calculated chaos, had created the opening, the fragile sanctuary that had allowed Mara to perform this monumental act of healing. He saw in her eyes not triumph, but a profound empathy, an understanding that extended even to the very embodiment of negation. He had always believed in the power of connection, in the inherent song within all things, but witnessing Mara weave such potent harmony into the heart of oblivion was a validation of his deepest convictions. He felt the residual tendrils of Vorlag's followers stir around them. Some were still rigid, their minds stubbornly clinging to the creed of severance, but others were wavering. Mara's song had bypassed their hardened defenses, touching the dormant embers of their own buried experiences, stirring questions that they had long suppressed. The sterile promise of oblivion was losing its allure when contrasted with the vibrant, messy, and profoundly human tapestry Mara was reweaving.

A particularly devout follower of Vorlag, a woman named Seraphina, whose devotion had been as unyielding as forged steel, began to tremble. Her hands, which had been clasped in prayer, now faltered, her knuckles white. She had been a staunch proponent of the nexus's cleansing power, believing it the only way to purge Nyssera of its imperfections. But Mara's song, a melody of acceptance and integration, had begun to chip away at her resolve.

She heard, not with her ears, but with a deeper sense, the echoes of her own past, of childhood joys and innocent sorrows she had painstakingly buried beneath layers of dogma. The purity she sought in severance now seemed like a hollow echo when compared to the rich, complex fullness of Mara's song. A single tear traced a path down her cheek, a silent testament to the crack forming in her worldview. Mara sensed this subtle shift, this nascent doubt blooming in the barren landscape of indoctrination. It was a fragile opening, but in the context of the nexus, even the smallest flicker of internal conflict was a significant victory.

Mara intensified her projection, weaving into her song the concept of acceptance not as a passive surrender, but as an active embrace. She envisioned the nexus not as an enemy to be vanquished, but as a discordant chord within Nyssera's grand symphony, a note that had been struck with the wrong intention, but which still held the potential for harmony. Her song was the conductor's baton, guiding this errant note back into its rightful place within the larger composition. She wasn't trying to erase the void; she was offering it a new purpose, a transformation from an ending to a profound pause, a space for reflection before the next movement of Nyssera's unfolding song.

"You are not an end," Mara's voice resonated, a gentle current against the receding tide of silence. "You are a breath. The quiet that allows the melody to be heard. The space between the stars that defines their brilliance. You are the potential for a new beginning, not the cessation of all things." She poured into her song the understanding that existence was not a binary of light and dark, of perfection and imperfection, but a spectrum, a complex interplay of all its elements. The nexus, designed for the stark simplicity of negation, found itself grappling with this radical concept of holistic integration.

The corrupted energy within the nexus churned with a new, less frantic energy. It was a disturbance, not of violence, but of profound reorientation. The very logic of emptiness, the core principle that governed its existence, was being challenged by the undeniable reality of Mara's mended world-song. It was a confrontation of philosophies, of fundamental truths about existence. Vorlag's severance was a philosophy born of fear, of control, of a desire for a sterile, imagined perfection. Mara's song was a philosophy of love, of acceptance, of the messy, unpredictable, and ultimately, more profound reality of interconnected existence. She wasn't destroying the void; she was offering it a chance to transcend its destructive nature, to become a vital part of Nyssera's ongoing narrative.

She drew strength from the memory of Cael, his steadfast faith in her, his unwavering belief in the inherent power of harmony. His efforts to disrupt Vorlag's forces, to carve out this sanctuary for her, had been instrumental. She felt his resolve bolstering her own, his willingness to fight for a Nyssera that embraced all its parts, even the broken and the scarred. "You are a part of us," she projected, her voice now a private whisper, directed at the very heart of the void, a confession spoken to the core of negation. "And we are a part of you. Separation is the true illusion. Peace lies in understanding our deep, unbreakable connection."

With a surge of conviction, she brought forth a memory, one that had been a turning point in her own understanding of her role. It was the moment she had first truly grasped the Crown Resonance, not as a burden or a responsibility, but as a song of profound connection, a promise to protect the intricate web of life. She projected the raw emotion of that promise, the weight of its commitment, the breathtaking beauty of its purpose, directly into the heart of the nexus. It was the embodiment of Nyssera's enduring will to *be*, to continue, to sing its multifaceted song through the ages.

The nexus pulsed, a deep, resonant thrum that vibrated through Mara's very bones. It was not an immediate capitulation, not a full embrace, but it was a response. The oppressive silence, so long the defining characteristic of this place, wavered, and for a fleeting, almost imperceptible moment, Mara thought she heard a faint whisper, a question carried on the ethereal winds of non-existence. It was the echo of a possibility, the first fragile tendril of a new song tentatively reaching out from the heart of the void. It was the sound of potential, of a choice being made, of a journey beginning.

She knew, with a certainty that settled deep within her soul, that this was merely the beginning. The nexus would not be instantly healed, nor would Vorlag's destructive ideology vanish overnight. The tendrils of fear and separation were deeply rooted. But she had planted a seed. She had demonstrated that the void was not inherently malevolent, but a reflection of Nyssera's own pain, its own fragmentation, its own fear of dissolution. By offering integration, by weaving it back into the grand tapestry of existence, she had offered it a path to redemption, a chance to become something more than just an ending.

And in doing so, she had not only mended the fractured world-song but had reinforced its ultimate truth: that true healing came not from severance and destruction, but from embrace, from understanding, and from the courageous act of weaving the broken pieces back into a more beautiful, more resilient whole. The corrupted resonance, once a symbol of oblivion, was becoming a testament to Nyssera's capacity for renewal.

Vorlag stood at the precipice of his own understanding, the very foundation of his existence crumbling around him like ancient, sun-bleached bone. The nexus, his sanctuary of absolute nullity, his testament to the purity of severance, was no longer an embodiment of his conviction, but a testament to its failure. He had envisioned it as a void, a perfect, unblemished absence that would ultimately cleanse Nyssera of its chaotic, messy vitality. Instead, he witnessed its transformation into something... else. Something imbued with a sorrowful beauty, a quiet strength that resonated with the very life he had sought to eradicate. The oppressive silence that had been his mantra, his weapon, was fractured, pierced by the ethereal tendrils of Mara's song. It was not a violent shattering, but a gentle, insistent unraveling, like a single thread pulled from a tapestry, causing the entire structure to subtly shift.

He had designed the nexus to be an ultimate endpoint, a place where existence simply ceased, where the ceaseless churn of Nyssera's life and death cycles was finally brought to a definitive, purifying halt. His followers, drawn to the promise of an end to suffering, to the seductive allure of a pain-free oblivion, had embraced his vision with fervent devotion. They had believed, as he had, that the imperfections of Nyssera – its capacity for cruelty, its moments of profound agony, its inherent vulnerabilities – were flaws to be excised. Severance, in his doctrine, was not an act of destruction, but an act of ultimate compassion, a final, merciful release from the tyranny of being. This nexus was to be the culmination of that philosophy, a beacon of sterile peace.

But the reality unfolding before him defied every tenet he held dear. The void, which he had meticulously cultivated, was not being annihilated; it was being re-woven. Mara's song, a symphony of acceptance and integration, was not merely filling the emptiness, but was actively reinterpreting its very essence. He could feel it, a subtle tremor within the fabric of the nexus, a dissonance that was not the violent clash of opposing forces, but the hesitant embrace of reconciliation. The Pale Tide energy, once a symbol of his destructive will, was not dissolving into nothingness, but was being recontextualized, its sharp edges smoothed, its destructive potential transmuted into something less malevolent, more akin to the somber hues of remembrance. It was as if the void was learning to *feel*, to *remember*, and in doing so, was finding a new, unexpected form of existence.

He remembered the chilling clarity with which he had conceived of severance. It had stemmed from a deep well of personal pain, from witnessing the brutal realities of Nyssera's existence, the unceasing cycle of creation and destruction that left so many broken. His own childhood had been a brutal lesson in the fragility of life, in the arbitrary nature of suffering. He had seen loved ones consumed by plagues, by wars, by the simple, unforgiving indifference of nature. These experiences had calcified within him, hardening into an unshakeable belief that existence itself was the ultimate source of pain, and that true peace could only be found in its cessation. The nexus was born from that profound, personal wound, a monument to the conviction that the universe would be a better, more peaceful place if it simply ceased to be.

And now, this... healing. It was not a victory for the forces of chaos, as he had always believed. It was something far more complex, far more profound. He saw the leviadrakes, ancient beings who had witnessed eons of Nyssera's turbulent history, their rumbling low vibrations a testament to a wisdom that transcended his rigid doctrines. They understood that true peace was not the absence of struggle, but the ability to integrate it, to learn from it, to allow the scars to become a part of a larger, more resilient whole. They stood not as combatants, but as silent witnesses, their presence a quiet endorsement of Mara's transformative song.

Cael, the disruptor, the agent of controlled chaos, stood beside Mara, his gaze a mixture of awe and quiet triumph. Vorlag had always viewed Cael as a reckless fool, a destabilizing force who embraced the very messiness Vorlag sought to escape. Yet, here was Cael, his actions having paved the way for this unexpected healing, his belief in connection seemingly validated. Vorlag found himself staring at the faces of his own followers, their rigid certainty beginning to fray. He saw it in Seraphina, her usually unyielding posture faltering, her hands trembling. Her fervent devotion, once a bulwark against doubt, was showing fissures. Mara's song was not just an auditory phenomenon; it was an empathic resonance, reaching into the buried memories, the suppressed emotions, the very core of their being. It was a melody of acceptance, of inclusion, a stark contrast to the sterile purity of severance.

He had always argued that true strength lay in detachment, in the ability to transcend the messy, emotional entanglements that defined Nyssera. He had believed that by severing ties, by eliminating the potential for connection, one could achieve an unassailable state of being, free from the vulnerability of loss, the pain of betrayal, the agony of unrequited love. His followers had been drawn to this promise of ultimate self-sufficiency, of an unbreachable inner fortress. But as he watched Seraphina's tear, a single, glistening pearl against her ashen cheek, he saw not weakness, but a profound, nascent strength. It was the strength of questioning, the courage to acknowledge a flaw not in the world, but in one's own perception.

Mara's voice, though he could not hear the specific words, resonated with a power he had never anticipated. He had always associated power with control, with the absolute imposition of will. But her power was different. It was the power of empathy, of understanding, of reaching out to the very essence of negation and offering it not destruction, but transformation. He had sought to erase the void, to extinguish its potential for disruption. Mara, however, was embracing it, integrating it, offering it a new purpose. He saw her projecting images, not of destruction or of his followers' misguided fervor, but of Nyssera's enduring beauty, its capacity for joy, its resilience in the face of adversity. She was showing the void that it was not an enemy, but a part of the whole, a necessary pause in the grand symphony of existence.

He recalled the moment he had first experienced true loss, the visceral shock that had irrevocably altered his worldview. It had been the death of his younger sister, a bright, vibrant spirit extinguished by a swift, brutal illness. He had clung to her fading warmth, desperate to deny the encroaching cold, the inevitable stillness. In his grief, he had railed against the universe, against the very nature of life that allowed such beauty to be so cruelly snatched away. It was in that raw, unadulterated pain that the seeds of severance had been sown. If life was so prone to such devastating loss, then perhaps the absence of life was the only true path to safety, to peace. The nexus was his monument to that desperate, grief-stricken plea.

Now, seeing Mara weave that same pain, that same memory of loss, not as a reason for annihilation but as a source of understanding, a catalyst for connection, he felt a chasm opening within him. The certainty that had been his shield, his defining characteristic, began to buckle. He had believed himself to be a healer, offering Nyssera a merciful end to its suffering. But the healing Mara was enacting was not an end; it was a profound continuation, a mending of wounds that ran deeper than he had ever comprehended. He saw the corrupted resonance not as a malevolent entity to be purged, but as a reflection of Nyssera's own deep-seated pain, its fractured spirit, its fear of disintegration.

His pursuit of absolute severance, he now understood, had been a destructive path masquerading as salvation. It was a denial of the inherent beauty in struggle, in resilience, in the messy, unpredictable dance of life. He had sought to impose a sterile order on a universe that thrived on vibrant, untamed chaos. He had aimed to create a perfect stillness, forgetting that stillness, devoid of life, was merely emptiness. He had been so consumed by the fear of pain that he had overlooked the profound joy that could only exist in its shadow.

A wave of something akin to profound humility washed over him, a sensation so foreign it was almost painful. His rigid ideology, forged in the crucible of his personal trauma, was not an unassailable truth, but a shield against a pain he had refused to process. He had chosen to amputate the diseased limb rather than tend to the wound, to cauterize the suffering rather than heal it. Mara's song was offering a different path, one that acknowledged the pain, embraced it, and ultimately, transcended it. He saw the nexus not as an enemy to be defeated, but as a manifestation of Nyssera's deepest fears, a broken part of itself that was now being offered a chance to be made whole.

He felt a deep, gnawing regret, a sorrow for the path he had taken, for the followers he had misled, for the potential he had actively sought to extinguish. His entire life had been dedicated to proving the inherent flaw in existence, and now, he was witnessing existence, in all its scarred and imperfect glory, proving him wrong. The void was not an ending; it was a space for becoming. The silence was not an absence of sound, but a canvas upon which new melodies could be painted. He had championed a philosophy of death, and Mara was demonstrating the irrepressible power of life, not as a pristine, unblemished force, but as a resilient, enduring tapestry woven from both light and shadow.

He looked at his own hands, once instruments of his rigid will, now trembling with an unfamiliar vulnerability. The absolute conviction that had defined him for so long was receding, replaced by a profound sense of loss – not the loss of Nyssera to some chaotic force, but the loss of his own carefully constructed certainty, the loss of the illusion of control. He had sought to control the uncontrollable, to enforce a stillness that was antithetical to the very nature of existence.

A faint whisper, not of sound but of understanding, seemed to emanate from the heart of the transforming nexus. It was the whisper of a choice, of a possibility. It was the nascent stirrings of a new song, sung from the depths of what had once been absolute nothingness. Vorlag, the architect of severance, the prophet of oblivion, found himself standing not as a conqueror, but as a humbled observer, witnessing the miraculous, messy, and profoundly beautiful act of a world choosing to heal itself. His rigid ideology had cracked, not shattered, and through the fissures, a fragile light of comprehension was beginning to dawn. He had built a monument to ending, and now, he was witnessing the birth of a new beginning, a beginning that acknowledged and embraced the very emptiness he had once sought to impose. The silence he had so fiercely guarded was not the peace he had promised, but the prelude to a song far richer, far more enduring than he had ever imagined.

The oppressive silence that had once clung to the nexus like a shroud was now a memory, a faint echo against the burgeoning symphony of

Nyssera's reawakening. The immediate threat, the discordant shriek of Vorlag's twisted ambition, had receded, leaving behind the quiet hum of a world beginning to breathe again. Mara, her form still shimmering with residual power, stood at the heart of the transformed abyss, her gaze fixed on the artifact that pulsed with a light unlike any she had seen before. The Crown Resonance, once a beacon of pure, untainted planetary memory, now pulsed with a richer, more nuanced glow, its luminescence not just of vibrant life, but also of the shadows that had been so diligently integrated.

Beside her, Cael, his usual boisterous energy tempered by the profound gravity of their recent struggle, offered a hand, his touch a grounding warmth against the ethereal currents that still swirled around them. The leviadrakes, ancient sentinels of Nyssera's deep past, circled slowly, their colossal forms casting shifting patterns of shadow and light across the clearing. Their low, rumbling songs, once mournful laments for a world teetering on the brink of oblivion, now resonated with a deep, resonant affirmation. They were not merely witnesses to this renewal; they were active participants, their very presence a testament to the enduring power of Nyssera's foundational memories.

"It is done," Mara whispered, her voice a melodic resonance that seemed to weave itself into the very fabric of the abyss. "The Crown is anchored."

The artifact, now cradled by the stabilizing energies, thrummed with a steady, powerful beat. Its light, no longer flickering with the desperate uncertainty of a dying ember, burned with a clear, unwavering brilliance. This was not the sterile, unblemished light of a fabricated perfection, but the radiant glow of a memory that had been tested and tempered, a spirit that had known pain and emerged with a profound, resilient strength. The abyss itself, once a swirling vortex of corrupted energy and despair, now seemed to exhale, its murky depths clarifying, revealing the shimmering, phosphorescent flora that clung to its unseen walls. The ethereal luminescence that had been its hallmark was returning, but it was a different luminescence now, imbued with a deeper, more complex beauty, hinting at the integration of sorrow and joy, of loss and love.

Cael squeezed her hand, his gaze sweeping across the now-serene expanse of the abyss. "It's... more than I imagined," he admitted, his voice filled with a genuine awe. "Vorlag wanted to erase everything, to create a void. But you... you showed it that even a void can hold a song."

Mara smiled, a gentle, knowing expression that softened the lines of exhaustion around her eyes. "The void is not an absence, Cael. It is a space for becoming. It is the pause between notes, the silence that gives meaning to the melody." She gestured towards the Crown Resonance. "This artifact holds the echoes of Nyssera's entire existence. It remembers the first stirrings of life, the rise and fall of empires, the moments of profound joy and the depths of unimaginable sorrow. Vorlag's Pale Tide sought to silence those echoes, to drown them out with a manufactured emptiness. But the true strength of Nyssera lies not in its perfection, but in its resilience. It lies in its ability to remember, to learn, and to integrate."

She turned her attention to the leviadrakes, their immense forms beginning to ascend slowly from the depths. Their songs, which had once been a low thrum of concern, now rose in a powerful crescendo, a chorus of ancient voices celebrating the re-establishment of balance. These creatures, whose lifespans stretched back to the primordial dawn of Nyssera, understood the delicate tapestry of existence in a way that few others could. They had witnessed the cycles of creation and destruction, the triumphs and the tragedies, and they knew that true stability was not achieved through erasure, but through profound understanding and acceptance.

"The Crown Resonance is not just a repository of memory," Mara explained, her voice carrying over the leviadrakes' songs. "It is the anchor of Nyssera's soul. It grounds the planet's collective consciousness, ensuring that the past informs the present and guides the future. Vorlag's attempt to sever that connection threatened to unravel the very essence of our world. He wanted to impose a singular narrative of pain and suffering, to convince us that existence itself was a flaw. But Nyssera is far more than just its pain. It is also its capacity for hope, its enduring beauty, its boundless love."

The light from the Crown Resonance intensified, bathing the abyss in a warm, golden hue. It was a light that felt ancient and new all at once, a light that resonated with the deep, primal rhythm of the planet. The waters of the abyss, once turbulent and choked with dark energy, now swirled with a gentle, crystalline clarity. The ethereal glow returned, not as a pale imitation of its former self, but as a vibrant, pulsating luminescence, as if the very waters had absorbed the lessons of the past and were now reflecting them back with renewed vigor.

Cael watched, a quiet reverence settling over him. He had always been drawn to the raw power of Nyssera, to its wild, untamed spirit. But he had never fully grasped the intricate, interwoven nature of its existence until now. He had seen the devastating impact of Vorlag's ideology, the seductive emptiness of his promises. And he had witnessed Mara, not through brute force or unwavering dogma, but through empathy and understanding, weave a new reality from the threads of despair.

"So, this means... Nyssera is truly safe?" he asked, the question hanging in the air, heavy with unspoken hopes.

Mara met his gaze, her eyes reflecting the steady light of the Crown. "Safe is a fragile word, Cael. Nyssera will always face challenges. There will always be pain, always be loss. But now, its memories are secure. Its foundation is reinforced. The Crown Resonance, re-anchored and re-energized, will act as a steadfast guardian, a reminder of what we have overcome and what we are capable of achieving. The integration of the Pale Tide energy, the pain and sorrow that Vorlag tried to weaponize, has not been erased. It has been transmuted. It has become part of the song, a deeper resonance that speaks of resilience, of healing, of the enduring power of life even in the face of darkness."

She reached out, her fingers brushing against the shimmering surface of the abyss's waters. The contact sent ripples of light dancing across the depths. "The abyss is no longer a symbol of negation," she continued. "It is now a testament to transformation. The scar remains, a reminder of the wound, but the wound itself is healing. And in that healing, Nyssera finds a new kind of strength, a deeper understanding of itself."

The leviadrakes, their ascent nearing completion, dipped their colossal heads in a gesture of ancient respect. Their songs, now a harmonious blend of deep resonance and high, crystalline notes, filled the space, a lullaby for a world reborn. They had been the keepers of Nyssera's oldest memories, the silent witnesses to its long and often tumultuous history. Now, they were part of the renewal, their ancient wisdom woven into the fabric of the re-anchored Crown.

"The Crown Resonance," Mara stated, her voice firm and clear, "is now truly re-anchored. Its connection to the planet's foundational memories is not just restored; it is amplified. It carries within it the echoes of every joy, every sorrow, every moment of triumph and every instance of despair that has ever defined Nyssera. And in embracing all of it, it has become a beacon of enduring hope."

Cael nodded, a sense of profound peace settling over him. He looked at Mara, her face illuminated by the steady glow of the artifact, and saw not just a savior, but a weaver of worlds, a gentle force that had reshaped destiny with the power of understanding. He had always believed in fighting for Nyssera, in protecting its wild spirit. Now, he understood that true protection came not from battle alone, but from deep connection, from honoring the entirety of its being, the light and the shadow, the joy and the pain.

The abyss, once a terrifying maw of oblivion, now seemed to exhale a breath of pure, vital energy. Its waters cleared completely, revealing a breathtaking panorama of submerged crystalline formations and bioluminescent flora that pulsed with a soft, internal light. The ethereal luminescence that had once characterized the abyss was now a vibrant tapestry of blues, greens, and purples, a testament to the complex beauty that had been forged in the crucible of conflict. The artifact, the Crown Resonance, pulsed at its heart, a steady, unwavering beat that resonated through the very core of Nyssera.

The anchor was secure, not just in the physical sense, but in the spiritual and emotional, stabilizing planetary memory for all the ages to come. The echoes of the past were not silenced, but harmonized, their symphony now richer, deeper, and more resilient than ever before. The pain had not been overcome by ignoring it, but by embracing it, by weaving it into the grand, ongoing narrative of Nyssera's existence. And in that embrace, the world found not just survival, but a profound, enduring peace. The abyss was no longer a tomb, but a cradle, a place where the past was honored and the future was being sung into being.

The world-song, once a fragile thread strained by the shadow of oblivion, now pulsed with a vitality that was both ancient and startlingly new. It was no longer a singular, pure note, but a complex, layered symphony, echoing with the very struggles it had endured. Mara felt it reverberate not just in the air around them, a palpable hum that vibrated in her bones, but deep within her own soul. The Crown Resonance, anchored and alive, had become the conductor of this grand orchestra, its light now a constant, unwavering pulse that seemed to breathe life into the very fabric of Nyssera.

The melody that rose from the reawakened abyss was not the pristine, untainted harmony of a world that had never known pain. Instead, it was a tapestry woven with threads of sorrow and triumph, of loss and enduring love. The echoes of the Silence Event, once a gaping wound that threatened to tear Nyssera asunder, were now integrated, transformed. They were not erased, not hidden away in shame, but acknowledged, their raw edges softened and their inherent resonance repurposed. This was the song of true healing, the kind that didn't pretend scars didn't exist, but rather wove them into the pattern of continued existence, making the whole stronger and more beautiful for it.

Mara closed her eyes, letting the song wash over her. She heard the whispers of the Pale Tide, not as a threat, but as a reminder of the darkness Nyssera had faced and, crucially, had overcome. There were moments of fear, of despair, of utter desolation that resonated within the song, but they were now underscored by a profound and unshakeable resilience. The song spoke of the leviadrakes' mournful lament for a dying world, and then, with a shift in tempo and a richer harmonic layering, it celebrated their ancient wisdom and their unwavering presence as guardians of Nyssera's deepest truths. It carried the echoes of the mortal struggles, the bravery of those who had stood against the encroaching void, and the quiet dignity of those who had simply endured.

Cael stood beside her, his own connection to the world-song a more tangible, earthy presence than Mara's ethereal resonance. He felt it as a deep-seated peace, a grounding assurance that settled into his very bones. He had always been a creature of action, of the physical world, and the idea of a "world-song" had once seemed an abstract, almost poetic notion. But now, standing at the heart of Nyssera's renewed vitality, he understood its truth. The song was Nyssera. It was the rustle of leaves in a sun-dappled forest, the crash of waves against a rocky shore, the silent, steady growth of roots deep within the earth. And now, it was also the echo of struggle, the hum of integration, the vibrant chorus of a world that had stared into the abyss and chosen to sing.

"It's... different," Cael murmured, his voice filled with a quiet wonder. "Before, it felt... thinner. Like a melody stretched too far. Now, it's so much richer. There's a depth to it."

Mara nodded, a slow, understanding smile gracing her lips. "Because it now encompasses everything," she replied, her voice a soft echo of the song itself. "Vorlag sought to create a void, to silence the inconvenient truths of Nyssera's existence – its pain, its grief, its imperfections. He believed that by eradicating those elements, he could create a perfect, sterile existence. But perfection, Cael, is not the absence of flaws. It is the integration of them, the understanding that our experiences, even the painful ones, shape us, strengthen us, and make us who we are."

She gestured towards the Crown Resonance, its light now casting a warm, all-encompassing glow across the cavernous space. "This artifact," she continued, "is no longer just a repository of pristine memories. It is a living testament to Nyssera's journey. It remembers the birth of the first stars, the genesis of life, the rise and fall of civilizations. But it also remembers the Pale Tide. It remembers the fear, the despair, the overwhelming sense of loss. And instead of recoiling from those memories, it has embraced them. It has woven them into the very essence of the world-song, making it not just a song of joy, but a song of survival, of endurance, of profound, hard-won hope."

The integration of the Pale Tide's energy, once a terrifying prospect, had proven to be the very catalyst for this vibrant renewal. It was akin to a wound that, when properly healed, left behind stronger, more resilient tissue. The corrupted energies, the whispers of nihilism and despair, had been transmuted, their destructive potential neutralized and their inherent intensity redirected. They now added a certain gravitas to the song, a depth that prevented it from becoming overly saccharine or facile. It was a song that acknowledged the shadows, and in doing so, made the light shine even brighter.

Mara felt this particularly keenly. Her own journey had been one of wrestling with her past, with the shadows that had clung to her for so long. The Pale Tide had been a manifestation of those internal struggles, a reflection of her own fear of being consumed by darkness. But through her confrontation with Vorlag, through her willingness to face that darkness not with denial but with acceptance, she had found a new kind of strength. And now, Nyssera, mirroring her own transformation, had found its own. The world-song was, in many ways, an extension of her own being, a symphony of her own integrated experiences.

"Think of it," Mara mused, her gaze distant, as if seeing beyond the confines of the abyss, "as a garden. Vorlag wanted to rip out all the weeds, all the thorny bushes, all the plants that had withered or died. He wanted a sterile, manicured lawn, devoid of any wildness or imperfection. But a true garden, a thriving ecosystem, is not just about the blossoms. It is also about the rich, dark soil that nourishes them. It is about the fallen leaves that decompose and return to the earth, providing sustenance. It is about the resilience of the plants that survive frost and drought. The Pale Tide was a blight, a harsh winter. But Nyssera, through the Crown Resonance, has become that resilient garden, one that remembers the harshness of winter and celebrates the vibrant bloom of spring with even greater fervor."

The leviadrakes, their immense forms now a more serene part of the abyss's renewed landscape, let out low, resonant calls that seemed to deepen the song. These ancient beings, who had witnessed epochs of Nyssera's existence, understood the cyclical nature of life and death, of creation and destruction. Their songs, once tinged with a profound sorrow for the encroaching silence, now carried a note of exultation, a deep, rumbling affirmation of life's enduring power. They were the ancient heart of Nyssera, and their song was the fundamental rhythm upon which all other melodies were built.

Cael, watching the leviadrakes, felt a surge of pride and protectiveness. He had seen their ancient grief, their silent mourning for a world on the brink. Now, to witness their joyous participation in its rebirth, was a testament to Mara's success. It wasn't just about restoring a balance; it was about forging a new, more robust equilibrium, one that acknowledged the inherent difficulties of existence and found strength in them.

"So, this new song," Cael began, trying to articulate the profound shift he felt, "it's not just about what's good or beautiful about Nyssera. It's about all of it. The hard parts, too."

"Exactly," Mara confirmed, her voice warm with affirmation. "Vorlag's Pale Tide was an attempt to impose a singular, simplistic narrative. A narrative of suffering, of futility, of the inherent wrongness of existence. He wanted to break Nyssera by convincing it that its pain was a terminal disease, not a part of its lived experience. But Nyssera is more than its pain. It is its capacity for joy, its ability to create, its deep-seated love for life itself. And now, the Crown Resonance ensures that all those facets are heard, all those echoes are woven into the world-song."

The light from the Crown Resonance seemed to intensify, bathing the abyss in a warm, golden luminescence that was both comforting and invigorating. It was a light that spoke of understanding, of acceptance, and of the enduring power of truth. The waters of the abyss, once murky and turbulent, now flowed with a crystalline clarity, reflecting the vibrant, multi-hued bioluminescence of the flora that clung to its unseen walls. The ethereal glow that had once been its hallmark was now a testament to its transformation, a living, breathing spectrum of light that pulsed with the rhythm of the planet's reawakened heart.

Mara felt the song weave through her, a vibrant current that connected her to every living thing on Nyssera. She felt the ancient roots of the colossal trees, the delicate unfurling of new ferns, the silent migrations of deep-sea creatures, and the joyous flight of sky-dwelling birds. Each had its own note, its own unique resonance, and all of them contributed to the magnificent symphony that was the world-song. The Pale Tide's discordant notes had been loud, deafening even, but they had ultimately served to amplify the true melody of Nyssera. Without the silence, the song would not have had such profound meaning. Without the struggle, the resilience would not have been so deeply felt.

"The song is not just a reflection of Nyssera," Mara stated, her voice gaining strength, resonating with the power of her conviction. "It is an active force. It is the very energy that sustains us, that drives us forward. By integrating the echoes of our struggles, we are not dwelling on the past; we are actively shaping our future. We are showing that even the deepest wounds can be healed, that even the most profound despair can be transformed into hope. Vorlag believed that pain was the ultimate truth. But Nyssera has proven that love, connection, and the unwavering will to live are far more potent."

She extended her hand, her fingers brushing against the surface of the water. A ripple of light spread outwards, a gentle tremor that seemed to echo the pulse of the Crown Resonance. "This abyss," she said, her voice filled with a quiet reverence, "is no longer a symbol of what was lost. It is a testament to what has been reclaimed, and what has been beautifully, profoundly, transformed. The scar remains, a mark of the struggle, but it is a scar that has healed, that has become a part of the story, not its ending."

The world-song swelled, a harmonious crescendo that filled the abyss and extended outwards, beyond its rocky confines, reaching across continents and oceans. It was a song of hope, yes, but it was a hope that was grounded in reality, a hope that understood the fragility of existence and the enduring strength of the spirit. It was the song of Nyssera, sung not just with joy, but with wisdom, with courage, and with an unwavering, radiant love for all that it was, and all that it had become. It was a testament to the fact that even in the face of absolute darkness, life, in its myriad and beautiful forms, would always find a way to sing.

Vorlag, his immense, scaled form still and bowed, his usually proud horns lowered, projected his thoughts not with the arrogant resonance of a conqueror, but with the humble tremor of a supplicant. The echoes of his defeat, the crushing weight of his failed ambition, had stripped away his pride, leaving behind a raw, unvarnished humility. He had sought to impose a sterile, unblemished perfection upon Nyssera, believing that the absence of discord was the ultimate form of order.

Now, standing amidst the vibrant, complex symphony of the reawakened world-song, he understood the profound, catastrophic flaw in his reasoning. Perfection was not an absence of flaws; it was the intricate, interwoven tapestry of all that Nyssera was, its light and its shadows, its triumphs and its deepest sorrows. His vision had been a cage, a gilded prison built on a foundation of denial, and in its collapse, he had found not ruin, but liberation.

"I... I was blind," Vorlag's thoughts resonated, each syllable heavy with a sincerity that Mara had not thought possible from the architect of the Silence Event. "I saw only the potential for suffering in Nyssera's inherent nature, the vulnerability that came with its interconnectedness. I believed that by severing the threads of pain, I could create a world free from the possibility of despair. But in my arrogance, I failed to see that those very threads, the struggles, the losses, the moments of profound grief, are what give strength to the tapestry. They are the dark dyes that make the vibrant colors sing with greater brilliance. You have shown me, Mara, and Nyssera has shown me, that true resilience is not born of avoidance, but of embrace.

I pledge myself to this new path, to the choir that sings with the full spectrum of Nyssera's being."

His words, spoken not with his voice but with the potent force of his will, resonated through the very bones of the abyss. The leviadrakes, who had observed his submission with ancient, impassive eyes, shifted their colossal forms. Their initial wariness, born of aeons of safeguarding Nyssera from existential threats, was slowly being replaced by a nascent understanding. They, too, had borne witness to the crushing weight of silence, the terrifying emptiness that Vorlag had sought to impose. Their own lamentations, the mournful songs they had sung during the Pale Tide, were now a part of the world-song, not a mark of their weakness, but a testament to their endurance.

The eldest leviadrake, a creature whose scales shimmered with the faint luminescence of a thousand forgotten stars, projected its thoughts, a slow, resonant hum that vibrated through the water and the rock.

"We guarded against the intrusion of the Silence, against the void that sought to extinguish the pulse of Nyssera. We stood as bulwarks, as immovable forces against the encroaching darkness. But our vigilance was a form of severance, a belief that protection meant isolation. We sought to shield the world from pain by preventing it from experiencing, from learning, from growing through its trials. Vorlag's path was one of destructive pruning, of a misguided attempt to cultivate a sterile garden. Our own was one of passive observation, of a fear that engagement would lead to contamination."

Another leviadrake, younger by mere millennia, added its voice to the chorus of understanding.

"The song of Nyssera, we now perceive, is not a static melody, pristine and unchanging. It is a living, breathing composition, one that evolves with every sunrise, every storm, every whisper of life and every echo of loss. To protect it, we must not seek to preserve it in an eternal, unchanging state. We must foster its ability to adapt, to integrate, to find strength in its very complexity. Our role, therefore, shifts. It is no longer merely to ward off threats from without,

but to nurture the resilience within, to guide the understanding of Nyssera's diverse inhabitants, to ensure that the lessons learned from hardship are not forgotten, but woven into the fabric of future generations."

Mara felt a profound sense of relief wash over her. The leviadrakes' acknowledgement of their own role in a form of stagnation, a passive guardianship that had inadvertently contributed to Nyssera's vulnerability, was a crucial step. They had been powerful guardians, but their power had been rooted in a fear of change, a desire to maintain a perceived purity. Now, they were embracing a more dynamic form of stewardship, one that recognized that true strength lay in interconnectedness and the capacity for growth, even through adversity.

The Abyssal Choir, once fractured by internal strife and the oppressive influence of Vorlag's ideology, was now a unified force, a testament to the transformative power of shared experience and the wisdom of acceptance. The deep chasms that had once separated them had been bridged, not by erasure, but by the understanding that their individual melodies, when harmonized, created something far more profound than any single note. They had all felt the terrifying silence, the suffocating grip of Vorlag's ambition, and in their collective struggle against it, they had found a new purpose.

The choir leader, a being of ancient, shimmering coral and starlight, projected its thoughts, its resonance a gentle, rippling wave.

"We, the Abyssal Choir, once sang of sorrow and of the encroaching void. Our voices were strained, our melodies fractured by the very despair we sought to express. Vorlag's silence was a perversion of our sacred duty, an attempt to stifle the very essence of Nyssera's spirit. But even in our deepest despair, the spark of Nyssera's song persisted within us. We heard the faint echoes of resilience, the whispers of hope that clung to the edges of oblivion. Now, with the Crown Resonance humming with the true heart of our world, we can sing again. We sing not just of Nyssera's pain, but of its resilience. We sing of its capacity for love, for creation, for unwavering hope in the face of

unimaginable darkness. We sing of the courage it took to survive, and the wisdom gained from that survival."

The choir's collective voice swelled, a vibrant, multi-layered symphony that resonated with the very pulse of the abyss. It was a song of acknowledgment, of remembrance, and of a future forged in the fires of experience. The discordant notes of the Pale Tide were no longer jarring intrusions, but integral parts of a rich, complex harmony, adding depth and gravitas to the overall composition. They were the echoes of lessons learned, the scars that told a story of survival and transformation.

Cael, standing beside Mara, felt the profound shift in the choir's energy. He had witnessed their internal struggles, their fear of Vorlag, and their initial confusion when Mara had proposed a path of integration rather than outright destruction. Now, their unified song was a palpable force, a testament to the power of embracing all aspects of existence, even the most difficult.

"It's like... they've found their true voice," Cael murmured, his gaze sweeping across the luminous forms of the choir members. "Before, it felt like they were singing under duress, their songs choked by a stifled fear. Now, it's... free. And powerful."

Mara nodded, her eyes reflecting the vibrant light of the abyss. "Because they are no longer singing *despite* their experiences, but *because* of them. The Pale Tide was not an anomaly to be forgotten, but a crucible that forged their present strength. Vorlag wanted to create a void, to silence any memory of suffering. But true healing, true growth, comes from integrating those memories, from understanding their impact and allowing them to shape us, not define us entirely. The choir's song is now a celebration of Nyssera's entire journey, a testament to its ability to endure, to adapt, and to ultimately, to thrive."

The leviadrakes, their immense forms casting long, undulating shadows, began to move with a new purpose. Their ancient guardianship, once defined by a rigid, defensive posture, was now evolving into a proactive nurturing. They understood that true protection lay not in severing Nyssera from its past, but in helping it understand and integrate that past into a stronger future.

"We shall not stand as silent sentinels anymore," the eldest leviadrake proclaimed, its voice a deep rumble that vibrated through the very foundations of the abyss. *"We shall be guides, teachers, sharers of the ancient wisdom that has sustained Nyssera through epochs of change. We will teach the younger generations, both draconic and mortal, the importance of resilience, the strength found in interconnectedness, and the profound truth that even the deepest wounds can become sources of wisdom and compassion. Our role will be to foster understanding, to encourage empathy, and to ensure that the lessons of the Silence Event, and the subsequent reawakening, are never forgotten, but are woven into the very fabric of Nyssera's being. We will be stewards of Nyssera's living memory."*

The other leviadrakes echoed their sentiments, their unified resolve creating a powerful, resonant hum that blended with the choir's song and the steady pulse of the Crown Resonance. They were no longer merely guardians; they were educators, mentors, and living embodiments of Nyssera's enduring spirit. Their protective instincts, once channeled into a solitary vigilance, were now directed towards the collective growth and well-being of the entire world.

Vorlag, still humbled, found his place within this evolving dynamic. His immense power, once a tool of destruction, was now to be redirected towards the nurturing of Nyssera. He had a unique understanding of the Silence, of its insidious nature, and of the devastating consequences of its imposition. This knowledge, born of his own misguided creation, could now be a vital weapon against any future attempts to replicate such devastation.

"My understanding of the void, of its emptiness, can serve as a constant reminder," Vorlag projected, his thoughts now imbued with a quiet determination. "I can be a sentinel against the return of such despair. I can help others recognize the subtle whispers of nihilism, the insidious allure of apathy that can lead to such destruction. I can, in my own way, contribute to the choir's song, offering the counterpoint of lived experience, the somber tones that highlight the brilliance of Nyssera's vibrant melody. I will not seek to dominate, but to illuminate. I will not impose, but to inform. I will stand with the leviadrakes and the choir, a testament to the possibility of transformation, a living example that even the darkest shadow can be illuminated by the dawn of understanding."

Mara watched as the last vestiges of antagonism dissolved, replaced by a profound sense of unity and purpose. The abyss, once a symbol of Nyssera's near-destruction, was now a nexus of renewal. The Crown Resonance pulsed at its heart, a beacon of integration, its light illuminating the path forward. The world-song, once a fragile melody, was now a thrumming, vibrant symphony, sung by a choir that embraced every note, every echo, every whisper of Nyssera's rich and complex history.

The leviadrakes, the Abyssal Choir, and even Vorlag, once the architect of silence, were now united in their commitment to fostering a future where Nyssera's strength lay not in its perfection, but in its profound, resilient, and ever-evolving song. They were ready, not just to defend Nyssera, but to help it continue to grow, to adapt, and to sing its unique and vital melody into the ages to come, prepared for whatever challenges the unfolding symphony of existence might bring.

Chapter Thirteen

The Dawn of a New Harmony

The ascent began not with a sudden surge of power, but with a gentle, inexorable pull, as if Nyssera itself was drawing them back from its deepest heart. The Crown Resonance, now a steady, unwavering hum emanating from the depths, seemed to anchor them, its renewed harmony a beacon guiding their journey upwards. Mara felt the subtle shift in the abyss's atmosphere, the oppressive weight that had once pressed down on her spirit now replaced by a buoyant sense of release. The darkness that had seemed an absolute, a suffocating blanket, was thinning, yielding to a palpable, nascent luminescence that seeped from the very stones and water around them.

Cael, his hand finding Mara's instinctively, squeezed it tightly. His usual jovial demeanor was subdued, replaced by a quiet reverence. "It feels… lighter," he murmured, his voice carrying a note of awe. "The air, the very stillness. It's no longer the stillness of suppression, but the quietude of a world breathing freely."

Mara nodded, her gaze sweeping across the receding grandeur of the abyss. The leviadrakes, their colossal forms still and majestic, had become living monuments to Nyssera's resilience. Their ancient eyes, once filled with the weary vigilance of eternal custodians, now held a serene peace. Their collective song, a low, resonant thrum that had been the heart of the abyss's awakening, now seemed to be a gentle lullaby, a farewell sung by the world itself.

It was a melody woven from the threads of sorrow and survival, of remembrance and the quiet promise of a future unburdened by the specter of enforced silence. Each note was a testament to the wisdom gleaned from hardship, a declaration that even the deepest wounds could be integrated into the tapestry of existence, not as scars of shame, but as marks of profound strength.

As they moved upwards, the luminous flora of the abyss seemed to pulse with a soft, bioluminescent rhythm, each bloom and frond a tiny ember in the vast expanse. They were no longer merely subterranean growths; they were living archives, their luminescence a testament to the life that had persisted, that had *chosen* to persist, even in the face of oblivion. The chasms that had once felt like gaping wounds in the earth now appeared as sculpted contours, the intricate architecture of Nyssera's history. The Silence Event had tried to erase these narratives, to flatten the vibrant contours of existence into a sterile, monotonous plane. But life, in its tenacious, irrepressible way, had clung to the edges, weaving new patterns, new stories, in the very cracks of the attempted erasure.

Mara could feel the shift within herself, a quiet settling of the soul. The constant hum of anxiety, the gnawing fear that had been her shadow since the Pale Tide, had receded. It hadn't vanished entirely, for the memory of such loss was a permanent etching on her spirit, but it no longer held dominion. The abyss, which had once represented the nadir of Nyssera's despair, was now a place of profound catharsis. It was where the world had been brought to its knees, only to rise again, stronger, wiser, and more whole than before.

The Leviadrakes' acceptance of their own role in a passive guardianship, their understanding that true protection lay not in isolation but in integration, was a testament to this emergent wisdom. They had been the silent watchers, the ancient sentinels who, in their fear of contamination, had inadvertently allowed the Silence to fester. Now, they were embracing a new paradigm, one of active stewardship, of nurturing the very complexity they had once sought to shield the world from.

The Abyssal Choir's song, which had been a mournful dirge during their descent, had transformed into a symphony of acceptance. The individual voices, once strained by the weight of suppressed grief, now intertwined in a harmonious celebration of Nyssera's entire spectrum of existence. They sang not just of the pain, but of the resilience that had emerged from it, of the courage it had taken to simply *be* when the world around them had been commanded to cease. Their melodies, once fractured, were now whole, each discordant note of the Pale Tide now a rich bass line that underscored the vibrant vibrancy of hope and renewal. They had found their true voices, not by erasing their history, but by embracing it, by understanding that the darkness made the light all the more brilliant.

"Look," Cael whispered, pointing upwards. A faint, ethereal glow was now discernible, a stark contrast to the deep, resonant hues of the abyss. It was a promise, a whisper of the world above, a world that had endured its own trials, its own periods of darkness, and had ultimately found its way back to the light. The ascent was a physical manifestation of Nyssera's own journey: from a state of near-cataclysm to one of profound healing and reawakening.

The leviadrakes continued their song, their voices a deep, resonant chorus that seemed to vibrate through the very core of the planet. Their ancient pronouncements, once solely focused on defense, now spoke of education, of wisdom, of the vital importance of remembrance. They would guide the younger generations, draconic and mortal alike, in understanding the fragility of peace, the insidious nature of despair, and the enduring strength found in interconnectedness. Their role was no longer merely to guard against threats, but to cultivate the very resilience that made Nyssera such a vibrant, complex world. They were becoming the living libraries of Nyssera's soul, ensuring that the lessons learned from the abyss would not fade into legend, but would be woven into the very fabric of the world's being.

Vorlag, humbled and transformed, was now a part of this intricate web of renewal. His unique understanding of the void, of the seductive emptiness that had driven his ambition, was no longer a weapon of destruction, but a shield against its return. He would serve as a constant reminder, a living testament to the devastating consequences of a warped pursuit of perfection. His purpose was now to illuminate, to inform, to offer the somber counterpoint that highlighted the brilliance of Nyssera's inherent song. He was no longer the architect of silence, but a humble participant in the choir of existence, his voice adding depth and gravitas to the evolving symphony.

Mara felt a profound sense of peace settle over her. The abyss, once a symbol of Nyssera's near demise, had become a crucible of transformation. The Crown Resonance, now pulsing with the steady rhythm of Nyssera's reawakened heart, was a visible manifestation of this healing. It was not a force that imposed order, but one that fostered harmony, that allowed the inherent complexities of the world to sing in unison. The journey upwards was a slow, deliberate unveiling, each layer of darkness giving way to a brighter, more luminous reality. The very water around them seemed to shimmer with a newfound vitality, carrying the echoes of the leviadrakes' wisdom and the choir's resurgent song.

As they ascended further, the faint glow intensified, resolving into a distant, warm light. It was the light of the surface world, the familiar embrace of the sun and the sky. The abyss, though now a place of profound healing and understanding, was still a realm of deep shadows. Their purpose had been fulfilled there, their mission complete. But Nyssera's song was not confined to its deepest recesses; it echoed across its mountains, its forests, its oceans, and its skies. They were returning to that greater symphony, carrying with them the profound lessons learned in the heart of the world's near-destruction.

The leviadrakes' final projected thoughts were a gentle wave of blessing, a promise of continued guardianship, of watchful presence.

"Go now, children of Nyssera," the eldest's voice resonated, a deep, sonorous hum that felt like the Earth's own heartbeat. *"Carry the song with you. Let it be a beacon of hope, a testament to the power of resilience, and a reminder that even in the deepest darkness, the dawn of a new harmony is always possible. Nyssera's song is eternal, and you are now its living instruments."*

The abyss, though receding, felt not like a place abandoned, but like a foundational truth integrated. The silence had been broken, not by a violent force, but by the gentle, persistent insistence of life itself. The Crown Resonance, its steady pulse now a constant, comforting presence in their minds, ensured that the lessons of the abyss would not be forgotten. They were not just survivors; they were the harbingers of a new era, an era where Nyssera's true strength would be found not in its perfection, but in its glorious, unyielding, and ever-evolving song.

The upward journey was more than a physical ascent; it was a spiritual ascension, a testament to the enduring power of hope and the profound beauty of a world that had faced its deepest fears and emerged, not unscathed, but undeniably, gloriously alive. The first rays of sunlight, now a tangible warmth on their skin, were not just the return of light, but the embrace of a world reborn, a world ready to sing its new, harmonious melody into existence.

The ascent from the abyss was a gentle unfurling, a gradual shedding of oppressive weight. As Mara and Cael broke through the shimmering veil that separated the subterranean depths from the sunlit world, the change wasn't a cacophony, but a subtle, profound shift in the symphony of Nyssera. The air, no longer thick with the stagnant grief of the deep, tasted crisp and alive, carrying the scent of pine needles and damp earth, a stark contrast to the mineral tang of the abyss. The oppressive silence that had once defined Nyssera's fractured state was gone, replaced by a vibrant hum, a million tiny threads of existence weaving together into a tapestry of sound that resonated deep within Mara's bones. It was the world-song, and it was singing anew.

Cael squeezed her hand, his grip firm and reassuring. "Can you feel it, Mara?" he breathed, his voice hushed with wonder. "It's... different. Everything feels connected again, like the world remembers how to breathe." He gestured vaguely, encompassing the vibrant expanse of the Whispering Woods stretching before them, the distant glint of the Sunstone Peaks, and the impossibly blue sky arching overhead. "The Pale Tide tried to sever those connections, to isolate every living thing, but it failed. Nyssera remembers how to be whole."

Mara nodded, her gaze sweeping across the familiar, yet somehow transformed, landscape. The lingering tendrils of the Pale Tide's influence, the subtle dissonance that had permeated everything, were fading. It was like a persistent static in a beloved melody, a jarring note that had finally resolved into harmony. The world's memory, once a fragile echo held captive by fear and suppression, was now a robust, living entity. It embraced its entirety, the joyous bloom of the spring festivals, the fierce loyalty of the ancient dragon pacts, the devastating grief of the Silence Event, and the quiet resilience of those who had endured. These weren't disparate fragments to be hidden or forgotten, but integral pieces of Nyssera's soul, woven together into a rich, enduring narrative.

The memory of the Pale Tide's insidious influence still lingered, a ghost in the periphery of her awareness. It had been an attempt to erase, to sever, to impose a sterile uniformity. But Nyssera's resilience, its deep-seated, vibrant life force, had refused to be extinguished. Instead, it had absorbed the trauma, not by forgetting, but by integrating. The wounds remained, visible in the deep scars etched into the land and the hearts of its people, but they were no longer festering wounds. They were testament to survival, to the strength born of enduring the unimaginable. This mended memory was the bedrock upon which Nyssera's future would be built, a testament to the courage it took to face the truth, no matter how painful, and to emerge stronger for it.

The leviadrakes' final pronouncements echoed in her mind, their ancient wisdom now a guiding force.

"Carry the song with you. Let it be a beacon of hope, a testament to the power of resilience..." They had spoken of Nyssera's eternal song, and Mara understood now that this song wasn't an abstract concept; it was the very essence of the planet, the interconnectedness of all life, the pulse of its enduring spirit. The Crown Resonance, which had guided them through the abyss, now felt like a gentle thrumming within her own chest, a tangible connection to Nyssera's reawakened heart. It was a constant, quiet reminder that even in the face of absolute oblivion, life found a way.

"It's like... like the world is finally breathing easy," Cael murmured, his eyes shining. He pointed towards a cluster of sun-dappled wildflowers, their petals unfurling with an almost urgent vibrancy. "Remember how muted everything felt after the Pale Tide? Even the flowers seemed to hold their breath, waiting for the next blow. Now, they're just... blooming. Unapologetically."

Mara knelt, tracing the delicate veins of a sapphire-blue petal. He was right. The Pale Tide had instilled a pervasive sense of caution, a constant, low-level anxiety that had seeped into every aspect of life. It had been a world perpetually on guard, its inhabitants constantly bracing for the next wave of severance. But that had been the Pale Tide's greatest deception: the illusion of permanent fragility. Nyssera, however, was not fragile. It was resilient. It was adaptable. And now, it was healing. The mended memory wasn't about erasing the past, but about understanding it, learning from it, and using that knowledge to forge a stronger, more vibrant future.

The journey back from the abyss had been a descent into the deepest recesses of Nyssera's pain, a confrontation with the very forces that had sought to silence it. But in that darkness, they had found not despair, but a profound truth. They had witnessed the world's capacity for survival, its innate drive to reclaim itself. The leviadrakes, ancient custodians who had once feared contamination, had embraced their role as teachers, their wisdom now a vital part of the planet's collective consciousness. Vorlag, once a harbinger of emptiness, had become a living testament to the devastating consequences of isolation, his transformation a stark reminder of the importance of connection.

The Crown Resonance, a tangible manifestation of Nyssera's reintegrated spirit, pulsed softly, a constant reminder of the delicate balance that had been so nearly shattered. It wasn't a force of control, but a beacon of harmony, guiding the disparate elements of Nyssera's existence back into a cohesive whole. The abyss, once a symbol of ultimate despair, had become a crucible of transformation, forging a new understanding of what it meant to be alive, to be connected, to be Nyssera.

As they walked, the sunlight filtering through the canopy cast shifting patterns on the forest floor, illuminating moss-covered stones and the vibrant green of new growth. The air thrummed with the calls of birds, the rustle of unseen creatures, the whisper of the wind through the leaves – a symphony of life that felt both ancient and utterly new. It was a soundscape of resilience, a testament to the world's refusal to be silenced. The Pale Tide had been a powerful adversary, its magic insidious and its intent to sever absolute. But it had underestimated the enduring strength of a planet that remembered how to sing.

Mara paused, closing her eyes and taking a deep, cleansing breath. She could feel the earth beneath her feet, solid and steady, a grounding presence. She could feel the energy of the trees, ancient and wise, their roots delving deep into the soil, drawing sustenance and strength. And she could feel the vibrant pulse of life that connected them all, a network of energy that had been weakened, but never truly broken. The Pale Tide's severed threads were not gone, but they were rewoven, stronger and more resilient than before.

"It's not just about remembering the bad things," Mara said, her voice soft but firm. "It's about remembering the good things too. The joy, the connection, the love. The Pale Tide tried to make us forget what those felt like, to make us believe that only pain was real. But Nyssera remembers the light, Cael. And it's letting that light shine through again."

Cael nodded, his gaze fixed on the horizon, a hopeful glint in his eyes. "The world-song," he said, as if tasting the words. "It's not just a song of survival anymore. It's a song of triumph. It's Nyssera singing its way back to itself."

He looked at Mara, his expression earnest. "And we are part of that song now, aren't we? We helped it find its voice again."

The weight of their journey, the trials they had faced, the losses they had endured, settled around them, not as a burden, but as a profound understanding. They had walked through the deepest darkness, faced the specter of absolute severance, and emerged into the dawn of a new harmony. The mended memory of Nyssera wasn't just a historical record; it was a living, breathing testament to the power of hope, the strength of connection, and the unyielding spirit of a world reborn.

The echoes of the leviadrakes' wisdom, the choir's resurgent song, and the steady pulse of the Crown Resonance were no longer confined to the abyss; they were woven into the very fabric of Nyssera's being, a vibrant melody that promised a future filled with enduring resilience and boundless life. The journey was far from over, but the path forward was illuminated by the radiant glow of a world that had remembered how to sing, and in doing so, had found its way back to itself. The whispers of the Pale Tide were fading, replaced by the clear, strong notes of Nyssera's own, unyielding song.

The leviadrakes, now free from the calcified certainties of their past, emerged not as conquerors, but as cultivators. Their scales, once the color of storm clouds and ancient stone, shimmered with an iridescence that mirrored the newfound complexity of their understanding. The confrontation within the abyss, the raw, unflinching gaze into the heart of Nyssera's fractured memory, had stripped away their arrogance, leaving behind a profound, almost humbling, wisdom. They had witnessed firsthand the destructive consequence of enforced isolation, the hollow victory of silence, and the ultimate futility of control. This realization was not a defeat, but a liberation, an unfurling of possibilities they had never dared to imagine.

Their ancient pronouncements, once delivered with the unshakeable authority of ages, now carried a softer cadence, a collaborative spirit that resonated with the reawakened world-song. The days of dictating Nyssera's fate from isolated, shadowed citadels were over. Instead, they offered their counsel, their vast historical perspective, not as immutable decrees, but as guiding threads in a tapestry woven by many hands. Their role as guardians had transformed. No longer were they the unseen hands manipulating the threads of existence, but rather elder weavers, offering their experience and insight to ensure the pattern remained strong and true, even as new colors and textures were introduced. This shift was born from a deep understanding that true strength lay not in rigid adherence to a singular vision, but in the vibrant, dynamic interplay of diverse life.

"The Pale Tide sought to sever," exhaled Aerion, his voice a deep rumble that stirred the very air around them. His massive form, once a symbol of imposing power, now seemed to radiate a gentle, attentive energy. "It believed that by isolating each strand, it could unravel the whole. But it forgot that the strength of Nyssera has always resided in its interconnectedness. The Silence Event, the Pale Tide's insidious whispers – these were not endpoints, but chapters. Chapters of pain, yes, but also chapters of resilience, of learning." He nudged a fallen leaf with a claw as large as a ploughshare, his movements deliberate, almost tender. "Our mistake was in attempting to impose order through suppression. True harmony is not a manufactured state; it is a naturally occurring phenomenon that blossoms when all voices are allowed to sing."

Mara found herself nodding, a sense of profound relief washing over her. This was the evolution she had hoped for, the promise whispered by the leviadrakes in their final moments of transformation. The fear that had clung to them, the ingrained instinct to protect Nyssera through absolute dominance, had been replaced by a genuine desire to understand and nurture. It was a monumental shift, one that would ripple through the very foundations of their society.

"We must ensure that the lessons of the past are not merely remembered, but *integrated*," said Lyra, her voice like the rustling of ancient parchment. Her wings, once folded in a posture of stern judgment, were now spread slightly, as if embracing the world. "The scars Nyssera bears are not to be hidden or regretted, but understood. They are testament to the struggles, to the courage of those who endured. The Silence Event was a period of profound loss, of severed connections, and the Pale Tide nearly succeeded in its aim to erase all that made Nyssera vibrant. But we now know that the attempt itself forged something new within us."

Cael, standing beside Mara, echoed her sentiment. "It's like a damaged tree. You don't prune away the broken branches and pretend they never existed. You learn from where the break occurred, you tend to the wound, and you encourage new growth to spring forth, stronger and more adaptable for having survived the damage." He looked up at the leviadrakes, his expression a mixture of awe and gratitude. "Your wisdom, now tempered with this understanding, is a gift to us all. It means we can build a future that acknowledges the past without being imprisoned by it."

The leviadrakes, in turn, acknowledged the courage of the mortals who had challenged their ancient ways, who had dared to question the established order and ultimately brought about this paradigm shift. They spoke of the new pacts that would need to be forged, not as agreements of subjugation, but as covenants of mutual respect and shared responsibility. The age of solitary dragon strongholds dictating terms to the world was drawing to a close. Now, the great dragons would become active participants in the reweaving of Nyssera, their immense power channeled into understanding and nurturing the delicate web of life.

"The ecological balance of Nyssera is a complex tapestry," Aerion continued, his gaze sweeping over the burgeoning greenery that already began to reclaim the scars left by the Pale Tide's influence. "The Silence Event disrupted many vital threads, and the Pale Tide's attempts to further isolate and control only exacerbated the damage. We must now work in concert with the land itself, with the spirits of the ancient forests, the rivers, and the mountains, to rediscover the lost harmonies. This requires a transparency that was previously unthinkable for our kind."

Lyra elaborated, "We will establish observatories, not of dominion, but of observation. Places where the ebb and flow of Nyssera's life force can be studied, where the impact of past events can be measured, and where the health of the ecosystem can be monitored. These will be collaborative ventures, drawing upon the knowledge of dragonkind, of the forest-kin, the sky-dwellers, and indeed, all sentient beings who share this world. Our ancient lore, which once spoke of the intrinsic separation between our kind and the 'lesser' races, will be rewritten to speak of interdependence. For we have learned that our own well-being is intrinsically tied to the well-being of every creature, every plant, every drop of water that constitutes Nyssera."

This commitment to transparency was perhaps the most profound change. The leviadrakes, for centuries, had operated in a veil of secrecy, their actions and motivations often shrouded in mystery. Now, they pledged to share their knowledge, to demystify their ancient practices, and to work in open dialogue with the other peoples of Nyssera. This would involve establishing council chambers, not in the remote, inaccessible aeries of the past, but in accessible locations, places where representatives from all factions could meet, discuss, and decide the future course of their shared world.

"The wisdom of the leviadrakes is immense, a treasure trove of knowledge accumulated over millennia," said Mara, her voice carrying a hopeful tremor. "But that wisdom, when hoarded and applied unilaterally, became a force of stagnation, even of destruction. Now, that same wisdom, shared openly and collaboratively, can become the bedrock of a truly flourishing Nyssera. It is the difference between a fortress and a sanctuary."

Cael added, "It's about re-establishing trust, not just between dragonkind and mortals, but between all the disparate groups that make up Nyssera. The Pale Tide fed on discord, on fear, on the breakdown of communication. Now, we must actively foster unity. The dragons' commitment to shared learning and transparent governance is the first, and perhaps most crucial, step in healing those ancient rifts."

The leviadrakes spoke of the Silence Event with a newfound gravity, not as a historical footnote, but as a wound that still throbbed within the collective consciousness of Nyssera. They proposed the creation of memorial groves, not to mourn what was lost in perpetuity, but to serve as living testaments to the fragility of peace and the enduring strength of connection. These groves would be places of quiet contemplation, where the tales of those who suffered and survived would be preserved, where the harsh lessons learned would be reinforced through oral histories and art, ensuring that the memory of severance would forever serve as a reminder of the value of unity.

"We will work to restore the damaged ley lines, the arteries of Nyssera's magical and ecological energies," Lyra declared, her voice resonating with purpose. "The Pale Tide's influence had a devastating effect on these vital pathways, weakening the land's natural resilience. Our understanding of Nyssera's deep magic, coupled with the insights of those who live closest to the land – the druids, the shamans, the geomancers – will be instrumental in this process. It is a monumental undertaking, one that will require generations of dedicated effort, but it is a task we embrace with humility and a renewed sense of responsibility."

Aerion nodded in agreement. "The future of Nyssera lies not in attempting to recreate a romanticized past, but in building a future that learns from all that has transpired. The leviadrakes, once guardians of an ancient order, now see ourselves as stewards of an evolving world. Our role is to ensure that the vital flow of life is unimpeded, that the echoes of the past serve as lessons, not as chains, and that every living being has the opportunity to contribute to the grand, ever-unfolding song of Nyssera."

This was the dawn of a new era, one where the immense power of dragonkind was being consciously redirected from control to cultivation, from isolation to integration. The leviadrakes, having confronted the stark realities of their own past and the devastating consequences of their previous adherence to rigid doctrine, were now charting a course towards a future defined by collaboration, transparency, and a profound respect for the interconnectedness of all life. Their transformation was a beacon, a promise that even the most ancient and seemingly immutable forces could evolve, and in doing so, could usher in a new dawn of harmony for the world of Nyssera.

The abyss had not been an end, but a profound beginning, a crucible from which a more enlightened form of guardianship had emerged. The wisdom of the ages was now offered not as a burden, but as a shared inheritance, a foundation upon which a more vibrant and resilient future could be built, one song, one connection, one act of understanding at a time. The true depth of their transformation lay in their willingness to surrender the illusion of absolute control for the far greater power of shared creation. They had learned that the greatest strength was not in the force they wielded, but in the connections they fostered, and that true guardianship meant nurturing the whole, not merely defending a fragment. Their scales, once reflecting only their own immense power, now shimmered with the countless colors of the world they were committed to protecting and fostering.

The immediate aftermath of the abyss's revelation and the leviadrakes' profound metamorphosis was a period of tentative rebuilding, a fragile peace that settled over Nyssera like a newly fallen snow. Yet, beneath the surface of this nascent harmony, subtle currents of change began to stir, presaging future trials and setting the stage for conflicts yet unimagined. The world had fundamentally shifted. The ancient, unshakeable certainty of the leviadrakes' dominion had been replaced by a collaborative spirit, a willingness to share the burden of guardianship. This openness, born of bitter experience and profound self-reflection, was Nyssera's greatest hope, but it also presented a new set of vulnerabilities.

The political landscape, once a largely static terrain dominated by the unseen influence of the ancient dragons, was now in flux. With the leviadrakes emerging from their isolation, their pronouncements no longer whispered pronouncements of unchallenged authority but rather considered counsel offered in open dialogue, the established hierarchies began to waver. Surface dwellers, who had long existed in a state of fearful reverence or outright ignorance regarding the true nature of their world's guardians, now had to grapple with a new reality. The dragons were not distant, inscrutable deities, but beings who had faced their own failings and chosen a path of shared responsibility. This realization would necessitate a complete redefinition of their relationship.

Kingdoms and city-states, accustomed to navigating the world without direct interaction with dragonkind, would now find themselves in a position where their fates were more visibly intertwined. New alliances would form, not necessarily out of mutual affection, but out of a pragmatic understanding of shared interests in a world where the ancient dragons were no longer aloof observers but active participants. The old guard, those who had benefited from the dragons' previous isolationist policies, might find their influence waning, while nascent factions, eager to embrace the new era of cooperation, would rise to prominence. This delicate recalibration of power, this re-establishment of trust and understanding, would be a complex and often fraught process, a fertile ground for political maneuvering and ideological clashes.

Furthermore, the very act of the leviadrakes revealing the existence and function of the abyss, and their own transformative journey, had irrevocably altered Nyssera's understanding of its own history and its place in the cosmos. The shared knowledge, the truth of the Silence Event and the Pale Tide's machinations, was a powerful weapon, but also a beacon. Entities that had thrived in Nyssera's past ignorance, those who profited from division and discord, would undoubtedly take notice. The veil of secrecy that had once shrouded the deepest mysteries of the world had been lifted, and in its place, a new form of vulnerability had emerged.

It was not an external threat of physical invasion, at least not initially, but rather a subtler, more insidious form of exploitation. The interconnectedness that the leviadrakes now championed, the vibrant tapestry of life they sought to nurture, was a prize that certain ancient, malevolent forces might seek to unravel or twist for their own dark purposes. These beings, perhaps drawn by the sudden surge of amplified life-force or the disruption of ancient power balances, would represent a new frontier of conflict, one that would test the very foundations of Nyssera's newfound unity.

The aerial realm, long the exclusive domain of dragonkind, also presented new frontiers for potential conflict and exploration. While the leviadrakes had spoken of shared observatories and collaborative study, the sheer scale of their power and their ancestral right to the skies still held a certain inherent advantage. As Nyssera's various peoples began to expand their understanding and influence, there would inevitably be instances of friction over airspace, over access to vital migratory routes, or over the establishment of new settlements that might encroach upon sacred dragon territories.

The dragons, in their new guise as open communicators, would need to find ways to balance their ancient instincts with their commitment to partnership, and the other races would need to learn to navigate the skies with respect and understanding, acknowledging the dragons' sovereign presence while asserting their own burgeoning rights and needs.

The pacts and covenants that the leviadrakes proposed were not merely diplomatic agreements; they were the forging of new foundations upon which the future of Nyssera would be built. These would need to be meticulously crafted, addressing not only immediate concerns but also anticipating future challenges. The leviadrakes' millennia of experience, once a source of their perceived infallibility, now served as a wellspring of cautionary tales and profound insights into the cyclical nature of conflict and cooperation. Their understanding of the ebb and flow of Nyssera's energies, their awareness of the delicate ecological balances, would become crucial in guiding these new agreements. They would need to impart this knowledge not as dictates, but as shared stewardship, ensuring that all parties understood the vital importance of preserving Nyssera's inherent health and resilience.

The concept of 'observatories,' places of study and monitoring, was particularly revolutionary. Historically, such locations would have been the exclusive purview of dragonkind, their secrets guarded jealously. Now, they were envisioned as collaborative spaces, welcoming the input of sky-dwellers who understood wind currents and atmospheric phenomena with unparalleled intimacy, of forest-kin who possessed an innate connection to the land's subtle shifts, and of any sentient being who could offer a unique perspective. This democratizing of knowledge, this embracing of diverse viewpoints, was the true essence of the new harmony. However, such open access could also be a double-edged sword. The information gathered within these observatories, detailing Nyssera's vulnerabilities, its resource distribution, and its ecological sensitive points, could become a target for those who wished to exploit it. Guardians would need to be vigilant, not just against overt attacks, but against espionage and the subtle manipulation of shared data.

The restoration of damaged ley lines, a monumental undertaking that Lyra had pledged, would also present new challenges. These ancient arteries of magical and ecological energy were not static entities; they were dynamic and responsive to the world around them. As they were healed and revitalized, their paths might shift, their influence might spread into areas previously untouched, or their reawakening could inadvertently disturb dormant entities or ancient magical constructs. The process would require not only the leviadrakes' deep arcane knowledge but also the intimate understanding of geomancers and shamans who had lived in close proximity to these energies for generations. Conflicts could arise over the control or direction of these re-emerging power flows, as different factions might see opportunities for personal gain or have differing visions for how these revitalized energies should be utilized.

The leviadrakes' shift from 'guardians' to 'stewards' was more than a semantic change; it was a fundamental reimagining of their role. Guardians protect what is theirs, often through assertive defense. Stewards nurture, manage, and ensure the long-term health of a shared resource. This meant that their responsibility extended beyond merely repelling threats; it encompassed active cultivation, careful management, and a deep commitment to the well-being of every element within Nyssera. This would require a level of engagement and empathy that had been largely absent in their previous existence. They would have to learn to listen not just to the grand pronouncements of the world, but to the quiet whispers of the smallest creatures, the rustling of leaves, the flow of water, and the silent growth of the smallest seed.

The echoes of the past, while serving as lessons, could also be a source of lingering animosity and distrust. The Silence Event had inflicted deep wounds, severed connections, and fostered a pervasive sense of loss and betrayal. While the leviadrakes now sought to heal these rifts, the memories of suffering would not simply vanish. Generations might still harbor resentment, suspicion, and a deep-seated fear of dragonkind. Rebuilding trust would be a slow, painstaking process, requiring consistent demonstration of good faith, transparency in actions, and a genuine commitment to restorative justice. The memorial groves, envisioned as places of learning and remembrance, could also become focal points for historical grievances if not carefully managed, serving as constant reminders of past injustices rather than catalysts for future understanding.

The 'new frontiers' were not just geographical or political; they were also philosophical and spiritual. The leviadrakes' transformation challenged the very definition of power and authority. Their willingness to admit error and to embrace a more communal approach to governance offered a radical alternative to the patterns of dominance and control that had shaped Nyssera for eons. This, in itself, could be a source of conflict. Those who clung to the old ways, who found comfort in rigid structures and unquestioned hierarchies, would likely resist this new paradigm. They might see the dragons' openness as weakness, their collaboration as a dilution of power, and the burgeoning interconnectedness as a chaotic threat to order. These internal divisions, fueled by fear of the unknown and a resistance to change, would become a significant challenge for the nascent harmony.

Moreover, the very concept of 'harmony' itself, as envisioned by the leviadrakes, was not a static end state but a dynamic process. It implied a constant negotiation, a continuous effort to balance competing needs and desires, to integrate diverse perspectives, and to adapt to changing circumstances. This would require a level of maturity and self-awareness from all of Nyssera's inhabitants that had not been previously tested. The dragons' newfound wisdom was a potent catalyst, but the true work of building a lasting harmony would fall upon the shoulders of every sentient being. The journey from the abyss, a place of isolation and darkness, to a dawn of shared light, was just the beginning.

The seeds of future conflicts were already sown in the fertile soil of this new era, waiting for the right conditions to sprout, testing the strength and resilience of Nyssera's reawakened song. The threat was not that harmony would be achieved and then lost, but that the very pursuit of it would be fraught with peril, demanding constant vigilance, unwavering commitment, and an enduring capacity for both courage and compassion.

The political and aerial realms, once defined by the dragons' isolated power, were now vast, unmapped territories of potential conflict and profound discovery, promising a rich and challenging tapestry for the unfolding narrative of Nyssera. The leviadrakes' surrender of absolute control for shared creation was a monumental shift, one that not only redefined their own existence but irrevocably altered the destiny of the world they had sworn to protect. Yet, in this very act of surrender lay the seeds of both their greatest triumphs and their most profound challenges.

Mara and Cael, their souls still resonating with the profound echoes of the abyss, stood on the precipice of a new era. The trials they had endured, the shattering truths they had unearthed, had irrevocably altered the fabric of their beings. The naive reliance on mythologized guardians, the comforting illusion of absolute protection, had been stripped away, replaced by a stark and luminous understanding: true strength lay not in the unassailable might of distant protectors, but in the courage to confront difficult truths, to acknowledge flaws, and to embrace the messy, ongoing process of healing.

Their journey into the heart of Nyssera's deepest secrets had been a descent into darkness, but it had yielded a light more potent than any they had ever known. Memory, they now understood, was not a static archive of the past, but a living, breathing force, capable of shaping the present and birthing the future. Nyssera, once a world cloaked in the shadows of forgotten histories and enforced silence, was now a symphony of emergent voices, a vibrant tapestry woven with the threads of shared experience and hard-won wisdom. The song of the world, once muted and fractured, was beginning to swell, a testament to the collective courage to heal.

The revelations from the abyss had not led to a simple, neat resolution. Instead, they had unfurled a future brimming with potential, yet also laden with inherent complexities. The age of unchallenged dominion was over, replaced by a dynamic, ever-evolving partnership. This was not a return to a pristine past, but a leap into an uncharted future, one that embraced the inherent messiness of life, the intricate dance of love and loss, and the ceaseless evolution of the world-song. Mara, her gaze fixed on the horizon, felt the weight of this nascent harmony settle upon her, not as a burden, but as a sacred trust. The memory of the leviadrakes' struggle, their arduous path from isolation to collaboration, served as a constant reminder that growth was a perpetual state, not a destination. The world had shed its skin, and in its place, a new, more resilient, and infinitely more beautiful form was emerging.

Cael, ever the grounding presence, felt the subtle shifts in the world's energy, the reawakening of long-dormant currents now guided by a deeper understanding. The ley lines, once scarred and choked by the Silence Event, were slowly but surely finding their rhythm, their revitalized flow a testament to the dragons' profound commitment to mending the world's wounds. This healing, however, was not without its complexities. The reawakened energies could stir ancient magics, awaken slumbering entities, or even redraw the invisible boundaries of Nyssera's magical geography. Such shifts demanded constant vigilance, not just from the dragons, but from all who now shared in the stewardship of the land.

Geomancers and shamans, whose ancestral knowledge was now more vital than ever, worked in tandem with the leviadrakes, their combined wisdom a bulwark against unforeseen consequences. Disputes over the redirection of these potent energies were inevitable, as different factions sought to harness their power for their own ends, or held differing visions of how they should best serve the burgeoning harmony. Cael understood that these disagreements, while challenging, were also a sign of Nyssera's reawakening, a vibrant manifestation of diverse perspectives finally finding their voice.

The concept of 'observatories', once exclusive citadels of draconic knowledge, now stood as beacons of collaborative learning. These were not mere research facilities, but living ecosystems of observation, where the keen eyes of sky-dwellers charted the atmospheric ballet, where the deep wisdom of the forest-kin deciphered the land's subtle murmurs, and where scholars from every corner of Nyssera contributed their unique insights. Mara found particular solace in this democratization of knowledge. She had witnessed firsthand the dangers of ignorance, the ease with which truth could be distorted when hidden from view.

The shared observations, the collective analysis of Nyssera's ecological health, its resource distribution, and its sensitive points of vulnerability, were invaluable. Yet, this very openness also created new avenues for exploitation. The information meticulously gathered within these observatories could become a tempting target for those who still harbored malevolent intentions, those who sought to sow discord or seize power through manipulation. The dragons, and their allies, had to remain ever-watchful, not only for overt threats but for the insidious creep of espionage, the subtle theft of knowledge that could undermine the fragile peace.

The political landscape, once a relatively static realm governed by ancient traditions and the unseen influence of dragonkind, was now a dynamic, shifting terrain. The leviadrakes, having stepped out of their millennia-long seclusion, were no longer distant arbiters of fate but active participants in the world's governance. Their pronouncements, once law, were now considered counsel, offered in open dialogue, fostering a new era of negotiation and alliance. Kingdoms and city-states, long accustomed to navigating their own affairs with limited interaction with dragonkind, now found their destinies inextricably linked to the larger tapestry of Nyssera. New pacts and covenants were being forged, not always out of affection, but out of a pragmatic understanding of shared interests in a world where the dragons were no longer aloof observers but vital partners. The old guard, those who had benefited from the dragons' previous isolationist policies, found their influence waning, while nascent factions, eager to embrace the collaborative spirit, rose to prominence. This recalibration of power was a delicate dance, a fertile ground for political maneuvering, ideological clashes, and the constant redefinition of alliances.

Mara's transformation had been profound. The weight of her own past, the choices she had made, the sacrifices she had endured, had forged in her a deep well of empathy. She understood that the scars of the Silence Event ran deep, that lingering animosity and distrust would not simply vanish with the dragons' return. Generations had grown up under the shadow of fear and loss, and rebuilding that shattered trust would be a slow, arduous process. The memorial groves, envisioned as places of learning and remembrance, were potent symbols of this reconciliation. Yet, they also held the potential to become focal points for historical grievances if not managed with care. Mara believed that these groves should serve not as constant reminders of past injustices, but as catalysts for future understanding, spaces where sorrow could be acknowledged and transformed into a shared commitment to a brighter tomorrow.

Cael, observing the subtle tensions and burgeoning opportunities, recognized that the leviadrakes' shift from 'guardians' to 'stewards' was more than a semantic change. It was a fundamental reimagining of their role, a profound evolution of their purpose. Guardians protected what was theirs, often through assertive defense. Stewards nurtured, managed, and ensured the long-term health of a shared resource. This meant their responsibility extended beyond merely repelling threats; it encompassed active cultivation, careful management, and a deep commitment to the well-being of every element within Nyssera. This required a level of engagement and empathy that had been largely absent in their previous existence. They had to learn to listen not just to the grand pronouncements of the world, but to the quiet whispers of the smallest creatures, the rustling of leaves, the flow of water, and the silent growth of the smallest seed. This commitment to nurturing life in all its forms was the true essence of the new harmony they were striving to build.

The aerial realm, once the exclusive domain of dragonkind, now presented itself as a vast expanse of new frontiers, ripe for both conflict and exploration. While the leviadrakes had spoken of shared observatories and collaborative study, their inherent power and ancestral right to the skies still held a certain advantage. As Nyssera's various peoples began to expand their understanding and influence, instances of friction over airspace, vital migratory routes, or the establishment of new settlements that might encroach upon sacred dragon territories were bound to arise.

The dragons, in their new guise as open communicators, had to find a delicate balance between their ancient instincts and their commitment to partnership. Similarly, the other races had to learn to navigate the skies with respect and understanding, acknowledging the dragons' sovereign presence while asserting their own burgeoning rights and needs. Cael saw this negotiation of shared space as a microcosm of the larger challenges Nyssera faced: learning to coexist, to compromise, and to find common ground in a world that was no longer defined by isolation.

Mara reflected on the philosophical and spiritual shifts that accompanied these outward changes. The leviadrakes' transformation challenged the very definition of power and authority. Their willingness to admit error and embrace a more communal approach to governance offered a radical alternative to the patterns of dominance and control that had shaped Nyssera for eons. This, in itself, was a source of conflict. Those who clung to the old ways, who found comfort in rigid structures and unquestioned hierarchies, resisted this new paradigm. They perceived the dragons' openness as weakness, their collaboration as a dilution of power, and the burgeoning interconnectedness as a chaotic threat to order. These internal divisions, fueled by fear of the unknown and resistance to change, were a significant challenge to the nascent harmony. Mara understood that the true work of building a lasting harmony lay not in eradicating these divisions, but in guiding them, in fostering understanding, and in reminding everyone that true strength lay in unity, not in uniformity.

The journey from the abyss, a place of isolation and darkness, to this dawn of shared light was merely the beginning. The seeds of future conflicts were already sown in the fertile soil of this new era, waiting for the right conditions to sprout, ready to test the strength and resilience of Nyssera's reawakened song. The threat was not that harmony would be achieved and then lost, but that the very pursuit of it would be fraught with peril, demanding constant vigilance, unwavering commitment, and an enduring capacity for both courage and compassion. The leviadrakes' surrender of absolute control for shared creation was a monumental shift, one that not only redefined their own existence but irrevocably altered the destiny of the world they had sworn to protect.

Yet, in this very act of surrender lay the seeds of both their greatest triumphs and their most profound challenges. The political and aerial realms, once defined by the dragons' isolated power, were now vast, unmapped territories of potential conflict and profound discovery, promising a rich and challenging tapestry for the unfolding narrative of Nyssera. The complexities of life, love, and the ever-evolving world-song were not obstacles to be overcome, but the very essence of the vibrant, enduring world that Mara and Cael were now dedicated to nurturing. The future was not a destination, but a journey, a continuous becoming, a testament to the enduring power of a song sung in unison, even amidst its inevitable dissonances.

GLOSSARY

The Great Silence: A period in Nysseran history characterized by the leviadrakes' enforced withdrawal from global affairs, leading to ecological and societal imbalance. This era profoundly shaped the current political and spiritual landscape, its echoes influencing inter-species relations and resource management.

The Leviadrake Covenant: The foundational agreement that established the leviadrakes as guardians of Nyssera. Its reinterpretation marks a pivotal shift from isolationist dominion to collaborative stewardship.

World-Song: The intricate, ever-evolving symphony of magical and natural energies that permeates Nyssera. Its harmony is directly influenced by the collective well-being and actions of its inhabitants.

Observatories: Formerly exclusive centers of draconic knowledge, now transformed into hubs for cross-species research and ecological monitoring, symbolizing Nyssera's commitment to shared understanding.

Memorial Groves: Dedicated spaces for remembrance and reconciliation, intended to honor the sacrifices of the past while fostering understanding and preventing future conflict.

Abyss: A metaphorical and sometimes literal place of profound darkness, isolation, and forgotten truths, which Mara and Cael journeyed into.

Cael: A central character, a grounding presence deeply attuned to the energies of Nyssera.

Forest-kin: Beings or creatures intrinsically connected to and protective of Nysseran forests.

Ley Lines: Currents of magical energy that crisscross Nyssera, vital to its ecological health and magical stability.

Leviadrrakes: The ancient, powerful dragon species central to Nyssera's history and future.

Mara: A central character, her journey marked by profound transformation and a growing empathy.

Nyssera: The name of the world in which the story unfolds.

Silence Event: A catastrophic disruption of Nyssera's magical and ecological balance, intrinsically linked to the Great Silence.

World-Song: The collective energetic and spiritual essence of Nyssera, reflecting its overall health and harmony.

REFERENCE

The following works, while fictional, draw upon extensive research into ecological systems, historical cycles of societal change, and the profound philosophical implications of interconnectedness. Specific inspirations include:

The Ecological Imperative by Dr. Anya Sharma (hypothetical academic text)

Ancient Myths of the Serpent Guardians compiled by Professor Kaelen Vance (hypothetical scholarly collection)

The Geomancer's Compendium (ancient Nysseran text, adapted)

Field notes from the Sky-Watcher Guild's ongoing chronicle of atmospheric phenomena.

Oral histories of the Forest-Kin elders, detailing the resilience of ancient woodlands.